SHADOW FAERIE

Also by Rachel Morgan

THE CREEPY HOLLOW SERIES

The Faerie Guardian

The Faerie Prince

The Faerie War

A Faerie's Secret

A Faerie's Revenge

A Faerie's Curse

Glass Faerie

Shadow Faerie

Writing as Rochelle Morgan

THE TROUBLE SERIES

The Trouble with Flying

The Trouble with Flirting

The Trouble with Faking

The Trouble with Falling

SHADOW FAERIE

CREEPY HOLLOW, BOOK EIGHT

RACHEL MORGAN

ISBN 978-0-9947154-4-9

PART I

dash

PROLOGUE

DASH HAD BEEN AT HIS DESK AT THE CREEPY HOLLOW Guild for less than ten minutes when his amber, sitting beside the goblin abduction report he was working on, shivered and emitted a chirp. Glowing gold words rose to the surface of the rectangular device. Recognizing Violet's handwriting, Dash quickly pulled the amber closer. His eyes darted up to check who might have been standing close enough to his desk to have seen the message. The open office area was filled with the bustle of morning activity: a junior guardian team returning from a night mission; two trainees delivering scrolls; and his own teammate, Jewel, hard at work on something. It was highly unlikely any of these people would know who the message on Dash's amber was from, but it still made him

3

nervous corresponding with Griffin rebels while beneath the Guild's own roof.

He leaned back in his chair, schooling his expression into one of nonchalance, and read the message: *Do you know where Em is? I can't find her.* Ice chilled Dash's veins as he struggled to keep his expression neutral. If Vi couldn't find someone, that meant serious trouble. Thanks to her Griffin Ability, she should be able to find anyone who wasn't concealed by some form of magic. Em's Griffin Ability, however, was a whole new story. Was she playing around with it? Testing whether she could hide herself? Dash reached across his desk, grabbed his stylus, and wrote a quick response on his amber. *No. Are you sure she left? Check orbs.*

Vi's reply came seconds later: *Checking now.*

I'm on my way over, Dash scribbled as he pushed away from his desk and stood.

"Leaving already?" Jewel asked. Dash looked up as she stood and walked around her desk. "You only just got here."

"I need to check on something. One of the witness reports from the goblin abduction case. A few details are missing." Dash cringed internally, hating having to lie to one of his best friends. "I'll get one of the guards downstairs to open a doorway for me," he added quickly. Like Jewel, he wasn't supposed to be able to open doorways to the faerie paths anymore. An annoyance Em's Griffin Ability was responsible for. Em had since reversed the magic's effect on Dash, but Jewel didn't know that. The only thing Jewel knew was that Em had escaped the Guild's clutches and disappeared.

"Do you need me to go with you?" Jewel asked.

"No, don't worry. It'll be quick." He gave her a smile, which he suspected looking nothing like his usual easygoing grin.

"Okay. Hey, is everything all right?" Jewel caught his arm before he could turn away. "You're not normally so serious first thing in the morning." Her hand lingered a moment too long on his arm, and the conversation he'd had with Em came to mind. She'd pointed out that Jewel clearly wanted to be more than just his friend, a fact Dash had somehow been oblivious to until this moment. How had he missed it? And why had Jewel never said anything to him about her feelings for him? She must have exceptional control over them. He hadn't noticed any random magical outbursts.

Not important right now, Dash reminded himself. "Yes, everything's fine. I'm just … more tired than usual." That, at least, was the truth. He'd been up late the night before talking with Chase, discussing when to return to Tranquil Hills Psychiatric Hospital to examine whatever records were on file for Em's mother. With unknown magic preventing her from waking up, she wasn't in a position to explain why she and her daughter had lived for so long in the non-magic world, masquerading as human. Hopefully Em's father could provide some answers instead. Em said she knew nothing about him, but if he was the one who'd been paying Daniela Clarke's medical bills, the hospital must surely have his name and contact details.

"Okay. See you later then." Jewel returned to her chair.

Dash should have left then—he *wanted* to leave—but he couldn't ignore Jewel's desire to be more than friends now that he knew about it. "Hey, do you want to hang out this evening?" he asked before he could change his mind. "We should … talk." It would no doubt turn into the most awkward conversation they'd ever had, but he needed to do it. It wasn't fair of him to allow Jewel to continue hoping for something that would never happen.

"Yeah, okay. Great."

"Cool." Dash hurried down the Guild's main staircase, across the foyer, and into the room with bare walls used for accessing the faerie paths. "Do you mind opening a doorway for me?" he asked the woman standing guard just inside the door.

"Still haven't found that Griffin Gifted girl, huh?"

"Nope."

"I hope you do," the woman replied as she walked to the wall and raised her stylus. "I heard she's a dangerous one."

"Yeah," Dash muttered. "Extremely dangerous. I plan to find her."

The woman stepped back as part of the wall pulled away to reveal the darkness of the faerie paths beyond. Dash walked forward. Once the light had vanished behind him, he focused his thoughts on the oasis hidden in the middle of a desert thousands of miles away.

Minutes later, he hurried up the porch steps of the little white house on one side of the oasis, past a few closed doors, and into the surveillance room. A row of glass orbs lined three of the four walls, and within each orb was a miniature form of a different part of the oasis. Magic connected each orb to the enchanted bugs that flew around outside, displaying everything the bugs saw. Vi was bent over, staring intently into one of the orbs, while Calla and Chase sat in front of another one. "What can you see?" Dash asked, not bothering with a greeting.

"Oh, Dash, hey," Vi said as she turned to face him. "The orbs show that Em left during the night. Just beyond the dome layer, she opened a doorway to the paths and went through it."

"She must have taken someone's stylus."

"Yes. There was one missing from our kitchen this morning."

"I just don't understand," Calla said, her finger swiping repeatedly across the orb in front of her as she moved backwards in time through the scenes it displayed. "Why would she leave?"

Vi shook her head as she shrugged. "Any number of reasons, I suppose. Maybe she wanted to see one of her old friends. Or maybe she remembered something that could help her mother. What's far more worrying is the fact that I can't find her. What could possibly be shielding her?"

"Nothing good," Chase muttered.

"Dash, you never told me what happened when I couldn't find you and Em yesterday," Vi continued. "Remember, when I came to meet the two of you at her aunt's house?"

"Oh yes." Dash cursed inwardly—with the kind of words his mother wouldn't approve of—at having forgotten, yet again, to mention that strange place and the people who had taken him and Em there. "I don't know where we were, but it was weird. Everything seemed drained of color, and parts of it were sort of … smudged. Unclear or unformed. And we couldn't access the faerie paths. We ended up running from some shadowy creature I've never seen before, and somehow we found ourselves near the tear in the veil. But not on the human side, and not on the fae side. Somewhere … I don't know. Maybe it wasn't even real. Maybe it was some kind of hallucination. Anyway," he continued with a deep breath, "we were there because of the Unseelies. The prince and princess."

"Seriously?" Chase looked away from the orb he'd been examining.

"Yes. That girl who was at Chevalier House for a few days—Aurora—is actually the Unseelie princess."

"So that's what she was doing at Chevalier House," a new voice said from the doorway. Dash looked around and saw Ryn standing there. "Aurora wanted Em to run away with her. She was obviously planning to take Em back to the Unseelie Court."

"You didn't think to mention any of this last night?" Calla said to Dash, an accusatory edge to her voice.

"To be honest, I didn't think of it at all. Em said she was going to tell me what happened later—since I was, uh, stunned and unconscious for part of the time—but then that glass faerie showed up, and we almost died, and then we raced off to get Em's mom, and … I didn't think of the Unseelies again until late last night when I got home."

"Great, so we have no idea what they told Em," Calla said, crossing her arms and frowning at the floor.

Dash said nothing. It was unlike Calla to be so ticked off at him, but he couldn't blame her. He was furious with himself for not asking Em about that strange shadowy world last night. She'd seemed distant and unhappy, and, like an idiot, he'd tried to distract her with dancing. What the hell was wrong with him? How could he just *forget* that two members of the Unseelie royal family had transported Em to a strange place and then mysteriously let her go?

"So …" Vi rubbed her temples. "The fact that we can't find Em now might have something to do with the Unseelies."

"Unless she herself doesn't want to be found," Chase said. "She left voluntarily. She might have used her Griffin Ability to shield herself somehow."

"Whatever her reason for leaving, she must be planning to come back," Ryn said, walking into the room and taking a closer look at one of the orbs. "Her mother is still here, after all."

Dash shook his head. "She may have left of her own accord, but what if the Unseelies got hold of her once she was out there? They let her go yesterday, but they definitely still want her. They might be holding her against her will now."

"So what do we do?" Vi asked. "Wait to see if she comes back? And if so, how long do we wait?"

"She has to come back," Calla murmured, chewing on her thumbnail as she stared unseeingly at the floor. "She has to."

Ryn looked across the room. "What's wrong?"

Calla lowered her hand and frowned at her brother. "Don't do that."

"Hey, I'm not *trying* to feel what you're feeling," Ryn said, holding his hands up in defense, "but your anxiety is just about giving me a panic attack. I've been trying to ignore it but it's practically assaulting me."

"Anxiety?" Chase moved closer to her. "About what?"

"Jeez, people," Calla exclaimed. "I'm just preoccupied with another case. Everything's fine. Can we focus on how we're going to figure out where Em is? Just in case she *is* someone's prisoner now?"

"I have some Unseelie contacts," Chase said. "I'll see what I can find out."

"Good. I'm getting back to work on other stuff then," Calla said. She crossed the room and left without a word, leaving several moments of awkward silence in her wake. With a frown, Chase followed her.

Dash cleared his throat. "The Guild also has Unseelie contacts. I'll ask if anyone knows anything. And I'll question our Seelie contacts as well. It's possible they found Em but haven't informed the Guild yet."

"Thanks," Vi said.

"Let us know as soon as you discover anything," Ryn added.

"Of course." Dash turned and strode out of the room, already reaching into his pocket for his amber and stylus so he could contact the Guild's Unseelie liaison. He paused near the front door as he wrote a quick message enquiring whether the liaison had received any news regarding a Griffin Gifted girl.

"... something going on?"

At the sound of voices, Dash leaned to the side and peered out the window. Calla paced back and forth across the porch. "She has to come back, Chase. She has to."

"Okay, seriously." Chase caught her arm and pulled her to a halt. "Tell me what's going on."

Dash knew he shouldn't be eavesdropping, but if it was something about Em ...

Calla took a deep breath. "I saw something. Last night. When I went up to ask Em if she wanted to join us this morning. It made me hope that maybe … somehow …" She shook her head. "I mean, I know it's crazy to even think it. My brain is still playing through everything that happened back then and how it could even be possible. But if it's true …" She grabbed the front of Chase's T-shirt in both fists. "Chase, if it's true, then we *have* to make sure Em comes back."

Chase took Calla's hands in both of his. "You're not making any sense. What did you see?"

"You can't tell anyone, okay? Not until I know if it's true. I don't want to be responsible for any more broken hearts."

"Broken hearts? When did you—"

She leaned closer to Chase and whispered, her words too quiet now for Dash to hear through the window. He watched as Chase's brow furrowed further. "Not possible," he said as Calla stepped back. "Or … is it? When I first saw her, I thought …"

"Thought what?"

Chase's gaze became unfocused as he stared over Calla's shoulder for several moments, clearly lost in thought. A small smile stretched his lips as he returned his attention to her. "I think you could be right."

Her answering smile lit up her face. "I think so too. But I don't know for certain, and I refuse to get excited until we confirm this. I know someone who can tell us beyond a doubt, but I don't know where he is. You need to help me find him."

"Vi can help if she has …" Chase's words trailed off as he shook his head. "But you don't want her to know."

11

"No. Not yet." Calla took his arm and pulled him down the stairs with her. "We first need to find out if it's true." Her voice grew fainter as she and Chase headed away from the house, leaving Dash with more questions and no answers. He had his own mystery to solve, though. *Where are you, Em?* he wondered silently as he opened the door and stepped onto the porch.

His amber shivered in his hand, and he stopped to read the Unseelie liaison's reply: *No recent info from the Unseelies. Nothing interesting anyway.* Of course not. The Unseelies would never *choose* to inform the Guild if they happened to be in possession of a powerful Griffin Gifted girl. But Dash had to check, just in case the liaison had heard something. Now he'd have to contact the Seelie liaison. After that, it would be time to move on to unofficial channels. "Somehow, Em," he muttered as he strode away. "Somehow, I'll find you."

CHAPTER ONE

THINGS I NEVER IMAGINED: ONE, ESCAPING THE MISERABLE town of Stanmeade long before I ever dreamed it possible. Two, becoming almost-friends with the guy I hated for years. Three, climbing the outside of a faerie palace tower with a stolen stylus in my pocket so I can hide at the top and open a faerie paths doorway with magic. Oh yeah. And I never imagined using words like 'palace tower,' 'faerie paths' and 'magic' without sounding like an inpatient at a mental institution. But that was before I discovered I'm a faerie, and that a hidden world of magic exists alongside the one I grew up in. That was before I landed at the top of everyone's most-wanted list for possessing a unique and dangerous faerie superpower. And that was before I took the biggest risk of my life and agreed to marry a faerie prince of the Unseelie Court in the hope of saving my mother.

So yes. I imagine things now that most people from my old life would consider impossible. Like a dark hole of nothingness materializing across the gold-veined marble walls at the top of the tower I've climbed. I needed to get away from the watchful eyes of the palace guards, and this turret forming the highest point of the Unseelie Palace seemed like a good spot. Unfortunately, the spell I've been whispering and the words I've written repeatedly across the wall seem to be producing nothing.

I heave a frustrated sigh and clench my fingers around the jewel-encrusted stylus. I stole it from Aurora's room yesterday. Only the best of the best for a princess, so I doubt there's anything wrong with it. Which means ... perhaps my magic is the problem? I place the stylus on the turret floor and cup my hands together, then breathe out slowly and feel for the core of power within me. Almost instantly, a roughly spherical shape of white glitter and wispy fragments hover above my hand. It seems almost easy to produce magic now, after having practiced so much in the past few days. No need to squeeze my eyes shut, furrow my brow, and imagine dragging the magic out of myself like a mouse tugging on a truck.

So if my magic and the stylus aren't the problem, and the spell itself is correct—which I'm certain it is, given I used it to leave the oasis—that leaves only one answer: the faerie paths are not accessible from this tower.

"Dammit," I whisper. I shove the stylus back into my pocket and stare out across the endless lands of perfect summer. Brilliant green lawns, flowers in every color, enchanted water features surrounded by shrubs clipped into ornamental shapes, and various areas for entertaining: a pergola here, a gazebo there, the queen's bower off to the right beyond that little bridge. And just beyond the palace grounds, the turrets of manor houses belonging to Unseelie nobles rise above the trees.

And almost none of it, according to Aurora, accessible via the faerie paths. No one leaves this palace and no one arrives except through the main entrance. "It's not as though you *need* to go anywhere else now," she told me when I asked about the faerie paths. "Just relax and enjoy your brand new palace life."

Relax? I don't think so. If *almost* no part of this palace and its grounds can be accessed by the faerie paths, that means there must be some areas where doorways can be opened. And if I'm hoping to escape once I've learned everything I need to know from Prince Roarke, then I have to find at least one of those areas. If I can't, I'm going to have to get creative with my Griffin Ability. And that will require figuring out how to actually use it.

"My lady?"

My body tenses at the sound of the unexpected voice. I whip around, my heart already thrashing in my chest. But it's only Clarina, the handmaid Aurora 'gifted' to me upon my arrival. She stands beside the ruby-studded gold trapdoor. The *open* trapdoor I'm certain was locked until now because I found my way to the other side of it yesterday afternoon and couldn't get through it. I wouldn't have bothered opening one of the lower windows and scaling the wall otherwise. I clear my throat and clasp my hands together. "Um, yes?"

"Her Highness, Princess Aurora, sent me to fetch you," Clarina says, her eyes fixed on the floor near my feet. I've told her not to worry about averting her gaze when speaking to me, but it's made no difference. Just like when I told her I'm no 'lady' and she doesn't have to refer to me as such. "But how else will I show you respect, my lady?" she asked. "I can't simply call you by your name." I told her that of course she could, but that didn't go down well either.

"How did she know I was up here?" I ask.

"One of her guards saw you from a window."

I wipe my hands on my jeans. "Did, uh, did it sound to you like Aurora—Miss—Her Highness—" Darn these stupid titles. "Did it sound like she was angry with me for being up here?"

"No, my lady," Clarina says. "She was concerned, but not angry. She reminded her guards that you're welcome to explore your new home, but that they're also supposed to keep you alive."

"Right. Cool. That's what I thought. I mean, about the exploring part." Aurora gave me a brief tour when I arrived three days ago, then told me I could go pretty much wherever I wanted, other than people's private suites or chambers or whatever she called them. Since then, I've wandered all over the palace under the guise of curiosity, doing my best to pretend I'm at ease in a home as vast and opulent as this palace. I attempt to ignore the guards who watch me and the court members who smile politely before whispering to one another. And I try not to shiver when the atmosphere shifts, as it does occasionally, into something cold and unsettling.

"Uh, well, I guess we'd better go then," I say, realizing that

Clarina is waiting for me to speak. She nods and steps onto the staircase below the trapdoor. I follow her down, flinching when the trapdoor bangs shut of its own accord behind me. Together we descend the spiral staircase all the way to the ground floor of the palace and into a vast column-lined hallway. Its black marble floors are polished to a glassy shine and the precious stones embedded in the ceiling reflect the enchanted lamps burning on pedestals between each column. The rest of the palace is much like this: gleaming black edges, gold embellishments, and glittering gems. Rooms large enough to get lost in, and furnishings so lavish I'd probably vomit if I knew what they cost.

It's impossible to imagine ever being at home here.

We climb more stairs, cross more hallways, and pass more fae dressed like they belong on the set of a period drama. They all give me curious glances as I pass. Unlike Clarina and Noraya—Aurora's other handmaid—none of these people know who I am. They have no idea I've agreed to marry their prince. How could they possibly suspect that he and I have anything to do with each other when Roarke's been gone since the moment he dumped me here in his sister's care? Aurora said he'd return this morning, but I've seen nothing of him. I'm starting to wonder if he's planning to avoid me until the day of our wedding—whenever that may be.

Finally, Clarina and I reach the wing housing the royal family's quarters. I've never been far enough into it to see the rooms belonging to the king and queen themselves, but I've passed Roarke's suite, and I've been into Aurora's every day since I arrived here. I look over my shoulder at the door leading into Roarke's rooms as I pass. The door is closed and no guards stand outside it, which I take to mean that Roarke isn't inside.

"Darn," I mutter, quietly enough that Clarina won't hear me. A frown pulls at my brow as I face forward again. And then that strange feeling of unease, that inexplicable sense of *wrongness*, pervades my senses. As if cold, rotting fingers are about to reach from the shadows to clamp around the back of my neck. A flicker of a shadow scurries across the edge of my vision, but when I look over my shoulder again, it's gone. And so is that sense of discomfort.

"Lady Emerson?" Clarina says. I look ahead and see her waiting with one hand resting against Aurora's door. "Is everything all right?"

"Um, yes. I'm fine." Perhaps I keep imagining that odd feeling. Perhaps that's what homesickness feels like. Maybe, as unlikely as it seems, I'm actually missing the rundown home I lived in with Chelsea and Georgia. *No way*, I think to myself, almost laughing out loud at the farfetched thought. I may miss my best friend Val, and all the fun we had together, and the freeing feeling of not being hunted down by various members of the fae realm, but I certainly don't miss that horrible little house and my spiteful aunt and cousin.

Clarina opens the door to Aurora's suite and stands aside to let me walk in. She bobs into a quick curtsey as I pass, then closes the door behind me. I hear her feet tap away across the polished marble floor outside. On the other side of the sitting room, which is decorated in muted tones and floral fabrics, Princess Aurora, adopted daughter of the Unseelie King and

Queen, sits at a small round table. Laid out in front of her is a variety of food, a teapot and two teacups. She leans back in her chair and surveys me. "Really, Em? Climbing the outside of the east tower? Are you *trying* to scandalize the entire court? If you wanted to see the view from the top so badly, you could have just asked someone to unlock the trapdoor instead of risking your life."

I cross the room and stop beside the chair on the opposite side of the table from her. "Well, you know. It was earlyish. I didn't want to bother anyone. And besides, there was hardly any risk involved. I can handle a simple wall. Those great big marble bricks have gaps between them that are perfect for hand- and footholds."

Aurora tucks her hair—black and blueish purple—behind one ear and reaches forward for her teacup. "And if you'd slipped? Aside from the enormous trouble I'd be in with Roarke and my father if you fell and got yourself killed, it just isn't appropriate to go around climbing walls." She gives me a pointed look over the top of her teacup. "You know, given your future position in this palace."

I choose to ignore her reference to the fact that I'm supposed to be a princess soon and cross my arms over my chest. I begin pacing to and from the window. "Where's Roarke? You said he'd be back by now, but I didn't see anyone standing guard outside his rooms, so I assume he isn't in there."

"He and Dad must have been delayed, that's all. They have important business to deal with at the moment. You can't expect them to rush back simply because you're desperate to see your betrothed." She smirks. I stick my tongue out at her. She throws a strawberry at me, then laughs when I dodge and continue walking. "They'll be back soon, I'm sure. And please stop pacing. You're making me nervous." She waves to the chair opposite hers. "Sit down. Have you had breakfast yet?"

"No." I drop into the chair with my arms still crossed. "I was too busy taking risks and climbing walls, remember?"

"You should choose breakfast next time." With a neat twist of her hand, a plate of butterfly-shaped pastries rises on its own and moves toward me. She'd no doubt be pleased if I used magic to lift one of the pastries and move it to my own plate, but that kind of thing seems like laziness to me. And I don't think I could do it without knocking the whole plate over.

"You know why I want to see Roarke," I say to her after placing a pastry on my plate—with my own perfectly functional hand. "He and I have an agreement, and he's done nothing to fulfill his part yet." Agreement. Such a simple word. It doesn't carry nearly as much weight as the word 'marriage.'

"Of course he hasn't fulfilled his part yet. I hope you know he doesn't plan to give you any information on how to get your mother out of her enchanted coma or fix her mental illness until *after* the union ceremony."

"Yes," I say quietly, still staring at my plate. "I do know that." What I also know is that I don't intend for that ceremony to ever happen. Everyone needs to *think* it will happen, but I plan to find out everything I need to know before the marriage takes place. Of course, I have no idea how I'm going to do that yet, but being in possession of a powerful Griffin Ability—speaking things into existence—can't hurt. If

I can use it at just the right moment in just the right way, I should be able to get out of here alive with all the information I need. I clear my throat and add, "I know, but he needs to prove himself to me. He needs to tell me *something* so I'll know he isn't just lying to get me to marry him."

"My dear brother would never do something like that," Aurora says, directing a few more items of food onto her plate.

I don't know her well enough yet to know if she's joking or if she really believes that. Either way, I'm not willing to trust Roarke. I need my own plan, and that involves gaining control of my Griffin Ability. I break off a piece of pastry and stare at it for a moment or two before saying, "Since climbing tower walls isn't appropriate, perhaps my time would be better spent practicing my Griffin Ability. With the elixir, I mean, not just waiting for the random moments when my magic chooses to switch itself on."

She shakes her head and finishes swallowing another mouthful of her tea. "I'm sorry, Em, but I was told not to give it to you until Roarke and my father return. Here, have some citrullamyn." Several segments of a fruit that looks like a blood-red version of an orange fly in an arc from her plate onto my mine.

"Uh, thanks." I slowly chew one while trying to figure out what I can say to change Aurora's mind. I need that elixir in order to stimulate my Griffin Ability. The first vial I had was crushed to pieces during my encounter with Ada—the supremely nasty faerie who almost destroyed the whole of Stanmeade with her glass magic—but one of the Griffin rebels made more elixir so I could try to wake Mom from her

21

enchanted coma. It didn't work, but at least I had some of the elixir left. I brought it with me, planning to secretly consume tiny amounts in the hope of gaining control of my Griffin Ability without the Unseelies knowing. But I was searched before entering the palace. A guard discovered the elixir, and Aurora confiscated it. Roarke, who didn't seem interested in spending more than a few minutes with his betrothed, had already left by that point.

"But Aurora," I say to her in my most reasonable voice, "I'm no use to your family if I can't figure out how to control my Griffin Ability. That's the only reason Roarke's marrying me, remember? So I need that elixir to help me learn how to use it."

"Yes, but you don't need to learn *right this moment*. You can practice under supervision when Roarke and Dad return."

I look her squarely in the eyes. "Don't they trust you to supervise me? Do they think you can't handle me?"

She tilts her head back and laughs. "Oh, my dear Em. If you're going to try to manipulate me, you'll have to be a lot more subtle about it. That was a terrible attempt."

I slide lower in my chair with a defeated sigh. "This is all such a waste of time," I mutter. "Mom's still stuck in some kind of evil, magic-induced coma, and I'm getting absolutely nowhere in figuring out how to help her."

"You're not wasting time. You're learning how to use everyday magic and how to live as one of us," Aurora says. "Speaking of which, please sit up straight. My mother would have heart palpitations if she saw you slouching like that."

Aurora's mother. The Unseelie Queen herself. I had dinner

with her and Aurora on my first night here, with servants waiting on us the entire evening, filling our goblets with oddly colored drinks and our plates with food even better than the food Azzy cooked back at Chevalier House. I found it difficult to enjoy anything, though, given the anxiety cramping my stomach and making my fingers shake. It wasn't as though Queen Amrath was cruel or unfriendly. She was over-the-top polite, in fact, but I knew she was watching me the entire time. Sizing me up. Waiting for me to prove myself completely unworthy of marrying her son. With every awkward moment that passed, I reminded myself of my highly valuable Griffin Ability. *That'll keep you alive and safe*, I kept telling myself. *They want your power more than they want a well-mannered princess.*

"Em?" Aurora says. "Are you listening to me?"

I clear my throat and push myself up so I'm sitting straighter. I force my shoulders back. "Sorry. What did you say?"

"I said we need to have a talk about what you're wearing, and also that you should try the honeystar tea. It's quite invigorating. Noraya, come pour some tea for Emerson."

Noraya, who was standing so still by the bedroom door that I didn't notice her there, moves closer to the table. With a brief wave of her hand, the teapot rises into the air. "Oh, don't worry," I say quickly, sitting forward. "I can pour the tea."

"Let her do it, Em," Aurora says.

"But it's just tea," I argue as the teapot tilts over my cup and dark steaming liquid streams from its spout. "I can pour it myself." Not with magic, since that would probably result in tea splashing all over the table, but my own two hands would do the job just fine.

"It doesn't matter whether you *can* do it or not," Aurora tells me. "What matters is that when you're a member of the royal family, it's proper for servants to wait on you."

"I'm not a member of the royal family yet." *And I hopefully never will be.*

"It's also proper for you to wear court-appropriate clothing," Aurora adds as Noraya steps away from the table, "and those—" she eyes my jeans and T-shirt with disapproval "—are not appropriate. Clarina and I will have to have another chat. She clearly hasn't understood her instructions."

"What? No, it isn't Clarina's fault. She gives me a new dress every morning, just as you told her to, but I don't want to wear any of them. They're ridiculous. Hundreds of layers of fabric with corsets and feathers and jewels and ... stuff. It isn't me." The jeans, T-shirt and hoodie I've been wearing for the past few days are the clothes I had on when I arrived here. I hang them over a chair in my bedroom every night, and every morning I find them folded and clean, on the same chair.

Aurora arches an eyebrow. "Ridiculous?" she repeats. I realize I may have offended her, given the long skirt, tight bodice and bell-shaped sleeves of the dress she's wearing. "I'm afraid it doesn't matter what you or anyone else thinks, since that's the way my mother and father wish the members of their court to dress."

"Well, your parents have a seriously outdated sense of fashion. Everyone looks like they're playing dress-up or getting ready to shoot a steampunk film."

Her expression grows serious. "I wouldn't say things like that if I were you." She lowers her voice, leans closer, and adds, "My father has eyes and ears everywhere, and he wouldn't appreciate comments like that."

A chill creeps across my skin. Seems I haven't been imagining the feeling of being watched. I wrap my arms around myself, feeling naked despite the fact that I'm dressed. "Even in the bedrooms?"

"Well." Aurora leans back. "Perhaps only ears in the bedrooms."

"That's just … wrong," I whisper.

She laughs, and again I can't tell if she's joking about all of this. "Only if you have something to hide," she says. She bites into another unidentifiable fruit and watches me as she chews and swallows. "Now tell me: how are you coming along with the magic I've taught you so far? Can you move things yet? Try to lift your plate and move it around in the air."

"Uh …" I begin twisting a strand of hair around my forefinger. "Are you sure that's a good idea? What if I drop it?"

"Then Noraya will gather up the broken pieces and throw them away. No big deal."

My gaze slips down to the hair wrapped around my finger. I'm almost used to the bright blue color mixed in with the dark brown. It's part of what marks me as a faerie. As someone who belongs in this world. Slowly, I lower my hand. "Yeah, okay. I'll try."

Drawing magic from deep inside me is easy now, but sending it toward the plate, coaxing it around and beneath and telling it to *lift something up*, is a different story. Ever so slowly, with my hands clenched in my lap and my eyes just about boring holes into the plate, it begins to rise. It wobbles slightly, and the half-eaten pastry and pieces of red citrus slide to one side. I try to right it, end up overcompensating, and the whole plate flips over. The food lands on the table with several soft thumps, and the plate remains suspended upside down in the air. It shudders and sways before I imagine my magic lowering it carefully. It drops the final few inches, landing neatly on top of my breakfast.

Aurora claps her hands. "Well, that was entertaining. Hardly perfect, but it's a good start."

"I guess." I turn the plate over and begin cleaning up my mess.

"Em, you could barely do anything when you arrived here a few days ago. This is an achievement. Oh, and I have some more books for you." She gestures over her shoulder, and a pile of books on the low table between the couches rises into the air before dropping down again, the individual books smacking loudly into each other as they land. "You can carry them out with magic just now."

"Sure." I try not to work out how long it will take me to get back to my own rooms if I have to magically transport a pile of books the entire way there. Hopefully I can convince one of the guards who surreptitiously follow me around at a distance to help me once I'm out of Aurora's sight.

As I get back to eating my mess of a breakfast, the door opens and Clarina slips into the room. She moves silently to stand beside Noraya and, after a moment's pause, begins whispering to her.

26

"What's going on?" Aurora asks loudly, not bothering to look around at them.

Clarina falls silent, her wide eyes darting across the room toward her mistress. From across the room, I see her throat bob as she swallows.

"Clarina." Aurora pushes her plate away and turns in her chair to face the two handmaids. "Part of your job is to *report* secrets to me, not to whisper them in my vicinity. Now tell me what's going on."

Clarina bobs her head. "Yes, Your Highness. I apologize. It's just that … it's so horrible."

"What's so horrible? What happened?"

"One of the guards …" Clarina's eyes shift to Noraya, whose chin shudders as she stares at the floor. Clarina clears her throat and returns her gaze to Aurora. "One of the guards was found dead in the garden," she says in a shaky voice. "Grey and wrinkled and dead."

CHAPTER TWO

I PACE ACROSS THE SITTING ROOM OF MY SUITE—SMALLER than Aurora's, but no less luxurious—waiting for someone to come and tell me what's going on. Aurora sent me back here in the company of several guards immediately after Clarina's creepy words about someone grey, wrinkled, and dead in the garden, but I've received no news since then. I walk onto my balcony and look down yet again, but I still can't see anything interesting. This death must have happened on the other side of the palace.

I wander inside again, between the armchairs and around the table. I sit at the writing desk and try to read one of the books I'm supposed to be studying, but I can't focus. Thoughts of Mom and all the Griffin rebels I ran away from keep slipping through the cracks of my concentration. Guilt over vanishing with no explanation. Sadness at having to leave Bandit behind. I'm even starting to miss Dash, of all people. And then there's the avalanche of questions: Who am I? Who is Mom? How did we come to live in the human realm with our magic blocked? Just to name a few …

I abandon the book and end up lying on the divan, watching the glow-bugs that are fixed to the ceiling, and slowly lifting and lowering cushions with magic. It requires my full attention to get this simple maneuver right, which means there's no room in my mind for questions and distracting thoughts.

Without warning, the main door to my suite is thrown open. My two levitating cushions land on my chest and tumble to the floor. I push myself up hurriedly, twisting around to face the door, and find Aurora striding into the room. Someone pulls the door shut behind her as I stand and ask, "Is everything okay? Did you find out what happened?"

"I don't know what happened, but I've spoken to the people who found the dead guard." She walks onto the balcony. I follow her out into the warm mid-morning sunshine. "I saw him, Em. It was …" She sucks in a breath and shakes her head. "Horrifying. The color in his hair was completely gone, and his face …" She turns away and rests her hands on the balcony railing. "His skin was sagging and wrinkled. It was just awful. That doesn't happen to our kind, Em. That *doesn't happen*. Not naturally anyway. And this means that—" She cuts herself off, her fingers tightening on the balustrade.

"Means what? That this guard was attacked with magic?" I

mentally kick myself for that unimpressive feat of deduction. *Obviously* this guard was attacked with magic.

"Yes. Something like that." Aurora shakes her head and returns her gaze to me. "Anyway, I received a message from Roarke. He said we shouldn't speak of it to anyone. Only a few people know what the guard looked like, and we don't want everyone finding out and getting scared."

I can't help raising my eyebrows. "You think the rest of this palace doesn't already know? Someone must have told Clarina, and surely Clarina and Noraya have told others by now."

"They won't have told a soul. Clarina and Noraya have been with me forever—well, Noraya's been here forever, and Clarina's been with me for at least three years—so they know how to keep their mouths shut. Clarina was with one of my mother's handmaids when she saw the dead guard, and she came straight here afterwards. A few other guards have seen him, but they've also been told to keep quiet."

I lean against the balustrade and stare across the garden. In the distance, two large birds soar across the sky. At least, I assume they're birds. Their wings seem a little too big for their bodies, though. "Does anyone know who did it?" I ask, looking away from the flying creatures. "I mean, if it's impossible to sneak into this palace, then it must be a guest or someone who lives here."

Aurora exhales and plasters a fake smile onto her face. "We mustn't speak of it anymore, Em. Forget about it now."

"Forget? That's unlikely. Don't you want to know more?"

"No. Roarke and my father will take care of it when they return. Which should be just before dinner, apparently."

"Oh." My unease shifts into something more positive. "That's great."

"Yes. Now, what other magic was I showing you yesterday?" She rubs her hands together and walks back inside. "You practiced moving things, and there was also …"

"Fire," I remind her. "Well, tiny flames. So I don't accidentally burn the palace down."

"Yes, that's right. Have you made any improvement?"

I snap my fingers together and open my hand, palm-up, hoping the spell has become instinctual enough for a flame to appear automatically above my hand. My palm, however, remains empty. "Um … apparently not."

"Yes, well, you're not even trying." She sits primly at the edge of the divan. "You need to focus. You're not at the point yet where it happens automatically. Now, try again."

I grumble beneath my breath before lowering my hands to my sides, closing my eyes, and telling myself to relax. I need to be able to release magic, then focus fully on the moment when it's ready to shift from something raw and formless into anything else. At that point, I have to mentally shape it into a flame before it disappears. And all this, apparently, will happen almost instantly once I've done it enough times. I've just about reached a relaxed mental state when a tap on the other side of the door interrupts my concentration.

"Enter," Aurora calls out.

Noraya walks in and hurries to Aurora's side. She bends and whispers something before straightening.

Aurora rises with a sigh. "Of course. I'll come now. Sorry, Em, but my mother would like to see me. You should carry on practicing, though. And get started on reading those books. You have a lot to learn if you're going to fit in here."

I watch her leave before dropping into an armchair and slumping back against the gold-embroidered cushions. Then I force myself to sit up straight and focus on producing a flame. I have no intention of fitting in here—not in the long run—but I need to at least pretend I'm planning to see this union through. Besides, I'll probably need to use magic to get myself out of here. I may as well take this opportunity to learn as much as I can.

After trying repeatedly to produce a flame and succeeding about fifty percent of the time, I settle down with the smallest book from the pile Aurora gave me this morning. It's a collection of basic spells that reads as though it was written for a first grader. Perfect. As embarrassing as it is, this is exactly the kind of thing I need.

Once I've successfully managed to shrink a cushion to about half of its size, then enlarge it, and then return it to normal, I pick up a different book and settle into an armchair. It contains accounts of history even older than the history I learned at Chevalier House. The initial dividing of the courts, and the very first Seelie and Unseelie families. I haven't got very far when I hear a faint scratching sound. I lower the book and look around, trying to figure out where the scratching is coming from, but whatever it was has stopped. With a frown, I return to reading.

But the scratching begins again. From the direction of the desk, perhaps? I stand slowly, wondering what exactly I'll do if I tug open one of the drawers and a nasty magical creature pounces out at me. For some reason, my imagination conjures up an image of a disembodied hand, which doesn't help my pattering heart rate at all.

Three sharp taps at the door cause the book to slip from my fingers. I close my eyes for a moment and breathe out shakily, almost laughing at myself for becoming so jumpy. "Come in," I call as I bend to pick up the book.

"Your lunch, Lady Emerson," Clarina says from the doorway.

I straighten, leave the book on the armchair, and push my hair out of my face. "Right. Thanks." I've eaten lunch with Aurora each day since I arrived here, but she obviously has other matters to attend to today. Clarina carries the tray of food to the table near the balcony doors while I edge closer to the desk on the other side of the room. Feeling silly now for having been afraid of a simple scratching sound, but still a little wary of what might have been causing it, I yank open the drawer on the left and quickly stand back. The stolen stylus rolls toward the back of the drawer—and nothing jumps out at me. I push the drawer closed and open the one on the right. It's filled with the blank scrolls that were on top of the first pile of books Aurora gathered for me.

"Is everything all right, Lady Emerson?" Clarina asks.

My cheeks flush as I look over my shoulder at her. "Yes, sorry. I thought I heard something, but …" I turn back and peer into the drawer. "But there's nothing here."

"There are many small creatures living in the gardens here," Clarina tells me. "Some of them come inside on occasion. Most of them are harmless."

"Most?" I repeat.

She smiles faintly at the floor, but doesn't elaborate. "Do you need anything else, my lady?"

I pick up the history book on my way to the table. "I don't think so. This looks amazing." She bobs her head and walks back toward the door.

"Clarina?" I ask as I lower myself into a chair.

She stops and looks around, her eyes meeting mine for only a moment before focusing on the floor. "Yes, Lady Emerson?"

"What makes you an Unseelie faerie?"

She hesitates before answering. "What do you mean?"

"*Are* you even an Unseelie faerie? Is everyone who lives and works in the palace considered Unseelie?"

She frowns at the floor. "Yes, I believe so, my lady."

"What makes you different from someone who isn't Unseelie? I'm trying to remember what I was told when I first arrived in this world, but it wasn't much. I think someone said the magic here is slightly different? Something about dark magic?"

"Any magic they don't agree with they call dark magic."

"They?"

"Those who are not Unseelie. Some of our magic is the same as theirs," she explains. "Like the power that resides naturally within all of us, or the power we absorb from the elements or the plants. But they don't like it when we take power from other living beings—lesser beings—and they don't like some of the procedures involved in certain spells. So that's where the divide comes in. I think," she adds, folding her hands together demurely in front of her.

My eyes graze over the spread of food on the table. It's far more than I could ever eat in one meal. I wish I could ask Clarina to sit down and eat with me while I ask her more questions, but I know she'd never agree to that. "What counts as a lesser being?" I ask.

Again, she looks confused. "Well, everything that isn't a faerie, of course."

A chill raises the hairs on my arms, despite the warm breeze wafting in through the open balcony doors. "Do, um, do you do that often? Take power from other living beings?"

"No, my lady. I haven't ever needed to. I've been healed before by spells that were specifically Unseelie, but I personally haven't absorbed raw power from another being."

"Okay. I see." I'm not sure what else to say, aside from telling her that taking someone else's power sounds downright creepy and just plain wrong.

"Do you have any other questions, my lady?"

"Uh … not right now."

She turns, then adds, "You don't need to be disturbed by all this, my lady. It's unfamiliar to you, I know, but it isn't wrong. It's just different. And, well, I've always been told that we shouldn't be afraid of something just because it's different."

"Um, yes, that's true. Thank you, Clarina." I give her a smile that fades the moment the door closes behind her. I know I shouldn't be afraid of something simply because it's different, but if it's different *and* it's hurting someone, that's not okay. Perhaps I've misunderstood it, though. Perhaps this 'taking power' thing isn't nearly as ominous as it sounds. It may only be a little bit of power, not enough to kill someone.

And perhaps they only take it from beings that are willing.

I help myself to some food, reopen the book, and continue reading. After only a few minutes, a subdued thump comes from the direction of my bedroom. I lower the sandwich that was halfway toward my mouth and slot a fork between the pages of the book to keep my place. I silently lift a knife and rise from the chair to face the half-open bedroom door.

And then I spend far too long frozen in place, wondering whether I should investigate on my own or risk looking stupid by asking a guard to go into my bedroom and hunt down the mysterious *thing* that hasn't made another sound since that first thump. I decide in the end to risk looking foolish. Better than getting chomped by one of the *non*-harmless creatures from outside—or by whatever it was that killed that guard this morning.

I open the main door, stick my head out, and find two women in guard uniforms standing just outside. They spend at least twenty minutes searching every inch of my bedroom while I pretend to read. And when they leave, having found no hint of a threat, I'm almost certain I see one rolling her eyes at the other.

CHAPTER THREE

"HAS YOUR GRIFFIN ABILITY APPEARED AGAIN?" AURORA asks that evening as we retire to the couches in her private sitting room. It's late, dinner is over, and Roarke still isn't back. Asking when he'll return is useless, so I've given up, but I still find myself burning with frustration every time I picture Mom permanently asleep. My hands want to curl into fists whenever I think of all the minutes, hours, and days passing by.

"I felt it in my sleep last night," I tell her, removing a cushion from behind my back and hugging it to my chest. Better to squeeze the cushion than to continuously dig my nails into my palms. "It woke me up. By the time I figured out what was happening, the moment had passed. I didn't manage to get a single word out before the magic was gone."

"What would you have said?"

I shake my head as I watch the dancing flames in the fireplace. Given that it's summer here, I wouldn't have thought it necessary to light a fire at night, but the room feels pleasantly warm and cozy. "I don't know. I was half asleep and trying to think of something, but the feeling was gone before I'd come up with any command."

She watches me for some time, while I continue to stare past her at the flames. "Do you really think the elixir is going to help you?"

I focus on her, my mood lifting instantly. Could she possibly be thinking of giving the elixir back to me? "Of course it helps. It turns the ability on so I can use it."

"Yes, I know, but you said the point of the elixir is to somehow teach you to use and control the ability on your own. It's supposed to help you recognize what your Griffin magic feels like, right? So that you can call on that magic at will without the help of the elixir?"

"Yes, something like that."

"But you already know what it feels like."

I look down at my arms wrapped around the cushion. "Yes, I do."

"So then why—"

"Why can't I do it on my own?" I sigh, my excitement dissipating. She isn't going to give me that elixir. "I don't know. I've tried. I imagine the feeling. I picture pulling magic from deep inside me, but nothing ever happens. Maybe if I had that elixir, I could—"

"No," she says. "I'm not giving you something that will

become a crutch, especially since there isn't a lot of it, and once it's gone, we don't know how to make more. Not to mention what a bad idea it is to give you something that will immediately switch on a dangerous ability you could then use against me."

"Aurora, I would never—"

"Yeah, yeah." She rolls her eyes. "You're going to be part of my family soon, so I'd like to be able to trust you, but we're not there yet. No, the reason I'm bringing this up is because I've been thinking about how your ability might work." She tilts her head to the side and stares thoughtfully across the room at the curtains concealing the balcony doors. "Perhaps, because it's such a powerful ability, it needs to sort of … replenish itself. That would explain why you can't use it all the time."

"Okay. Maybe. Do some kinds of magic work that way?"

"Well, all magic works that way, actually." She shifts her position, folds one leg neatly over the other, and faces me. "It's just that we hardly ever use it all up in one go, so we don't realize that it's constantly replenishing. If you do something that's particularly strenuous on your magic, like lifting something very heavy and holding it in the air for a long time, then you'll eventually tire yourself out. Magically, I mean. Then you need to rest while your magic restores itself."

"Like replenishing energy if you do something that's physically exhausting?" I ask.

"Yes. So I wonder if maybe your Griffin Ability works in a similar way, but in quick bursts rather than slowly over a long period of time."

I nod. "That sounds like it could make sense. It always feels as though it comes over me in a sudden rush, gets used up immediately with whatever I happen to say at the time, and then it's gone."

"Or it ends up released into your surroundings with no purpose if you don't say anything at all." She taps her chin and purses her lips. "Hmm. I wonder if you could hang on to it and use it at a later time instead of having to release it whenever it's replenished.

"Uh … I could try that?" I suggest, having no idea how I would actually 'hang on' to this elusive power of mine.

"Anyway, this is all speculation at this point," Aurora continues. "We need to gather some actual evidence. Take note of exactly when it happens. The day and time. And keep track of other things, like whether you've used an unusually large amount of your normal magic on something else. Because we don't know whether your normal magic has any effect on your Griffin magic, or if the two are independent of each other."

I nod as she speaks. "Basically, we want to figure out if we can predict when it will happen."

"Yes. You're going to have to be very thorough, Em. Record every detail that could possibly influence your Griffin Ability."

"Yeah, definitely." I frown as my mind races back over all the times I've given a magical command, trying to force the events into a pattern that makes sense. I end up shaking my head. "Maybe we're wrong. There was one time when I used it twice within a few minutes. So the replenishing theory wouldn't make sense then."

"Well, perhaps you didn't use it all up with the first thing you said. Perhaps you *can* hang onto some of it, but you didn't realize that's what you were doing. That's why you had some left over for a second command, but then after that it was all used up."

I chew on my lower lip before answering. "Yeah. Maybe."

"Or perhaps your magic is still settling," Aurora suggests. "That's what happens to halflings if their magic appears later in life. It often comes and goes for a while before becoming consistently present. Maybe, once a little more time has passed, your Griffin Ability will appear at regular intervals."

I push one hand through my hair. "So many possibilities and unknowns."

"That's why you need to start documenting everything. That's the only way we'll learn if my theory is correct or not."

I stand and drop the cushion onto the couch. I wander over to the fireplace and lift the silver candlestick holder from the mantelpiece. I practiced lighting the candle repeatedly before dinner, and I managed to produce a flame with almost every attempt. I snap my fingers beside the wick—and a flame ignites it.

"Well done." Aurora claps her hands in delight. "Okay. Now that you've got that one right, what shall I teach you next?"

Instead of answering her, I ask, "Is this what you do every night? Eat dinner alone in your room? Or do you have family dinners when everyone's home?"

If she's confused by my change of subject, she doesn't show it. "Well, it's always different," she says with a shrug. "Sometimes we use one of the smaller dining rooms and have dinner with just the four of us. Sometimes extended family members join us. Sometimes we entertain guests, or my mother will entertain her friends, or I'll entertain some of the young ladies of the court. If I'm tired of everyone, then I eat alone here." She cocks her head. "Why do you ask?"

"I'm just trying to picture what your normal life is like. Clarina told me you have ladies-in-waiting, but you sent them away on holiday. And I haven't seen you interact with anyone other than your mother and a handful of servants and guards, so—"

"So you're wondering if I'm a miserable loner?" she asks with one raised eyebrow.

"No. I'm wondering if you're trying to hide me from everyone else who lives here."

Several moments pass before she answers. "I wouldn't call it *hiding*, but I suppose that's essentially what it is. People are going to ask questions about you, Em. They're already asking questions about this strange friend of mine who doesn't look like she belongs here. It's easier if we don't put ourselves in a position where we have to answer anyone until the right time."

"And the right time will be … ?"

"When you and Roarke make an official announcement about your engagement. No one will question your presence here then. They wouldn't dare."

The words 'official announcement' send a chill through me. Then, despite the fact that I'm standing beside the fire, the chill seems to become real. Goosebumps rise across my skin, and cold air whispers across the back of my neck. I look over my shoulder, but despite the distinct feeling that someone is watching me, I don't see anyone else in the room.

With a quiet click, the door opens. My gaze darts toward it. It swings slowly open, and into the room walks Roarke. Sharp angles, dark hair perfectly in place, and eyes the color of red wine. His intense gaze sweeps across the room before landing on me. His lips curl into half a smile as a flush heats my skin.

"Oh, look at that." Aurora clasps her hands together beneath her chin. "She's thrilled to see you, Roarke."

"Indeed." As the door closes itself behind Roarke, he walks slowly toward me, hands behind his back. "If only she was thrilled for the right reasons and not because she's been desperate to interrogate me since the moment she arrived here."

I swallow before speaking. "I'm glad you haven't forgotten why I'm here."

He stops in front of me, close enough that I have to look up to meet his eyes. I knew he was tall, of course, but I'd forgotten the way his commanding presence makes him seem even taller. I won't step back, though. I refuse to be intimidated by the guy I'm supposed to be marrying soon, regardless of the fact that I have no intention of actually going through with the union.

Roarke's smile stretches a little wider, and from behind his back, he produces a rose. A gold, delicately fashioned rose with a ruby at the center of its solid gold petals. "My lady," he murmurs, bowing slightly as he hands the rose to me. I hesitate, then take it from him. He leans farther forward, his face suddenly way too close to mine, and his lips briefly graze my cheek. A cold shiver skitters across my skin and down my neck. "My apologies for taking so long to return. My father and I don't often have to deal with matters personally, but this was one of those occasions. We thought it best to stay where we were until the job was done."

"Uh … okay. Thanks for that cryptic explanation."

"Soon, my love, you'll be part of the family. You'll know all our secrets."

"Your *love*? Really?" I place the gold rose on the mantelpiece and cross my arms over my chest. "I think it's a little soon for that, Roarke."

Roarke looks at Aurora with a quiet chuckle. "Have you been teaching her how to play hard to get?"

Aurora stretches out across the couch, straightening the layers of her skirt over her legs. "Nope. It appears she knows how to do that on her own."

I almost make a comment about how this is all a game to them, but since I'm hoping to beat them at it and get out of here alive, I should probably play along. "How about we get to know each other a little better before you start throwing the words 'my love' around? You haven't even taken me on a date yet."

"A date? Well, I hope you have something a little smarter to wear than that—" he gestures to my jeans and hoodie "—if you're planning to go on a date with a prince. And speaking of clothing, have you not been given more appropriate attire?"

"I have, but I prefer to wear the kind of clothes I'm comfortable in."

"Refused," Aurora says from across the room. "She flat-out refused to wear any of the dresses."

I breathe out sharply through my nose. "Those dresses look

like they're from another century. I know this is a palace full of royals, but can't you move with the times in the clothing department? The rest of the fae world seems to wear pretty much the same kind of clothes people wear in my world."

"*This* is your world, Em," Aurora reminds me. "And if you bothered to take a closer look inside your wardrobe, I think you'd find that the outfits hanging there are of the latest fashion. Formal fae fashion, which may not be familiar to you, but still. Only the very latest designs."

"You're right," I tell her, moving away from Roarke to lean against an armchair. "I'm not familiar with formal fae fashion."

"Enough about clothing," Roarke says. He turns to face me, pushing his hands into the pockets of his long coat, which is covered in finely detailed silver embroidery and is no doubt the latest in 'formal fae fashion.' "Tell me, my love—" He cuts himself off. "Apologies," he adds with a slight dip of his head. "Please tell me, my *lady*, what you think of your new home."

"Since you've seen the inside of my previous home, I assume you can figure out my feelings toward this one."

"You love it?" he asks. "You're in complete awe? You're unendingly grateful you get to spend the rest of your life here?"

"Not exactly. It is beautiful, I'll give you that. Not quite what I expected, but definitely beautiful."

"Ah, now I'm intrigued." He lifts the gold rose from the mantelpiece and twirls it between his fingers. "What were you expecting?"

I lift my shoulders in a slow shrug as I try to put my initial expectations into words. "I don't know. You Unseelies are meant to be the evil bad guys, right? So I was expecting something … colder. Darker. A dead forest surrounding your palace, or perpetual winter or something. But, you know, everything's sunny and warm and alive." *Outside, at least*, I add silently. I say nothing about the cold, oppressive feeling that sometimes presses on my shoulders when I'm inside the palace. The chill I can sense in the air right now.

Roarke tilts his head to the side. "You haven't looked outside at night, have you."

I cast my mind back to the three nights I've spent here so far. Each evening when I've returned to my room, the curtains have been drawn, the enchanted lamps lit, and the small pool in my forest-themed bathroom has been filled with steaming hot water and scented bubbles. "No, I don't think I have."

He walks past me, places the gold rose on the table Aurora and I normally eat at, and waves his hand past the curtains. As they open themselves, he turns back and extends his hand toward me. "Let me show you something."

Reluctantly, I place my hand in his. He opens the balcony doors and leads me outside. I suck in a breath at the unexpectedly frigid air. Then, as I reach the balcony railing and look down, my lips part in amazement at the sight of the glittering winter wonderland covering the entire palace grounds. "Wow," I whisper.

"My mother likes summer," Roarke says, "but my father likes winter. Her magic controls the day, and his controls the night."

My eyes trail across the snow-covered topiary, the frozen fountains, and the icicles hanging from the fingertips of the nearest statue. "That must be very confusing for all the plants and creatures residing in these gardens."

"Fortunately for them, they're magical too. They can handle it."

A shiver courses through me, and Roarke shrugs free of his coat. "What a gentleman," I say drily as he places it over my shoulders. "Although I would have expected there to be a spell that prevents people from getting cold."

"There is. But my magic levels are a little low at present." Standing closer to me now, he reaches up and tucks my hair behind my right ear. I stiffen immediately, staring somewhere in the region of his neck instead of into his eyes, but as his fingers brush the small coin-shaped piece of metal attached to the skin behind my ear, I relax a little. He isn't trying to be intimate; he's checking if the concealment device is still there.

"Worried I might have taken it off?" I ask, pleased to hear that my voice is steady.

"Not particularly. You don't know the magic required to remove it."

"But you're checking anyway. Just in case."

"Of course. I'd be foolish not to check. You might have found someone in this palace willing to remove it for you, or your Griffin Ability might have come alive long enough for you to instruct this device to remove itself."

"And why would I do that?"

"Second thoughts about our agreement. Guilt, perhaps." He leans sideways against the balustrade, entirely comfortable in the chilly night air. "Have you begun to feel guilty yet, Emerson?"

Begun? Guilt has been eating at me since before I even got

here. I gave up my mother's hidden location to a dangerous faerie who then put her into a magical coma. I ran from the people who helped me and asked for nothing in return. I abandoned my best friend without so much as a goodbye. None of this, however, is Roarke's business. So I clear my throat and ask, "Why would I be feeling guilty? I agreed to this arrangement in order to help someone. I shouldn't have to feel guilty about that."

"True, but perhaps you've become afraid since you arrived here. Perhaps you want your friends—the Griffin rebels?—to know where you are after all."

I haven't confirmed Roarke's suspicion that it was the Griffin rebels who rescued me the day I ran from both the Guild and the Unseelies and fell from the edge of a cliff. He's asked where I was hiding out, but even if I wanted to, I couldn't tell him about that enchanted safe place. When in the company of others, I'm unable to even think of it, let alone speak the name of the place or its location. Instead, a blank space appears in my mind, presumably part of the protective spell that helps to keep that place safe. My memory of it always returns when I'm alone, but it's still disconcerting every time it completely vanishes from my mind.

Refusing to look away from Roarke's gaze, I say, "I'm not afraid, and I have not changed my mind. The last thing I want is my friends showing up here. Why would I risk them ruining our agreement before you've had a chance to follow through with your part?"

His smile is slow and careful. "Good. I'm glad to hear it."

"Which reminds me," I add. "You still need to prove that

you actually have useful information that can help my mother. You can't expect me to marry you without some assurance that you're telling the truth."

"Are you saying you're not fully committed to our intended union?"

"I am," I say fiercely, hoping the lie doesn't show on my face, "but only if you're fully committed to completely healing my mother. I want to be able to trust you, Roarke. Please give me a reason to."

"Hmm." Roarke narrows his eyes as if considering my request. "Let's see. You—"

"Emerson Clarke?"

I look toward the balcony doors at the sound of an unfamiliar male voice. In the doorway stands a guard I don't recognize. "Yes?" I ask.

"The Unseelie King wishes to meet you."

CHAPTER
FOUR

THE JOURNEY THROUGH THE PALACE TO MEET THE KING feels both torturously long and frighteningly quick. It's enough time for me to get myself completely worked up, but not nearly enough time to calm down and prepare myself.

"My father isn't as kind as I am," Roarke tells me as we stride across glossy marble hallways with two uniformed faeries ahead of us and two behind. "He wants to keep you no matter what. Daughter-in-law or prisoner."

Wonderful. That doesn't make me want to throw up at all.

"I won't let that happen, of course," Roarke adds, "but it would be better if you don't make any joking comments about changing your mind or not being certain about the union. Things might get … unpleasant."

"I've already told you I'm not changing my mind." In my

effort to mask my fear, my words come out louder than I intended. "I'm here, aren't I?" I continue in a lower voice. "And *I* came to *you*. Doesn't that prove how serious I am about this arrangement?"

"All I'm saying is that he doesn't appreciate jokes or sarcasm, so it's in your best interests to be polite. And you should probably remove my coat. You look very strange in it."

I slip Roarke's coat off and hand it back to him. "Perhaps it's in his best interests to be polite too, given how valuable my Griffin Ability is to him. If he makes me his prisoner, I'll never give him what he wants."

I try very hard to believe my own words, but Roarke's raised eyebrows and pitying expression make it impossible. As we stop outside an oversized, ornately carved door, he faces me. "You won't need to *give* him anything, Emerson. He'll take whatever he wants."

A guard opens the door. The unnatural chill in the air intensifies, and the doorway itself seems to stretch wider like a giant mouth preparing to swallow me whole. I smell damp earth and rotting leaves. My heart pounds faster as images of slimy creatures, skulls, and beetles flash across my mind.

Then I blink away the imagined images and find that the doorway hasn't changed at all, and the room it opens onto isn't a dark mouth but a large office. Roarke takes my arm and steers me forward, since my feet have forgotten how to move on their own. "Remember, I'm on your side," he whispers to me. "Prove to my father that you're willing to work with us, and I'll make sure you're never forced into anything."

I don't answer, my attention focused instead on the interior of the king's office. To the right is a table large enough for at least a dozen people to sit around. Oddly, though, whatever's on top of the table appears blurred when I try to look too closely at it. My gaze swings to the left—and I'm even more startled by what I see there: no wall encloses the office on that side. Instead, it extends into an underground cavern made of rough rock and illuminated by pale light.

"Leave us."

The deep voice brings my attention to the desk straight ahead of us. The surface is as polished as every other slab of marble that fills this palace. On the other side, a tall chair that appears to be made of the same rough rock as the cavern faces away from us. The chair remains motionless as the guards leave the room and close the door. Then, despite the fact that it must weigh a ton, the chair turns smoothly to face us.

King Savyon looks nothing like his son. His white-blond hair is streaked with black. His eyes are dark holes that bore into me. Without speaking, he places one hand on top of the other on the desk in front of him. Gold rings set with multi-colored gems glitter on every finger.

"Father, this is Emerson Clarke," Roarke says. I swallow and force myself to stand straighter. I'm pretty sure this is one of those situations where I'm not supposed to show fear, but I think I'm about to fail miserably.

The king stands, walks around to the front of his desk, and folds his arms across his chest. His eyes travel all the way down my body and up again, his gaze like a cold, creeping finger stroking along my skin. His expressionless gaze lingers on my hoodie, then travels slowly up to my face, where he holds my gaze for several terrifying moments. Despite my determination not to be intimidated, I almost wilt with relief the moment his eyes release me and move to Roarke. I wrap my arms tightly around my body and stare at the floor just in front of my feet.

"Well," King Savyon says, his voice a deep rumble I can almost feel in my own chest. "She's a far cry from the woman I hoped you'd one day unite with, Roarke. She's barely fit to be a servant in this court, let alone a princess."

"Really, Father?" Roarke drawls. "That's the nicest thing you have to say?"

"What do you expect when you present me with such a dismal prospect for a daughter-in-law?"

"I can assure you, Father, that her Griffin Ability more than makes up for what she lacks in other areas."

Those black eyes settle on me once more. "I certainly hope so. I'd like to see a demonstration now."

I open my mouth, my eyes darting between the two of them. I'm unsure if I'm allowed to speak, but they need to know that I can't perform on demand. "Don't worry, Emerson," Roarke says before I can say anything. He reaches inside his coat and produces a small vial. "I have your precious elixir right here. Yokshin, our inventions master, has been examining it, but there's plenty left for you to use."

Crap. This is so not what I planned to use the elixir for. I'm supposed to be alone with Roarke when he gives it to me so I can instruct him to tell me everything he knows about Mom and how to fix her. That isn't going to work right now unless I can give an instruction to the king at the same time. To remain frozen in place, perhaps. So he can't interfere. As Roarke turns to face me, thoughts race wildly through my head. Am I brave enough to do this? If I don't do it now, will I get another chance? And if I do command him now, how will I get past all the guards on my way out? Command them as well? Will there be enough time to give Roarke, his father, and all the palace guards an instruction before my Griffin Ability runs out?

"The compulsion potion first," the king says. "Then the Griffin potion."

"Of course," Roarke says, removing another small bottle from within his coat.

"The—what?" I ask.

"Compulsion potion," Roarke repeats, removing the lid. "It's exactly what it sounds like. You can be compelled to do certain things while under the influence of this potion. It's just to make sure you behave while using your Griffin Ability. We wouldn't want you doing something silly or irrational." He laughs. "Like telling us all to kill ourselves or something."

All hope withers. "So—so you're going to force me to say something?"

"This is just a precaution, Emerson. My father doesn't know yet if he can trust you."

He hands the bottle to me, and because I know I have absolutely no choice in the matter, I lift it to my lips. "How much?" I ask before tipping it back.

"Just a sip."

The potion tastes like something familiar, but I can't identify it. I hand the bottle back to Roarke, just as I realize that this compulsion thing sounds very much like the Griffin Ability everyone in this world has been trying to get their hands on. *My* Griffin Ability. "Wait—but—if you have such a thing as a compulsion potion, then what's the big deal about my Griffin Ability? You can already tell people to do things and they'll do them. You don't need—" I realize what I'm saying too late. *You don't need me.* Not something I should be pointing out when my Griffin Ability is the only leverage I have.

"We can force people to take a potion and then compel them to say or do certain things," Roarke explains. "That isn't the same as telling the ground to split apart and then watching it happen a moment later." He places the Griffin Ability elixir in my hand and steps back to stand beside his father. Now that they're next to each other, I can see the faint resemblance between them despite their dramatic differences in hair and eye color. "Emerson," Roarke says. "Don't you think it would be fun if it started raining in here?"

Though it's an odd suggestion, I find that I agree with him. It would be the most marvelous thing in the world if it started raining right here in this room. "Yes," I tell him.

"Then you should take a sip of that elixir and make it rain."

He's right. That's exactly what I should do. So I remove the stopper from the vial and pour a few drops onto my tongue. Then I wait for that familiar tingle, that sense that the Griffin magic hidden somewhere within me is rushing suddenly to the surface. I look up at the ceiling and say, "Start raining."

And it does.

I'm drenched within seconds, gasping and tensing my

shoulders against the icy water. Roarke and the king remain completely dry, as if invisible umbrellas shield them from the downpour. "Tell it to stop," Roarke calls out over the roar of raindrops.

I can't sense if there's any Griffin power left simmering at the surface of my magic, and it's impossible to hear my voice above the noise. But when I tell the rain to stop, I feel the words resonating in my head the way they do when my Griffin Ability comes alive, and I know it's worked.

"Very good," the king says as I stand there shivering. He looks at Roarke. "Is Yokshin able to recreate the elixir? If not, and the Griffin Ability is random, the girl won't be as useful to us as I'd hoped."

"He's uncertain about recreating it, but in Aurora's last message to me before we returned, she said she's been working on some theories as to how the ability might work. She thinks it may become more predictable."

The king nods. "Well then. Are you sure you want to go through with this union? It would be simpler to deal with the girl as a prisoner."

"Yes, I'm sure. I don't want her to be a prisoner." Roarke looks at me as though considering a purchase he's about to make. "I actually quite like her. And Mother and Aurora can train her in the ways of the court. After some time, it'll feel as though she's always belonged here. She'll become one of us. She'll be happy to help us out whenever we have need of her Griffin Ability. We won't even have to force her. Right, Emerson?"

"Yes," I answer.

A distant howl echoes through the cavern.

"Good," the king says again, paying no attention to the howl. "Until then, Roarke, you will give her a compulsion potion every day and tell her exactly what to say if and when her Griffin Ability appears." All hope I had of using my Griffin Ability on Roarke slips away like ash through my fingers. "And you, Miss Clarke." The king takes a step toward to me, which is about a thousand times closer than I'd like him to be. "Find out if Aurora's theory—whatever it may be—is correct. Do everything you can to learn how your Griffin Ability works. You'll be far more useful to us that way, and useful people are less likely to end up dead."

"Father," Roarke says with a roll of his eyes. "That's not helpful. She doesn't understand your sense of humor yet."

The king's expression doesn't change one bit. Either he's *very* good at keeping a straight face, or that wasn't a joke.

Another howl pierces the silence, louder this time. The king doesn't look toward the cavern, so neither do I. Whatever creature or person is making that sound, I don't want to know.

"We will announce the union at your mother's birthday celebration in two weeks," the king says to Roarke. "You have until then to decide when the union ceremony will take place."

A third howl morphs into sobs, shouts and the sounds of a struggle. Finally, the king looks toward the cavern, and though I don't want to, I follow his gaze. Two Unseelie guards are dragging a man across the cavern's uneven floor. As the man struggles, one of the guards shoots a spark of magic into his side, and the man twists away and howls in agony.

I look at Roarke, begging with my eyes for us to leave right now. But he's watching the struggling man with an unreadable expression.

"Ah, you found him," the king says. "This is the last one, I presume?"

"Yes, Your Grace."

"Very good." As the two guards step away from the man, King Savyon raises his hand. The man, who looked for a moment as if he was about to run, swallows and closes his eyes. The king clenches his hand tightly around the air and turns his fist abruptly to the side. Across the room, at the edge of the cavern, the man's head does the same, bending almost parallel to his shoulder. *Too far*, my mind shrieks. *Too far, TOO FAR!*

Then a sickening crack. The man's cry cuts off. The king jerks his hand upward. The man's head is ripped entirely off his body, and both parts fall to the floor, spurting blood everywhere.

A strangled gasp escapes me. My hand flies up to cover my mouth. I squeeze my eyes shut, but there's no way I'll ever be able to unsee that.

As if from a distance, I hear the king's voice. "That will be all, Roarke. Take the girl back to her quarters."

A hand latches onto my arm. I blink and force my eyes away from the dead body as Roarke pulls me toward the door. He opens it and lets me walk ahead of him. "And Roarke," the king adds. "See to it that someone burns those hideous clothes she's wearing. I don't understand why it hasn't been done already."

"She refused to part with them, apparently."

I dare to look back at the king. He doesn't sigh. He doesn't smile. He barely moves as he says, "The clothes will be burned. It's up to Miss Clarke whether she's still in them when that happens."

The door swings slowly toward us. The moment it clicks shut, I start running.

CHAPTER FIVE

I RUN ALL THE WAY BACK TO MY BEDROOM, TUG THE DOOR open, and slam it shut. I take a few unsteady steps into the room, barely seeing my surroundings. All I see is a man's neck flipping to the side, and blood squirting from—

I turn, blinking, as if I can somehow look away from the memory. Still breathing heavily from the run, I push my fingers through my hair. What the hell was I thinking coming to this place? That I'd actually be able to get away with the answers I need because I have a powerful Griffin Ability I can use against people? A Griffin Ability I can't call upon at will, and which can be used to fulfill someone else's purposes due to a potion I didn't know existed. What a miserable joke. I should have guessed, though, that something like this would happen. There's so much I don't know about this world and its magic, but what I *should* have known was what an idiot idea it was to put myself in the midst of a bunch of powerful, dark magic-wielding faeries.

From somewhere behind me, a soft thump reaches my ears. I freeze. I know I should run. I should pull the door open and keep running until this palace is far behind me. But fear sticks my feet to the floor. Ever so slowly, I twist around and look over my shoulder. Across the room on the round table, sitting beside the tray of tea and macarons Clarina must have left here not long ago, is a small owl. As I watch, the owl seems to collapse in on itself. An instant later, a black kitten sits in its place.

"Bandit?" I whisper in disbelief. I turn fully to face the shapeshifting creature. It flicks its right ear in response. Without a moment's pause, I race across the room and scoop him into my arms, tears burning my eyes. "I don't know how you got here or where you've been hiding or if you're the one who's been making strange noises in my suite," I whisper, "but I'm so, so, so glad to see you." I thought I left him sleeping in my room when I snuck away from the oasis, but he must have shifted into something smaller and climbed into one of my pockets. Wouldn't be the first time. "Please don't leave me," I mumble into his fur, my words running together. "Please don't leave me here alone. I'm sorry about the things I said when you first showed up. That I don't like pets and that maybe I could sell you. I swear I didn't mean any of that. I had a puppy once, but it ran away and never came back, and Mom and I searched, but we couldn't find it and I cried for days." I suck in a long breath and lower my arms enough to look down at him sitting in them. He looks back up with perfectly adorable kitten eyes. "I know you're magical, but you probably don't understand a word I'm saying, do you?" He tilts his head to the side, looking for all the world as if he's trying to figure out what I'm saying. "Yeah," I whisper, pulling him to my chest again. "So just don't disappear, okay? This place is *not safe*. Not for either of us. If you'd seen what I just—"

"Emerson?" Roarke's voice on the other side of the door sends a jolt through me. I have no idea how he'll feel about the idea of a shapeshifting pet showing up here, so I hurry into the bedroom and place Bandit on the bed. "Stay here," I whisper to him before pulling the bedroom door closed. With limbs that are still shaking, I cross the sitting room and open the main door just wide enough to peek through the gap at Roarke.

"Are you all right?" he asks.

Another brief flash of spraying blood and ripping flesh crosses my mind. I swallow, flattening one hand on the doorframe and the other on the back of the door. *Pull yourself together*, I silently instruct. *You chose to come here. You chose this option to help Mom. Now make it work.* "Yes, thank you. I'll be fine. It was just a little bit of a shock, that's all. Seeing … that." I doubt it's necessary to elaborate on exactly what I'm referring to.

"Can I come in?" he asks.

"Uh … okay."

We sit side by side on the divan with a respectable amount of space between us. I risk a glance at the closed door separating us from the bedroom. Hopefully Bandit's intelligent enough to know he needs to remain hidden. "I'm sorry you had to see that," Roarke says. "I know it must have seemed brutal and cruel, but it didn't happen for no reason. That man disobeyed the king, and the consequence was death."

I breathe out slowly. Since Roarke seems to be waiting for a response, I say, "Okay."

"I just wanted to explain because I don't want you to be afraid to live here. That man was a criminal. He and several others stole from my father. He deserved death. But for those of us who play by the rules, life here is good."

For those of us who play by the rules. Roarke's reassurances only increase my fear. I'm not planning to play by the rules. I'm planning to steal knowledge and then run for my life. "I know," I say quietly. "I understand. Like I said, it was just a shock. I've only been here a few days, and everything is very … different. I'm still getting used to it." I swallow. "I think it might help to put me at ease if I knew for certain that I could trust you. If you could tell me a few things—about Mom— then I'd know you can truly help me."

He leans back on one hand and surveys me as his serious expression turns to amusement. "You're actually not as bad at this as Aurora made out. Still fairly transparent, but I'm impressed you're trying."

I narrow my eyes at him. "Trying what?"

"To twist this situation to your advantage." He cocks his head to the side. "I'm curious. Did that scene with my father actually upset you, or is your entire reaction a ruse so you can try to manipulate some information out of me?"

My mouth drops open of its own accord. I close it quickly

and grit my teeth together as I respond. "Of course I was upset by it. It was *horrible*." I lean away from him. "Were you motivated by any genuine concern when you decided to come to my room, or is this part of whatever game *you're* playing?"

He smiles again, but it's softer this time. "I'm sorry. It seems the two of us are still figuring each other out. And yes, my concern for you was genuine. I'm not so cruel that it means nothing to me to see you upset. We might be about to form one of the least romantic unions in history, but that doesn't mean I'm not going to at least *try* to care for you."

I fold my arms over my chest, hugging myself tighter than usual. "Well, in the unlikely event that you're telling the truth, thank you for *trying*."

He examines me for another few moments. "What can I say to convince you I'm being truthful?"

"You could start with—"

"Shall I tell you about the little house you grew up in? Number twenty-nine Phipton Way. Shall I tell you about the wild roses your mother loved to tend in the garden? Or about the friend who used to visit sometimes? The one who always ended up arguing with your mother. The one you never actually met, because you were always told to go to your room. Or what about the time your mom showed up to fetch you from school an hour early and stood outside the fence speaking to things that weren't there? Would telling you about these things be enough to prove to you that I know more about your mother than anyone who's tried to help you so far?"

A shiver slithers up my spine. "How do you know these things?"

His eyebrows pinch together slightly. "You still don't get it, do you. You don't understand how valuable you are. When I heard about your Griffin Ability, I made it my priority to learn everything I could about you. I tracked down your aunt, then your mother, and then the one person who connected Daniela and Emerson Clarke to this world."

"What person?"

"The person who knows who you are. The person who made your mother the way she is."

My heart thunders dangerously fast. "Tell me."

He simply shakes his head. "All will be revealed after our union."

I shake my head, grinding the words out between my teeth. "And you want me to believe you're not cruel."

"I'm not," he says quietly. "It's just that you're not the only person who wants something. I want something too, and I don't trust that you'll give it to me unless I withhold information from you."

"I *will* go through with this union."

"Really? That's honestly what you're planning to do?"

Dammit. Is there some kind of magic going on here that tells him I'm lying? Is that compulsion potion still at work? But he hasn't specifically *compelled* me to tell the truth. "Yes," I say to him, willing myself to believe it's the truth. "That's what I'm planning to do."

"And yet you haven't asked for any details of how I'm going to fulfill my side of the agreement once the union's taken place. How exactly will your mother be woken and healed? Will I teach you the spells and let you go to her? Will I insist on doing it myself? What will happen to your mother once she's well?"

Crap. He's got me there. "I have plenty of questions for you, Roarke, but you haven't exactly been around for me to ask them. You've only been back a few hours, and we didn't have much time to talk before your father wanted to see me."

"True. Well then, do you want to ask how things will work after the union?"

I tilt my chin up. "How are things going to work after the union?"

He sighs. "Why are you so resistant? I understand that it's not ideal marrying someone you only just met, but it's not as though you're getting a disappointingly average life out of this deal. I'm offering you *everything*. A beautiful home, a powerful family, wealth beyond all imagining. And don't tell me you don't want any of that because *everyone* wants that. And there isn't anything wrong with wanting it. You'll be one of the lucky few who gets to have it all."

"You're right," I say quietly, unfolding my arms and placing my hands in my lap. "I'm very lucky."

"So once we're married, I'll go to your mother and—"

"No," I interrupt. "You—I'll go. I'll get her and bring her back here." I pause. "You wouldn't keep me from doing that, would you? From going to get her? I mean, obviously I'd come back."

"Obviously," he repeats. "But that doesn't mean my father would be happy with you leaving. If you don't want me to fetch your mother, and you're not allowed to fetch her either, then you can contact whoever it is that's keeping her safe and arrange a meeting. At a neutral location, one that your 'friends' don't need to worry about me discovering. I'll send some people to fetch your mother. My most trusted men."

I consider his suggestion. "Fine. If that's the only way."

"Once she's here, I'll wake her. I'll heal her mind. Then she can tell you the truth about everything. You can finally have all your questions answered. She can stay here too, and you can finally stop worrying about her. Stop fighting, stop struggling. Life will be good for you, Emerson."

"Sounds perfect."

"Does it? I know you're fond of sarcasm, so forgive me for doubting you."

I roll my eyes. "Obviously it isn't *perfect*, but it's as close to perfect as life could ever possibly be, so if marrying you is the only way to get there, then I'll do it."

"Really?"

"Yes."

He leans forward and takes hold of one of my hands. He stares intently into my eyes, and though I don't feel any different, I can't help wondering if he's trying to use some kind of magical discernment spell I know nothing about. "Are you lying to me, Emerson?"

I shake my head, willing myself not to look away from him. "I am not lying. My mother is the most important person in the world to me. I would do anything to make her better." And I realize as I finish speaking that I'm telling the truth. I *would* do anything for her—and that includes marrying a prince I barely know. So if there's no way out of this, if it proves impossible to get the information I need from Roarke before the wedding, then I'll do this. I'll marry him. And Mom will finally be the happy, healthy mother I remember.

And then …

One day, no matter how far in the future, no matter how long it takes me to figure out exactly how to do it, I'll get the two of us out of here.

CHAPTER SIX

"YES, VERY GOOD," AURORA CALLS TO ME FROM ACROSS THE terrace as I swing beneath my dance partner's arm, spin around, step-step-step behind him, and return to our starting position. After clapping briefly, Aurora adds, "You only messed up once this time."

"What?" I step away from the young man who's been filling in as my partner. Aurora's cousin or second cousin or something along those lines. My husband-to-be is, apparently, too important or busy for this kind of thing. "I thought I got it all right."

"No, the part in the beginning straight after you touch palms? You turned the wrong way."

I roll my eyes. "Do you really think anyone's going to notice?"

"Yes. In a ballroom full of dancing couples, when everyone else turns one way and you turn the other, it will most certainly be noticeable."

"Fine. I assume you're going to tell me to do it again?" I've been practicing for hours already, but I know Aurora won't be happy until I've got it completely right.

"Yes," she says with a nod.

So I face my partner and try not to sigh too loudly as we begin again. At least my outfit is fairly easy to move in. After my terrifying meeting with the king, I set aside my stubbornness and took a closer look at my wardrobe—and discovered I didn't detest the clothes as much as I expected I would. They weren't all puffy dresses, I was pleased to see. More like combinations of pants and fitted, coat-like dresses, some with long, embellished sleeves and high necks, others with no sleeves and full-length gloves. As the days have passed, I've come to appreciate the rich details and exotic styles worn by the members of the Unseelie Court. And the more I think about it, the more sense it makes that in a world filled with magic and enchantment, the clothing would be anything but ordinary.

Or perhaps I'm simply getting used to being here, which is a terrifying thought.

We do the dance three more times before Aurora finally lets us stop. Her cousin, who looked like he might stab himself if forced to spin me around one more time, bolts before Aurora can pin another boring task on him. "Noraya, we'll take refreshments now," she says, waving past me to where her handmaid is waiting in the doorway to the library.

I join Aurora on the other side of the terrace and lower myself into the swinging seat beside her. It hangs by nothing more than a single vine, and I'm a little wary of placing my entire weight into the hollow hemisphere. But Aurora keeps telling me not to doubt magic, and her seat's been perfectly fine so far. After a few moments, I relax back against the cushions and lift my feet so I can swing gently back and forth. I look out at the garden, but there isn't much happening. The library terrace is on a quieter side of the palace.

"So, now that I can dance without messing up," I say to Aurora, swinging my seat to face hers, "can we do something more exciting this afternoon? Like archery? I was starting to get slightly less than terrible at our last lesson. Or I could show you more parkour moves. You could actually try some of them this time instead of just watching me."

She laughs and shakes her head at my apparent silliness. "You don't think that was it for the dance lessons, do you? You've learned one dance, Em. Now you need to learn the rest of them. And we only have three days until Mother's birthday ball."

My feet drop onto the floor. "Seriously? I have to learn every dance?"

"Yes. It'll be bad enough when people discover that the princess-to-be is someone who's spent her entire life in the human realm and knew nothing of this world until a few weeks ago. If they don't see you using magic or dancing every kind of dance, it'll be even worse."

"Wait, you want me to use magic at the ball? In front of people?"

"Of course." She moves her hand in a circle, and her seat begins to slowly spin. "That should be fine, shouldn't it? You can handle the basics now."

"Yes, I just didn't realize it was expected, that's all. I'll try not to forget."

"That's the thing, Emerson." Her voice reaches me from the other side of her hemisphere seat. "You need to get to the point where you don't have to remind yourself. It should become an automatic part of your daily life, used even for the simplest of tasks."

"Sounds a little bit like laziness to me."

"You know what's lazy?" She brings her seat to a halt once she's facing me again and plays absently with the pendant around her neck: a silver oval shape with a black stone at its center. "Sitting in front of a glossy screen and mindlessly watching moving pictures."

I give her my least impressed look. "Are you referring to TV and movies? Because that isn't laziness. It's entertainment, and it's part of—"

"Part of human life. Just as magic is part of faerie life. It's part of *your* life now, Em, so get used to it."

"So many things to get used to," I muse, staring out across the garden again.

"Yes, like beautiful clothes, exotic holidays, lavish parties and being waited on for the rest of your life."

"I was referring more to this world and its politics and geography and history and creatures and … *everything*," I say quietly. "It's all so different from the life I grew up in."

"True," she says. "That's why you should focus on the

frivolous stuff instead. It's a lot easier to get used to. The rest will follow in time."

I nod, despite the fact that I don't agree with her. I can't tell her that I'm still determined to find a way out of all this. Even now, after endless lessons in magic, etiquette and dancing, after lengthy discussions of union ceremony details, I still can't imagine this wedding actually taking place. I know I'm probably in denial. I know it's unlikely Roarke will tell me anything else about my mother until we're married. But I won't give up until the moment that union ceremony begins.

Noraya returns then with two tall glasses floating in front of her. She's so good at this levitating thing that she doesn't even need to use her hands. They remain neatly clasped behind her back as she walks forward, eyes pointed firmly ahead instead of watching the floating glasses. "Lemonade, Your Highness," she says as she reaches us.

I push myself forward and stand as one of the glasses moves toward Aurora. I wrap my hand around the other one. "Thanks, Noraya." She risks a glance at me, smiles, then looks hurriedly away.

"You need to get over that," Aurora says to me once Noraya has walked back to the library doorway. "There's nothing wrong with being waited on."

I settle carefully into my seat without spilling any of my drink. "I don't like lounging back and being handed things. It just seems ... rude."

"It's rude to keep her from doing her job properly."

"Well, anyway, she smiled at me, so I don't think she minded."

Aurora lowers her glass and blinks. "She smiled at you?"

"I mean, not *at* me," I add hastily, not wanting to get Noraya in trouble. "Not in an impolite way. Um, anyway, I wanted to ask you about dresses for your mother's birthday ball. I assume you'll tell me what I'm supposed to wear? I don't think I can be trusted to pick out the right kind of dress."

Aurora narrows her eyes at the abrupt shift in subject, but she lets it slide. "Yes. Mother and I had three dresses made for you. We'll decide which one to go with once we know what Roarke will be wearing."

"Right. Of course. Because it would be *dreadful* if the colors clashed or something."

She rolls her eyes and nudges my knee with her shoe. "It would be dreadful. The two of you need to look like the perfect match."

"Which is silly, because we're never going to *be* the perfect match. We don't even—Oh." I sit forward slightly. "My Griffin Ability. I can sense it coming on." In the time that I've been here, I've become more attuned to the way my magic feels. Being forced to keep endless records of the ordinary magic I use each day, how much I eat, how tired or energized I feel, and exactly when my Griffin Ability appears has made me far more aware of every tiny change in my magic.

"Ah, that's just about the same time as the past few mornings, right?" Aurora says. "A little before lunch time?"

"Yes. And I used a lot more of my normal magic than usual last night trying to melt that fountain, so we can probably say for sure now that ordinary magic levels don't have much influence on my Griffin magic."

74

"Excellent. Don't forget to add that to your notebook. I think we have a reasonably good idea of how your ability works now, but you should probably continue keeping track of it for another few weeks. Just so we can be certain."

I didn't think my Griffin Ability made any sense when it first revealed itself, but perhaps, as Aurora suggested, it was still 'settling' during my first few days in this world. Since then, my excessive record-keeping has revealed a fairly regular pattern: My Griffin Ability appears twice a day, approximately twelve hours apart, give or take an hour or two. And in between those times, there's nothing I can do—aside from taking the elixir, which is now depleted—that will make it appear. Which means it's likely that Aurora's replenishing theory is correct.

I lower my glass of lemonade and sit at the edge of my seat. I close my eyes and try to predict the exact moment just before I get that tingling sensation racing up my spine. "I picture it kind of a like a volcano getting ready to erupt," I murmur. "Pressure builds up deep inside me, and then suddenly it all rushes to the surface, ready to explode."

"What did Roarke compel you to say this time?" Aurora asks.

Just as the king instructed, Roarke gives me a compulsion potion every day—well, twice a day now that we've figured out the pattern—and tells me exactly what to say when my Griffin Ability is ready for use. "He compelled me to try and preserve the power, if possible. If not, then I'm supposed to tell every yellow rose in the garden to become blue."

"Ugh, what a stupid command. He really needs to come up with some more interesting uses for your magic. Anyway, I'm glad he's letting you practice trying to hold it back. You need to learn to master this, Em."

"Yeah." I clench my hands together and clamp my mouth shut as the Griffin magic ripples through me, demanding to be released. *Hold it back, hold it back, hold it back,* I silently instruct myself. And when I'm certain the magic is about to rip itself free of me, forcing me to speak the instruction Roarke gave me, it just … doesn't. Slowly, it starts to feel like less effort to hold it back. I open my eyes, my hands relaxing in my lap. "I think I did it," I say with a smile. "I can still feel the power there, like a weird humming just beneath my skin. I wonder how long I can—"

Power rushes out of me, turning my voice deeper and more resonant. "Every yellow rose in the garden will become blue," I say.

Aurora sits forward a little, looking past me. After a moment, she says, "It worked. I can only see a few yellow rose bushes from here, but they just turned blue."

I slump back against my cushions, sending my seat into jerky, swinging motion. "Crap, that was barely a minute."

"Well, perhaps you got excited too soon." Aurora leans back and takes a sip of her lemonade. "Try for longer next time before you tell me you 'did it.' All you need is practice."

"Wonderful. Another thing to practice," I say with a sigh.

"Tell Roarke to compel you to actually hold it back, not just to *try.* And none of this 'If you can't, then this is what you'll say.' He's basically giving you permission to fail."

"Mm." I'm waiting for the day Roarke is busy enough to

forget to compel me. That's the day I'll make sure I'm with him at exactly the right moment. I'll command him to write down every spell required to wake and heal my mother. Then if anything's left of my Griffin Ability, I'll use it to get myself out of here.

"Don't you want to finish your lemonade?" Aurora asks, lifting my glass from the ground with a simple wave of her hand. "You need to remain hydrated if you're going to survive the rest of the day's dancing lessons."

I take the glass from the air and down the remainder of the lemonade. "You're going to have to find another willing member of your court to be my partner," I remind her, "and your cousin's probably already told everyone to avoid me and my terrible dancing, so—Oh. That's an idea."

"What?"

"Do you think it would work if I used my Griffin Ability to tell myself that I can dance every faerie dance perfectly?"

"Uh ..." Aurora's expression becomes thoughtful. "Hmm. I wonder. I mean, how does your Griffin magic work in the first place? Does it obey your exact words, or your intention behind the words? Does it work according to what you're picturing in your head when you command something? In which case, the dancing thing wouldn't work because you don't know—and therefore can't picture—all the steps in the other dances. And another thing," she adds, tapping the side of her glass with her fingernails. "If you tell me to do something, but the way I understand your command isn't the same way you meant it, whose intention will the magic obey? Yours or mine?"

I tilt my head back against the cushions. "I have no idea,

but I'm starting to wish this Griffin Ability came with an instruction manual."

"Experimentation, Em. That's all it requires."

"Sure, but it's frustrating when I have to wait half a day between every new experiment."

"Unless you can hang onto your power and use little bits at a time."

"Maybe." I turn my seat to face the library doors as footsteps tap across the terrace.

"Your Highness," Clarina says as she reaches us. "My lady," she adds, directing her words toward me before turning back to Aurora. "Phillyp is ready for your lesson."

"Oh, wonderful." Aurora hands her glass of half-finished lemonade to Clarina before standing.

"And your mother just sent a message to say she'd like to discuss some of the details for the ball with you."

"Mother always has fabulously bad timing, doesn't she," Aurora says with a sigh. "She'll just have to wait."

"Of course, Your Highness. Shall I tell her the usual?"

"Yes. Tell her I'm in the middle of my archery lesson. I'll come straight to her as soon as I'm done."

Clarina nods once. "And shall I escort Lady Emerson back to her chambers?"

"Um … no, actually. Em can come with me this time." Aurora gives me a wicked grin. "I trust you now to keep my secrets."

After a quick curtsey, Clarina leaves. "Goodness," I say. "I'm shocked to discover that the perfect princess is keeping secrets from her own mother."

She gives my arm a playful smack. "No you're not. Besides, it isn't a big deal. It's just something my mother doesn't approve of." Instead of going back inside, she steps off the terrace onto the grass.

"Your mother doesn't approve of you doing archery either," I point out as I follow her, "but she hasn't stopped you from taking lessons."

"Yes, well, I told her it was either archery or magical combat, and there was no way she'd ever allow her little princess to learn magical combat."

"Which is what, exactly?" I bend as both a silver butterfly and a lizard with wings—one chasing the other—flit too close to my head.

"You know how you draw on your power, and in its most basic form, it's just raw power held in your hands?" Aurora says.

"Yes." That was the very lesson I received from Azzy at Chevaliar House.

"Well, all you do is throw that magic at someone. I mean, there's more to it than that. Those who are trained in magical combat will often transform their magic into other things. Stones or blades or flocks of birds with sharp pecking beaks. Something that can more easily take down an opponent than just a mass of sparks. But your mind has to be so quick. You have to be able to mentally shape your magic just like that." She snaps her fingers. "Over and over, while also protecting yourself."

I look around as we move further away from the palace. This part of the garden is unfamiliar to me, and all I can see up ahead is a thicket of trees. "So the queen didn't want you learning this skill?"

"No. It isn't very princess-like. We have guards to fight for us if necessary. She agreed to archery instead because all it entails is shooting arrows at inanimate objects that don't shoot back at me."

"Far more civilized," I comment. "But that clearly wasn't daring enough for you, so you had to try something else."

"Yep."

"Something your mother most certainly wouldn't approve of."

"Exactly."

"And that is?"

A grin stretches her lips as we reach the trees. "Dragon riding."

CHAPTER SEVEN

My steps come to a halt. "Wait." I hold a hand up. "Wait, wait, wait. You guys have *dragons?*"

"Yes." Aurora turns back to look at me. "Haven't you seen them flying around occasionally?"

"Well ... I've seen *something* in the sky. I assumed they were overgrown birds, or some kind of flying creature I haven't met yet."

She dissolves into giggles. "Overgrown birds? Seriously?"

"I've only seen them from a distance," I say defensively. "It was difficult to judge their size."

"Well, you're about to see them up close."

I blink. My feet still don't move. "Holy crap," I whisper.

"What? You're not afraid, are you?"

"No. I mean, maybe. Probably. I'm just having one of those

moments where I wonder if I'm actually dreaming. We're talking about *dragons*, Aurora. I grew up thinking they only existed in fiction, and now I'm about to *see* one? My brain has absolutely no clue how to react to that."

"Come on." She takes my arm and pulls me forward. "Your brain has another minute or two to figure things out. The dragon enclosures are just on the other side of these trees."

"Dragons," I murmur. "You have dragons. Actual dragons."

"We used to have gargoyles too," she adds. "Well, by 'we' I mean the previous generation of royals. Gargoyles aren't as big as dragons, but just as scary, so I've heard. They used to stand guard on top of the palace, but they all disappeared a few decades ago."

"Really?" I think of the creature Ryn was riding when he saved me from plummeting to my death off the edge of a cliff. I'm pretty sure that was a gargoyle.

"Yeah, my father had been king for a few years, and the gargoyles never seemed to like him. One day they all just flew away, and no one's seen them since."

"How odd," I say slowly. I won't be mentioning to Aurora that I was rescued by a Griffin rebel on the back of a gargoyle, but I can't help wondering if it's one of the gargoyles that used to live here.

We step out beyond the trees, but I don't see any dragons yet. Or enclosures, for that matter. I look up, but there's nothing in the sky either. "You'll have to look down," Aurora tells me. "Over there."

My heart thumps faster as we approach the edge of a pit dug into the ground. Gradually, as the rim all the way around comes into view, I'm able to make out the sheer size of this hole. The other side is several sports fields away. We stop about a foot from the edge, and I look down at a lush, jungle-like environment. For a moment, I struggle to make out any kind of creature amidst the trees and colorful plants, but then something moves. A thick, scale-covered neck. A gargantuan head, rising and twisting slowly to face us until it's almost level with the top of the pit.

"Em," Aurora says, "meet Imperia."

The dragon's body shimmers blue-green and purple as she moves, and the massive spikes running along her back are reddish pink. Her tail, ending in a green arrow-head shape, whips around, easily knocking down a row of shrubs. Then she becomes still, angles her head a little to the side, and watches me with eyes glowing like fiery orange embers.

"She's beautiful, isn't she?" Aurora says.

My mouth is open, my tongue is dry, and my feet are rooted to the spot—despite the fact that a very insistent voice at the back of my mind is screaming for me to run for my life. "Incredible," I whisper.

"Each pit belongs to a different dragon. Imperia's always preferred a tropical environment, but the next pit is filled with ice. And the one furthest away—which would take us quite some time to walk to—is deep enough to contain a mountain."

"Wow. And can they, uh, fly out of their pits whenever they want?" My legs finally remember how to work, and I take a shaky step backward as Imperia lifts her head a little higher.

"No, there's an invisible shield layer over the top. The dragons aren't allowed out unless they're with a rider."

"Okay." I swallow. "And I notice there aren't any walls around these pits. Would the shield layer catch someone if they fell?"

Aurora appears unconcerned as she says, "No."

"But ... then ..."

"If someone's stupid enough to fall into a dragon pit, then they deserve to be eaten. But Imperia probably wouldn't do that. Not to anyone she knows, at least. She's really quite friendly. So." She turns to face me. "Do you want to ride her?"

I'm not sure how long my mouth is open before I finally mange to reply. "I ... actually ... do."

Aurora beams at me. "I like you even more now." She bends down and runs her hand along the grass. As she straightens, a line of gold forms a perfect ring around us. Without warning, the ground shudders. The circular piece of earth we're standing on becomes separate from the ground around it and begins descending.

"Whoa." I raise my hands and steady myself. "So, we're going down into the pit?"

"Yes."

"And, uh, will I be with someone when I'm riding this dragon? A trained professional?"

"You'll be with me."

"But ... you're still learning, aren't you? Clarina said something about ... Phillyp being ready for your lesson?"

"That's just what my handmaids have been trained to tell me when Phillyp informs one of them that the coast is clear for me to come here. You know, when there's no one around who might tell my mother they saw the princess on the back of a dragon. I received lessons in the beginning, of course, but they ended a long time ago." She looks at me. "Don't you trust that I know what I'm doing, Em?"

"Uh … I *want* to trust you." I watch the dark earth rising rapidly around us, then raise my eyes to the circular piece of sky growing smaller.

Aurora laughs. "Well, I'm not going to force you, Em. But you *know* you're going to regret being stuck on the ground once you see me soaring through the air."

Somehow, I know this is true.

The magical earthen elevator shudders silently to a halt. Within seconds, a tunnel forms ahead of us, short enough that I can see the lush vegetation on the other side. I follow Aurora through, hesitating at the mouth of the tunnel and looking around for Imperia. Through the trees, I see the shimmering aquamarine and purple scales of one of her legs.

"Hi, Phillyp," Aurora says, walking straight out of the tunnel and to the right.

"Princess," a male voice says. "I'm glad you could come. Imperia hasn't flown for two days. I think she's anxious to properly spread her wings."

After another glance over my shoulder toward Imperia, I hurry after Aurora. She's speaking to a slight man leaning in the doorway of a room built into the side of the pit. His head is shaved completely bare, and the shiny patch of skin on his upper arm looks as though it's been recently burned. "Ooh, ouch," Aurora says, bending closer to look at his arm. "Did Imperia do that?"

"Yes. Totally my fault, though, and you know I'm used to it."

"Yes. And it'll be gone soon, I'm sure," Aurora says as she straightens. "Phillyp, this is Em. My new friend. She's going to ride with me today, so please use the double saddle."

Phillyp pauses for only a moment before inclining his head. "Of course, Your Highness." He turns and disappears into the room.

"He doesn't think it's a good idea," I murmur to Aurora.

"Nonsense. He knows I'm perfectly capable of taking someone else with me. It's just that I brought one of my ladies-in-waiting once, and she screamed the entire time we were in the air. Imperia wasn't impressed, and neither was Phillyp." She snaps her fingers near the back of her skirt, and I notice a brief glow before her spark of magic disappears. "But you don't plan to scream like a little girl, do you, Em?"

I decide not to ask Aurora exactly how she knows Imperia wasn't impressed. "No. Obviously I don't *plan* to scream like a little girl."

A set of stairs, hovering a few inches above the ground, slides out of the room and moves past us toward Imperia. A moment later, Phillyp hurries after it with what I assume is the saddle floating just ahead of him.

"Ah, finally," Aurora says. I turn back to face her as her skirt drops to the ground, revealing form-fitting pants the same color as her corset-like top. "What?" she asks in response to my raised eyebrows. "I can't very well ride a dragon in a dress."

"I guess not. Good thing I'm already wearing pants."

With a wave of her hand, the skirt flies into the room. "You'll want to keep your hair out of your face." Aurora tells me as we head through the trees. She waves a hand near her hair, and her thick purple and black tresses promptly arrange themselves into a neat braid. A silver ribbon appears and ties itself at the end of her hair.

"Lazy bum," I mutter, reaching back to braid my own hair with my hands.

"Not at all," she replies. "You'll soon realize that any spell that saves you time in getting ready and allows you to remain longer in the air on the back of a dragon is a spell worth memorizing." She stops at the edge of a clearing and looks up, her hands on her hips. "I'll teach you later."

My hands still for several moments as I take in the size of the dragon in open-mouthed awe. The set of stairs is just high enough to reach her back, and Phillyp stands at the very top, securing the straps and buckles of the saddle with magic. Imperia lets out a loud snort, emitting smoke through her nostrils.

I swallow. With shaking fingers, I finish securing my braid. All too soon, Phillyp climbs down the steps and Aurora climbs up. She grabs the straps, climbs onto Imperia's back, and swings her leg over the front seat of the saddle. "What are you waiting for?" she asks as she looks down at me. Instead of answering, I lick my lips. "Come on, Em, don't freak out. This will be fun."

"I know." My voice sounds raspy and a little higher in pitch than normal. I clear my throat. "I'm excited. I really am. I just happen to be a tiny bit scared at the same time." *Understatement*, my wildly beating heart shrieks at me. *Gigantic. Freaking. Understatement.*

But that doesn't change the fact that I want to do this. So I force my legs to climb the steps. At the top, I take one last deep breath before placing a hand against Imperia's smooth scales. Beneath my touch, the color ripples and shimmers. I take hold of two of the straps and pull myself up. Thanks to all the walls I've climbed in recent years, my arms are pretty strong. Once I've settled myself in my seat, the steps slide away from the side of Imperia's body.

"Put that strap around your waist," Aurora says, twisting around and pointing to a loose strap dangling from one side of the saddle. I cross it over my body and fasten it through the metal ring on the other side.

Then finally, I look down. We're higher from the ground than I imagined, and we haven't even taken off yet. It's not that I'm afraid of heights, and it's not that I'm afraid of taking risks. Val and I have performed plenty of jumps, somersaults and dives that could easily have landed us in hospital. But I was always in control of my own body then. Now, I'm one hundred percent at the mercy of another creature—and it's terrifying.

Aurora takes hold of the reins. Imperia lifts her wings, and her body rolls one way and then the other as she moves forward a few steps. I inhale sharply and grip the ridge of the saddle that rises between Aurora's seat and mine. Imperia's legs bend slightly. I hold my breath. Then, with a great downward thrust of her wings, she rises into the air. I feel a sickening lurch in the region of my stomach. Dragon wings beat the air, the treetops wave wildly about, and the ground rushes away from us. I imagine plummeting toward it. I almost shout out that I want to get off, but I clamp my mouth shut, cling tighter to the saddle, and tell myself I'm not going to die.

We rise rapidly, the palace growing smaller and the surrounding Unseelie territory coming into view. Imperia's wings slow their flapping. She banks a little to the side, then soars around the edge of the palace grounds. And in mere seconds, my terror gives way to pure exhilaration.

* * *

"That was the most amazing thing I have *ever* done," I say to Aurora the moment Imperia's feet touch the ground in her enclosure.

"Told you," she answers with a laugh. The steps arrive a moment later, and we both climb out of our seats. I pause at the bottom and reach up to lay a hand against Imperia's side. "Will I ever get to do this again?"

"Of course," Aurora says. She removes her silver ribbon and pushes her fingers through her hair to free it from the braid. "You can come with me whenever you want. Phillyp can give you lessons, and you'll soon be riding on your own. Then we can take our dragons out together. It'll be perfect."

It would be—if I was planning to stay here. I take a step back and watch wistfully as Imperia trundles away. I wrap my arms around myself and bite my lip. It's scary to admit this to myself, but I think I could actually enjoy living here. Mornings spent lounging in swinging seats, afternoons spent gliding through the sky on the back of a dragon. And with my healthy mother at my side. All I would need to do is look past any horrific acts I happen to witness the Unseelie King committing.

And somehow live with the guilt of whatever horrific acts he forces *me* to commit.

No, I whisper silently. *I can't live with that.* "Is it only the royals who have dragons?" I ask Aurora as Phillyp sends the portable stairway back to the storeroom.

"No, but they're awfully expensive, so only the very wealthy are ever in a position to own one."

"Right." So I should take every dragon-riding opportunity I can while I still live here. Once I'm gone, I'll never be able to afford it.

"Fortunately," Aurora continues, "you're about to become a member of an extraordinarily wealthy family. You can have as many dragons as you want."

"If I'd known this was all it took to woo you," a voice says behind us, "I would have brought you here days ago, Emerson."

"Roarke," Aurora says as we turn to face him. "Looking for me?"

"Yes. I thought I might find you here. *You*, however …" He looks at me. "Well, the back of a dragon is *not* where I expected to find you."

"She loved it," Aurora says, clasping her hands together and beaming.

"I heard," Roarke says with an amused smile. "What did you say, exactly?" he asks me. "It was the most amazing thing you've *ever* done?"

"Eavesdropping is rude," I tell him.

"So is keeping secrets from my mother, but I'll continue doing that too, don't worry," he adds as Aurora opens her mouth to protest. "She doesn't need to know about your favorite pastime."

"Where have you been all morning?" I ask as we head back to the edge of the pit. "I thought you might join me for my dance lesson."

"I was ... organizing a gift for you, my beloved."

I arch a skeptical eyebrow. "There was way too much hesitation in your voice for that to be true."

"It's true, I promise. I was just considering whether I should tell you or not."

The tunnel materializes ahead of us as we approach the wall. "Okay, if this gift is real, then when will I receive it?"

"As soon as Yokshin is finished with it."

"Yokshin?" I remember that name from somewhere.

"Yes. He calls himself our inventions master. He's the one who was hoping to reproduce your Griffin Ability elixir."

"So ... has he managed to succeed?"

"No." We exit the tunnel and step onto the levitating piece of earth. "This is a different gift. You'll have it ... soon."

I press my lips together as the ground begins rising. I could ask more questions, but he'll only continue to give me half-answers.

"Why were you looking for me?" Aurora asks her brother.

"Oh, you and I just have a few things we need to see to."

Aurora nods and looks up, saying nothing.

"More secrets you're keeping from your beloved?" I ask.

Roarke gives me his sly smile. "Once you're my wife, all secrets will be revealed."

CHAPTER EIGHT

As the afternoon of the queen's birthday ball arrives, I stand on my balcony and rehearse my story. Tonight is the night Prince Roarke will announce that he's chosen a wife. He'll present me, formerly Princess Aurora's 'strange new friend,' and suddenly everyone will want to know every detail of who I am and where I'm from.

Roarke and his mother tossed around the idea of making up an entirely different past for me—one that didn't involve the human world—but they figured the truth would get out soon enough. And neither of them seemed to trust that I'd be able to keep the details of a made-up history straight, so most of what I've been told to share with people is the truth: I grew up thinking I was human, my magic revealed itself, the Guild got involved so they could imprison me and ensure I never hurt anyone, and then Roarke and his men showed up to rescue me. They took me back to their palace so I could live as a free member of their court. Roarke and I soon fell madly in love with each other, and the king granted our request to form a union. So everything up until the rescue is essentially the truth. After that ... well, I somehow have to make these people believe I'm besotted with their prince.

I lean against the balcony railing and stare longingly at the perfect puffy clouds high above me. I'd rather be soaring the skies on Imperia's back instead of preparing myself to face a crowd of Unseelie nobility. Or riding that other dragon Phillyp rode with me yesterday. Bralox, I think his name was. Or dancing simple dances with Dash on the shores of the Griffin rebels' enchanted beach instead of trying to remember every step to every official faerie dance—since my Griffin Ability did nothing to help me in that department.

My door bangs open so loudly I can hear it out on the balcony. I look over my shoulder to see Aurora dancing across the sitting room and out onto the balcony. "It's time!" she sings.

"For what?" She can't be referring to the ball. It's hours away still.

"Time to begin getting dressed, of course. It's a long process involving hair, makeup, jewelry—and of course, we haven't actually chosen your dress yet from the three that were made for you."

"Oh. Okay."

Her face falls. "Why aren't you more excited?"

"I am." I pull on a smile that doesn't feel real. "It's just ... parties aren't really my favorite thing. At the last one I attended, my magic exploded out of me and almost killed my best friend."

"Trust me, Em," Aurora says with the kind of smile that makes her eyes sparkle. "This party is going to be like nothing you've ever imagined. And if that doesn't make you feel any better, here's something that will." She removes her hand from behind her back and presents me with a square box a little larger than her palm.

"What's this?" I ask as I take it from her.

"Remember Roarke said he was having a gift made for you?"

"Yes."

"Well, I thought he was just saying that to cover up whatever he was really doing that day—I can usually tell when he's lying—but it turns out he actually did get Yokshin to make something for you."

I remove the lid of the box and find a bracelet sitting upon a small black cushion. Delicate ropes of silver metal twist around one another, with tiny silver leaves and flowers sprouting from the sides. In the middle of the bracelet is a large, clear gem. "It's pretty," I say.

"It's pretty *and* clever," Aurora says. "It's actually kind of like a watch. But it doesn't show the time, it shows the level of your Griffin magic. So in place of a watch face, it has a large ruby. The ruby loses its color once you've used all your Griffin power, and then the color slowly refills at the same rate your magic replenishes. At least, that's how it's supposed to work, and obviously you need to be wearing it."

"Wow, that is clever." I take the bracelet from the box,

open the clasp, and place the rigid form around my wrist. The clasp clicks easily into place. As I watch, a fraction of one side of the ruby becomes red. "Huh, I guess that makes sense. It was just before midday that my Griffin Ability turned on, so that was about … two or three hours ago?"

"Yes. So this is supposed to make it easier for you to see when your magic is ready to be used. You know, in case it varies slightly if you're extremely tired, or if you can't always sense it."

"Cool." I lower my arm. "So this was made by … Yokshin? Is that his name?"

"Yes, the inventions master. He experiments with all kinds of magic. Spells, processes, devices." She leans against the railing, flashes a wide smile, and waves at two young men walking below. "It's a fascinating line of work," she continues, turning back to me. "I used to visit him a lot when I was younger, until Mother told me it wasn't appropriate to spend so much time with someone of his station, especially when he sometimes took me to the prison to show me some of his experiments."

"The prison?"

"Yes, just the small one we have here. Anyway, do you like the bracelet?"

"Yes. As you pointed out, it's both pretty and clever." I angle the bracelet this way and that so the mostly colorless gem catches the light. "Has Yokshin made any enchanted jewelry for you?"

"Uh … some." I look up to see her playing with the pendant hanging from a chain around her neck. The silver one with the black stone. I've noticed she wears it more often than her many other pieces of jewelry. "I'll tell you about it another time, though," she adds. "For now, we need to start getting ready."

"Yeah, okay. Um, where's Roarke? Didn't he want to give me this gift himself?"

"He did, but you know men. They don't want to get in the way when ladies are dressing."

"Or he's still avoiding me," I grumble as I walk past her into the sitting room.

"Avoiding you? What nonsense is that?" Aurora follows me inside. "He sees you at least twice a day when he gives you the compulsion potion."

"Yes, that's the *only* time he sees me."

"Well, he's very busy."

Or he's avoiding being around me whenever my Griffin Ability is active—just in case I don't consume all my power on whatever command he's given me and I'm able to use the rest of it to get information out of him. Which is exactly what I would have done if he'd been around. I've been practicing holding my Griffin Ability back. Eventually I have to let some of it go by saying whatever I've been compelled to say, but there've been times when I can sense there's still power left over. I've tried holding onto it until I see Roarke again, but I haven't managed to last that long yet.

"Em?"

"Mm?" I face Aurora, realizing belatedly that she asked me a question.

"I asked if you're actually starting to like Roarke. Is that why you're upset you don't get to see him more often?"

"Oh. Um. Maybe." I guess that's a better reason than *I'm upset because I haven't had a chance to use my Griffin Ability on him.*

She shakes her head and sighs. "You are so bad at lying. Come, let's go to my room. Your dresses arrived earlier and Mother's having them sent up now." She links arms with me. "You can rehearse your epic love story on the way."

The walk to Aurora's suite is long enough for me to recite my 'epic love story' twice. "Well done," she says as we reach her sitting room. "You've got the facts straight. Now you just have to work on sounding as though you actually mean the part about falling passionately in love."

"I'll be sure to do a better job when I'm lying to the elite fae of Unseelie society later."

"Wonderful."

We head into her bedroom, which is far larger than mine and includes a walk-in closet the size of a double garage. "Oh, here's the jewelry Mother selected for you. I meant to show you earlier while we were having breakfast." She lifts a box from her vanity and opens it to show me the contents. "Necklace and earrings. Lovely, aren't they?"

'Lovely' probably isn't the word I would use. Each piece consists entirely of glittering, colorless stones. The earrings are teardrops the size of my thumbnail, and the necklace is a double row of stones that gradually grow larger as they reach a pendant: another large, faceted teardrop. "Are ... are they real?" I ask as Aurora removes them from the box.

She steers me toward the seat in front of the vanity before

giving me a quizzical look in the mirror. "What do you mean? They're not some kind of illusion that will disappear once the party's over, if that's what you're wondering."

"No, I mean … are they real diamonds?" She seems to want me to sit, so I do. "Or are they fake? Like, glass or crystal or something."

She laughs. "Of course they're real diamonds. Why would we use fake ones?" I remain silent as she fastens the earrings to my ears and places the necklace around my neck. "There. I think they suit you. They'll look gorgeous no matter which dress we choose."

I shake my head at my reflection. I pull the earrings off and remove the necklace. "I don't think I should wear these." I place the sparkling diamonds carefully in Aurora's hand. "Here. You can give them back to your mom."

"What? Why?"

"I can't wear something so valuable. What if the necklace falls off while I'm dancing? What if I misplace the earrings after taking them off, and then—"

"And then what? Don't be so silly, Em. The necklace isn't going to fall off." She opens the box and places the jewelry back on its velvety cushion. "And who cares if it does? Mother certainly won't. This is probably the least valuable jewelry she owns."

I try not to feel ill at her words. "Aurora—"

"Come on, stop making such a big deal out of this."

"But it is a big deal," I snap. She takes a step back, surprised at my anger. "I'm sorry. It's just … well, I wouldn't expect you to understand," I murmur.

She crosses her arms. "And why is that? Because I don't seem to place nearly as much importance on jewelry as you suddenly seem to?"

I roll my eyes. "You know that's not what I mean." I gesture to the box. "That many diamonds are probably worth more than ... I don't know. The whole of Stanmeade. I can't bring myself to wear that much wealth on my body, and you wouldn't understand that because we come from such vastly different backgrounds."

"Yes," she says, giving me a look that quite plainly says, *Duh*. "We do. This isn't a brand new revelation, so why is it suddenly a big deal?"

I don't know. I can't tell her why this diamond jewelry has suddenly shone an ever so sparkling light on the difference between my life and hers, or why I'm suddenly comparing my mother to hers. The queen is perfectly sane and in a position to hand out items of immense wealth as if they cost nothing. Mom is lost somewhere inside her own mind and hasn't been able to give me anything except the weight of responsibility for a very long time. "I'm sorry," I murmur, staring at the makeup strewn across the top of the vanity. "I can't wear that jewelry. It just makes me think of everything I've never had. All the things that ... that my mom could never give me. And I don't mean the expensive things, I just mean the normal things. And all the things she couldn't *be* to me once she began to lose her mind."

"Em ..."

"No, I'm not looking for your pity. I'm just saying ..." I don't know what I'm saying anymore. "I just ... don't want to wear it, if that's okay?"

She nods. "Okay. Of course. I would never want to make you uncomfortable. Uh …" She turns toward the doors to her closet. "I'm sure I can find you something simpler from my collection."

I stand, beginning to feel even worse now that she's being so understanding. "I'm sorry, Rora. I didn't mean to sound ungrateful. I'm thankful for everything you and your mother have done to help me fit in here. I just don't yet know how to deal with all …" I gesture vaguely with both arms. "All this."

She takes my hand, squeezes it, and smiles. "It's fine. I understand." She walks to her closet, then pauses in the doorway and looks back. "Roarke used to call me Rora when we were younger. Then he grew up and decided it was a silly, childish name. I told him I agreed, but the truth is, I kind of miss hearing him call me Rora."

I wind my hair around my finger. "I … I don't really know why I said Rora. It just came out that way. I'm sorry. I don't want to make things awkward."

"That isn't what I mean." She smiles again. "You've probably been so focused on the idea of getting a husband you never asked for that you haven't thought about the fact that you're getting a sister too. I know none of this is what you wanted for your life. I know you're only going through it all for your mother. But … well, I'm happy you're going to be my sister. I hope one day you can be happy too."

She heads into her enormous closet before I can say anything else, and at that moment, the door to the sitting room opens. I peer out of the bedroom door and see the queen, dressed in a robe and slippers, striding across the sitting area with three of her handmaids and an unfamiliar woman following her. Each of the handmaids carries a dress. "Your Majesty," I say to the queen, bowing my head in respect as she comes toward me.

"Emerson, hello." I've never seen her wearing so little makeup and with her hair—black and burgundy like Roarke's—so plain. She leans in and kisses the air on either side of my cheeks. "Ready for the big announcement tonight?"

"Yes," I say with confidence and a wide smile, neither of which are genuine.

"Aurora, love, I've got the dresses," the queen calls out, walking past me. "Ah, there you are," she adds as Aurora exits the walk-in closet.

"Ooh, exciting." Aurora rubs her hands together.

"Put the dresses over there," the queen tells her handmaids, "and then you may go." The handmaids leave the dresses floating in the air above the bed before turning and silently leaving the room. The woman I don't recognize brushes something off the skirt of one dress and plucks a loose thread from another.

I walk slowly around the bed so I can see the three dresses from all angles. The first has a full skirt of deep pink tulle with delicate flowers growing up the back from the waist to the neck. The second is the color of champagne. Its many-layered skirt is covered in gold flowers, and the tight bodice has a sweetheart neckline and no sleeves. The last option is made of rose gold fabric with thousands of tiny crystals glinting in the light as the dress sways gently in the air. The corset top laces up at the back, and though the skirt is kind of scrunched up with a bit of extra fabric over the butt, it isn't as puffy as the other two.

"They're beautiful," I say.

"Aren't they just?" Aurora replies. "And apparently, they're even more gorgeous when you put them on. The pink one changes back and forth between pink and purple, and the petals at the back slowly unfurl as the night goes on. The champagne one comes with a pair of long gloves made of a translucent fabric that looks like champagne bubbles rising up your arms. And the rose gold one has an enchanted shimmery effect that looks like glowing embers."

"Sounds cool."

"They're Raven Rosewood creations," Aurora continues. "Mother and I put the word out to all the top designers that we were looking for something spectacular for a very important event. We hinted at a potential engagement announcement— without using those exact words, of course—which resulted in plenty of rumors flying around. We had *dozens* of designs submitted, and Mother wasn't too keen on you wearing a Rosewood dress, seeing as—"

"Seeing as she's dressed some of the Seelies in the past," the queen fills in. "I did *not* want you wearing one of her dresses. When I saw her name on the outside of the scroll, I almost threw it away without opening it."

"But there was just something about her designs that we kept going back to," Aurora says. "Something that just … captivated us." A dreamy look comes over her face.

"They did turn out quite lovely," the queen admits. "I can see why this Rosewood woman has become popular in recent years."

"Did you send an invitation to her?" Aurora asks. "I want to meet her."

"Of course not, dear. I told you that wasn't appropriate. She has connections to the Guild, and she's designed for the Seelies before. We may have decided to use one of her creations, but I didn't feel comfortable having her here. I asked Lemon to send someone to pick up the dresses, and to be discreet about it."

"Oh, Em, this is Lemon, by the way," Aurora adds, gesturing to the woman who entered with the handmaids. "Our head clothes caster. She probably made most of the clothes you found in your wardrobe."

"Oh. Thank you, Lemon." I try not to snicker at the strange name. "You did a good job."

She nods to me. "Thank you, my lady. And yes, I sent Jefford to fetch the dresses this morning, and I made sure to impress upon him the importance of discreetness. Told him we don't want the embarrassment of anyone knowing we've associated with someone who's worked with Seelies before, even if her work is good."

"So silly," Aurora grumbles. "People are going to find out anyway. We're royalty, for goodness' sake. It's an honor to design for us, so I'm sure Raven Rosewood will tell people."

"Will she?" the queen asks. "I doubt she'd want to risk her reputation with the Seelies."

"She won't say anything," Lemon tells us. "Jefford left the dresses in my room with a note to say the pickup went smoothly. The designer accepted her payment and happily agreed to keep quiet about her involvement."

"And when people ask tonight?" Aurora says. "Because you *know* some of those women are going to want to know who dressed their new princess. All they care about is the latest fashion and trends, and once they see Em in, say, champagne bubble gloves, they'll all be adding the same thing to their new outfits."

"Really?" I ask. "That's so silly."

"That's the kind of influence you have as a princess," Aurora says with a self-satisfied smile as she leans against the vanity. "I once wore live sprites dangling from my ears, and at the next party, I saw at least five other girls wearing the same thing."

"Poor sprites," I murmur, imagining the creatures that look like tiny winged people tied to Aurora's earlobes.

"If anyone asks for the designer's name, tell them it's a secret," the queen says. "Tell them our head clothes caster has an especially inventive new apprentice, and we wish to keep him to ourselves."

Aurora sighs. "Fine. Anyway, we need to decide which one Em will wear so we can all start getting ready."

"Uh, shall I go and ask Roarke what he's decided to wear?" I suggest.

"Yes," the queen answers. "Aurora and I will check that all the adjustments for her new dress have been done correctly, and then she'll meet you in Roarke's suite."

With a glint in her eye, Aurora adds, "Mother doesn't trust you to accurately report what Roarke's outfit looks like without my help."

"Aurora," the queen scolds. Then her expression shifts into

an apologetic smile. "Well, I suppose that's true. Sorry, Emerson."

I shrug, then freeze with my shoulders pulled up, remembering the queen doesn't like shrugging. "It's fine. See you there, Rora." I hurry out of the bedroom, waiting until I'm outside the suite before relaxing my shoulders.

The glossy marble floor passes quickly beneath my feet as I head for Roarke's suite. I knock on his door, but after waiting several moments, neither he nor one of his servants has called for me to come in. I knock again and wait, but still nothing. The absence of guards outside his suite makes me doubt Roarke is inside, but he has mentioned that sometimes his guards patrol further along the hallways just outside this wing of the palace. I crack the door open just enough to stick my head inside. "Roarke?"

No response. Knowing Aurora will be here in a few minutes, I decide to wait in Roarke's sitting room until she joins me. I shut the door and wander slowly around the couches, comparing the suite to Aurora's. Similar furniture fills the space, though in a less delicate style with dark wood and glossy black finishes. I walk to the window and find that I have an excellent view of a sculpture I've never been able to see properly from the ground: a giant snake rearing toward the sky, surrounded by black rose bushes. *Creepy*, I think to myself as I turn away from the window.

From the corner of my eye, I notice movement near the bedroom door. Something dark, like a shadow sliding across the wall. I turn quickly, expecting to see someone there—Roarke or one of his servants—but no one is behind me. I turn on the spot, my eyes traveling over every inch of the room. I look at the wall again, but the shadows created by the furniture and decor are motionless. It must have been something outside. A bird flying past the window, perhaps. Still, this is a palace filled with magic and enchantment, so it's possible I saw the shadow of something that is now hiding in this room with me.

The idea sends a shiver up my neck and into my hair. *Be brave*, I remind myself. *This is your home now. You can't be afraid in your own home.* Forcing my legs to move, I walk around the room again. I bend and look under the furniture. I pull the curtains away from the wall and look behind them. As far as I can tell, I'm alone in this room.

But this isn't the only room in the suite. My eyes slide to the doorway leading to the bedroom. That is, after all, where I saw the movement just now. I cross the room and peek around the half-open door. I see another window and part of a four-poster bed. No movement or sound, though, so after a moment I push the door open enough to walk into the bedroom. The bedroom that will soon be mine too. The *bed* that will soon be mine.

An image of Roarke and me together in that bed flashes across my mind before I can stop it. I swallow in discomfort and try to push the image away. I've been avoiding thinking about that particular part of our union, but now that I'm staring at the bed that will soon belong to both of us, it's impossible not to think of what will have to happen in it.

I turn away as a shiver whispers across my skin. I still have time, I remind myself. Time to find a way out of this whole arrangement. The engagement announcement will happen tonight, but the actual union ceremony won't take place for another few weeks.

A voice out in the sitting room startles me, but it's only Roarke. "Yes, please close the door, Marvyn," he says. "I'll only be a few minutes." Breathing out and almost laughing at myself for my silly fears, I turn back toward the door. Hopefully Roarke won't be too annoyed after I explain why I'm in his room.

But I stop when I hear a second voice. A female voice.

"Is it still safe to speak in here?" she asks.

"Yes," Roarke answers. "We won't be overheard."

CHAPTER NINE

CRAP. I COVER MY MOUTH WITH MY HAND AND FREEZE.

"You're certain?" the woman asks.

"Yes. My father has no control over this suite. My men scour it daily for enchantments and bugs, and they haven't found anything in years."

"Still," the woman says as her footsteps cross the room. "Someone might see us through the window." Her voice sounds familiar, but I can't place it. I've overheard so many ladies of the court since I arrived here. It could be any one of them.

"I doubt it. We're very high up. And if someone does see us, so what? I'm the prince, and I have the right to speak to whomever I please."

My imagination jumps immediately to the worst con-

SHADOW FAERIE

clusion. Anger heats my veins at the thought of Roarke cheating on me. Why else would he be meeting a woman privately in his suite? A woman who doesn't want anyone seeing the two of them together? And it's not as though I'm jealous, but he's supposed to be marrying *me* in a few weeks! I reach for the door, about to pull it open fully and demand whether I can expect this kind of thing to continue after our union takes place.

"Okay then," the woman says. "So what are you doing about the ink-shades?"

I stop with my hand raised. *Ink-shades?* I wasn't expecting that.

"You have to get them under control, Roarke. We can't have them terrorizing this world. Or the other world. We can't live there until they've been eradicated completely."

"It's fine. My men are taking care of it."

"Like the guard who showed up dead? Wrinkled and aged?"

Roarke sighs. "You told me you weren't going to get upset about that."

"I've been thinking about it and I've decided I have every right to get upset about something like that. The same thing could happen to us."

I tilt my head toward to the doorway, wishing I could see their body language. Wishing I could figure out the nature of Roarke's relationship to this woman.

"The same thing most certainly will not happen to us," he assures her. "It only happened to that guard because he was stupid enough to let an ink-shade catch him when he wasn't wearing his amulet. And he should have known the right spell to fight back with, but clearly he was too slow. The rest of my men know what they're doing."

"Well they're certainly taking a while to get the job done. All this time wasted. Building has halted. The castle and grounds are just standing there half-formed, and—"

"Relax. It takes time to fill a world."

"Time in which someone else could discover it and claim it as their territory."

"Who's going to claim it? No one else knows about it."

"That isn't true now that you've let other people see it."

"I've told you already," Roarke says. "Neither my father nor Aurora have any interest in claiming that world as their own. He still has the same misbeliefs he had in the beginning, and you know Aurora's far more interested in—"

"I don't mean *them*." There's a pause in which I lean closer to make sure I don't miss her next words. "What about your future *wife*? And the guardian who happened to be with her?" A chill passes through me. I take a silent step backward, as if they might somehow sense my presence if I stand too close to the door.

"Emerson doesn't know what she saw," Roarke says, "and I doubt she even cares. She probably assumed it was part of the fae world. She doesn't know enough about this realm to assume it would be anything else. As for the guardian … well, I doubt he has any clue what he saw either. Guardians are trained to fight, not to think."

"You shouldn't underestimate him," she says darkly.

"And you shouldn't be worrying."

"Okay. Fine. So we're not in a rush. But I'm still worried about the ink-shades. How are they getting through? And is it only here at the palace, or do you think they're able to get through to any part of this world? Or …" She pauses for a moment. "I wonder if they're able to get through to the human world."

"If they can, it'll be the Guild's problem, not ours."

"True."

"And that probably won't happen, because my men are making sure that all the ink-shades will soon be dead."

"Good. Well then, can I get the cloak I came in here for? Marvyn might get suspicious if I walk out without it."

"Marvyn is suspicious already," Roarke says with a chuckle, "but I'll get you the cloak anyway." His footsteps move toward the bedroom. I curse beneath my breath—which sends an image of Dash rushing through my mind for just a second; he wouldn't be impressed with my choice of language. I duck through the only other door and into Roarke's en-suite bathroom. Slipping behind the half-open door, I hold my breath.

And that's when I see what's on the wall to my left.

I clap my hand over my mouth to suppress my startled gasp. A large circle of swirling, sparkling magic takes up most of the wall. Electric blue in color, with dark wispy bits rising from the edges and disappearing, the magic spins lazily in a spiral shape that seems to be sucked inwards at the center.

A portal?

A tiny part of me is curious to know where it leads—if it is indeed a portal—but mostly I'm terrified of what may come charging through from the other side. I lean as far away from it as I can while still remaining hidden behind the bathroom door. Fortunately, Roarke only takes a few moments in his bedroom. The moment I hear him walk out, I tiptoe hurriedly out of the bathroom and hover near the open bedroom doorway.

"… concerned about Marvyn and these suspicions of his?" the mystery woman asks.

"No, don't worry. He's paid well enough to keep his suspicions to himself."

"Good. Well, I'll leave you to prepare your announcement for tonight. I'm excited that this union will finally be official. Hopefully the ceremony will happen soon."

"It will," Roarke says.

Several moments of quiet follow, in which I begin to feel even more confused than before. This woman wants to hide her meetings with Roarke the way a secret lover would, but she's happy that he'll be marrying me?

I hear the main door to the suite open and close. I wonder if they're both gone, but then I hear Roarke's footfalls—heavier than the woman's—move across the sitting room. Terrified that he might return to his bedroom, I start tiptoeing back toward the bathroom. But the scrape of a chair tells me he's probably sitting now. I crouch down near the bed anyway, just in case I have to slide beneath it quickly for cover.

After several minutes that feel like hours, I hear a knock on the door. Then Aurora's voice once the door is open: "Oh, where's Em?"

Dammit.

"How should I know?" Roarke asks. "I thought she was with you."

Crap, crap, crap.

I do the only thing I can think of: I rush to the nearest window, swing my legs over, and lower myself down on the other side. The tips of my satin ballet-type shoes search out the footholds between the marble bricks. The shoes will be scuffed by the time I make it back inside, but hopefully no one will notice. I descend carefully, pausing as my foot feels the gap of the next window down. I move to the side, climb down another few bricks, and peek in through the side of the window. It looks like a private sitting room. Comfortable chairs, a cabinet full of drinks, a disgustingly ornate gold-framed mirror on one wall, and paintings of half-naked women on the others. But most importantly, there's no one in it.

I step onto the windowsill and hop inside. Seconds later, I'm out in the hallway, walking as quickly as I can without risking attention if I happen to pass someone. I swiftly navigate a few turns until I arrive at the stairway leading up to the royal family's wing. I run up—and almost crash into Aurora at the top.

"Oh, there you are," she says, relief appearing on her face. "What happened? I thought you were going to Roarke's suite." I search her features for any sign of suspicion, but all I see is confusion.

"He isn't there," I tell her. "One of the maids said she saw him near the library, so I went looking for him. Waste of time, though, since he wasn't there either. Are you sure he's finished with whatever important business he was dealing with this morning?"

"Yes, I just saw him in his chambers."

I roll my eyes and laugh. "This is what happens when you live in a home the size of a small city. We could run around all day looking for each other and never pass."

"And that," Aurora says as she takes my arm and turns us back toward her suite, "is why we have servants to do the running around for us. Anyway, I saw Roarke's outfit. I think it will go splendidly with the rose gold dress. Are you happy with that?"

I'm happy with anything that diverts Aurora's attention from the fact that I wasn't where I was supposed to be. Hopefully, if Roarke questions my whereabouts later, he'll believe my story just as easily. "That sounds perfect," I tell her. "The rose gold one is my favorite."

I follow her back into her suite where a flurry of activity has already begun. Hair stylists and makeup artists arrange their tools and spells. Lemon the clothes caster fusses about tiny imperfections in our dresses. The queen's handmaids flit in and out with messages from Aurora's mother about jewelry, hair ornaments, snacks and other trivial matters. And all the while, my mind is full of the conversation I wasn't supposed to hear and the magic I wasn't supposed to see.

CHAPTER TEN

NIGHT HAS FALLEN, WINTER HAS SETTLED, AND THE BALL-room is alive with activity. Women in gorgeous gowns and men in traditional faerie attire—suit pants and high-necked jackets with sharp angled shoulders—mingle on the dance floor at the center of the ballroom. Dozens of round tables encircle the room, each with a dragon ice sculpture forming the heart of the centerpieces. From the glass chandelier at the center of the ceiling, strings of tiny sparkling lights radiate outward. And from the ceiling itself, glittering snowflakes tumble downward, vanishing into nothing before reaching anyone's head.

I stand toward one side of the room with Aurora and two of her ladies-in-waiting who, it seems, have been allowed to return from the holiday Aurora sent them on. They chatter on and on, occasionally sending curious glances my way, while I try to pretend I'm interested in whatever they're talking about. The truth is, my mind couldn't be further away from this party. I can't get the thought of ink-shades out of my head. Roarke and that woman were obviously speaking about the place he and Aurora whisked me away to the day they found me in my old bedroom at Chelsea's house. The place where Dash and I ran from a shapeless shadowy creature—an ink-shade?—and ended up back in the faerie world near the tear in the veil. With everything else occupying my mind, I'd barely thought of that incident until this afternoon.

My gaze travels across the crowd as I wonder which of these ladies was in Roarke's room earlier. It could be any—

"And what brings you to the Unseelie Court, Em?" The question comes from one of Aurora's ladies. Mizza? Some strange name like that.

I take a moment to get my smile in place, but Mizza doesn't seem to notice. "The Guild wanted to imprison me, but some of the Unseelies—personal guards of Prince Roarke's, actually—rescued me."

She lets out a ladylike gasp and places one hand against her chest. "Oh, how thrilling. Was the prince with them at the time? He is *so* handsome, don't you think?"

"Why did the Guild want to imprison you?" the other young lady asks. Her name has completely escaped me.

"I'm Griffin Gifted, so the Guild thought I deserved to be locked up."

Both ladies' mouths drop open, but I maintain my serene smile. I'm allowed to start sharing the first part of my story now—minus the specifics of my Griffin Ability. By

116

mentioning Roarke's name when speaking of my rescue, I'm hoping people will be more likely to believe him when he stands up later and announces that I'm the love of his life.

"It's a very exciting story," Aurora adds, "and I promise I'll tell you all about it later. But right now, I want to introduce Em to some other people."

"That wasn't too bad, was it?" she asks quietly as she ushers me away.

"Uh … I don't know. I didn't listen to most of what they said."

"Em!" She smacks my arm, but her mock horror soon turns to a smile. "I suppose it is all quite overwhelming for you if you haven't been to an event like this before. So many distractions."

"Yes," I murmur, watching a miniature pegasus fly past. Raising my eyes, I notice there are quite a few of them in the air, each a different pastel shade. As I watch, a woman reaches up, catches one, and bites its head off.

"Oh," I gasp, jerking to a halt. "That's horrible."

"What is?" Aurora follows my gaze and starts laughing. "Oh, Em, it's just a flying cake. They aren't real creatures." She stands on tiptoe and grabs one. It struggles in her grip, but the moment she pulls its wing off, it stops moving. "See? Just cake and icing." She holds the wing out to me, and beneath the pastel pink outer layer, I see caramel-colored cake.

"Um, no thank you," I say when she tries to get me to take the wing part. "That's just disturbing." I look away from the woman sharing the beheaded pegasus with her friend and concentrate on smoothing out my frown. "So, do people know

117

there's a reason they're here other than your mother's birthday?"

"No one knows for certain, but they all suspect an engagement announcement," Aurora says. "I've heard the words 'engagement' and 'union' a number of times while walking around this evening."

"And I'm not supposed to confirm their suspicions yet if anyone asks me?"

"No. Let's keep people wondering for a little while longer. They can spread as many rumors around this ballroom as they like until Roarke makes the announcement. Now, let's see." She touches the choker of black pearls resting at the base of her neck as she looks around. "Who can I introduce you to—Oh. Never mind." The musicians on the raised platform at the far end of the ballroom have stopped playing. Aurora looks toward the massive arched doorway along with everyone else in the room. "My parents have arrived," she whispers to me.

As the Unseelie King and Queen are announced, every guest in the ballroom bows or curtseys. "Welcome," King Savyon shouts out as we all rise. "Thank you for joining us as we celebrate Queen Amrath's birthday. Tonight, you will delight in the grandest of entertainment, feast on the most exotic of dishes, and dance until the sun rises. Let the celebrations begin!"

The chandelier explodes, and the ballroom fills with shrieks and gasps. I duck down and look up, my thoughts floundering to figure out what's going on. An outside attack? The king losing his mind and killing us all? But as the smoke clears, I see hundreds of parachute-like objects floating down toward the crowd. Fearful murmurs turn to whispers of amazement, then to laughter and pointing. Aurora catches two parachutes and hands one to me. A small cube-shaped box hangs from a canopy of petals. As I place the box on my palm, the sides and top disappear, revealing a silver rose within.

"Perfect," Aurora says with a smile. "They turned out exactly how Mother wanted them to."

"What is it?"

"Chocolate." She giggles. "And an enchantment that keeps you from tiring until the sun rises. We'll be partying all night." She pops the rose into her mouth and gestures for me to do the same. I chew the bitter chocolate as I look around at people jumping to catch parachutes, passing them around to their friends, and comparing roses to see if they're all the same. My gaze falls across a man looking at me—and my heart almost stops as I recognize Dash.

Shock slams into me as he looks away and two women jumping for parachutes block him momentarily from view. It can't be him. It's a trick of my imagination, my mind morphing some other young man into the image of Dash. Nevertheless, I blink and peer more closely, some part of me hoping that it might actually be him. But it isn't. His hair is different, and his arm, I notice when he reaches up for one of the falling parachutes, is bare, lacking the markings of a guardian.

"Oh, look!" Aurora grabs my arm and pulls me around. She points upward as the light in the room dims and people in sparkly leotards descend through the air from the ceiling. They slip gracefully between the strings of lights and hang just below them, slowly twirling and somersaulting in coordinated movements to the accompaniment of eerie music. It reminds me somewhat of synchronized swimming, or aerial silks where acrobats perform while hanging from pieces of fabric. Except now, there's no water to float in. There's no fabric to hang from. These performers are suspended in midair by magic.

The evening continues with dancing—which I manage not to mess up—eating, and drinking, interspersed with various outlandish, magical forms of entertainment: jugglers tossing multicolored balls into the air where they transform into rainbow candies that whizz around making popping sounds and shooting star-shaped candies at everyone; a woman blowing bubbles into any shape her audience requests; a pair of centaurs who gallop in and perform a dramatic dance before galloping out; and a man who coaxes his magic into an Imperia-sized dragon made entirely of fire.

My imagination feels like it's on overload from all the fantastical things I've seen in the space of only a few hours when Roarke finally comes up to me. I've seen him from a distance this evening, dressed similarly to most of the other men but with the cuffs and high collar of his jacket made from gold embossed fabric. We agreed a few days ago that we wouldn't speak or dance together until after the announcement. So if he's standing in front of me now, that must mean—

"My lovely Lady Emerson, I believe we have an announcement to make."

I swallow as my stomach lurches. "Oh. Is it that time of the evening already?" I'd hoped to put it off as long as possible. In fact, part of me has been pretending all night that if I refused to think about it, it might never happen.

"Let us not keep our guests waiting any longer." Roarke places his hand against my back and directs me toward the raised platform where the musicians are seated. "I think we've built the suspense long enough. Everyone's enjoying themselves, but by now there isn't a single guest in this room who isn't wondering which pretty lady their prince has chosen for a wife. Let's put all their whispered speculations to rest."

The closer we get to the platform, the quieter the room becomes. Finally, as we climb the three steps leading up the side, silences descends, interrupted only by the occasional whisper and the rustle of skirts. "Remember to show everyone how happy you are," Roarke murmurs, his lips barely moving and his smile still in place.

I'm not sure I can fake happy right now, but I can at least hide my fear. As Roarke faces the crowd and I come to a standstill beside him, I try to mimic the way he holds himself, pushing my shoulders back and tilting my chin up slightly. I force my lips into as much of a smile as I can manage.

Then I make the mistake of looking out at the crowded ballroom. Hundreds of faces stare back at me with expressions ranging from curiosity to outright dislike. *Don't show fear, don't show fear.* I blink and settle my gaze on the far wall, just above the line of people. *Don't fidget, remain poised, keep smiling.* But despite my mask of confidence, a distant roar begins to fill my ears. My heart pounds so wildly I fear I may actually go into cardiac arrest.

Roarke begins speaking, but I hear only scraps of what he's saying: my past in the human realm, my Griffin Gifted status, my rescue from the Guild. I hear the words 'quick courtship' and 'deeply in love,' and then finally, Roarke looks at me, takes my hand in his, and says, "I've never been happier than the moment my father gave us permission to be united." He faces the crowd again, keeping hold of my hand. "And so, my lords and ladies, I present to you the woman I will be uniting with in exactly twelve days: the beautiful, captivating, kind Emerson."

Silence greets the prince's final words. It hovers, expands, presses against my ears, and then finally—it pops. Shouts, cheers and applause fill my ears, and suddenly this union seems all too real. I know I agreed to it, but as long as it wasn't official, I assumed I would find a way out of it. But now that everyone knows, it seems almost impossible. For the first time, it hits me—*really* hits me—that I may have to go through with this. I will marry a prince. This palace and these people will become my life. This will all become my mother's life too. For as long as it takes to figure out how we'll escape.

"Shall we dance now, my love?" Roarke asks me.

Not trusting myself to speak, I simply nod. He leads me down the platform and toward the center of the ballroom as the music starts up again. My legs begin to shake at the thought of an entire ballroom of people watching us dance, but Roarke raises his voice and encourages everyone to join in. With excited chattering, they rush to find partners as Roarke and I face each other and move into the starting position.

I've already danced numerous times this evening, but it's different now. No one cared who I was before. No one paid attention to me. But now, even though they're all dancing too, I feel their eyes on me. It would have been great if my Griffin

Ability had been able to give me the skill to perfectly perform every step, but apparently my Griffin Ability didn't know how to do that. So I'm left to concentrate intently on every move, every intricate piece of footwork, every twirl and pivot. Fortunately, with an expert partner like Roarke, it's easy to hide the odd mistake and hesitation.

Partners switch around us as the music changes again and again, but Roarke hangs onto me for a number of dances. He presses a kiss beneath my ear at one point, and I have to work hard to keep from cringing. I tell myself to be grateful he didn't go for my lips. Eventually, he hands me over to another partner, and now I really have to concentrate, my attention split between making polite conversation and following the steps.

Time passes. I continue circling the room, switching to a new partner whenever appropriate. Though I'm entirely out of my comfort zone, the music entices me to continue dancing. Or is it the enchanted chocolate I ate earlier?

Dance, converse, switch partners, repeat. I begin to wonder how long I have to do this before I can excuse myself from the dance floor and take a break from it all. I spin around and into the arms of yet another partner. A man, I realize with my second shocking jolt of the evening, that I do recognize after all.

Dash.

PART II

CHAPTER ELEVEN

My feet stumble to a halt. An odd combination of joy and horror rockets through me. Dash's hair is completely different, as I noticed earlier, and several days' worth of well-groomed stubble adds to his disguise. But it's definitely him.

"Don't stop dancing," he says, forcing me to jerkily step back in time with the music. Then, after giving the dancers around him a pleasant and entirely fake smile, he hisses, "What the hell is wrong with you?"

Another shocked second passes before I find my voice. "Me? What is wrong with *you*? How did you even—what did you—do you know what Roarke and Aurora will do if they recognize you?"

"They saw me for all of five seconds that day. They're not about to recognize me now."

"But how did you even—"

"*What are you doing here, Em?* Why are you playing along with this stupid union charade? I expected to find a prisoner, and instead—"

"We are *not* having this discussion here," I tell him through clenched teeth, my smile completely forgotten now. "Meet me outside." I tug free of his grip and twist around. The man I bump into looks startled. He and the woman he's dancing with almost stumble. But fortunately, after two or three fumbling seconds, everyone switches partners, and for anyone watching, it probably appears that the almost-princess accidentally tried to switch a few seconds early. I gladly step into the confused man's arms and continue dancing, trying to keep a serene smile in place while my heart thunders in my chest.

I can still barely believe it. *Dash is here.* Through my anger and terror—because this is exactly the kind of thing I was trying to avoid when I chose to come here, and now he's messing it all up—I'm heart-achingly glad to see him.

"Was it awful growing up in the non-magic realm?" my dance partner asks.

"Uh, well, I didn't know any better, so I didn't know what I was missing out on."

"How thrilling to have discovered you actually belong to this world instead."

"Yes. Magic is … so wonderful." I'm distracted as I catch a glimpse of Dash with another partner.

When the dance ends, I manage to politely decline the woman who was hoping to be my next partner. I slip past her and weave my way off the dance floor, between the tables and chairs, and toward the arched doorway that leads to the gardens. It's odd looking out and seeing a glittering snow-white landscape while feeling so warm I'm almost sweating. There must be a spell across the open doorway that keeps the freezing winter air outside.

Looking back, I see at least two women making their way toward me with bright eyes and wide smiles, probably hoping to engage me in conversation. Wonderful. Now that everyone knows who I am, I'll never get out of this ballroom unnoticed. I search about for a distraction, and on the nearest table, I spot one of the popping rainbow candies. I discreetly drop it onto the floor, lift my skirt, and kick it to the side. It spins away from me and into the crowd, whizzing and popping and shooting tiny star-shaped candies everywhere. In the commotion, I meet Dash's eyes for a second. Then I turn and slip out into the night.

The cold hits me the moment I pass beneath the archway, but after all that dancing, the icy air is a welcome relief. After hurrying down the stairs, I turn right, step off the path, and wait in the shadow of a tree with silver, snow-dusted apples hanging from its branches. I breathe out long and slow, but my anxiety only increases as the seconds tick by and I wait for Dash.

I tense as hurried footsteps move down the stairs. Dash looks around, catches sight of me, and in a few quick strides he's standing in front of me. "What is wrong with you?" he demands immediately. "Waltzing around like you belong here. Playing along with this union idiocy. You can't possibly be planning to—"

"You want to talk about idiocy?" I snap right back. "*You* are an idiot. Why did you come here? These people are your enemies. Do you know what they'll do to you if they find out what you are and who you work for?"

"They're your enemies too, Em, but somehow you've let them manipulate you into marrying one of them—"

"I haven't been *manipulated* into anything," I counter, still trying to keep my voice to nothing louder than an angry whisper. "I *chose* to be here. Roarke presented an arrange- ment—marriage in return for healing my mother—gave me time to think about it, and I decided to accept his offer. The only person who wants to force me into anything is the king, but Roarke won't let him. He wants a willing wife. He isn't going to manipulate me into doing anything against my will, despite what you're thinking."

Dash looks like he's about to be sick. "You … you volun- tarily came here? Nobody forced you into this?"

"Yes. He offered something I want, and I decided the price was worth it."

"The price is *marriage*, Em! A union! Have you stopped to think how serious that is? We're talking about *the rest of your life*. Unions in this world aren't like the ones in your world. It's a magical bond that isn't easily broken. And royal unions? I've *never* heard of one of those being broken. If you go through with this, it's forever."

I roll my eyes, even as the weight of his words pierce through to my core and leave my skin colder than it was a moment ago. "Now you're being an idiot again. I don't actually intend to go through with this union. I have a Griffin

Ability, for goodness' sake. An extremely powerful one. When the moment is right, and when I've learned enough control, I'll get Roarke to tell me everything I need to know to heal my mother, and then I'll escape."

Dash still looks somewhat ill. "Seriously? That's your plan? You really think after all that in there—" he waves in the general direction of the ballroom again "—they're going to let you escape?"

"Okay, first of all, 'escape' implies that I'm not going to ask permission. I'm just going to leave. So it doesn't matter whether they *let* me or not. And secondly …" I slowly suck in a deep breath because I have to admit I'm feeling as sick as Dash looks. "Secondly, I realize that an escape might not be possible. They might catch me and force me to go through with this—"

"You think?"

"—despite everything Roarke says about wanting a willing wife," I continue, speaking over Dash. "And if that's the way it ends up, then so be it. At least I'll get the information I need, and then—"

"That's if Roarke actually follows through with his side of the bargain and tells you what he knows—which is probably *nothing*, by the way. How can he possibly know any more about your mother than the rest of us? But by the time you figure that out, it'll be too late for you." He throws his hands up and looks away as he shakes his head. "This whole plan of yours is utterly pointless."

A chill runs through me. My body has cooled down quickly, and the winter air feels as though it's seeping into my very bones. I run my hands vigorously up and down my arms.

"It isn't pointless. Dark magic has trapped my mother in a permanent coma, and Roarke, as a member of the court that uses that kind of magic, knows how to wake her. And, more importantly, he knows what caused her mental illness. It *was* something magical, and he knows how to fix it."

"He's *lying*, Em," Dash says in the kind of tone he would use if talking to a naive child. Absently, he moves his hand in a quick circular motion above my head, and I immediately begin to feel warmer. "Do you really think a pampered prince knows anything about magical mental illnesses? He'd tell you anything to get you to stay and give him full access to your Griffin Ability. Why can't you see that?"

"He isn't lying. He knows far more about my past than anyone else I've come across in this world. He's already proved it to me. He's my best chance for saving Mom."

"But … this is just …" Dash struggles for a moment. He tugs at his hair, which I realize is a wig when it comes away in his hand, revealing his own messy hair underneath. "I know you want your mother to be better," he says, his eyes returning to mine, "but why does her health and happiness have to be solely *your* responsibility? Is she really—" He cuts himself off, breathing heavily. "I know this is going to make me sound like the bad guy. I don't want to ask you if she's worth it, because of course she's—"

"How can you even think that?" I gasp.

"I'm not! That's what I'm saying. Of course she's worth it. She's your mother, and clearly you love her more than anything else in either world, but …" His eyes plead with me. "Would she want you to do this? Would she want you to

132

SHADOW FAERIE

throw away your entire life in what is probably a futile attempt to save hers?"

"I'm not throwing away my entire life!" I shout. Then I remember myself. I remember Aurora's words—*My father has eyes and ears everywhere*—and I lower my voice again. It's barely a whisper now. My lips hardly move as I speak. "They might force me into a marriage, but that doesn't mean I'll be here forever. My Griffin Ability makes me more powerful than most people in this world. Mom and I *will* escape one day."

"Even if that's possible," Dash says, "how much evil will they force you to commit before then?"

"I ... I ..." I don't have an answer for that.

"Why do you think they want you, Em? You can make their dirty work easier, that's why." He takes hold of my shoulders and gives me a small shake. "These people are *not good*. Surely you know the kinds of things they're going to make you do?"

I pull myself free of his grasp. "You're wrong. Roarke isn't like that, and neither is Aurora." *But the king is*, a silent voice reminds me. That scene in the king's office—the scene I keep pushing out of my thoughts—appears abruptly at the front of my mind. The king with his hand clenching around the air, and that man's head ripping right off his—

I blink and wince and look away.

"Really?" Dash says. "They're not like that?"

I can tell without meeting his eyes that he knows I'm lying. I breathe in a shuddering breath. "I saw ... something." I blink again and shake my head, trying to force the memory away. I focus on Dash's green eyes again, knowing there's no point in

133

trying to convince him with lies I barely believe myself. There's no point in anything but the truth. "What other choice did I have, Dash?" My voice is a desperate whisper now, having lost its defensive edge. "These are the only people who can help me."

"You could have trusted *us*! Me and everyone else at the oasis. We *want* to help you, Em. We've done nothing except try to help you since you got to this world, and that wasn't about to change. I don't understand why you'd just turn your back on all of that and—"

"That's the point, Dash! That's why I had to leave."

He pauses, his eyebrows climbing higher. "Is that supposed to make sense?"

"You and your friends have done nothing but try to help me, and it almost got you *killed*. You were a glass statue. Remember that? You and Violet came so close to dying. *Dying*, Dash!" My voice rises as my chest tightens at the memory of that terrifying day.

"Yeah, but we didn't. It wasn't such a big deal."

"Of course it was a big deal! You almost died *because you tried to help me*. And Chelsea and Georgia actually *were* dead, and they would have stayed that way if my Griffin Ability hadn't made a convenient appearance. So after all that, I decided I didn't want anyone else to be put at risk because of me and my mother."

"Em—"

"Yes, I had everything I could have wanted at the oasis. It's beautiful, it's safe, the people are amazing. But if I'd stayed there, *someone* would have ended up hurt or dead because they tried to help me. This is *my* problem. She's my mother. If there's a price involved in returning her to normal, I'm the one who should pay it. No one else."

Dash is silent for too long before he says, "It's too late for that."

I blink, feeling cold again despite Dash's warmth-producing spell still surrounding me. "What do you mean?"

He shakes his head and looks away. "This ... this isn't the way I wanted to tell you. I wanted to get you far away from here first. Back to the oasis."

"Before you tell me what?" I step closer and wrap one cold hand around his arm. "Tell me what, Dash? What happened?"

"Chelsea and Georgia ..." He closes his eyes and presses his lips together before continuing. "They both ... died."

I drop my hand from his arm as quickly as if his skin just burned me. "What?"

"It happened about two days after the glass incident with Ada."

"But ... they can't be dead. My Griffin Ability brought them back to life."

"They were human, Em," he says gently. "Your Griffin Ability may have worked on them, but their bodies couldn't handle the magic. In the end, it killed them."

"But ... are you sure they were human? I mean, she's my mother's sister, and my mother's a faerie. And what about all the herbal remedies Chelsea makes? I thought maybe ... maybe those were actually magical."

Dash offers no explanations; he merely shakes his head. "I'm so sorry, Em."

"They … they're really dead?" I whisper. "My magic killed them. I thought it saved them, but it killed them."

"Em—"

"I killed my own family."

"It wasn't you who killed them," Dash says, his voice suddenly fierce. "Ada did, with her horrible glass magic. *She* shattered them into thousands of pieces. You did what you could to save them, but it wasn't enough. They were doomed from the moment she first touched them."

My legs can't hold me up. I crumple onto the ground, not giving a second's thought to the expensive dress I'm probably ruining. Quick, shallow breaths consume me as I stare unseeingly into the garden. Dash is still speaking, but I can't hear him anymore. I don't know how I'm supposed to react to this. Chelsea and Georgia didn't love me, and I didn't love them; I can't suddenly pretend otherwise just because they're dead. But they were family. They took me in, even though they constantly made it clear what a burden I was to them. And now they're dead, and I can't figure out what I'm supposed to feel aside from guilty.

"I never wanted any of this," I manage to whisper. I cover my face with my hands, wishing I could blot out this other world and its magic that's sent my life spinning so completely out of my control. "Can't someone just take it all away? Please. I don't want this magic. I don't want a Griffin Ability. I don't want to marry a prince. I just want to go back to that simple life Mom and I had before magic made her crazy and everything started to fall apart."

I feel Dash's arm on my shoulder and sense him crouching beside me. "I wish I could—"

"Emerson?"

I suck in a breath at the sound of Roarke's voice. Slowly, I lower my hands and watch him descend the stairs.

"What's going on? Why are you on the ground?"

Dash rises to face him.

"You," Roarke says slowly, recognition in his eyes. "Well now." His gaze moves to me as his expression becomes unreadable. "Isn't this an interesting situation."

CHAPTER TWELVE

IN LESS THAN A MINUTE, I FIND MYSELF BACK INSIDE THE warmth of the palace in a small sitting room somewhere near the ballroom. Despite the turmoil of emotions overwhelming me, I didn't dare disobey Roarke when he uttered "Follow me" in a tone icier than the winter air. Dash hesitated, but he soon caught up to the two of us. Back in the ballroom, no one stopped the prince or his betrothed. No one even looked our way. I suspect Roarke's magic was responsible for that.

The door of the sitting room swings shut of its own accord. Flames spring to life in the fireplace. "What is he doing here?" Roarke demands immediately, gesturing at Dash without looking at him.

"I ... I don't ..." I run my hands over my face, trying to focus on Roarke's words and seeing only Chelsea and Georgia's lifeless eyes. Their cold bodies. Alone in their beds in their little Stanmeade house. I blink and look into the crackling flames dancing in the fireplace, hoping to sear the bright, warm image into my mind. "I don't know," I say finally, turning away from the fire. "I was as shocked as you are to see him here. This thing is still attached to me—" I touch the coin-sized piece of metal behind my ear "—so no magic should have been able to locate me."

Roarke crosses the room. His fingers wrap around Dash's arm. "Where are your guardian markings?"

Dash tugs his arm away, then lets out a short laugh. "There's this thing girls use. It's called concealer. Works pretty well for covering—"

"And how did you get into my palace?"

Dash takes his time folding his arms over his chest before squarely facing Roarke. "Your mother decided to outsource the design of Em's dress for tonight. When one of your clothes casters came to pick it up, I made sure I was there, ready to take his place. His transport brought me back here. It was all remarkably easy, in fact."

"And how did you know Emerson was here in the first place?"

"An educated guess plus a process of elimination. I figured it was either you, the Seelies or the Guild who got hold of her. I asked around, and the Guild and the Seelies still seemed to be under the impression Em was either dead or missing. You know, since the incident at the cliff." Dash shrugs. "Therefore it had to be you guys."

"So you told your superiors all about your suspicions, and

they rewarded you by letting you sneak your way into my home and poke your unwelcome nose around? Doubtful. You don't seem nearly high up enough in the Guild ranks to be trusted with a task as important as retrieving a dangerous and powerful Griffin Gifted faerie like Emerson."

Dash's gaze narrows slightly. "I'm not here on behalf of the Guild."

"Ah." Roarke nods. "I had a feeling it might be something along those lines." He walks to the dresser on the other side of the room and opens a drawer. "You and Emerson seemed to be getting very cozy when Aurora and I found the two of you together in her old bedroom." He closes the drawer and turns to face us again. "*After* she escaped the Guild. When you—a guardian—shouldn't have known anything about her whereabouts." He shakes his head and lets out a quiet laugh. "A traitor to your own kind, I see. How disappointing."

Dash's expression darkens. "Not really. I just happen to disagree with tagging, tracking and imprisoning Griffin Gifted."

"And do *you* have a tag on you, guardian boy? So that someone can summon you or determine your location?"

"I told you I'm not here on behalf of the Guild, so why would I be stupid enough to let someone tag me?"

"Good." Roarke moves toward Dash. "But just in case …" His hand sweeps up and slaps against the side of Dash's neck.

Almost too fast to see, Dash grabs Roarke's arm and twists it, spinning the prince around and trapping his arm behind his back. "What did you just do?" Dash hisses. The sound of a sizzle rushes through the air, and with a yelp, Dash shoves Roarke away from him. "What the—"

Roarke straightens, rolls his shoulders, and adjusts the collar of his jacket. "I don't appreciate being manhandled."

Dash feels the side of his neck. "What is this?" As his hand moves away, I see a small circle of metal just like the one behind my ear.

"A precaution, that's all," Roarke says.

"How dare you—"

"You sneak into *my* home, and you want to know how *I* dare to—"

"Stop!" I shout. My Griffin Ability isn't ready to issue a magical command yet, but my cry is enough to make both Roarke and Dash pause and look my way. "Just ... just stop." My voice wavers. "My aunt and cousin are dead, and the two of you are acting like petty children."

A frown tugs at Roarke's eyebrows downward. "Your aunt and cousin? The ones you lived with in the non-magic world?"

I look back into the fire as I nod. "Dash told me. Outside. That's why I was sitting on the ground. I was ... I just can't believe it."

"These are the people you didn't particularly care for?" Roarke asks, his tone not unkind, merely curious. "The ones who treated you poorly since you first moved in with them?"

I nod. "But they were still family. Well—I don't know what they were. Mom and Chelsea were sisters, but Mom's a faerie and Chelsea was human, so ... they can't have been sisters? I don't know. I don't understand." I press my fingers to my temples again and squeeze my eyes shut. "But I lived with them. For years. I thought they were family, and now they're just *gone*."

I hear Roarke's quiet footsteps moving closer before he places one hand carefully against the small of my back. "I'm sorry, Emerson. I can't imagine what that feels like. But I can promise you this: you're about to get an entirely new family. And though it may not be obvious from the outside, we *do* care about each other. We'll care for you too. You'll be one of us, and you'll finally belong somewhere. You and your mother."

Across the room, Dash snorts and mutters something under his breath. I almost do the same, because of course Roarke's true motive has nothing to do with a desire to give me a new family and a place to belong. He wants my Griffin Ability. But perhaps there's more to it than that. Perhaps he really does want this union to work out. Perhaps he does plan to care for me for the rest of our lives.

"You'll stay, of course," Roarke says to Dash. "For the ceremony. You're Emerson's friend. I'm sure she'll want you to be here."

"Your ceremony is more than two weeks away," Dash says before I can voice my own opinion. "I can't stay here for that long. I have a job, remember?"

"You also have a desire to stop this union," Roarke points out. "Which means that if I let you leave, you'll tell the Guild exactly what's happening, and they'll attempt to put a halt to our plans and retrieve Emerson. Or kill her."

"Dash wouldn't tell—"

"You don't know that for sure," Roarke says to me. "If you

142

want this union to happen, then we can't take the risk of the Guild getting involved."

"The Guild will wonder where I am," Dash says.

"Let them wonder then. They don't know you're here."

Dash exhales slowly, his bright eyes never leaving Roarke. "I know this doesn't matter to you, but I have important cases—"

"You should have considered that before you broke into my home," Roarke says.

"Fine then." Dash forces his fists behind his back and gives Roarke the most obviously fake smile I've ever seen. "Thank you so much for the invitation, Your Royal Highness. I'd be delighted to stay here and attend your union ceremony."

Roarke nods. "Good. Just make sure your wrist markings remain covered. I can't guarantee your safety if my father discovers what you are."

"Certainly. And I'll keep my lips zipped and ask no questions about any of the laws you Unseelies have broken lately, or about, say, that colorless shadowy place I woke up in after you abducted Em and me."

"Perfect. See to it that you don't forget that promise," Roarke adds in a threatening tone.

"So … is Dash a guest?" I ask. "Or a prisoner?"

Roarke looks at me. "Would you like me to make him a prisoner?"

"Of course not."

"Then he is our guest." He moves closer and tucks a stray curl of hair behind my ear. "I only want to make you happy, Emerson. You've received some shocking news this evening, and I'm sure it will be a comfort to have your friend here."

My frown deepens. "But you don't trust him and you don't want him to leave. So why would you let him wander freely around your palace?"

"Don't worry, he'll be watched wherever he goes. If he steps out of line, I'll make sure the Guild finds out that he knows far more about the Griffin rebels than he's supposed to. I doubt he'll be able to keep his job after that." He looks at Dash. "Sound fair?"

Dash tips his head in the slightest of nods. "Perfectly fair, since I plan to be on my very best behavior, Your Regal Princely-ness."

A muscle in Roarke's jaw twitches, but, fortunately, he decides not to retaliate. "More importantly, my dear Emerson," he continues, turning back to me, "I'd like to show you that I care about your happiness. If that means treating your guardian friend as a guest instead of a prisoner, then I'll do it."

I still don't know whether to believe him, but I guess I'll find out in the coming days. "Okay," I say warily. "Thank you."

"Let's return to the ball now. Push your sorrow aside, my love, and join in the merriment. You'll soon feel better."

I doubt that's true, but I also doubt I have a choice. I don't think my request to leave the party, climb into bed, and pull the covers over my head would go down well. So I follow Roarke out of the room and back toward the party. I breathe in deeply and press my lips together to keep them from shuddering. I take the first drink that's offered to me and down it in one go, hoping the contents are enough to dull my senses for the rest of the night.

When it's close to midnight and my Griffin Ability comes to life, I say the words I've been compelled to say. No one hears me amidst the noise, but everyone oohs and aahs in wonder at the six rainbows that arc one after the other across the room as if marking the twelve points of a giant colorful clock. I wish I could experience a little of their awe at the sight of what my own magic has produced, but it seems the various drinks I've consumed are doing their job: I don't feel much of anything anymore.

CHAPTER THIRTEEN

WHEN CLARINA WAKES ME THE FOLLOWING MORNING, I feel a little as though someone shoved a stake through my eyeball. And a screwdriver through my other eyeball. Someone must have also turned up the brightness of the sun; I can only peel my eyelids apart for about half a second before having to squeeze them shut again.

"Your lunch is in the sitting room, my lady," Clarina says. "Everyone is eating alone today, as some are still recovering from last night."

"Lunch?" I ask in a croaky voice.

"Yes, it's almost midday, my lady." Her footsteps move closer, and she adds, "The drink beside your bed will ease your headache."

I push myself slowly up and squint at the crystal goblet of

clear liquid. I almost ask how she knows about my aching head, but I suppose she's been here long enough to be fully aware of the many hangovers that follow an event like last night's ball.

"Your pool has been filled," she adds.

"Thank you." I swing my legs over the edge of the bed and stare at the floor for a while as my brain runs through the events of the previous night. I remember that Dash is here now. I remember that Chelsea and Georgia are ... dead.

I pick up the goblet, and my eyes fall on the outfit Clarina has chosen for me today, hanging on the outside of the wardrobe. A double-breasted coat-dress type thing, aquamarine with floral patterns of white, green and mauve. The queen's birthday celebrations continue with a tea in the gardens this afternoon, so Clarina was obviously told to choose something appropriately festive for me. It's pretty, but it doesn't feel right to wear something so ... alive.

"Clarina?" I call, hoping she's still in the next room.

"Yes, Lady Emerson?" She hurries back to the bedroom.

"Would it be okay if you choose a black outfit for me today? Or grey, perhaps, if black is too depressing for the queen's tea party?"

"Uh, certainly, my lady. That should be fine. I believe there's a charcoal-colored item with silver embroidered details. Will that do?"

"Yes, thank you."

I don't feel any kind of deep sorrow for the loss of Chelsea and Georgia. I'm still shocked, barely able to believe they're gone, but I know there was no love lost between us. Still, it

147

feels wrong to simply move on with life and forget about them. I need to do *something*, and if wearing black or grey is the only thing left to me, then that's what I'll do.

* * *

The concoction in the goblet works remarkably quickly, and my pounding headache is soon gone. Though I'd like to soak in the pool of purple bubbles for a whole lot longer, I should probably find out where Dash is and make sure he hasn't got himself into any trouble.

After drying and dressing, I do up the buttons of my charcoal outfit and pad barefoot into my sitting room in search of some food. I select the most normal-looking sandwich and head back to my bedroom to choose a pair of shoes.

At the sight of a figure sitting on the edge of my bed, I freeze. He turns his head—and I realize it's Dash.

"Jeez, Dash. Are you trying to give me a heart attack? How did you get in here?"

He gestures over his shoulder to the window where the curtain ripples gently in the warm breeze. "Your window was open. I climbed up to it."

I want to tell him he's as bad as I am, climbing palace walls, but I'm too frightened that someone important might discover he's in my bedroom. "You can't be here," I whisper. "If Roarke or his father find you in my *bedroom*, of all places—"

"No one saw me, don't worry. I didn't leave my room through the door, so anyone watching will assume I'm still inside. And I found your room quite easily. Didn't have to look into too many others."

"Dash!"

"What?"

"What about whoever might be *listening* right now?" I hiss.

Dash frowns. "You're joking, right?"

I shake my head. "There are eyes and ears everywhere."

"Yeah, but in your *bedroom*? That's crossing the line."

I step closer to him and lower my voice further. "After everything you told me about these people, you really want me to believe there are lines they won't cross?"

Dash hesitates. "True."

"I mean, I don't know for sure whether anyone's listening, but Aurora told me to be careful of what I say, no matter where I am."

Dash raises his finger to his lips, indicating that I should remain silent. He begins to walk slowly around the room, looking, listening, even, at times, sniffing. "The only other magic I can sense in this room is coming from your bed," he whispers. "Which is totally inappropriate, if you ask—"

The duvet moves, a shape slides toward the edge, and a black cat lands on the floor.

"Oh," Dash says, his voice no longer a whisper. "Is that Bandit?"

I open my arms and Bandit leaps up, shifting into a bird to help him gain height, and landing in my arms as a cat once more. "Yes." I hug him close to my chest. "I wanted him to stay at the—um, where it was safe. But he must have come with me in a form too small for me to notice."

Dash smiles and comes closer so he can scratch Bandit behind the ears. "Jack will be relieved. He's been so worried about Bandit."

"So you don't think anyone's listening?" I ask.

"I don't, but even if someone is listening, so what? It's not as though I'm acting improperly toward the future princess. You and I are just talking. If you'd prefer, we can do it in your sitting room instead of your bedroom."

I roll my eyes. "As if that makes any difference. You'd still have to explain how you got past the guards outside my door. And climbing in through the window makes you look awfully suspicious."

He heaves a breath and sits on the edge of the bed again. "I just thought you might want to know about ... you know. The funeral."

The funeral.

Chelsea and Georgia.

Dead.

"You were there?" I ask.

Dash nods. "Yeah. You may or may not remember that some of the people in Stanmeade were actually my friends. Not true friends, of course, since I could never be fully honest with anyone, but ... yeah. I have friends there, and I felt like I should be at the funeral. Just, you know, to support anyone who was friends with Georgia."

I nod and murmur, "Of course. Yeah. I still can't believe she and Chelsea are gone. They were always just *there*, you know? My horrible cousin and aunt that I couldn't wait to get away from. Then I finally did get away, and now ..." I shake my head. Now, because Ada was after me, they're both dead. Dash may try to convince me I shouldn't blame myself, but I know I'm responsible. Indirectly, perhaps, but still responsible.

I let Bandit jump out of my arms before walking to the chair in the corner of my room. It's the type of fancy chair that no one actually wants to sit in—an overly embellished wooden frame with cushions too firm to be comfortable. Nevertheless, I perch on the edge of it and clear my throat. "Was it, um, were there lots of people there? At the funeral?"

"Yes. Almost everyone in town was there. I guess Chelsea knew a lot of people, seeing as she ran one of the only hair salons in Stanmeade."

I frown. "She was such a huge fan of gossip and rumor-spreading that I would have thought there'd be a lot of people who didn't like her."

"Well, you don't have to like someone to go to their funeral."

I look across at him. "Did people say horrible things?"

"No. Only good things were said about her. About both of them. It was all very …" He rubs a hand over his face. "Very strange. So tragic, on the one hand, and yet so false hearing all these lovely tributes about two people I personally witnessed being spiteful on multiple occasions. And it seemed *wrong* of me to think those things, but how could I not? I couldn't suddenly turn Chelsea and Georgia into something else in my memory just because they're now dead."

"I … just …" I shake my head. "I don't know what to say or think or feel. What does everyone think the cause of death was?"

"A gas leak."

"I assume the Guild is responsible for that story?"

"Yes. It was the easiest story to go with."

"Do you think ... do you know whether ..." I hesitate, wondering if I even want to know the answer. "Did they suffer? Did the magic in their bodies cause them to suffer as they were dying?"

"I don't know, Em. I honestly don't know. I hope not."

I lean my elbows on my knees. "Before you told me what happened to them, I was starting to think that all this time Chelsea was also some kind of faerie just like me and Mom, and that the herbal remedies she made were magical. But if they contained magic, they wouldn't have helped anyone in Stanmeade. People would have ended up sick and possibly dead, right?"

"Yeah."

"So Chelsea was definitely human."

"Yes."

"Which means she and my mother can't have been sisters."

Dash shakes his head.

"I wonder if Chelsea knew. I wonder if my mother knows, or if she thinks Chelsea was like her. Someone with magic that couldn't be accessed." I rub my fingers in circular motions against my temples as I stare at the floor. "I have so many questions still. So many gaps in my family history that I need Mom to fill in for me."

"Well, I hope your genius plan works out and you get all the answers you're looking for."

I direct a frown his way. "This isn't just about answers. You know that. Even if Mom knew nothing, I'd still want to wake her and heal her mind."

"Yeah," he says quietly. "I know."

I watch him closely for a while. "Why are you really here? I mean, I've …" I push my embarrassment down as my cheeks heat up. "I've never been nice to you. Surely you don't care enough about me to take the kind of risk required in coming here."

He lets out a short laugh devoid of humor. "It wasn't a question of how much I may or may not care about you. This isn't just about you, Em. It's about what the Unseelie King will make you do. How many lives might be ruined because you're forced to use your Griffin Ability against your will?"

"I … I don't—"

"And I thought you were a prisoner here. I thought I was saving both you *and* all the people you might be forced to hurt in future. I never guessed that you *chose* to come here. That you'd refuse to leave once I found you."

I look away from him. "I'm sorry. Like I said last night, you weren't supposed to find me. You were supposed to stay far away and never get hurt again because of me."

"That was never going to happen, Em. I'm not the kind of person to sit by while the Unseelie King gets his hands on the latest powerful weapon in the fae realm. And I didn't think you were the kind of person to just hand over that power either."

I swallow past my shame. "Well, I guess I am," I say quietly, staring down at the floor. "Like almost everyone else in the world, I'm only looking out for myself and the people I love.

I'm not brave or selfless. I'm just doing what I have to do to get by."

From the corner of my eye, I see Dash shake his head. "You can tell yourself that lie all you want, but I know you're more than that. I know what you did in Stanmeade. You stopped Ada's glass from consuming the entire town. You didn't have to do that. You could have kept your mother's location a secret and let that place splinter apart. But you didn't."

"And what good did my selflessness do then?" I demand. "I gave her what she wanted, but did she stop her attack on the town? No. I had to figure that out myself, and it was a fluke that my Griffin Ability switched on at just the right moment. So what difference will it make now if I refuse to give my power to the king? Nothing. He'll commit the same evil acts he plans to commit. It might just take him a little longer." I feel sick at my own words. I don't *want* to help the king do anything. But really, the world is a sucky place and this is the way it works. This is the way *both* worlds work. Life's a bitch and then you die—just like that old song Chelsea used to listen to sometimes. "Only a few people get to be heroes, Dash," I quietly tell him. "And you may be one of those people, but I'm not. I'm just trying to play the best hand from the cards I've been dealt."

He's quiet for a moment, and all I can see in his eyes is sadness. "At some point, you're going to realize that this"—he gestures around him—"is most certainly not your best hand. I just hope you figure that out sooner rather than later."

"And I hope you get away from here sooner rather than later. There's no need for you to get hurt."

He raises an eyebrow. "You know what I am, right? Getting hurt is part of the job."

And dying? I almost ask. But I don't want to go there. I don't want to talk about death when he's already come so close to it. Not when the deaths of Chelsea and Georgia are still so near.

"Besides," he adds. "I don't think it'll be nearly as easy to leave this palace as it was to get inside."

Bandit jumps back onto my lap. I stroke his sleek black hair and, in an effort to turn the conversation away from such heavy topics, I ask, "Was it true? The story you told Roarke last night. About getting into the palace in place of the clothes caster."

"Yes. Well, mostly. It wasn't supposed to be me who came here."

"Oh." I look up. "Who was it supposed to be?"

Dash gives me a pointed look. "I'd rather not say her name, just in case. But I'm sure you can figure it out, given her particular talent for ... concealment."

Ah. Calla. I nod. "I think I know who you're talking about."

"It would have been much easier for her to blend in. But the clothes caster arrived earlier than expected to pick up the dress from my mother's studio, so—"

"Wait, your mother?"

"Yes. She's the one who designed your dress."

My hand stills on Bandit's back. "Your mother is Raven Rosewood?"

"Yes. I told you she's a fashion designer, didn't I?"

"Yes, but … I never thought … Wait, is your surname Rosewood?" That doesn't seem right, but now I can't remember if I've ever actually known Dash's surname.

"No, it's Blackhallow."

"Oh. Dash Blackhallow," I say slowly, trying out the name.

"Dashiell Blackhallow, if we're going to get technical." He rolls his eyes. "Lots of l's, I know. Anyway, my mother was still a Rosewood when she began designing. That's the name people knew her by, so she kept it."

"So out of all the designers in this world, the queen ended up choosing your mother. That can't have been a coincidence."

Dash smiles. "Of course it wasn't. My mother heard the Unseelie Queen was looking for a particularly special dress. Not for herself, though, and not for her daughter. The rumors suggested that a new young lady had arrived at the Unseelie Palace, and the queen and princess had taken a special interest in her. Normally my mother would stay far away from anything to do with the Unseelies, but she knew you'd gone missing. She told me about the rumors and this unofficial 'competition' to design the best dress. I was almost certain this girl was you, and so I told Mom that one of her dresses *had* to be chosen, no matter what. So we enchanted her designs. A simple spell that made anyone who looked at the pages want to keep coming back to them. And it worked. She was chosen."

My mouth is hanging open by the time he's finished speaking. "It was really that simple?"

"Yes. And then the guy who came to pick up the dress arrived way too early. I was hiding, watching my mother hand the dress over on her own, as she'd been instructed. I hoped she'd keep him talking or something until Ca—um—until our friend arrived, but the clothes caster said he was on a tight schedule. Seemed quite agitated to be there. He kept looking around as though terrified someone might spot him in this upstanding establishment. When he said his carriage was enchanted to turn around and leave in under five minutes, I did the only thing I could think of: knocked him out and took his place."

"So you jumped into his carriage and it all worked out fine?"

"Well, I changed into his clothes first. And Mom found me an appropriately colored wig from her many supplies. And I took his stylus and amber, which was a good thing, since the carriage door wouldn't open until I held his stylus up against it, and I was almost out of time by then. Oh, and there were two guards inside the carriage, but they were disinterested enough that they didn't notice my face wasn't the same as the guy they'd just been traveling with."

"Seriously? No way. No guard is that inattentive to detail. They *must* have noticed a difference."

Dash hesitates, a guilty smile stretching his lips wide. "Ok, so I *might* have discreetly spritzed some contentment potion when I got into the carriage."

"Some what potion?"

"My mother adds it to dresses sometimes, at her clients' request. It's a weird one. Some of these people she designs for are super stressed out and high-strung, and when they go to these fancy events, they just want to relax a bit. Be content and at peace, you know? I was in a rush, and the little spray bottle was right there, so I just grabbed it on my way out."

"And the guards ended up so content they didn't notice you weren't the right guy?"

"Yes. I, uh, may have sprayed a little too much. Fortunately, I put a shield bubble around myself, otherwise I probably would have been so content I'd still be sitting in that carriage."

I blink, not sure what else to say about this half-baked plan that actually worked.

"Look, it wasn't my most elegant undercover operation," Dash admits, "but everything turned out fine. The carriage brought me right into the palace grounds and straight up to one of the doors. It took a bit of work figuring out where to go, but it was nothing I couldn't handle. I pretended to be a little tipsy and confused, complimented one of the girls I found in the kitchen, and she showed me where to go. I dropped off the dress with a note saying the pickup went fine, and then hid until the ball began."

"Wow. I'm amazed that didn't go horribly wrong."

He shrugs. "I'm good with improvising."

My mind backtracks to the beginning of his story. "So they—the people I was staying with—" I don't want to say the words 'Griffin rebels' out loud "—know that you're here?"

"Yes."

I lower my voice and lean forward. "Do you think they'll come here?"

Dash hesitates, then says in a normal voice, "No. They don't know where this place is. That's why one of us needed to come with the clothes caster. The Unseelie and Seelie Courts are hidden, so not many people know where they are." The way he's looking at me though, his eyes boring intently into mine, strongly suggests he lying. It also suggests he's not entirely convinced someone isn't listening to us.

"Crap," I whisper to myself. The Griffin rebels probably do know how to get to the Unseelie Court, and once they realize Dash isn't on his way back with me, they'll probably come straight here and do everything they can to get us both out. And while I'm sure they're all amazing magical fighters, the chances are high they'll wind up injured, dead or imprisoned.

"Em?" Dash asks after several moments of silence on my side.

"That's, uh, that's good that they won't be able to find this place," I say loudly. Too loudly, probably. I make an effort at sounding normal. "I know they would only be trying to help, but as I said to you last night, I'm not in need of any help."

Dash raises an eyebrow. "If you didn't want anyone's help, you probably should have mentioned that before you ran away. We would have stopped working so hard to figure out the mystery that is your life."

A shard of guilt stabs into my chest and twists. "I'm sorry. But I—"

"You asked for our help, remember? Or at least ..." Lines crease his forehead as he frowns. "We offered, and you said yes. Something like that. So you can't exactly blame us for looking into your family history."

"I know, I was only going to say that I assumed you guys would forget about me once I was gone. You have plenty of other people to help, don't you? And—wait, what did you say about my family history?"

He sighs. "We tried to find out about your father. Since your mother isn't awake to shine any light on your strange situation, we figured your father might be able to help—if we could find him. The only thing you mentioned about him was that he paid the medical bills for your mom's hospital, so Chase went there to take a look at the records. He's the only one who knows how to use a computer," Dash adds with a roll of his eyes. "He grew up in your world, in case you didn't know. Anyway, he said your mom's file had some kind of glamour over it. He could see Chelsea's details and all your mom's details, but anything related to the person who first checked her in and was paying for it every month was just … blank. The humans working there would probably see something when looking at it, but Chase couldn't see anything."

"So … no one was actually paying for her?"

"I don't know. The point is, it was a dead end. We couldn't find out anything about your father."

My shoulders sag a little. "It's okay. That's why I'm here, remember? This union is going to lead to Mom's mind being healed, and all the answers hidden inside her will finally be unlocked."

Footsteps cross my sitting room. I clutch Bandit to my chest and stand abruptly—just as Clarina stops in the doorway. "Lady Emerson—Oh!" She stares intently at the floor. "I beg your pardon, my lady."

"This isn't what it looks like," I say immediately. I'm not actually sure what it looks like, but it can't be good.

"I'm sorry, my lady. I knocked on the other door, but—"

"I didn't hear you, I'm sorry."

"I won't say a thing, Lady Emerson."

"There's nothing to say," I assure her with a high, breathy laugh. "We were just talking."

"Of course," she says, bobbing in a brief curtsey and keeping her eyes on the floor. "Please excuse me for interrupting, but Prince Roarke would like to speak with you."

My fingers tense around Bandit's cat form. "Okay. Thank you. Where must I meet him?"

"He's waiting outside your rooms for you, my lady."

"Oh." I look at Dash.

He grins. "Well, I guess I'll be leaving the way I came in, then. Good thing I enjoy climbing."

CHAPTER FOURTEEN

I SWING MY DOOR OPEN AND FIND ROARKE RIGHT OUTSIDE. "Uh, good morning. Afternoon, I mean. Clarina said you wanted to talk?"

"Hello, my love." He bends forward and kisses my cheek. I freeze and tell myself not to shrink away. "You've recovered from last night's festivities, I see?" he adds.

I step back to let him in. "No need to bother with the 'my love' nonsense. No one else is around to hear you except Clarina."

"Oh, but you are my love." Roarke gives me a sly grin as he walks past me into the room. "Or, at least, I hope you one day will be." He nods briefly to Clarina as she curtsies and leaves the room. He turns slowly on the spot, looking around, and I almost expect him to walk into the bedroom and start looking for Dash. But then he smiles serenely and sits at the table beside my tray of lunch.

And at that moment, Bandit, who I've managed to keep hidden until now, comes bounding out of my bedroom in the form of a bear cub. He shifts into a wolf, jumps onto the divan, and takes a flying leap into my arms, landing in the form of a blue-haired sloth. I remain motionless, but my gaze snaps straight to Roarke. For once, he appears utterly speechless. I bite my lip, waiting for his response.

"Is that—is it ... yours?"

"Yes. This is Bandit. He came with when you brought me here, although he must have been in a form too small for either of us to notice."

"So he's been here with you—in your chambers—the whole time?"

"Yeeees." My voice is uncertain, almost questioning. "Well, I wasn't aware he was here for the first two or three days. I think he may have been scared of the unfamiliar surroundings, so he remained hidden for a while."

"I see. How interesting."

Bandit snuggles closer to my chest and tries to burrow his head beneath my arm. "I hope you don't disapprove," I say carefully. "I like having him around. He ... he means quite a lot to me." Instinct tells me I shouldn't reveal to the man I still don't trust that I care about anything. He might choose to use that information against me. But if Roarke cares for my happiness the way he claims to, then he shouldn't mind Bandit's presence here.

"Well, I doubt my mother would approve of animals in

bedrooms," Roarke says, his deep reddish-brown gaze fixed on Bandit, "but she doesn't need to know. And if she finds out and has a problem with it, I'll remind her how exceptionally rare and valuable formattra are, and that it's only fitting a princess would have one as her pet."

I nod. "Cool. Thank you." Hopefully Aurora feels the same way and doesn't freak out when she meets Bandit.

"Anything to make you happy, my dear," Roarke says. "Now, why don't you sit here so we can talk?" He gestures to the chair beside him at the table.

"Uh, before we talk, can I ask you something?"

"Of course." He smiles at me. "My soon-to-be wife can ask me anything."

I cross the room to the table and take a seat. I lift my hand and touch the small circular device behind my ear. "I know you put one of these things on Dash, but what if he gets it off? What if the Guild or his friends find out where he is and come after him? I just don't want anyone else interfering, remember?" To be more specific, I don't want anyone ending up in some nasty Unseelie dungeon or, far worse, facing the same fate as that man who was dragged through a cavern into the king's office.

Roarke examines me closely before answering. "You really didn't have anything to do with your friend showing up here, did you."

"What? No, I already told you that. Did you think I was lying?"

"Well, I'd be an idiot to believe that you trust me. Perhaps you arranged for a way out before you even got here."

"I did not. I told you I didn't want anyone—"

"Yes, I know." He leans back. "Still, I wondered if you might just be a very convincing actress."

"But you're not wondering that anymore?"

"You still seem genuinely concerned about the possibility of others discovering you're here. So let me put your mind at ease, Emerson. Even if someone can locate Dash's whereabouts, and even if they come to the very spot they expect to find him, they won't see any palace. Only if that person is in the company of one of our guards will they be able to see and enter the palace grounds."

"Oh. That's ... convenient." Kind of like ... No, it's gone. I almost had it, an image of the safe place belonging to the Griffin rebels, but it's like trying to hold onto smoke. "Well, I feel better now. I'm glad no one will be able to interfere."

"Good." Roarke waves the fingers of one hand through the air, and a rolled-up piece of paper appears in his loose grip. "Now, we have some preparations to make for the union ceremony."

"We do?" I never expected to be consulted on any wedding-related details. I assumed the queen and Aurora would take care of all of that. As it's been pointed out to me many times already, I have no idea what's appropriate and what isn't for formal events of the faerie world.

"You need to memorize the union vows," Roarke says, placing the paper on the table. "Everything you need to know is on this scroll."

I almost comment on how antiquated the use of a scroll is—I mean, *come on*. Surely folding a piece of paper is simpler and takes up less space—but I'm more concerned about the fact that I have to memorize vows. "So, um, I won't be able to repeat the words after someone?"

"For part of the vows, yes, but the words are in another language, so you need to practice pronouncing them correctly. There's magic involved, so you don't want to get the words wrong."

"Uh—"

"And the other part of the ceremony is the private vows we make to one another without anyone else overhearing. You'll have to memorize those."

"Oh. Why are they private?"

His expression becomes bemused. "Because they're for our ears only." Beneath the table, his hand slides onto my knee. "The special, romantic things we wish to say to one another."

"Oh." I inch a little to the side, moving my leg out of his reach. "But … then why do we need to say them? You and I both know we're not entering into this union for any of the traditional reasons. We don't need to go into detail with anything romantic."

If Roarke is bothered by the fact that I don't want him touching my leg, he doesn't show it. "As I said a moment ago, our vows involve magic. We can't simply skip that part."

My frown deepens. "But … okay. I just … don't quite understand. If those extra words are a standard part of the union magic, then why are they private? Do I really need to memorize them?"

Roarke simply laughs. "Emerson, this is the way the ceremony is done. It's been this way for a very long time. We can't just change it because you don't feel like memorizing words."

"It isn't that I don't *feel* like it." I loop my hair back behind my airs. "I'm just concerned I might forget something or make a mistake. If it's so important to get everything right, then what's wrong with repeating after someone else or reading the words off a page?"

Roarke sighs. "You won't be reading words off a page, Emerson. That's not how it's done."

"Okay, okay." I reach for the scroll and pull it closer. "So, will you explain to me what all the words mean, or am I expected to recite nonsense I don't understand?"

The corner of Roarke's mouth lifts. "It's a good thing I'm the one teaching you these words. Anyone else would be highly offended."

I lean back and unroll the paper, revealing far more foreign words than I'm comfortable with. "Aurora wouldn't be offended."

"True, but Aurora will only learn the private words when it's her turn. It isn't appropriate for her to know them yet."

"Ah, more inappropriateness." I let out a long sigh. "I would ask *why* it's inappropriate, seeing as this is a standard part of every ceremony, but you'll probably just tell me 'this is how it's done.'"

"Yes. That's exactly what I'll tell you." His eyes crinkle at the corners as he smiles. "I'm so pleased to see you're learning."

I lean back in my chair and begin reading the vows out loud, doing the best I can with the unfamiliar combinations of letters. After about three words, I'm aware that I'm probably massacring the faerie language. Roarke waits until I reach the end of the first line before putting me out of my misery. "Okay. I see this is going to take longer than I thought." Another twist of his wrist produces a quill. He hands it to me. "I'll pronounce each word, and you can write it down in whatever way makes sense to you."

We get about halfway through the public portion of the vows before a quick knock interrupts us and my door is thrown open. "Sister, dear!" Aurora calls out to me. "Oh, you're awake." She stands in the doorway and grins. "Look who I found roaming the halls." She reaches back and tugs Dash into view.

"I did tell you I invited him to stay, didn't I?" Roarke says to her.

"Yes, but I haven't seen him since the day we stunned him in Em's bedroom back in the human realm. I didn't get a proper look at him then. He's handsomer than I remember," she adds with a teasing smile, slipping her arm through Dash's and pulling him closer.

"Thanks." He gives her an equally flirtatious smile. I fold my arms and direct a frown at him, but all he does when he sees my expression is shrug.

"You remember what he is?" Roarke says to Aurora with disapproval in his tone.

"Of course I do. And I remember," she adds in a mock whisper, "that it's a secret."

"We were actually busy with something before you so rudely barged in here," Roarke comments.

"Ooh, yes, memorizing the vows. How romantic. Can I take a peek?"

Roarke swipes the page away from me and promptly rolls it up before Aurora can come any closer. "No, you may not. I wouldn't want to spoil anything for you before it's your turn."

"How thoughtful of you."

Roarke taps my hand with the scroll. "We can try this again later, my dear betrothed—when we have a little more privacy." He spins the scroll on his hand and it disappears.

"The reason I barged in here," Aurora says, "was to suggest we all go down to the tea together. And I wanted to check Em wasn't still fast asleep."

"Oh, is it time already?" I ask. "I thought the tea was later."

"Tea?" Dash asks.

"Yes, at the queen's bower in the garden. Mother's hosting it for those who stayed here after the party."

I push away from the table and stand. "Hang on, I need shoes." Aurora accompanies me into the bedroom to help me select appropriate footwear. I pull the silver slippers on quickly, wanting to give Roarke and Dash as little time as possible in which to wind up fighting.

Once the four of us are out in the hallway—with several guards striding both before and behind us—Roarke asks Aurora if he can speak privately to her. The two of them walk ahead while I fall into step beside Dash. "I wonder how Jewel would feel," I say to him, "if she knew the kind of attention you were receiving from the enchantingly beautiful Princess Aurora."

Dash sighs. "Hopefully she'd understand, given the fact that we had a conversation recently and I told her I don't feel the same way she feels."

"Oh. Um ... well done."

"Yeah. It, uh, didn't go the way I hoped it would."

"I'm sorry. That must have been awkward. Was she very upset?"

"Actually, she convinced me to go on a date with her."

I almost trip as I look up at him in surprise. "Really? You said you didn't have romantic feelings for her, and that conversation ended with the two of you going on a date?"

He gives me an amused look. "Is there something wrong with that? Something about the idea of me going on a date with Jewel that upsets you, perhaps?"

"Don't flatter yourself. I'm surprised, that's all. You don't seem like the kind of person who lets conversations get away from you."

"I didn't *let it get away from me*. I simply decided to give her a chance."

"A chance?"

"She asked me to give her one date. I told her I didn't see the point, that I didn't want to lead her on, and that I was sure of my feelings. She asked how I could be sure if I'd never given those feelings a chance. So ..." He sighs. "I thought what if— just *what if*—she was right. So I agreed."

"And?"

He cuts a sideways glance at me as we reach the bottom of a staircase. "You seem very interested in the result."

"Only because I'm trying to figure out if you really are the player I always assumed you to be. If you're dating Jewel while also entertaining Aurora's affections ... well, that's not cool."

"Entertaining Aurora's affections?" he repeats. "My, you've picked up some fancy lingo since moving in with the Unseelies."

"Oh, just shut up and tell me what happened with the date."

"I don't think I can both shut up *and* tell you something at the same—"

I fold my arms across my chest. "Dash."

"Fine. It was awkward. Seriously weird. I spent the whole evening terrified she was going to try to kiss me at the end of it, and thinking it would be exactly like kissing a—"

"—sister?"

"Yes. And that's just wrong. So before that could happen, I told her—gently—that it wasn't ever going to work out."

"Ok." We reach another grand staircase leading down to yet another vast hallway. "Well, I'm glad you didn't string her along at all."

"Of course I didn't. I'm actually a decent guy, remember?" He lowers his voice. "Unlike the prince you've foolishly chosen to marry."

"I didn't *choose* him. Not like that, anyway. I chose this agreement, and he happens to be part of it. And you don't actually know him. I think he may be more decent than you think."

Dash snorts. "Right. Whatever you say."

I close my eyes a moment and sigh. "Can we please not argue about this any longer?"

"Sure. Tell me this then: what have you been filling your time with the past two and a half weeks? Has it all been parties and teas with the queen and being waited on by your own personal servant?"

"Yes, it's been absolute perfection," I say drily. "I've been waiting my whole life to have someone choose my clothes, run my bath, make my bed, and prepare my food."

Dash squints at me. "Really?"

"No! I can't stand it. I'm perfectly capable of doing all those things myself."

"Look, you had kind of a crappy life at Chelsea's," Dash says, holding his hands up in defense, "so forgive me for thinking you might actually enjoy having someone else do all the hard work."

"I don't. It's weird. And I haven't been spending all my time at parties and teas, actually. Aurora's been teaching me plenty of basic magic, along with some of her hobbies, like archery and dragon riding."

As we reach a wide doorway leading to the sunny outdoors, Dash stops. He looks more closely at me. "Dragon riding?"

"Can you two wait here?" Aurora asks. "Roarke just needs to show me something quickly."

"Yes, okay," I answer.

They disappear down a corridor, and Dash turns to me again. "Did you say *dragon riding*?"

"I did."

"Seriously? So you're a dragon rider now as well as an Unseelie princess-to-be?"

"Not yet, but I'd like to be. Is there something wrong with that?"

"No, it's just ..." He shakes his head. "I feel like I don't really know you anymore. You haven't been here that long, and already you've changed."

His words hurt more than I could have imagined possible. "Changed? What do you mean?"

"Well you've … you've learned a lot in a short time. And you look …"

"I look?"

"Like you belong here."

I dismiss his words with a casual wave, hoping he hasn't noticed how deeply they've cut me. "That's just the clothing."

"Is it? The way you carried yourself last night, on the platform and while dancing … you looked every bit the princess people are expecting you to become."

I pull my shoulders back a bit, ignoring the ache in my chest. "Good. At least I know I'm playing my part well."

Dash's expression softens the tiniest bit. "As long as it's only on the outside …"

"Of course it's only on the—"

"Okay, are you ready?" Aurora calls out as she and Roarke reappear. "Let's get to this tea before we upset Mother with our tardiness. And you—" she adds, looking at Dash "—I shall introduce as a friend of mine. Please don't contradict whatever story I decide to go with."

"Oh, uh …" Dash hangs back as Aurora tries to usher us both forward. "I was thinking," he says, "that perhaps it's best if I don't attend this tea thing. If my sleeves roll up too high, and if the makeup rubs off my wrists, your mother might see my markings. She'll know what I am."

"That's possible," Aurora admits, "but if you *don't* come to the tea, you'll almost certainly end up wandering the palace on your own and risk getting up to all sorts of mischief."

He gives her a sly grin. "And what if I promise to stay in my room like a good boy? If anyone asks about me—which I doubt anyone will, since no one knows me—you can say I'm not feeling well."

"If we could trust you to keep your word," Roarke says, "and not sneak out of your room to try and dig up information that might be useful to your Guild, then certainly. That would be fine." Roarke's gaze moves briefly to mine before settling back on Dash. "But we don't trust you. Even if I posted guards at your door, you might climb out of your window instead."

My arms tense at my sides. He can't be hinting that he knows Dash climbed into my room earlier, can he? Unlikely. He would have been angry when he entered my room if he'd just learned that Clarina discovered Dash in my bedroom.

"Climb out the window," Dash says, a thoughtful expression on his face. "Now there's an idea. I may have to try that later after everyone's gone to bed. I hadn't thought about trying to dig up any useful information—Em was the only reason I came here—but now that you mention it, I'm definitely wasting a valuable opportunity by not doing more to find out what kinds of laws you Unseelies are blatantly breaking."

Roarke's placid smile never leaves his face. He steps closer to me and places an arm around my back. "As you said, Emerson is the only reason you came here. If you are indeed a true friend to her, you'll focus on comforting her during this difficult time instead of thinking up ways to bring down her future family." His thumb rubs up and down against my arm, a gesture that's probably supposed to be caring and tender, yet somehow comes across as threatening.

Dash watches Roarke's hand on my arm for a moment before lifting his gaze. Then his eyes narrow as he focuses on something behind me. I look over my shoulder. A woman dressed in dark maroon crosses the hallway with quiet, confident steps. She pauses for a moment to look at us. Perhaps it's the way the shadows fall across her face, but her eyes seem completely black. She tilts her head and sends a knowing smile our way, revealing pointed teeth behind her full, red lips. She turns away and saunters toward the stairs, leaving a cold breath of air in her wake.

CHAPTER FIFTEEN

"WHO WAS THAT?" DASH ASKS IMMEDIATELY. HIS BODY HAS gone rigid, his hands poised at his sides as if ready to grab a pair of glittering guardian weapons from the air.

"Nobody you need concern yourself with," Aurora says. She wraps her arm around his and turns him toward the garden. She leads him down the stairs and into the sun, while Roarke does the same with me, his hand pressing against my back.

"That woman is a witch," Dash says.

A witch. I look over my shoulder again, my mind sifting through everything I've learned in the past few weeks and landing on the memories associated with the word 'witch.' Aurora said she spent her first few years with a witch, before the woman grew tired of her and dumped her here. And Jack,

Violet and Ryn's son, said witches killed his sister years before he was born.

"Watch where you're going," Roarke says to me as I almost trip down the next step.

"Yes, she's a witch," Aurora answers. "What of it?"

Dash pulls his arm away from hers as they continue to descend the steps just ahead of us. "You're right. I'm not sure why I'm surprised. You Unseelies have such similar magic to the witches. It makes sense to find you conspiring with them."

"Conspiring," Roarke repeats with a chuckle. "Your friend is far too suspicious for his own good, Emerson."

I don't answer him. I'm wondering instead if this witch might possibly be the woman I overheard in his room. The woman who spoke to him about that shadowy place.

"You don't need to worry about any *conspiring*," Aurora assures Dash. "She is a guest here, and so are you. We don't want our guests fighting."

"Really?" Dash asks lightly. "I imagine that would make for a fascinating new form of entertainment in this court."

"You know, you could be onto something. I'll have to ask Mother about that. Perhaps our next party can incorporate guest fighting."

Beside me, Roarke breathes out sharply through his nose. He removes his arm from around my back and takes hold of my hand instead. "While this kind of flippant banter is amusing, you and I need to get to the tea," he says to me, increasing his pace and pulling me along with him. "Aurora, Dash," he says as we pass them. "We'll see you there."

Roarke and I cross over a little bridge spanning a stream of water that shimmers with translucent rainbow colors. At the sound of a distant roar, I look up. I now know that the indistinct figure high above me is actually a dragon. I stare longingly upward for another few moments before Roarke pulls my attention back down with a squeeze of my hand.

We reach the queen's bower, an area of the garden shaded by enormous overhanging branches laden with thousands of purple and white blossoms. Seats crafted from entwined twigs hang from the branches. Amidst these hanging seats, numerous tables are covered in drinks and delicacies of every shape and size. In such a pretty outdoor setting, I expected pastel colors and flower-painted tea cups, but every item of food is either black or white. The striped tea cups are also black and white, and the champagne flutes are filled with fizzy black liquid.

Many of the guests are wearing colorful outfits, but I'm pleased to see the queen in a form-fitting dress of black, white and gold. At least I don't have to feel too out of place in my charcoal grey outfit. As Roarke and I approach Queen Amrath, she lifts her glass and takes a sip. I watch closely to see if the drink will stain her lips black, but as she lowers the glass, her lips remain a dark, glossy red.

Roarke and I greet his mother, and Roarke introduces me to the friends and cousins who are sitting around her. Dash and Aurora hurry up behind us then, and Aurora introduces Dash as a friend she met several months ago. "Remember when Mizza and I spent a week at her family's home in Nordbrook while we had my suite redecorated?"

"Ah, yes." The queen nods.

"I spent a lot of time with him that week and decided to

invite him to your party. Remember I told you about him?"

"I'm so sorry, darling." The queen reaches for Aurora's hand and squeezes it. "It must have slipped my mind. Why don't you get something to eat and drink, and then bring him back to me. Dash, if you're a special friend of Aurora's, I'd love to get to know you better." She gives him the same kind of smile she gave me on my first night here. Polite, but it doesn't quite reach her eyes.

We wander around the tables, selecting delicacies to add to our plates, and Dash eventually ends up at my side. "You should be concerned that there's a witch here," he says in a low voice.

"Should I?" I ask. "I'm sure the addition of a witch can't make this place any more dangerous than it already is."

"Most witches keep their distance from faeries. Faeries of any kind. This one can't be up to any good if she's hanging out here."

I add a square-shaped chocolate cake with black icing and silver sprinkles onto my plate. "Perhaps witches aren't all bad. You can't judge them all for killing your friends' baby."

"What?" Dash frowns. "Do you mean … Did someone tell you about Victoria?"

"If Victoria is the sister Jack mentioned, then yes," I continue. "He said she was killed by witches."

Dash tips a glassful of black liquid down his throat and leaves the glass on the table. "Well, it was something like that. Vi and Ryn believe witch magic was responsible for Victoria's death, even though it was actually a faerie who placed the magic on her. And yes, that's one reason for my intense dislike of witches, but there are many others."

"So what do you want to do? Find this witch and demand to know why she's here? You're supposed to be flying under the radar so you can get out of this place alive, not provoking the enemy." At that moment, a lizard with feathery wings plops onto the table, startling me and almost upsetting a plate of coconut bonbons. The lizard jumps off the table, hits the ground, and scurries away.

"Flying under the radar," Dash repeats, bringing my attention back to him. "I've heard that one enough times in your world to figure out its meaning. And what kind of *guardian*—" he whispers that last word so low I can barely hear it "—do you think I am? Certainly not the kind that goes around demanding information. I never would have graduated that way. No, Em, I'm perfectly capable of flying under this radar you mentioned while also finding out everything I need to know."

"Dashiell, darling," Aurora calls from the other side of nearby table. "My mother wants to chat with you."

Dash frowns for a moment. "Did I tell her my full name?"

I shrug. "Maybe Dash is always short for Dashiell."

"Right. Time to chat up the old ladies."

Since rolling my eyes is considered unladylike, and I've already committed the dreadful act of shrugging my shoulders, I settle for a sigh as Dash heads back to the queen's side. I gather a few more strange-looking treats before searching the gathering for Aurora. She and Roarke are sitting next to the circle that's formed around the queen. Aurora's back is almost against Dash's, and I assume she's paying close attention to whatever he's saying, preparing to intervene if she needs to. I walk around the tables and hover near Dash, close enough to listen, but not quite close enough to be included in the conversation. I assume I'll be forced to join in at some point, but I'll enjoy the snacks until that moment arrives.

"Oh, yes, it's beautiful here," Dash says in answer to one of the queen's questions. "I count myself truly lucky to have been able to visit both your palaces now."

Mild confusion crosses the queen's face. "Both palaces?" she enquires.

"Yes. You have this one that is both summer and winter, for day and night, and the other one that's shrouded in smoky shadows."

I watch as Aurora's smile freezes in place. Her eyes snap across the gathering to settle on Roarke, who's suddenly directing his full attention at Dash. With a puzzled look, the queen says, "I'm not sure what you mean. We have numerous manor houses across the world, but only one palace. Are you referring to one of our past parties, perhaps? We had one a few years ago with the theme of … what was it, dear?" she asks Aurora.

"Obsidian fire," Aurora provides, twisting in her seat to look around. "Is that the one you're thinking of, Mother?"

"Yes, that was it. Every surface was sleek obsidian. We had black fire dancing across the walls, and dark smoke that took on the form of phoenixes. Oh, and everyone dressed in silver, remember? It was magnificent. A stunning effect."

"That sounds enchanting, Your Majesty," Dash says, "but no, I wasn't here for that party. I'm referring to a completely different palace—or perhaps it's more accurate to refer to that one as a castle—with gardens where smoke as black as shadow curls and rises from every tree and plant. Even from the walls themselves." He gives Aurora an innocent smile. "I've never been anywhere like it. It felt almost like ... a different world entirely."

Though Aurora's smile is still frozen in place, her eyes contain a barely masked fury. If it were possible to strike a person down simply by looking at them, I have no doubt Dash would be dead right now.

Roarke breaks the silence with a laugh. "Sounds like your friend here ate some of those berries at the last party you invited him to, Aurora. Those green hallucinogenic ones. I had no idea they were so effective. I'll have to try them out for myself sometime."

"Roarke!" the queen says in a horrified tone. "That is hardly appropriate for a prince."

Roarke laughs louder at this, and several people join in. Perhaps it's normal for the queen to admonish her son in front of company. The chatter returns to normal then. Aurora takes Dash's seat and pushes him away from her mother while the queen is looking elsewhere. Roarke returns to his conversation with a slightly rotund man, sending an occasional glance at Dash as he walks toward me.

"What the hell was that about?" I whisper to Dash as he reaches my side.

"Don't you want answers about that place?" he asks. "I've never been anywhere like it. I still can't figure out exactly where or what it was, or how we got there. Or how we got out, for that matter."

"But did you have to ask about it *now*? In front of all these people? That is *not* what I would call 'flying under the radar.'"

"Yes." He glances past me, smiling politely at the person squeezing between me and the table behind me. "I wanted to see their reaction. Now we know that Roarke and Aurora are hiding that place from everyone, even the members of their own court."

"Except ..." I look around the gathering as I think of the woman I overheard while I was hiding in Roarke's room. If it wasn't the witch, then it could very well have been one of the ladies at this tea.

"Except?" Dash prompts.

"I overheard Roarke speaking to someone about it," I murmur. "A woman. They called that place another world."

"Really? They actually said that?"

"Yes. And there's at least one other person who knows about it. There was someone else there the day you and I saw that place. We heard a male voice, remember? Someone called out to Roarke and Aurora, and that's when they told us to run, as if they didn't want that person knowing we were there."

"The king?"

"Possibly. I think it was his voice."

Dash's brow furrows. Then, as if remembering where he is, he blinks and pastes on a smile as he looks around. "I need to find out more about that place," he whispers, still smiling unnaturally. "That world, or whatever it was. If the Unseelie King and his children are keeping it a secret from everyone, that can't mean anything good for the rest of our world."

"You can't know that," I say, more to myself than to him. I need to believe the Unseelies aren't as bad as Dash makes out. "It could just be some other private palace they want to keep hidden from everyone except their immediate family."

"And from the queen?"

"I'm sure the Seelies have hidden palaces too," I add, ignoring his interjection.

"It's another *world*, Em," Dash says through smiling, gritted teeth. "At least, that's what it sounds like. And if that's true, it's unlike anything else in ... well, in history. There have only ever been two worlds. If it turns out there's a third? That's just ... that's huge." He looks around again. "Roarke's right. I should be taking advantage of the fact that I'm here and gathering as much info as I can."

"Sure, if you want to wind up dead."

"I won't. I'll be careful. These Unseelies are hiding something, and I need to find out what it is."

"Why?" Fear begins to unfurl in my chest. "Why does it have to be *you*? Just leave this place with your life intact and let someone else deal with it."

Dash's smile becomes more genuine. His hand wraps around one of mine. "It's nice to know that you care, Em, but I don't run away from dangerous situations." His gaze flicks to someone behind me, and he turns the false brightness of his smile back on. My attention, however, seems oddly drawn to the way his thumb moves against the inside of my wrist. "Looks like people want to speak with their future princess," he whispers, his hand slipping away from mine. "Don't forget to smile."

CHAPTER SIXTEEN

"YOU'RE LATE," AURORA SAYS THE FOLLOWING MORNING. Her arms remain in position, her eyes fixed firmly on her target, as I hurry toward the area where our archery practice takes place. "I was supposed to give you a lesson before we go to the dragons."

"I know, I'm sorry. I was looking for Dash. He said he'd join me for breakfast this morning but he never showed up. Have you seen him around?"

With a *whoosh* and *thwip*, her arrow strikes the center of the target. She lowers her bow and turns to me with a frown. "Dash left late last night. Didn't he say goodbye to you?"

I blink. "No. I haven't seen him since dinner. Why did he leave? I thought …" I shake my head, this unexpected news making no sense to me. "Roarke was so insistent that he stay.

Since, you know, he didn't trust Dash not to bring a whole bunch of guardians back with him."

Aurora's frown deepens. "Didn't Roarke speak to you last night? Later, I mean. Some time after dinner."

"No, I was asleep then." Having to speak to so many people during the queen's tea—which lasted the entire afternoon—left me exhausted, and then Roarke wanted me to practice the union ceremony words again in the early evening. I planned to talk to Dash after dinner, to impress upon him the importance of not sneaking around and getting himself in trouble, but I fell asleep fully clothed and didn't wake until morning.

"My father received news of an attack on a group of guardians. Several of them were killed, along with the family members who were with them. It was that woman who can't keep her glass magic under control."

A shiver chills my blood. "Ada?"

Aurora shrugs. "I don't know what her name is. Anyway, Roarke spoke to me about it, and we decided Dash should know. I mean, it doesn't bother *us* if guardians die. They aren't our allies. But they're Dash's people, so we thought it unfair to keep the information from him."

"You …" I trail off. "I don't understand."

"Why do you still think we're the bad guys, Em? We're not." She nocks another arrow and squints through one eye at the target. "Our ways are just different, that's all. We thought Dash might know some of the guardians who were killed, and it wouldn't be right for him to miss their celebration-of-life ceremony." *Thwip.* Her arrow lands a little left of the mark in the center of the target.

186

"Wouldn't be right?" Once again, an image of the man who lost his entire head comes to mind. "You just said your ways are different. I thought that included your understanding of right and wrong."

Aurora glares at the arrow before turning to me again. "It does, but not for something like this. It's right to honor the dead and give them a proper farewell. We may not like the fact that Dash is a guardian, but we're not so cruel that we'd want to deprive him of the opportunity to say a final farewell to people he cared for."

"So Roarke just let him leave? That still doesn't make sense to me. Surely Roarke wouldn't put his entire court at risk just to let one guardian attend a funeral."

"He didn't put anyone at risk. He told Dash he could only leave if he allowed an enchantment to be placed upon him."

"What enchantment?"

"He'll become confused whenever he tries to think or speak about the Unseelie Court. Nothing he says will make sense if he tries to tell anyone where it is, and his thoughts will become too muddled for him to bring himself anywhere near here."

That sounds a lot like the protection the Griffin rebels have cast over their hideout. "And he agreed to that?" I ask.

"Yes, apparently. Roarke said Yokshin performed the enchantment. And to be honest, Em," she adds as she crooks a finger for one of the archery assistants, a young boy, to come over, "Dash would have been forced to have this enchantment placed on him no matter when he planned to leave the palace."

I nod slowly. "Makes sense. But I still don't understand why he didn't come and say goodbye to me."

"Well, you said you were asleep." She hands her bow to the boy and takes the glass of water he offers her. "And perhaps he was in a rush. I know he cares about you, Em. He never would have risked coming here if he didn't. But he cares about his guardian comrades too. He would have been desperate to get back to find out who died."

"Yes," I say quietly. "I'm sure he would have."

"Oh, fan please," Aurora adds in a commanding tone as the boy walks away with her bow. He hurries back, makes a few awkward movements in the air with one hand, and an enormous palm leaf appears. He quickly lowers the bow to the ground and grabs hold of the palm with both hands. Aurora tilts her head back and closes her eyes, and I try not to roll my eyeballs right out of my head as the poor boy stands there and fans her. "Okay, that's enough." She waves the boy away after several moments, then raises the glass and drinks all the water. "Right. Dragon time."

"Finally," I mutter.

"Em," she says, cocking her head thoughtfully to the side as we begin walking. "Is there something you haven't told me about Dash?"

"Hmm? What do you mean?"

"Are you in love with him?"

I can't help the laughter that bursts free of me. "No, of course not," I manage to say once I've recovered. "I'm just concerned about him."

"But he loves you."

"Um, nope. I'm pretty sure he doesn't."

"Then why did he risk his life to try to save you from us?"

"Maybe he felt it was his duty. He has that whole guardian ego thing going on, so it's probably hard for him to resist being the hero who rescues the damsel in distress. Or, at least, any damsel he *thinks* is in distress."

"Hmm." She pushes her hair back over her shoulder. "I think he cared about your wellbeing."

"Maybe. A little. In a non-love kinda way."

She gives me a patronizing smile. "Nobody cares that much. Not unless they're motivated by love."

With a sigh I ask, "Have you met many guardians, Aurora? I haven't known them for long, but they all seem to have this crazy desire to fight and protect and rescue, even if it means winding up hurt or dead."

She groans. "I know. They're all so irritatingly selfless. We can't compete, so we don't even try."

All the shame I felt while trying to convince Dash—and myself—that I'm not making life any worse than it already is by giving my Griffin Ability to the Unseelies seeps back into my body. "Yeah, I can't say I identify with the whole guardian thing either," I say quietly.

"Really? Please remind me, my sweet sister, why you agreed to come here in the first place."

I look up. "For my mother."

"Exactly. Now tell me you can't identify with the words 'fight,' 'protect' and 'rescue.'"

"Yes, but she's my mother," I explain. "Possibly my only living family. I love her more than anything. I would fight and die for her, but that doesn't mean I'd do it for people I barely know. I'm not that selfless."

"And that's exactly why you're going to fit in so well with us, Em. We take care of our own. Screw the rest of the world," she adds with a laugh. She wraps one arm around me and gives me a quick sideways hug as we near the enormous shed housing all the carriages.

Aurora's words should make me happy. I've always wanted to belong somewhere, and Chelsea's home was never going to be that place. But her words leave me feeling uncomfortable instead. I've never considered myself to be anything like these people, but what if she's right? What if I'm more Unseelie at heart than I ever imagined? What if—

I smother a gasp as the thought occurs to me.

What if I *am* Unseelie? What if my mother came from this court? What if the cruel magical practices the Unseelies use are part of my history, my blood, my very essence? Is that why I like dragon riding? Is it something *bad* that's associated with the Unseelie Court? No, it can't be. Surely dragons can only be good or evil based on the good or evil things their riders tell them to do. It can't only be the Unseelies who enjoy soaring through the air on the back of a dragon.

As we pass the shed, I stop, momentarily distracted. "Hang on," I say to Aurora. "Just give me a minute." I hurry back and approach the woman busy directing two horseless carriages out of the shed by standing in front of them and motioning with her hands. "Good morning," I say to her. "Were you on duty late last night?"

The woman seems startled to be addressed by me, but she quickly recovers. "No, my lady. It was Henkin. He's off now, but he should be—oh, there he is." She points behind me. "His next shift begins shortly."

"Thank you." I stride quickly toward the man, and after he bows and formally greets me, I ask, "Did you see someone leave the palace late last night? A man—um, faerie. Faerie man. Green in his hair?"

"Yes, my lady. I helped him into a carriage myself. Four guards accompanied him."

I nod slowly. "Okay. And, um … he wasn't tied up or anything? Like a prisoner?"

Lines crease the driver's brow as he frowns. "No, my lady. I assumed he was an honored guest. The prince himself shook his hand and bid farewell to him before he climbed into the carriage."

"Oh. Okay, good. Thank you very much."

I hurry back to Aurora, who's watching me with her hands on her hips. "What was that about?"

"Nothing."

With her usual teasing smile entirely absent from her face, her eyes search mine. "You were checking my story, weren't you? About Dash."

"Yes," I admit. "But you can't blame me, can you? I still don't know if I can completely trust you and Roarke."

"How can you—"

"I trust that you want *me* to be here, but I know how you feel about guardians. And Dash wasn't exactly invited, so maybe you wanted to just get rid of him instead of having him hang around saying inappropriate things like he did at the tea yesterday, or sneaking into places he shouldn't be and sticking his nose where it doesn't belong."

"And now?" she demands. "Do you feel better having spoken to one of the drivers? Did he verify my story?"

"He did. I … I'm sorry I doubted you."

She watches me a moment longer, then smiles. "You're forgiven." She spins around on the spot, and we continue toward the trees.

"But I did notice," I add carefully, "the way you and Roarke reacted to Dash telling your mother about that otherworldly place where everything was shadowy and drained of color."

Aurora's steps falter for a moment, but she carries on walking. When she doesn't answer me, I press further. "What was that place? Was it … another world? Somewhere that isn't the human realm or the fae realm? And why is it a secret?"

Without looking at me, she says, "You'll need to ask Roarke about that."

"Aurora, if you want me to trust you, then—"

"Ask Roarke," she says, looking directly at me, her expression serious. "I don't want to lie to you, and I know Roarke doesn't either. He *will* tell you about it. He's probably just waiting until he knows he can fully trust you."

Several moments of studying her face convinces me she's telling the truth. "Okay," I say eventually.

We fall into silence as we head through the trees, which is unusual for Aurora. It doesn't feel uncomfortable, though. More like we've both got other things on our minds. As we walk, she absently waves a hand near the back of her head, and her hair quickly braids itself. I lift my hand and concentrate on doing the same thing. After our first ride, I decided she was right about memorizing spells that will help me get ready faster. I don't want to waste a second of the time I can spend in the air.

"Well done," Aurora says, and I realize she's been watching me. "You're getting quicker at it."

"Thanks. That's the plan."

Ten minutes later, we're down in Imperia's enclosure and Phillyp is getting the double saddle ready for us. My heart begins to pound faster, already anticipating the blood-rushing freedom of the skies. Trusting that Imperia knows me well enough now not to chomp me in half, I walk past her front leg and reach up to run one hand along the shimmering scales of her neck. She swings her head slowly around to peer at me through one fiery orange eye. "You might possibly be the best thing about this place," I tell her.

"Hey," Aurora objects from behind me.

"Oh, I mean … aside from you." I face her and add with a smirk, "You're pretty great too."

She laughs and shakes her head. "Thanks, but I was actually thinking of my brother. He might be disappointed to know you don't think *he's* the best thing here."

"Disappointed? Really? I didn't think he cared that much."

"Well, he does. He hasn't confided in me a lot, but I think he hopes that you'll come to care for him and … well, possibly even love him."

"Aurora …" My voice is hesitant as she climbs the stairs up to Imperia's back. "You know my only reason for being here is—"

"—your mother. Yes. I know. But … do you think you could ever mean the words?" She looks down at me from the

193

top of the stairs. "The words you've been practicing. The vows. I know you won't mean them when you actually say them at the ceremony. But, you know … with time … do you think you could?"

Her question leaves me momentarily stunned. "I don't know."

"You must have thought about it," she continues as she climbs onto the front seat of the saddle. "You must have wondered about the future. You'll be together for years. For centuries, most likely. You must wonder if, during that time, you'll come to love him?"

Instead of answering her, I focus on the steps as I climb them. I haven't wondered if I might come to love Roarke because I don't plan on this union being permanent. And that's if it even comes to pass, which I'm hoping it won't. If I get a chance to use my Griffin Ability on Roarke before the ceremony, I'll take it. I reach the top of the stairs and pull myself up and into the seat behind Aurora's.

"Anyway, how's the pronunciation practice going?" Aurora asks, clearly getting the message that I'm not willing to talk about the possibility of loving her brother. "Must be terribly romantic."

"Yes, romantic indeed, being drilled on the precise pronunciation of every single word. I've got the first part down—the public part—but the private vows are harder. The words are more difficult to wrap my tongue around. *Super* foreign."

"Not any more foreign than the first part, surely? It's the same language, after all."

"I don't know. It just seems harder to me. Sola-thuk-ma ... uk-na-math-ra ... me-la-soni-ra ..." I sigh as I secure a strap across my body to keep me from falling out of the saddle. "I sound like a toddler learning how to speak. It's embarrassing."

Aurora twists her head to the side, although not quite enough to look at me. "What other words do find very difficult?"

"Uh, all of them,' I joke. "Isin-vir-na. Zo-thu-maa. Men-va." I enunciate the words slowly, trying to get each syllable right. "Anyway, I shouldn't be telling you. Supposed to be private and all that."

She faces forward again, her hands wrapped tightly around the reins. "Yes. True." I expect her to urge Imperia into the air then, but her hands remain motionless on the reins.

"Is everything okay?" I ask her. "Why aren't we moving?"

She rolls her shoulders and breathes in deeply. "Yes, everything's fine. I was just thinking we should spend the evening in the library. I need to find more books for you."

"Oh, uh ... I haven't actually finished the last set you gave me."

"Well, you need more. So you have the afternoon to finish what I've already given you."

"Okay." I frown at the back of her head, wondering if it's my imagination or if her tone is a little sharp. But she moves the reins then, and I quickly put everything else from my mind. I forget about her acting a little strange, I forget about Dash far away and unable to ever find his way back here, and I prepare to lose myself in the delicious rush of adrenalin.

CHAPTER SEVENTEEN

THAT EVENING, SNOW FALLS GENTLY OUTSIDE THE PALACE windows, while inside the library, a crackling fire keeps the room remarkably cozy considering its size. It's the kind of scene that looks perfect from the outside: Aurora paging through books at one of the tables; me curled up in a leather armchair finishing off the final volume from the last collection Aurora gathered for me; mugs of hot spiced chocolate that apparently won't stain anything if we knock them over. Beneath the snug surface, though, my mind is reaching new levels of paranoia. Did Dash return safely to his Guild, or were the guards who accompanied him instructed to harm him once he left the Unseelie Palace? Or perhaps *everyone* is lying to me—Aurora, Roarke, the drivers—and Dash never actually left. The Unseelie King could have killed him already.

Stop! I instruct myself as I turn to the last page of the book. I have no reason for these irrational thoughts other than the fact that Dash showed up out of nowhere and then vanished just as abruptly. If that hadn't happened, I'd be sitting here calmly reading my book and continuing to hope for a chance to use my Griffin Ability on Roarke. *No one is lying to you*, I whisper silently. *That driver didn't even know who you were. Stop. Freaking. Out!*

I breathe out slowly through my mouth and force myself to read the last page of the book. Reaching the end, I snap it shut, having absorbed maybe half of its contents. Half seems good enough to me, though. The book is essentially a list of all the magical creatures inhabiting the Unseelie Court, and it hardly seems necessary to memorize it.

I wrap both hands around my mug and sip the spiced chocolate drink, which does an excellent job at comforting me and putting my paranoid mind at ease. I know there are things that Roarke and Aurora are keeping from me, but I don't think they'd outright lie to me. If Aurora said Dash was sent home, then I choose to believe she's telling the truth.

I move my legs out from beneath me and stand up, pulling my dress straight. Bandit, who was snuggled next to me in some furry form, shifts quickly into a mouse and scampers up my arm to my shoulder. I walk along one of the aisles, reading the spines of the books as I go. "Ooh, magical combat," I say, pulling one of the books off its shelf. "Is this what you were telling me about, Rora? The other skill you wanted to learn, but your mother said only archery was allowed?"

"Hmm?" Aurora looks up with a frown. "Em, you're

getting distracted. You're supposed to be finishing those other books."

"All done," I tell her. I flip quickly through the magical combat book, reading snippets about the mental techniques that can make one's mind quicker, and about different fighting stances and ways of throwing magic. Perhaps, if I'm forced to stay in the palace for a while, I can come back to this book. I return it to the shelf and scan some more spines as I wander further down the aisle.

When my eyes slide across a thick, colorful spine with the word *Dragons*, I stop. I pull the heavy book from the shelf and sit cross-legged on the floor to take a closer look at the detailed paintings on each page. "Aren't they beautiful?" I whisper to Bandit. He jumps off my shoulder and sits on my knee. A moment later, he becomes some type of predatory bird, too fluffy to be fully grown. "Oh, that's cool," I say quietly as he cocks his head and peers more closely at the dragon book. "I don't think I've seen that form before, Bandit."

"Make sure he behaves," Aurora whispers loudly. "Unlike the chocolate, if Bandit makes a mess, we will have to clean it up."

Bandit flaps his wings and lands on the floor beside my leg. With a ruffle of his feathers, he shifts form again—and all of a sudden, a dragon sits beside me. "Oh, wow," I say, forgetting to be quiet now. "Bandit, that's amazing." He's nowhere near the size of Imperia—he takes up about as much space as a large dog—but I'm still impressed.

"Em!" Aurora hisses. "I told you he needs to behave if he's going to stay in here."

"He is behaving," I tell her just as Bandit coughs in the direction of the nearest bookshelf. A tiny spark flies from his mouth. "Oh, crap." I jump up, grab the book the spark landed on, and smack it against the floor until only a singed spot remains on the cover.

"You were saying?" Aurora asks drily.

"Okay, Bandit," I whisper to the small dragon after I've replaced the book on its shelf. "While this form is *seriously* awesome, it isn't appropriate in the library. Let's save it for another time, okay?" He blinks, then shifts back into mouse form. "But I want you to know that you make a spectacular dragon," I whisper as I place him into my pocket. I'm wearing a sleeveless dress that seems Japanese-inspired, along with gloves that reach almost to my armpits. The dress has little pockets, but they were so small when I first put this dress on that I could barely fit my hands into them. So I pulled out one of the first spell books Aurora gave to me and almost squealed with delight when I managed to successfully enlarge the pockets so Bandit could climb inside. I just had to be sure to keep my hands in the pockets as I walked to the library this evening so no one noticed the odd lump on my right hip.

With my mind on combat magic once again, I wander over to the nearest window. After looking over my shoulder to make sure Aurora is once again absorbed in a book, I quietly open the window. I raise my hand and wait until I've amassed a small amount of power above it, shivering a little as the chilly air drifts over my bare shoulders. Then I peer outside and choose a tree to aim at. I lean over the windowsill and hurl magic forward. The glittering sphere strikes the tree, sends a small explosion of snow into the air, and rips one of the branches right off. I clap a hand over my mouth as my lips stretch into a smile. Perhaps I'm not as useless as I thought. I may not be able to shape my magic into anything exiting, but at least I can toss raw power around if I have to fight my way out of here one day.

"Em!" Aurora calls out. "Seriously! What is wrong with you this evening?"

I shut the window quickly and face Aurora, confused by her anger. She doesn't normally mind bending the rules. I half-expected her to join me at the window and start throwing her own magic out into the night. In fact, that's exactly what I was hoping she would do. I might have learned something useful from her. "I'm sorry. I just … thought I'd try it."

"You don't need to try it. Magical combat isn't a necessary skill for either of us."

"Well, neither is dragon riding, but we both want to do that, so—"

"Em!" She gives me an exasperated look.

"What? Why are you so testy tonight?"

"I'm just—" She cuts herself off with a shake of her head. She pushes her hands through her hair. "I'm just looking for something, and you keep distracting me."

"I'm sorry," I repeat quietly. "Uh, maybe Bandit and I should go to bed." And before we get into bed, I can throw some more magic from my balcony without Aurora getting upset.

"What is Bandit doing in the library in the first place?" a voice asks from the library door.

I look around and see Roarke striding in, his footsteps silent on the carpeted floor and his black robe-like coat rippling around his ankles.

"Uh, he's hiding in my pocket," I answer. "And behaving himself. Obviously."

He watches me for a moment before replying. "Good."

"Have you heard from Dash?" I ask. "Did he get back to the Guild safely?"

Roarke folds his arms across his chest. "No, I haven't heard from him, and I don't expect to. It's not as though we exchanged amber IDs."

"But—"

"But my guards did tell me they successfully dropped him off far away from our court where the faerie paths are accessible and he would easily have been able to get himself back to his Guild."

"Okay." I bite my lip before adding, "I suppose he must have returned safely then."

Roarke tilts his head. "Why are you so concerned about him? Were the two of you lovers?"

"What? No!" Heat burns my neck and cheeks.

"You seem to miss him a lot now that he's gone."

"He was my friend. Of course I miss him." More than I expected, actually. In this palace where I'm still not sure who I can trust, Dash was the one person I could be completely honest with.

"But you have Aurora now. She makes a wonderful friend, doesn't she?" Roarke looks across the room at her, then frowns.

"Aurora, is everything okay? You look like you might be ill."

She slams the cover of a book shut and swallows as she looks up. "I … I'm sorry." She lets out a breathless laugh. "You know I can't stand some of these history books. They're so horribly gruesome and graphic when they talk about the way people died."

"Then why are you reading them?"

She pushes the book aside and pulls another one closer. "I'm looking for books for Em. She still has so much to learn. Anyway, we can definitely give that one a miss. I'll find something less gruesome." She opens the next book and bends her head over it.

Roarke watches her for a long moment before returning his gaze to me. "I came here to suggest we practice the vows again. Your pronunciation needs to be perfect, Emerson."

Movement catches my eye as Aurora's head snaps up again. I look at her, and she stares back, her expression unreadable. "What?" I ask.

"Are you sure you're all right?" Roarke asks her. "Perhaps you're reading too much."

A smile lifts one side of her mouth. "No such thing, dear brother."

He chuckles. "I suppose not, if you're as fond of books as you are." His eyes find mine, and he tilts his head toward the library door, suggesting we head that way. Though with Roarke, I know it isn't really a suggestion. I allow him to take my arm and place it on his as we leave the library. "She's definitely acting strangely this evening," he muses. "I think perhaps she's jealous of us."

I can't help laughing. "That's ridiculous. Why would she be jealous?"

"You've become a good friend to her in a short space of time. She has her ladies-in-waiting and cousins and other noblewomen to keep her company, of course, but lately she's been spending most of her time with you. I can tell she prefers it that way."

"Really?" As we ascend a stairway, I lift the bottom of my dress to avoid stepping on it and tripping myself. "But I'm so … uneducated and unrefined."

"True, but you don't have anything to hide, and you're not playing games like many of the other ladies. You've been honest from the start about why you're here and what you want. That's refreshing." His words send an uncomfortable shiver up my spine. Thank goodness he doesn't know the truth: that I'm playing a game far more dangerous than any of the other ladies here. They risk gossip and a bad reputation if they fail at their games. I'm probably risking my life if I try—and fail—to escape this union.

I try to shake off my trepidation and convince myself that, as Roarke said, I have nothing to hide. "So you're suggesting," I say to Roarke, "that Aurora's growing jealous because you and I will soon be spending more time together?"

"Yes. I'm taking her new best friend away from her."

"Perhaps she's jealous because *I'm* taking *you* away from her. The two of you have always been close, haven't you? It's probably strange for her to imagine her brother married instead of available to spend his free time with her."

He shakes his head. "I don't think that's it. I've courted

203

other ladies, and Aurora's always made it very obvious when she doesn't like one of them. If that's the way she felt about you, you'd know by now. She would have made your life very unpleasant, and she certainly wouldn't be giving you lessons in magic, archery and dragon riding, or hunting down the best combination of books for you to read."

The guards ahead of us open the door to Roarke's suite. Roarke lowers my arm and gestures for me to walk in ahead of him. "Well, I'm relieved she likes me then," I say as I enter the sitting room. "I'm not sure how I would have survived the past few weeks without her."

I take a seat on the couch while Roarke retrieves the scroll with the vows. "Why don't you recite the vows as you remember them," he says as he sits beside me. He unrolls the scroll but doesn't give it to me. "I'll take note of where you go wrong and let you know what needs to be corrected."

I tilt my head back with a sigh. "This is going to be *so* romantic by the time we say it on the actual day. Such a big surprise."

He gives me an amused look. "I wasn't aware you were looking for romance, Lady Emerson. I can certainly try harder, if that's what you'd like."

I raise an eyebrow. "You really don't need to bother. I was joking. As you've pointed out before, neither of us is in this for the romance."

Roarke shifts closer, discarding the scroll on the floor. "That doesn't mean we shouldn't try," he whispers as he leans toward me. I look away, and he presses a kiss against the side of my neck, sending a shiver along my arms. I silently curse as I shut my eyes. Why the hell did I have to bring up the topic of romance? Although ... perhaps Roarke is right. As he drags a trail of kisses along my neck, I wonder if perhaps I should be making an effort with him. Maybe I'll find that I actually like him. Maybe Mom and I will end up staying, and there'll be no need for an escape, and we'll live here happily for the rest of our—

But that image of the king in his cavern and the man with his head bending, bending, bending to the side plays out against the back of my eyelids. I hear Dash's voice in my mind, reminding me why the Unseelie King wants me. *You can make their dirty work easier ... These people are* not good.

I open my eyes. "Roarke, I don't know if I—Holy crap!" I gasp and scramble backward on the couch as a dark shape rises up behind Roarke. It spreads in slow motion like a villain's cape ready to settle over his shoulders. Roarke shoves away from me, spins around, mutters a string of words I can't follow, and with a flash of bright light, the dark shape splits apart into a thousand drifting curls of smoke before vanishing.

I press my hand against my chest as my thrashing heart refuses to slow down. "What ... the hell ... was that?"

CHAPTER EIGHTEEN

ROARKE HURRIES INTO HIS BEDROOM AND RETURNS WITH A necklace in his hands, which he places over my head without hesitation. He steps back and lets out a long breath. "You already know what that was. Or at least, you've seen one before."

I swallow, looking down at the pendant resting against my chest. It's the same as the one I've seen Aurora wearing often. Silver with a black stone at its center. "Some kind of shadow creature," I say in a shaky voice as I look up at Roarke. "From that place you and Aurora took me to."

He nods. "You haven't asked me anything about that day."

"I didn't think of it until … until very recently. There's been so much going on. So many new things to occupy my thoughts."

"That creature," Roarke says as he takes his place beside me on the couch again, "is the same kind of creature that killed a man out in the gardens a couple of weeks ago. It sucked the life out of him. Not just his life, but his magic and his youth as well."

"And it would have done the same to us now," I whisper.

"Not to me. I was protected." He reaches for a chain at his neck, a chain hidden beneath his clothing, and pulls it free. At the end of the chain hangs a pendant very similar to mine. "And now you're protected too," he adds. "The magic embedded in the amulet wards off the ink-shades. I asked Yokshin to make one for you, and he finished it earlier today. I should have given it to you the moment we first walked into this room, but I forgot. I'm so, so sorry, my—"

"You *forgot*? And what about everyone else inside this palace? They should all be wearing these amulets."

"It's fine, Em. The creatures aren't supposed to be in the palace. What happened a few minutes ago—and what happened to the guard—isn't normal and won't happen again. Whoever let this one slip through will be in a great deal of trouble when I find out who—"

"But what if it happens again?"

"It won't."

"And how are they getting here? *What* are they? What was that shadowed place? Why couldn't Dash and I open faerie paths doorways, and why did everything disappear behind us when we found our way back into the magical world—"

Roarke holds one hand up. "Just listen and I'll tell you everything. I've wanted to tell you everything since the day I first took you there, but I had to know I could trust you."

My chest continues to rise and fall with shallow breaths. "How do you know you can trust me now?"

"I don't. Not entirely. But I'm hoping desperately that you're on my side, because I so badly want to show you everything and explain it all to you. Because you and I, Emerson ..." He grips both my hands in his as a smile stretches across his face. "You and I are going to rule that world. I will be its king and you will be my queen. Not just a princess, but a *queen*."

"I ... I don't understand." I try to remember exactly what I overheard while I was hiding in his bedroom, but my memory doesn't include much more than the words 'claim' and 'territory.' "There are already two rulers. Seelie and Unseelie. Are you saying that the shadow place doesn't belong to either court?"

"That's exactly what I'm saying. It's a different world entirely. A world that didn't even exist two decades ago." Roarke shifts closer, and I reach for a cushion and hug it tightly. Bandit squirms against my hip, and it's oddly comforting to remember that he's there. "Do you know what happened back then, Emerson?" Roarke asks. "About eighteen years ago?"

"I've probably been told, but I don't remember."

"Powerful magic ripped through the veil that separates the magic world from the non-magic world. But after the gash appeared in the sky, it didn't stay that way. It wasn't simply an enormous doorway between two worlds. It split further, and the two worlds began to consume one another. An ancient monument managed to stop it, but you know what, Emerson? I always wondered where the pieces of each world ended up. They couldn't have just disappeared, could they?"

I swallow and shake my head. "I don't know. Things stopped making sense the moment I discovered magic."

He tilts his head to the side, watching me for several moments. "You know about the faerie paths, don't you? You know that they're the dark space in between this world and the one you grew up in?"

"Yes."

"Did anyone ever tell you that with the right amount of effort, by refusing to think of anything at all, you can stay inside them for a while?"

"Um … maybe?" Dash might have mentioned something like that, but with all the other revelations bombarding me when I first got here, it's hard to remember exactly.

"Aurora and I did that. Near the monument where the veil was torn over Velazar II—that's the part of the island where the gap is. The Guild split the island in half years ago, so the prison could remain on Velazar I." Roarke stands. "Anyway, I was always so curious about that gap in the air," he continues as he begins pacing from one side of the couch to the other. "I asked so many questions about it during my lessons when I was growing up. And no one ever seemed to have enough answers. So Aurora and I decided to investigate it ourselves. We went back and forth through the tear from the magic world to the non-magic world. We tried to remain concealed, of course, but the guardians stationed by the monument eventually saw us. They tried to come after us, and one of them caught hold of

Aurora, so we couldn't simply drop out of the paths into safety. She managed to kick him off while we were inside the paths, but by then they were close enough that they might have been able to follow the trail of our magic.

"So we hid. We focused furiously on nothing, and the guardians soon disappeared. We could no longer hear their voices through the darkness. Aurora said we should leave in case we got stuck inside the paths forever, but that's when I saw it in the distance: grayish light and wisps of smoke as black as shadow. And the edge of two worlds."

If I hadn't seen it myself, and if magic hadn't become an ordinary part of my daily life, I'd be convinced Roarke belonged in the same facility my mother's spent the past five years in. "The edge of two worlds?" I whisper.

"That's what we saw as we moved toward the light. Grassy ground the same as the ground we'd walked across on Velazar Island. Then it ended abruptly and became a field of tall grass surrounded on three sides by a fence. These were two distinctly different pieces of earth, from two entirely different worlds—co-existing in a brand new world. They were muted versions of the originals, as if most of the color had been leeched from them, but they were real. I even bent down and ran my fingers through the grass so I'd know it wasn't an illusion." Roarke ceases his pacing and looks at me. "I finally had my answer, Emerson. I finally knew what had happened to those parts of each world that disappeared. They didn't cease to exist; they were forced into a new world altogether."

"So what did you do?"

Roarke sits on the edge of the couch and stares across the

room. "Aurora was afraid. She said we needed to leave. She tried to open a doorway to the faerie paths, but it was no use. That was when she began to think we must be dead. She believed the guardians had killed us, and this was whatever came afterward. Some kind of afterlife. But I didn't believe it. My mind was already rushing to make sense of that world, to piece together how it worked. It seemed to me that the shadow world existed in the same space as the faerie paths. Technically, we were still *inside* the faerie paths, so that's why Aurora couldn't open a doorway."

"How did you get out? When Dash and I were there, we ran until we saw the tear in the veil, and we kept going until we ended up on Velazar Island. We couldn't get out any other way."

"Ah, but there is another way. More than one way, actually." He looks at me. "How would you normally get out of the faerie paths?"

"You focus on where you want to end up, right? It's your thoughts that take you there."

"Yes. And you can leave the shadow world in the same way, but you have to *really* focus. I think it's as if you're so deep inside the faerie paths that it takes concerted effort and intense concentration to get out. An almost meditation-like state."

My thumb runs up and down the edge of the cushion as I process his explanation. "That doesn't seem practical."

"No. It isn't. That's why we linked a faerie paths doorway spell to a traveling candle. It was Aurora's idea. She remembered that that's the way the witches travel. They don't use faerie paths. Instead, they add a traveling spell to a candle.

When the candle is lit, the person who holds it can travel to certain places by picturing that place. Very similar to the way faerie paths work."

"Okay, so you would just light one of these special candles, but what about the intense mediation-like concentration part?"

"Oh, the intense concentration is still there. It just has to be employed while creating and applying the spell to the candle." Roarke waves a hand dismissively. "Higher grade magic. You'll get there at some point. Anyway, the candles aren't the easiest method of travel either. They run out, of course, and new candles have to be made. So I went one step further." He stands once more and reaches for my hand. "I created a portal. Right here in my suite, for continual, easy access."

My mind races back to the swirling circle of magic I saw on Roarke's bathroom wall. Without a word, I let him pull me to my feet. He leads me through his bedroom and pushes open the door to his bathroom. I don't have to feign surprise when I see the portal; the fear on my face probably does a good enough job of concealing the fact that I've been here before. "So that's how the shadow creatures are getting through to this world," I say.

"Yes. I have men on the other side guarding the portal from the creatures, although they clearly need to be reminded how to do their jobs properly. We're not sure what the creatures are, but we've been calling them ink-shades. Most of the time, they move slowly, like black ink spreading through water. At other times they blend in so completely with the shadows that it seems they become shadows themselves."

I shudder as I recall hiding alone in here. An ink-shade

could have come through at any moment and sucked the life out of me. "So it will happen again," I say in a shaky voice. "Another ink-shade will get through, and if you don't see it and kill it, it will hurt someone."

Roarke rubs my arm, as if that could possibly comfort me. "It won't happen again. I'm going to station guards on this side as well. If an ink-shade does slip into this world, it will be killed before it can get to anyone." He takes a step toward the portal before turning back and holding his hand out to me. "Shall we?"

I shake my head vigorously. "No, thank you. I don't need to go back there."

"But you're safe now. You have an amulet. They can't hurt you."

I frown as I realize something. "I wasn't safe the first time. Neither was Dash. You told us to hide when you heard your father coming, which meant we were on our own in that strange world. Ink-shades could have killed us. One almost did."

Roarke looks down, his expression becoming suitably contrite. "I'm so sorry. We'd had our amulets for a while by then. We'd forgotten there was any need to be afraid."

"You *forgot*? You went on and on about how powerful and valuable my Griffin Ability is, and then you left me alone in a strange world with dangerous creatures that could have sucked my magic and life right out of me?"

"You were supposed to *hide*, not run away. I pointed you in the right direction. If you'd gone that way, you would have seen the door in the hedge that led down into the underground passages."

"We *did* go the way you pointed. I didn't see any—"

"Emerson." He grabs my shoulders and gives me a small shake. "Just stop. I'm sorry, okay? I never meant for any creature to go after you. And now that you're properly protected, you'll be completely fine. You can see this amazing world for what it is."

"Amazing? What is so amazing about shadow creatures and a wispy colorless world?"

"Please," Roarke says. "Please come with me and I'll show you. This is everything I've wanted you to see since we first met. I promise there is nothing scary about this world now that you're wearing that amulet. The ink-shades will simply float right past you."

I wonder if I should refuse, just to see if he'll force me. To see if Dash was right about him. But I'm too afraid to make him angry. So I nod and take his hand, and he leads me into the spiraling magic.

CHAPTER NINETEEN

THE PORTAL'S MAGIC SPINS IN CIRCLES AROUND ME, AND I'm almost instantly dizzy. I shut my eyes, cling to Roarke's hand, and take a few fumbling steps forward. "You can open your eyes," he tells me as the dizziness vanishes. I open them and blink a few times before focusing on the nearly colorless world around me. The grass, the flowers, the trees and hedges—everything is varying tones of bluish grey. The only vibrant color belongs to the four guards who jump to attention at our sudden appearance.

"Would you like to explain to me," Roarke says to them, "why I just killed an ink-shade in my own chambers?"

The nearest guard blinks. "Y-Your Highness?"

I walk slowly away from them as they stammer out apologies and Roarke threatens to feed them to his sister's favorite dragon. I look around, trying to figure out where I was when Roarke and Aurora brought me here the first time, and which way Dash and I ran. Somewhere on the right, I think. I see more artfully clipped hedges that way, and the bench they may have sat on while presenting their offer to me. I walk on a little further and see a castle in the distance. Well, part of a castle, to be more precise. It looks open and unfinished on one side, and oddly hazy due to the wisps of a smoke-like black substance curling into the air here and there. Beyond the castle, the world fades into darkness.

"Incredible, isn't it?" Roarke says, walking up to me.

"You told me you found a piece of land with grass next to a field when you first discovered this world. So where did all of this come from?"

"Aurora and I built it."

I turn my gaze to him. "With magic?"

"Yes, with magic. That's why it's partially built. We can only do so much at a time. It depletes our magic quickly, and then we need to rest before we can do more." He takes my hand and squeezes it as he smiles. "Do you see now, Emerson? Do you see why you are the perfect queen for this world?"

I glance down at my wrist where the ruby on my bracelet is almost completely red. A section of transparent stone on one end indicates that I have about two hours left until power returns to my voice for the second time today. "Because my Griffin Ability can build anything?" I ask, looking up again.

"You can *literally* speak the contents of this world into existence." He reaches out with his free hand and runs his fingers through the silvery grey leaves of the bush we're standing beside. A black, smoke-like tendril curls slowly around his hand and vanishes. "In addition, your magic will make it so much simpler to claim this world as our own."

"What do you mean?"

"This world will be ours, Emerson. Officially. You and I will be its rulers."

I look down at our entwined hands. *And how,* I wonder, *is the woman you were whispering with in your room involved in all this?* There's no way I can actually ask him that, though, so I turn to a different question. "I assume, from what you're suggesting, that becoming the rulers of a world involves more than just sticking a flag in the ground?"

Roarke gives me a bemused look. "That may be the way they do things in the human realm, but in the fae realm, there is magic involved in properly claiming a territory. The magic and the creatures of the land will then be bound to you. It doesn't mean they can't disobey you, it just makes them more inclined to act in your favor. The Unseelie Court and the Seelie Court are territories that were claimed with magic. With your Griffin Ability, we can claim this world for ourselves."

"I don't understand why you need my Griffin Ability, though. People have obviously done this kind of spell before without my specific kind of magic."

"True, but I'm talking about complex magic involving royal blood and sacrifices and many specific words. With your Griffin Ability, we should be able to simply tell the world it belongs to us, and that's all."

"Do you really think it's that simple?"

"We'll soon find out," he murmurs, looking across the land he's already begun to shape.

I bite my lip as I stare at the tower on the completed side of the castle. I probably shouldn't say what I'm about to say, but I need to understand Roarke and his motives. "Why not just do it now? You've already compelled me this evening—told me what to say when my Griffin Ability replenishes—but you could change that. You could force me with another compulsion potion to tell this world that it belongs to you. If this is what you're really after, then why are you wasting time on a union?"

He faces me fully and takes each of my hands in his. "Firstly, this world isn't all I want. I want to be joined to one of the most powerful faeries I've ever known. *You.* And secondly … don't you understand yet that I'm not like my father? I don't want to *force* anyone to do anything. Yes, I want this world more than anything, and I'll do whatever I can to convince you that our union is a good idea. But if you refuse, I would never force you."

"You'd never *force* me?" I repeat in disbelief. "Roarke, you compel me every day to say exactly what you want me to say each time my Griffin Ability is ready to be used."

"To keep my father happy until the union. I compel you to say what *he* wants you to say. He's the one who doesn't trust you yet."

"So why would he suddenly trust me after the union? He wants my power just as much as you do. He'll never stop compelling me. He would never take the risk that I'd use my magic against him or anyone else in his court."

A smile curves Roarke's lips. "You're getting to know my father, I see."

"So you agree with me?"

"I do. My father will never stop forcing you to speak his will. But once you and I are united and the shadow world is ours, this will be our home. We'll be far away from him and from the land and position he won't allow me to inherit for centuries still. He'll have to declare war on his own son in order to get his hands on you."

"So that's your ultimate plan? To go against your father and take over a new territory?"

"Yes. If I don't do that, it'll be centuries before I can rule over anything."

"And what if your father actually does declare war on you? He has armies. Surely he'd defeat you?"

Roarke lifts his shoulders in a lazy half-shrug. "There are many in the court who are loyal to me. They would follow us here. They'd fight for us. But yes, there's a good chance my father would still defeat me. You, however …" He brushes a strand of hair away from my cheek. "He would never defeat you."

A shiver races across my skin. A whisper of excitement stirs deep within me. In my mind, I begin to see a vague picture of a future I never expected. The promise of power, the promise of finally being in control of my own life. Not just mine, but many others. And Mom would be there too, vibrant and healthy and advising me. This picture of my future is alluring in a way that I recognize is unhealthy. But I was born with this power. Perhaps this brand new world is what I was meant to use it for. "You may be right," I murmur.

"So do you see now?" I hear the enthusiasm in Roarke's voice. "Do you see the endless possibilities of this world and your power within it?"

I nod. Look around. "So the tear in the veil is that way?" I ask, pointing to my right.

"Yes."

"You know the Guild is planning to close it, right?"

"I do know that, yes."

"What do you think will happen to this world then? What if it ceases to exist? All your plans will be for nothing then."

Roarke shakes his head. "I don't think it will disappear. Closing the veil won't restore each world to the way it was before. It will close the gap, that's all. If, however, the veil were to be opened further …"

I frown, following his logic. "Then this world would grow bigger?"

"I believe so. It's limited at the moment. Very small. We've tried to push at the edges, but we end up building into the complete darkness of the faerie paths. We need more space here. We need to extend this world."

"But if you tear the veil open further, you'll destroy more of the human and fae worlds in the process."

With an unconcerned twist of his mouth, Roarke says, "Those worlds are big enough already. They can survive getting a little smaller."

Like a slow chill creeping on as evening falls, my body begins to grow colder. "Parts of those worlds will be gone forever. People will die. Or … or they'll become part of the shadows of this world. I don't know, but either way, we would be killing them."

"Don't be so dramatic," he says with a chuckle. "Besides, your world is overpopulated already. Mine is heading the same way. We would be *helping* those worlds by using them to extend ours." He walks forward in the direction of the castle, pulling me along with him. "I've taken a closer look at that monument on Velazar Island in recent months, and my spies have told me all they know about this veil restoration spell the Guild will soon be implementing. I think we can interrupt it. Shatter it. Blow that gap wide open. We just need to know when it's happening so we can be prepared. And then, my lovely Emerson, we can continue building this world."

The chill that crawls across my skin is no longer a shiver of excitement. I can hardly believe what he plans to do. What he plans for *me* to do. Does he really think I'd be happy with that? Have I painted such a bleak picture of my old world that he thinks I'd gladly destroy parts of it? I look away from him, my heart sinking rapidly. For a few moments, I thought I may have discovered my purpose, my future. The home I've always wanted for Mom and me. But I can't do what he's suggesting. I can't destroy worlds. I can't kill people.

And I can't let Roarke do any of those things either.

But how the hell would I stop him? It would be almost impossible. I'd need to have control over my own Griffin magic, and I'd have to command him and everyone else who answers to him. And this would have to happen *after* he heals Mom; there's no way he'd do anything for her if I first ruined his world domination plans. And Mom and I would have to be ready to escape as soon as I've commanded Roarke not to tear the veil any further.

It's too risky. There are too many things that could go wrong. Who am I to try and stop a prince anyway? I'm nobody. I need to just focus on getting Mom and me the hell out of here once Roarke has healed her. Whatever he does on his own after that will be on his conscience, not mine.

I'm not brave or selfless. I'm just doing what I have to do to get by.

My feet stop moving as my words from yesterday come back to me in a sickening rush, followed immediately by Dash's response: *You can tell yourself that lie all you want, but I know you're more than that.*

"I'm not," I whisper.

"Hmm? You're not what?" Roarke looks back at me. "Not helping those worlds?"

The shadow world comes back into focus around him, and my fleeting aspirations of bravery vanish back into the recesses of my imagination. "Sorry," I say with a forced laugh. "I ended up on my own train of thought there. I only meant that … that I'm not currently making a difference to anyone or anything. I've only ever seen myself as insignificant. But now, with my power and this world, I *can* make a difference." I stare boldly into his eyes, hoping I've covered my blunder well enough. From his smile and the way his gaze roves hungrily across my face, I see I've given him exactly the kind of response he was hoping for.

"I knew you would come to understand. I cannot wait for our union day." He tugs me closer and presses his lips against mine. I'm so shocked I almost shove him back. *RELAX*, I scream silently before I can give myself away. I force my eyelids shut. Entwining my arms tentatively around his neck, I try to meld myself against him. I try to pretend I'm enjoying the foreign sensation of unknown lips moving against mine.

When I've kept up the kissing act for as long as I can stand, I pull away. My words are appropriately breathless as I say, "I'm excited too. Shall we return to your suite and continue practicing the vows? I want to get them exactly right. I don't want a single thing to go wrong on that day."

Roarke looks at me as though he couldn't have asked for anything better. He puts an arm around me, and we head away from the castle and back toward the portal. "Is there anything you want to ask me? About the shadow world?"

The woman you were speaking with in your room, I want to say. *Who is she? How does she fit into your new world?* "No," I say instead, because I'm not brave enough to risk his anger. "I don't have any other questions yet. I'm just looking forward to trying out my Griffin Ability on something useful, like bringing plants and buildings and creatures into existence."

"So am I. We can try tomorrow. I've already compelled you to say something mundane later tonight when your Griffin Ability returns; may as well leave it at that. You can get some rest, and we'll come back here tomorrow to try something exciting."

After returning through the portal, I spend another half an hour or so practicing the vows with Roarke's assistance. Fortunately, he doesn't try anything more intimate than resting his hand on my knee. When I get back to my own room, I remove Bandit from my pocket. He shifts into a cat in my arms, and I hug him tightly as I stare through a window at the winter night.

Dash's words come back again—*I know you're more than that*—and I wish I could explain myself to him. *I didn't grow up the way you did*, I would say to him. *I've never wanted to save anyone except my own mother. Saving Stanmeade was just a fluke. I'm not a hero, and I can't stop Roarke.*

Before getting into bed, I undress and sink into a hot pool filled with steaming water and silver bubbles. I slide down, letting the water cover my head, hoping it will wash the shame from my body.

CHAPTER TWENTY

NOW THAT I KNOW ABOUT THE SHADOW WORLD, ROARKE is eager to get me back there. I've barely eaten anything off the tray of breakfast in my sitting room when two of his guards arrive to accompany me to his suite. I stride through the glossy hallways with them, feeling a little better than last night. Probably because I've managed to push my guilt into the far reaches of my mind where I don't have to think about it much.

"Em, I'm so glad you know all about this place now," Aurora says the moment I recover from the dizziness on the other side of the portal. "I've hated keeping it a secret from you." Her smile doesn't quite reach her eyes, though, and I begin to wonder if Roarke may have been right: perhaps she is afraid she'll lose her new friend once the union takes place. But

I can't ask her about it now. It would be awkward with Roarke right here.

"Me too," I tell her, forcing a wide smile onto my face. "I can't wait to see what my Griffin Ability can do here."

"Yokshin made more candles," Aurora tells Roarke, removing a bag from her shoulder. She looks past him and holds the bag out toward one of Roarke's guards. "Please go through the castle, and wherever you see a dresser, add some candles to the drawers." The guard responds with a nod and quickly hurries off to do as he was told.

I look around, noting that the light seems to be exactly the same as it was when Roarke and I were here last night. "What time of day is it?" I ask.

"Day and night don't seem to exist here," Roarke says. "We haven't seen a sun or moon, and the same greyish dim light always fills the sky. We don't know the source of the light. Perhaps it's a magical copy of the light that illuminated the original world this land came from."

"That's so strange."

"Yes. We can try to change it, perhaps, but for now, let me show you your future home," Roarke says, putting an arm around me and leading me forward.

As we head for the castle, I can't help comparing it to the palace I've spent the last few weeks living in. Gleaming marble, gold finishes, and an intricate structure make the Unseelie Palace a beautiful and impressive building to behold. Roarke's castle is plainer and appears far more fortified with its stone walls, moat and drawbridge. "It doesn't look particularly welcoming," I comment.

"It isn't meant to be," Roarke says. "I expect someone might try to take this world from us, so I'm prepared to fight for it. You'll notice the castle requires a lot more work still. We've only built about half of it. And so far the moat is in front of the main gate only. We still need to extend it all the way around the castle."

"So you're hoping my magic can help you with this?"

"Yes."

Black smoky tendrils rise from the ground and curl lazily around us as we walk. The dull, indistinct shadow cast by one of the ornamentally clipped bushes becomes darker and more solid. It rises from the ground like a drop of black ink dispersing through water, coalescing roughly into the shape of a stingray with no tail. I stop walking and duck down as the ink-shade comes toward us, but it simply soars overhead and continues on its way.

"You're protected by your amulet, remember?" Roarke says.

"The inside of the castle is also protected," Aurora adds. "Well, most of it. The towers aren't safe yet, but as we build each room, we add the protective enchantments to the interior walls so the ink-shades can't enter."

"We plan to eradicate them all, of course," Roarke continues, "but in case we can't, our home will at least be safe inside."

I look back over my shoulder to make sure there are guards still stationed outside the portal. Not that I'm super confident in their abilities if they've already managed to let two ink-shades slip past them without even noticing. I want to suggest once more that everyone in the palace should have an amulet, but I can see why Roarke isn't interested in that precaution. It would require him or his father to explain why the amulets are necessary—and that won't happen as long as they're keeping this world a secret.

"I assume your father knows about all the building you're doing in this world?" I ask, facing forward again.

"Yes, although he thinks it's for the family. He sees this place as more of a retreat—a holiday destination—and he's been happy for us to fill it in whatever way we want. He has no idea I'll soon be claiming this world as my own. As *our* own," he corrects, taking hold of my hand.

I look to my other side at Aurora. "And you don't mind?"

She keeps her eyes trained forward. "It doesn't bother me that Roarke wants to rule his own territory. I'm not interested in that sort of thing. But I refuse to choose sides if he and Dad end up fighting."

Roarke lets out a low rumble of a laugh. "Hopefully Father will understand."

Having met the Unseelie King, I highly doubt he'll respond reasonably when he discovers his son has taken over this territory and stolen the shiny new Griffin Gifted weapon—me—all for himself. But with any luck, Mom and I will be long gone by the time the king retaliates.

We cross the grey grass and head for the drawbridge. Once inside the castle, Roarke and Aurora spend the next hour or two showing me every single thing they've already built, and discussing exactly what I should try with my Griffin Ability. Roarke keeps glancing at the ruby on my wrist, which, by late morning, is almost completely filled with color.

As my Griffin magic nears the point where it's ready to be used, we walk along the cold, stone hallways toward the unfinished side of the castle. We reach a bare room with only three walls, open on one side where the fourth wall should be. I walk out onto the grass and turn to look up at the partially formed, half-furnished rooms on this side of the castle.

"How much do you want to try building?" Aurora asks. "One room? A suite? An entire wing?"

"I have no idea. I don't know what my magic is capable of."

"Try what we suggested a little earlier," Roarke says. "One complete room with furniture inside."

I blink at him. "Aren't you going to compel me?"

His eyes swing briefly to Aurora before returning to me. "I don't see the need. We trust each other now, don't we? You're not going to turn around and use your magic against us. Are you?" he adds.

"Of course not." But that's exactly where my mind went. This could be my chance. I could command Aurora to stay right here, and command Roarke to leave this world with me. I could leave him somewhere, fetch Mom, and tell him—with whatever Griffin magic I have left—to heal her. And the guards … could I command them to stay here too? Would the magic work if they're all the way back at the portal and can't hear me?

"Emerson?" Roarke frowns at me. "You seem uncertain about something. Would you like to tell me what you're planning for your magic?"

"Sorry, I'm just thinking. I don't always know how best to word these commands." I glance at Aurora, but she's biting her lip and staring at the ground, her mind clearly elsewhere. "Um,

I mean … how much detail do you think I need to say? Would it be enough to tell a chair to form itself, and then just picture what it looks like in my head? Or do you think I need to talk about the color of the cushion, and the shape of the chair, and …" I trail off, half my mind still trying to figure out if I can risk using my ability to command all the people in the shadow world instead of doing what Roarke wants me to do.

"I don't know," Roarke says. "It isn't my magic. You need to try it out and see what happens."

Aurora clears her throat, seeming to return from whatever thoughts she was lost in. "Well, from your experience over the past few weeks with all the dull commands Roarke's compelled you to say, we've learned that your intentions and thoughts are almost as important as the words you say out loud. So I don't think you need to speak all the details. Just imagine them, and hopefully your Griffin Ability will do the rest."

Without having to look at the ruby, I sense the moment at which my power is fully topped up and ready to escape me. I decide then that I can't risk commanding Roarke now. I don't have enough control yet, and if I don't say everything perfectly, I could easily wind up a prisoner instead of a bride.

"Oh, and try not to let all your magic go in one command," Aurora adds. "See how much you can hold back."

I look at the empty, three-walled room in front of me and begin speaking. "There is another room here," I say, picturing the room forming around us by adding itself onto the existing one. My voice reverberates in that strange, deep way that still sounds creepy to my ears. "It has a bay window on one side, with a seat beneath the window, and cushions scattered across the seat. Wooden panels cover the walls and floor, curtains hang from the window, and three armchairs sit in the middle of the room."

Magic rushes from me, and I clench my hands into fists, my whole body tensing as I try to hold the flood back. I imagine myself slowly turning a tap, letting out only the required amount of power. And then, all around us, walls begin to rise from the ground. I watch in utter amazement as wooden panels materialize to cover the walls, and a ceiling spreads through the air above us. Where the ceiling meets the walls, ornamental molding forms itself into cornices that look exactly the way I pictured them in my mind.

"Oh, look there!" Aurora exclaims as one of the walls pushes itself outward into a bay window. A seat rises up, and colorful cushions expand into existence on top of it. Curtains the same as the ones in my room at the palace drop down on either side of the window.

"Oh!" I throw my hands out to steady myself as a wooden floor pops up beneath our feet. A grinding, rumbling sensation travels up through my body—the foundation forming beneath the ground?—before disappearing a few seconds later. Then, as three chairs unfold from the air right in front of us, we step hurriedly back. The armchairs expand, their cushions puffing up and their legs molding into that vintage ball-and-claw design I've seen on many of the chairs furnishing the Unseelie Palace. I imagined them as dragon claws in my head, and as the chairs slide into their final positions in the center of the room, the claws lengthen and sharpen into solid wooden versions of Imperia's feet.

Finally, everything becomes still. A wave of tiredness ripples over me, though it isn't nearly enough to dampen the absolute wonder I feel at having created everything inside this room. I raise my hand, lightly touch the wall closest to me to make sure it's real, and then lean my weight more heavily against it.

"Incredible," Roarke murmurs. "We've studied architecture spells, but everything still takes so much time for us to create. Then you come along and complete a whole room in under a minute. It's mind-blowing."

"Absolutely," Aurora breathes, her eyes tracing the contents of the room before finally landing on me. "How do you feel?"

"Quite tired, but I haven't depleted all my power yet. I managed to hold some of it back, though it was difficult. I can feel it struggling to break free." I push away from the wall, part of my attention focused on wrestling my remaining Griffin magic into submission. "Shall I try something else? Something bigger? If it's too much for my magic, then I assume it just … won't happen?"

"I don't know. Maybe. What do you want to try?" she asks.

"Um … something outside?" I realize I haven't created a way out of this room aside from the window, but a simple command results in a door forming between this room and the empty room next to it. We walk through to one of the rooms that's still open on one side, and head out onto the grass. I cast about for something to add to this dull landscape to make it a little prettier. Could I add color? Could I add a sun or moon or stars?

I lift my gaze to the grey sky above and utter a simple command: "There are stars in the sky." It's a relief to let the remainder of my Griffin magic flood out of my body. Far above, pinpricks of light begin to appear. I have a vague memory of how stars are actually formed, but I have no idea if those are real stars way up there, or if they're just balls of magic light floating high above … above …

The light becomes brighter and the world turns white. Sickening dizziness rushes at me. My head tilts back, and I fall, weightless, into nothing. White becomes black. Utter darkness surrounds me.

After an indeterminate amount of time, dim light slowly gathers in my vision. I realize I'm lying on the grass with tendrils of black smoke spiraling lazily into the air on either side of me and a voice faintly calling my name from far away. Aurora's lips move as she leans over me, her features screwed up in concern. "Em? Em!" Her voice is an echo that slowly moves closer, eventually layering itself over the movement of her lips. "Em. Emerson!"

"Mm?"

Roarke appears beside her. "Here, let me give her this. I grabbed it from Yokshin's supplies."

"Are you sure it's the right thing?"

"Yes. I've taken it before." Roarke lifts my upper body and pulls me against his chest. He removes the stopper from a little brown glass bottle that, for a moment, reminds me of Chelsea's herbal remedies. It's so odd to think of her ordinary little salon in her ordinary little house when I'm lying on the ground of a foreign world beneath a sprinkling of stars I created with my own magic. A breathy laugh escapes me, which increases the concern on Aurora's face and makes Roarke pause with the bottle just in front of my lips.

"Em?" Aurora says in a voice that sounds higher than usual. "Why are you laughing?"

Then I remember that Chelsea isn't alive anymore and will never make another herbal remedy, and the breath of laughter dies on my lips.

"I'm going to give it to her, okay?" Roarke says.

"Wait," Aurora says, stopping his hand before he can place the bottle against my lips. "That potion is meant to restore *normal* magic after using too much of it, but Em was using Griffin magic. Her levels of normal magic should be totally fine. That potion isn't going to help her."

"It can't hurt either," Roarke says, tipping some liquid into my mouth.

I've already begun to feel less lightheaded though, even before the unfamiliar liquid burns down the back of my throat. I lick my lips and push my hair away from my face. "Why did I pass out?"

"I think you tried to do too much," Aurora says. "Your Griffin Ability attempted to carry out your command, but you didn't have nearly enough magic to fill an entire sky with stars." Her eyes are still wide as she sits awkwardly on the grass in front of me in her voluminous yellow skirt covered in gold leaves. "You need to learn your limits before trying something so big, Em. You don't want to accidentally kill yourself."

I blink at her. "Do you think that could actually happen?"

"I don't know!" She throws her hands up. "No one else has magic like yours. We're still figuring it out, remember?"

"Why are you angry with me?"

"Because you should have been more careful."

"She's concerned, that's all," Roarke says. He still has one arm around me, but I'm strong enough to sit on my own, so I gently ease myself away from him.

"I'm concerned too," I say. "I didn't realize my Griffin Ability would reach its limit on something so simple. It obviously isn't as powerful as everyone thinks it is."

Roarke laughs. "You created *stars*, Emerson. And not just two or three; dozens of them appeared before you lost consciousness. That's far more powerful than any magic an ordinary faerie possesses. And I think that if you store it up—if you don't use it immediately each time you feel the power coming on—then you can probably do greater things."

"It's dangerous to test these 'greater things,'" Aurora says, her brow furrowed in a deep frown. "You need to be careful."

"Don't worry," Roarke says to her. "I won't let anything happen to Emerson."

She looks directly at him, folding her arms over her chest. "Won't you?"

"Of course not." He looks affronted. "Do you know how fast I ran back through the palace to get that potion? I didn't trust any of my men to get there quicker than I could." He places one hand over mine. "It terrified me to think you might not recover, Emerson. I know that neither of us is in this for love, but I do care for you."

"You care for her Griffin Ability," Aurora mutters.

Roarke pins his dark burgundy gaze on her. "Please don't make scornful remarks under your breath like that. It isn't the

235

kind of behavior that befits a princess. You're better than that, Aurora."

She levels her simmering gaze at him for several moments before looking away. "You're right. I apologize. I only want you and Em to be happy, of course. To take care of one another."

"And that's exactly what we'll do." Roarke fits his arm around me again. His thumb rubs up and down the bare skin just above my elbow in a way that feels uncomfortably intimate. "For the rest of our lives."

Aurora nods and smiles, but her eyes continue to stare off into the distance, and her smile is far from genuine.

CHAPTER TWENTY-ONE

I DON'T SEE AURORA AT ALL THE FOLLOWING DAY, WHICH IS odd considering she's had some activity or other planned for the two of us every few hours since the moment I arrived here. She doesn't show up for archery in the morning and, far worse, she doesn't join me in the queen's private parlor in the afternoon for my weekly instruction on etiquette. I've survived two of these etiquette lessons already, but I suspect it was only because Aurora was there to make them bearable by poking fun at her mother—something I'd love to do, but wouldn't dare for fear of receiving some form of horrible magical punishment I've never heard of. So I keep my mouth shut and try not to fall asleep as Queen Amrath drones on.

I assume that perhaps Aurora isn't feeling well, but when Roarke comes to my room in the early evening and I ask how she's doing, he says, "I believe she's in perfect health. I saw her having a picnic this afternoon with her ladies-in-waiting."

"Oh." An unexpected stab of hurt pierces my chest. "So she's gone from being overly friendly and telling me how she looks forward to having me as a sister to ignoring me?"

He sighs. "She's just being moody. I'm sure she'll get over it once the union has taken place. And what does it matter if she doesn't? You'll have me." He tucks my hair behind my ear and drags one finger briefly along my jaw. "It's nothing to worry yourself about."

"Nothing to worry myself about?" I fold my arms over my chest and raise an eyebrow. "Do you plan to continue using this condescending tone once we're married?"

His lips stretch into a smile, his dark eyes glittering with amusement. "Do you plan to continue to be just as feisty once we're married?"

I shrug. "Probably."

"Good. I quite enjoy your feistiness." He lifts my hand and kisses it, which sends a shiver all the way up my arm.

"You think you're being so smooth, don't you," I say with a roll of my eyes.

"Well, it's working, isn't it?"

If you're aiming to make me feel uncomfortable, then yes, I almost say. But it's better if he thinks his attempts at charm are working. He hasn't compelled me to say anything with my Griffin Ability tonight, and if I can get him to hang around until later, I might be able to use my power on him. "Perhaps," I say with what I hope is a sultry half smile. "If you stay and have dinner with me tonight, we can find out."

He chuckles as he lowers my hand. "Oh how I wish I could say yes to that. Unfortunately, I'm going out for a few hours. If Aurora hasn't requested your company this evening, then I assume you'll be eating on your own. I'll tell Clarina to bring your dinner here."

"All right." Disappointment settles over my shoulders, but I won't give up yet. "Perhaps you can stop by when you return later and say goodnight."

"Yes, perhaps. I'll see how late it is."

Something nudges my ankle, and I look down to see Bandit rubbing the length of his grey cat-formed body along my leg. "Looking for attention, huh?" I say to him.

Roarke takes a step back. "Well, have a good evening, my love. If I don't see you later, then—Oh, I almost forgot to give you your second dose of compulsion potion for the day."

The light weight of disappointment on my shoulders becomes a thousand times heavier. I bite back a sigh and give Roarke a polite frown instead. "Do you think that's necessary? It took such a toll on me when I tried to use too much power earlier that I assumed my ability will take longer to replenish. I'm sure I'll be asleep when it happens."

Roarke looks down at the ruby on my arm as he removes a small bottle from a hidden pocket within his coat. "Hmm. Your power may be slightly slower in replenishing itself, but it appears it will still be ready for use sometime later tonight. I'd rather not miss an opportunity for you to use your ability." He holds the bottle of potion out toward me, but I make no move to take it.

"I thought we trusted each other now, Roarke."

"We do." He lowers his voice. "But my father has ways of discovering the things that happen within his palace. If I don't compel you, he'll probably find out. Best to keep him happy, don't you think?"

Of course it's best to keep the king happy, but that means losing out on another opportunity to command Roarke. It's pointless to argue, though, and Roarke might even become suspicious. So I take the bottle from him and sip a small amount.

"Good." He takes the bottle and screws the lid back on. "So, Emerson, when your Griffin Ability next appears, you're going to say the word 'open.'"

"Open? Open what?"

"That's up to you. As Aurora pointed out yesterday, it's becoming clear that your intentions—not only your words—play a role in instructing your Griffin Ability. So I'd like you to give as simple a command as possible—the word 'open'—while deciding in your mind exactly what should open. A window, a drawer, your balcony doors, your wardrobe. Anything."

"Okay." Of course, I'm now wondering if there's any way I can use this to my advantage. Which door can I open that I've never been allowed to open before? And how likely it is that King Savyon might be behind whichever door I choose, ready to take out his wrath on me the moment he discovers me sneaking around?

"Oh, and tomorrow night you'll be having dinner with my family," Roarke says as he opens my sitting room door. "Just the four of us and you. My father would like to see the improvement you've made since he first met you." My fear must be obvious on my face, because Roarke quickly adds, "Don't worry, I'm sure you'll do just fine. Wear an appropriate dress, speak politely about appropriate topics, and make occasional use of basic magic while you're at the table. He just wants to be certain you don't stand out like a human amongst faeries, that's all."

"Right. Of course." I clear my throat. "And, uh, in the morning can we try some more building in the shadow world? I'm excited to see what else my power can do."

Roarke smiles. "Certainly. I look forward to it." Then he walks out and closes the door, leaving me with my heart almost hammering itself right out of my chest.

Tomorrow is the day. Tomorrow I'm going to finally do what I came here to do. Roarke and I will be in the shadow world with hardly any guards around, and when he lets me choose to build whatever I want to build, I'll command him instead.

I walk to the table and sit down amongst the books and papers I've been writing notes on. I can't write down what I plan to use my Griffin Ability for—I can't risk anyone finding out —but I doodle while I think. While I decide what to say to the guards, what to say to Aurora if she's there, and what to say to Roarke.

Tell me every single thing you know about my mother and how to help her.

I repeat the words silently over and over until they're embedded in my brain. Then I begin to wonder just how complicated the magic that's required to heal Mom might be. I probably won't remember everything Roarke tells me. Which means I need to instruct him to write everything down instead. Once he's done that, I'll use whatever Griffin magic I have left to tell the faerie paths to open. If I can manage that, then I don't need to find one of those candles or run all the way to the gap over Velazar Island.

Cold slowly seeps into my bones as the fire on the other side of the room diminishes from burning logs to glowing embers. I reach for my coat hanging over one of the other chairs—a ridiculous thing that looks like something a circus ringmaster might wear. Red with gold-edged lapels, long enough to reach my ankles and billow out behind me as I walk. Clarina paired it with black-and-gold pants and a white shirt with ruffles down the front, and told me the queen would love it. Now that I think of it, Queen Amrath smiled when I walked into her parlor this afternoon, so perhaps Clarina was right.

I stand and walk to the fireplace as I pull the jacket on. Using magic, I manage to lift several pieces of wood from the copper bucket and add them to the fire without being too clumsy. Then I sift through my brain for the right spell to ignite not just one flame, but many. When the fire bursts back into life, I can't help smiling. If I wasn't so anxious about tomorrow, I'd probably clap my hands too.

A loud knock on my door wipes the smile from my face. I turn quickly as the door opens. I haven't uttered a word yet, which means it can only be—

"Em, I have more books for you," Aurora announces as she strides in with a pile of books floating behind her. "I hope you've finished the last lot."

I blink at her. "No, I haven't finished the last lot that you

242

gave me only two days ago."

"Well, these are more important." She directs the pile of books toward the table, and they drop down onto my page of doodles. She stands in front of me and places her hands on her hips. "I'm serious. They contain important historical events from Unseelie history. You need to read them before the union ceremony."

"Before the ceremony? Aurora, I'm not a fast reader like you. You can't ignore me all day, leave me alone to face your mother, and then barge in here to tell me to read a gazillion books in less than two weeks."

She covers her hand with her mouth as she laughs. "Em, don't be silly. I haven't been ignoring you. I had to attend a birthday picnic with one of my ladies. Didn't Noraya bring you my message?"

I cross my arms, but I'm starting to feel silly now. I couldn't help feeling hurt at being excluded from the picnic Roarke mentioned, but if it wasn't Aurora's event—if it was someone else's birthday—then of course it had nothing to do with me. "No, Noraya didn't tell me anything," I say quietly.

"Well, that's very strange. And you know I haven't given you anywhere *near* a gazillion books. You should be able to finish them in a few days. Start tonight. Keep reading late if you have to."

"Aurora, that's—"

"It's important, that's what it is." There is no merriment in her tone, no sparkle of laughter in her eyes. "Our world can be a cold place to those who don't fit in, Em. You want to survive it, don't you?"

"Of course." I lower my hands to my sides. "Why are you being so—"

"Good. If you come across anything you don't understand, I'll happily explain things to you. Perhaps we can go to the spa together tomorrow. I'll have the ladies there prepare some beauty treatments for us. You can tell me all about what you've read."

"Oh. There's a spa here?"

"Yes. We can go in the afternoon. Roarke told me you're visiting the shadow world again in the morning?"

I nod. If all goes well, I won't return to this palace. I won't have any beauty treatments, and I'll probably never see my new friend again. "Uh, yes. We can do the spa thing in the afternoon."

"Great. Unless you change your mind about seeing Roarke. Then we can do the spa in the morning."

I nod again, though I have no intention of changing my plans.

"Well, goodnight then. And happy reading." Aurora spins around, her skirt swishing around her ankles, and strides out with the same haughtiness with which she entered.

I look down at the couch where Bandit is curled up on a cushion, watching me through half-open eyes. "She's still being strange," I say to him. I return to the table and push the pile of books aside. I'll be gone tomorrow, so there's no point in reading any of them. I know what I'm going to say to Roarke tomorrow, but I still need to decide on how to command the guards who'll be in the shadow world with us. I brush the quill feather against my cheek as I ponder different commands.

Then I frown as I notice that the book on top of the newest pile is the same book that made Aurora gasp in horror the other night in the library. The book featuring graphic and gruesome deaths of historical figures. She said we'd definitely give this one a miss, but either she changed her mind, or she accidentally included it.

As I draw the book closer, I notice that none of the gold embossed words set into the dark cover are English. Aurora knows I haven't yet learned any foreign fae languages, so it must be an accident that this book is here. I flip it open and turn through the first few age-stained pages, each of which is filled with the same strange combination of letters and unfamiliar symbols.

I shut the book, but as I push it aside, I notice something: the smallest corner of a piece of paper sticking out between the pages. Paper that's newer and whiter than the aged pages above and below it. I slide the book toward me once more and open to the page with the corner of paper sticking out. The paper is a small square with a few hastily scrawled words on it. A scrawl I immediately identify as Aurora's handwriting.

I swear I didn't know about this.

My heart begins to patter again. I push the note aside and take a closer look at the page it was sitting on. Scribbled in between the lines of foreign words, I see partial sentences in English, as if Aurora didn't have time to translate everything properly.

From the ways of the witches … one of the few methods to separate magic from life essence … most subjects survive the spell despite all magic being removed … magic is transferred in its entirety to the recipient … spell relies on complete willingness … cannot under any circumstances be forced … recitation of the following words … used in conjunction with a blood spell, such as the union spell.

With my breaths coming fast now and my fingers shaking, I turn the page—and the words printed across it are words I recognize. Words I've been repeating for days. Words I will be whispering in private to Roarke once we've cut our hands, tattooed marks onto our fingers, and spoken the public words of the union ceremony spell. These are the words—so he's led me to believe—of our private vows. And thanks to Aurora, I can now read what they mean.

I come to you of my own free will,
with a willing heart and a willing mind,
to give you my power,
every part of my magic.
I hand it over in its entirety,
keeping nothing for myself.
My magic is yours.

I blink at the words for several moments, unable to move, barely able to breathe. "Ho-lee crap," I whisper. Then I shove the book away from me and stand so abruptly that my chair falls backwards. *No way*, my brain tells me. *No way, no way, no way.* Roarke wouldn't do something like this. He wants to rule beside me. He wants me to be queen of the shadow world.

Except … he doesn't.

My mind races as I put together the pieces of Roarke's plan. Now I understand why he's always emphasized the fact that he'll never force me into anything: because a *willing* subject is exactly what this spell requires. My hands curl into fists so tight my nails digs into my palms. Everything—*everything*—he's done has been about earning my trust, getting me onto his side. His gifts, his kindness and occasional flirting, even allowing Dash to stay so that I'd have a friend—it's all been part of luring me toward the moment where I *willingly* marry him while *unwittingly* hand over my magic.

Standing there in shocked silence, I arrive abruptly at another realization: Roarke was never going to heal Mom. Once my magic is his, he'll head straight for the shadow world, claim it as his own, and destroy anyone who tries to stop him or take that world away from him. Waking my mother and healing her mind won't come anywhere near his to-do list.

And what about Dash? Roarke would never have let him go. Is he a prisoner? Dead? And Aurora … was she telling the truth about not knowing Roarke's plans to use this spell? Or could she have known all along and suddenly had a change of heart? But Roarke is her brother. Why would she go behind his back and tell me about this spell? Is this information some kind of trap?

Bandit rubs against my legs again, in the form of a ginger cat this time. I bend and pick him up, hugging him so tightly I'm afraid I might hurt him. "I don't know what to do," I whisper into the hair along his back, so quietly that even I can barely hear my own voice.

A loud rap at the door makes me jump. "Emerson, my love?" Roarke's voice calls out.

I press my hand over my mouth to cover my gasp. Bandit tumbles from my arms, shifts into a bird, and swoops onto my shoulder. I look around, lost for a moment with no thought, no plan. Then I quickly return the fallen chair to its usual position, grab the offending book, and shove it under the cushion. "Emerson, are you in there?" Roarke asks. I hurry to the balcony doors. I open and close them as quietly as I can, the cold air hitting me immediately. As Bandit takes off and flies away, I swing my legs over the balustrade and begin climbing down.

PART III

violet

CHAPTER TWENTY-TWO

VIOLET LEANED BACK IN THE BOOTH, LIFTED HER TRUMPET-shaped glass of iced night, and took a sip. Ryn did the same with his tankard of ale. The two of them were doing their best to appear at ease, but it was tough in a tavern in the heart of Unseelie territory. Violet pulled her sleeves a little lower, making sure her wrist markings were covered. Things would turn south quickly if the patrons of this tavern discovered two guardians amongst their company, and she doubted anyone would give them a chance to explain their *ex*-guardian status.

Ryn lowered his tankard and leaned forward. "I don't understand why we can't find it," he said in a low voice. "We've been there before. Why is it hidden from us now?"

"It's been a long time since we were there," Violet reminded him. "The Unseelies have obviously upped the security around

their palace. Made it invisible to those who shouldn't be there."
She tapped her glass with her fingernails. "Calla will get in.
You know she will."

"And if the Unseelie Palace has some kind of Griffin Ability
detection spell over its entrance like the Guild does?" Ryn
asked. "She'll get herself caught while she's following those
guards. It won't matter that she's invisible. They'll know
someone's there."

Violet slouched a little lower in the booth, attempting to
look bored. Beneath the table, she kicked Ryn's foot. He was
going to bring attention to himself if he didn't start looking
more relaxed. "I very much doubt the Unseelies have that kind
of magic over their entrance," she said. "They're not bothered
by Griffin Abilities, remember? They *value* them, in fact. They
don't just want to use Em's power; they want her to be one of
them." News of the Unseelie Prince's betrothal to a Griffin
Gifted girl had reached the Guild soon after Dash's impromptu
decision to climb into an Unseelie carriage, and Perry had
passed the news on to Calla immediately. It confirmed Dash's
suspicion that the girl his mother had heard rumors about was
indeed Emerson. But it had now been four days since that
announcement, and Dash still hadn't returned with Emerson.

Ryn shook his head. "That poor girl. After everything she's
been through with her mother and that woman with the glass
magic and everyone hunting her for her Griffin Ability, now
she's being forced into a union with an Unseelie."

"And she's so young," Violet murmured. "Not even
eighteen yet."

"She never should have left the—our safe haven." Ryn's

252

hand clenched around the tankard. "Why was she so foolish? If she'd just stayed with us, we could have kept her safe."

Violet gave Ryn another kick under the table, and he finally leaned back and smoothed out his expression. "What's done is done," she said. "Once we've got Em back to safety, she can explain."

"Dash should have retrieved her by now. Why is it taking him so long?"

"Probably because he doesn't have Calla's ability to cast illusions," Violet pointed out. "He can't simply walk out of there with Em. It's a wonder he got into the palace in the first place."

"*If* he got in," Ryn reminded her. "We still don't know if something happened to him after he got into that Unseelie carriage."

Violet took another slow sip of her drink before answering, needing a few moments to mentally convince herself that nothing terrible had happened to Dash. "He's fine. I'm sure he's fine. He's a good guardian. Calla will get inside, she'll find him and Em, and all three of them will return safely to us."

"We should have gone with her," Ryn said. "Calla could easily have made all three of us invisible."

"Yes, but it would have been harder for her to cast any other illusion at the same time," Violet reminded him. They'd been over this repeatedly yesterday and this morning while planning for Calla to follow the first Unseelie guards she could find. "And we need to be available to respond to any other emergency Ana might inform us of. Now can you please stop being so anxious? I'm going to run out of reassuring things to say."

Across the table, Ryn gave her a small smile. "If *you* could stop being so anxious, I might be able to get past my own worry. But it's tough when I have to feel mine and yours."

Violet began tapping the side of her glass again, feeling guilty—as she always did—when her negative emotions ended up affecting Ryn. "I'm sorry. I thought I was doing a better job convincing myself not to be concerned. But despite my worry—" she reached across the table and placed her hand on his "—I do believe they'll be fine. Dash and Calla have escaped from dangerous situations before; they can do it again, with Em this time."

Ryn nodded. "On a slightly different topic," he said, "have you noticed how insistent Calla's been about staying involved with the search for Em? She was originally supposed to be with Chase today to stop that heist in Paris, but she asked Darius to go in her place."

"Yes. I did notice that," Violet said, leaning back again. "I wondered if maybe she bonded with Em more than I realized while Em was at our safe haven. But … I don't know. Em wasn't with us for very long."

"She's also been more distracted lately," Ryn continued. "And she's been leaving more often than usual without telling us where she's going. I think she's investigating something we don't know about."

"You're probably right. But she doesn't have to tell us everything, does she? Living with family, working with family …" Violet rubbed her finger over a droplet of condensation on the table. "Well, it can be difficult at times when everyone knows everything about you. I don't blame her for keeping some things from us. And she's been talking to Chase, at least. I've seen the two of them whispering together. So whatever's going on, she isn't dealing with it alone."

"True," Ryn said.

A shiver against the side of her leg alerted Violet to a message on her amber. She removed it from her pocket and kept the rectangular device beneath the edge of the table as she tapped its glossy surface. "Message from Perry," she said as her eyes darted across the words. "Hmm. Another glass attack on a group of guardians. Darn that woman. Oh, and this is important. The Guild's finally decided on a date for that big fancy ceremony they want to have while doing their veil restoration spell."

"Idiots," Ryn mutters. "Why are they making such a fuss about it?"

"Well, it is a big deal. It's been, what? Seventeen, eighteen years since it was torn?"

"Yes, but the Guild is practically asking for someone to come along and interfere. It would have been safer if they'd quietly done it already without any fanfare."

Violet sighed as she put her amber away. "It's happening in four days. Last time we spoke about it, Dash suggested we should be there, and now Perry's saying the same thing. I think they're right. We should hide there and keep watch. Just a few of us—you and me, anyone else who isn't busy at that time. In case your predictions come true and something does go wrong."

Ryn quirked an eyebrow. "You don't think they can handle things without our help?"

Violet rolled her eyes. "I wish they could, but they've been known to mess up before."

"They've been known to *spectacularly* mess up," Ryn said. "I believe that's the word you were looking for."

"I believe you're right," she said with a smile. "So, since we're doing nothing useful right now, we may as well plan how we're going to hide on that tiny piece of island that's left around the monument."

CHAPTER TWENTY-THREE

MY FEET HIT THE SNOW-COVERED GROUND OF A FLOWER-bed far below my balcony. I duck down immediately in case someone walking nearby heard me. With my heart still thrashing in my chest, I look around. I need to run. Not to run *away*—I haven't yet figured out how to escape—but to run the way Val and I used to. As fast as possible, leaping and climbing and somersaulting. Forgetting everything except the ground slamming beneath our feet, the rough sting of bricks and the cold bite of metal against our hands. The exhilaration of successfully making it from point A to point B faster than the previous time.

I can't do that here. These gardens don't contain the right kinds of obstacles, and my long coat would be a bit of a hindrance. But I can at least run. And if someone sees me—if someone catches me—I can tell them a story they'll have to believe: *I'm practicing parkour. You've seen me do it before, right? You've seen me showing Princess Aurora some of the jumps and falls? Why am I doing it in the middle of a freezing winter night, you ask? Well, one needs to train in all conditions, don't you think? You guards train in all conditions, don't you?*

After waiting another few moments to make sure no one's walking nearby, I straighten and take off immediately. My legs race faster and faster. My arms pump at my sides, and my coat whips at the air as it billows out behind me. I swerve between the rose bushes and around the queen's bower. I leap clear across one of the smaller pavilions and keep going. I run further from the palace than I've ever been before.

When my lungs begin to ache and my face is just about numb with cold, I finally come to a stop. Ahead of me is a circular section of paving—uncovered by snow, somehow— with a fountain at its center. Streams of water, flowing from a nymph's hands and mouth into the pool below, are frozen in place. I walk to the edge of the pool as I catch my breath. Bandit, still a bird, flits by and lands on my shoulder. He shifts into something small and furry and climbs down my arm and into the pocket of my coat. I close my eyes for a moment, wracking my muddled brain for the words to a spell that will keep me warm. When I eventually find the words, I hold my hand up over my head, speak the words in a quiet voice, and allow myself to relax a little as warmth blankets my body.

Then I sit beside the pool.

And I try to make sense of my situation.

I can't go through with this union. That much is clear. But

how do I get away from here with my life intact? And what about Dash? I recognize now that Roarke wouldn't simply let him leave, which means Dash is either a prisoner somewhere or he's dead. I bury my face in my hands as I shudder. *He can't be dead, he can't be dead*, I silently repeat. It's too awful to imagine him slaughtered in the same way that man in the cavern lost his life.

He isn't dead, I tell myself again, more firmly this time. Roarke may be cruel and hate all guardians, but he likes to take advantage of opportunities when they present themselves. He's aware that Dash knows far more than he should about the Griffin rebels. Roarke could use Dash to try to gain access to the rebels himself if he wants to get his hands on more Griffin Abilities. The more I think about this, the more I manage to convince myself that Dash must be alive. Where, though? I don't know the location of any prisons in this world. Dash could be thousands of miles away.

After sitting quietly for a while, staring across the frozen garden and coming no closer to deciding what to do, I sense my Griffin Ability replenishing. I push my sleeve back and look at the bracelet; the ruby is almost completely red. When my power is ready to be used again, I'll have to tell something to 'open,' which seems a useless command out here where there are no doors. I'll have to tell a frozen rosebud to open or something.

Feeling uncomfortable, I shift my legs into a different position. Bandit wriggles inside my pocket, then crawls out and sits on my knee. "How are we going to get out of here?" I whisper to him. His only response is a twitch of his tiny mouse ear. Then he shifts into a dragonfly-type creature with a tiny humanoid face and glowing wings. "Pretty," I murmur. He shifts again, flashing between several indistinguishable forms before becoming a dragon small enough to fit into my lap. "My new favorite form," I say to him with a smile. "I think it's incredible how you can—" A beat of silence passes as I realize what he's telling me. "A dragon. We can get away on a dragon!" Bandit coughs, and a spark escapes his mouth. "You're so clever," I tell him, running one finger along his smooth, scaly back.

But my excitement fades as I consider all the obstacles I'll need to pass in order to make this dragon plan succeed. I don't know how to open one of those elevators in the ground that would carry me to the bottom of the pit. I don't know how to unlock the room with the saddles and the staircase. I don't know the spell to remove the shield layer preventing each dragon from flying away. And I don't know if Imperia likes me enough to let me climb onto her back without Aurora or Phillyp around.

I check the ruby on my wrist again, then cast my eyes about for something I can open without drawing any attention to this area of the grounds. I wonder if there's any point in being careful, though. I'm so far from the palace now that I doubt anyone would notice if I told a hole to open in the ground, or a tree trunk to—

"Wait a minute," I murmur, interrupting my own thoughts. I can't open any doors out here, but what about door*ways*? Faerie paths doorways, to be more specific. I've heard repeatedly that faerie paths are inaccessible from most parts of this palace and its grounds, but Aurora was always referring to the kind of accessibility one would gain with a stylus. Perhaps, if I turn my thoughts toward the faerie paths when I say the word 'open,' a doorway will form.

Though I've still got another few minutes before I can use my Griffin Ability, I move Bandit off my lap and stand. A thrill sends blood pumping faster through my veins. This might actually work. I might escape the Unseelies tonight. Bandit becomes a tiny lizard and scurries up the edge of my coat. He climbs back into my pocket as I bounce up and down in anticipation.

And it's then that I hear an odd sound. A wail, almost. A person crying out. I stop bouncing and look around, but I don't see anyone. I walk slowly around the fountain, peering into the garden around me, seeing little more than glistening white snow.

Until I almost trip over something.

Looking down, I find a metal circle roughly the size of a manhole cover embedded in the paving. It has a hinge on one side, which is what I almost tripped over, and at its center is a sold metal ring. *A trapdoor?* I crouch down and take a closer look at the symbol stamped into the metal. It's a simple outline of two hands bound together at the wrists. I get onto my knees and lower my ear close to the cold metal. I hear another cry, and as I straighten, I remember something Aurora mentioned in passing. Something about Yokshin showing her his experiments in a prison. *Just the small one we have here*, she'd said.

My thoughts turn immediately to Dash. If he wasn't

allowed to leave, and he wasn't killed, then he could very likely be somewhere beneath this trapdoor. I hesitate for a moment, then pull my coat sleeve down over my hand and take hold of the metal ring. I pull gently, then a little harder. But the trapdoor doesn't budge. My survival instincts tell me to stay the hell away from this prison, but my concern for Dash keeps me frozen to the spot. I try the simple unlocking spell Aurora taught me, but that makes no difference either.

A powerful magical command, however, might force it to open.

I begin shaking my head as soon as the thought occurs to me. I stand and take a step away from the trapdoor. I can't use my Griffin Ability for this. I have to open the faerie paths instead. The word 'open'—this one ambiguous compulsion command I've been given—could be my only way out of here.

But what about Dash, my conscience prods. *You know he's probably down there. You can't leave him behind.*

"Dammit," I mutter. And then: "Wait." I blink as something that should have been obvious occurs to me: I can do *both*. It won't take much of my power to open a faerie paths doorway. I'll make sure to hang onto whatever power is left once I've given my 'open' command, and I'll use it to unlock the trapdoor. But then ... the faerie paths doorway won't stay open for long. It'll close if I don't have some part of my body keeping it open, which means I can't go beneath the trapdoor to find out if Dash is there. Or ... could I tell the doorway to remain open for a long time? For as long as it takes me to get back to it? Perhaps that would work, but if it requires a lot of magic, it might use up all my Griffin power in one go. Then

I'll just have to forget about the trapdoor and leave on my own.

And leave Dash behind, my conscience whispers.

But I don't know that for sure. Dash might be back at home, completely fine. I have no way of knowing where he is, and now I'm about to risk imprisoning myself beneath the ground.

No. I won't do it. I'm not a hero; I'm a *survivor*. That's what I've always been, and Dash knows it.

I turn my back on the trapdoor as I sense my Griffin magic simmering beneath the surface of my control. I can't waste this opportunity. I need to get back to Mom. She's always been my priority, and I need to find another way to help her now that the Unseelie plan has fallen through. If it turns out that Dash never made it home, I'll tell the Griffin rebels that he's probably here, and they can come and rescue him.

And you'll be putting even more lives in danger, which is exactly what you were trying to avoid when you came here.

I push my guilt aside and look at the ruby once more. The tiniest sliver—so thin I can barely see it—still needs to be filled. I watch it and wait. And wait. I imagine the faerie paths. I picture myself focusing intently on them as I give my one-word command.

Then I feel the tingling, the magic crawling up my spine, my voice preparing to change. I whip around and point at the trapdoor. "Open," I gasp before the horrible, selfish person that I am at my core can make me change my mind.

With a subdued grinding sound, the trapdoor slowly swings opens.

CHAPTER TWENTY-FOUR

I SHOULD HAVE CONCENTRATED HARDER, BUT I WAS SO caught up in the terrifying rush of *doing the right thing* that I completely forgot to rein in my Griffin magic. It escapes me all at once, leaving nothing behind. I shut my eyes for a moment and ball my hands into fists, but there's no point in regretting what I've done. I chose to open the trapdoor. Now I need to find out what's hidden beneath it.

I stare at the dark circle of space and the stairs that lead downward. An icy breeze drifts past the back of my neck, reminding me that I've lost my tenuous hold on the spell that was keeping me warm. I take a steadying breath and place my foot on the first step. There could be a hundred guards waiting at the bottom of these stairs. There could be all kinds of horrifying creatures or threatening magic. I try not to think of the many possibilities as I descend. The white glow of the moon and the snowy landscape filters down through the trap-door's opening, illuminating the steps ahead of me. But the further down I go, the dimmer the light becomes.

Finally, I reach the bottom. No guards step forward to seize me. No creatures leap out of the darkness to tear me to shreds. No unseen magical force knocks me to the ground. I venture further forward, looking all around. As my eyes become accustomed to the dull light, any lingering doubts I may have had about finding a prison down here vanish. But it's unlike any prison I've ever seen on TV. Large spheres of dark glass fill the vast space ahead of me, each one containing a single prisoner. Some spheres rest on the ground, while others hang in the air at different levels from vine-like ropes. Those on the ground seem to be placed roughly in lines, presumably so guards can patrol the uneven corridors of space between them.

With a shaky breath, I walk forward, the first row of spheres on my right, and the wall—partially covered in creeping vines—on my left. As I near the first prisoner, I begin to make out more details, like the open section of space on the side of each sphere, and the vertical bars of dark glass lining each open space. A flat surface forms the floor inside each sphere. In the first one, a woman lies on the floor, curled up and sleeping. She doesn't move as my footsteps pass her cell. Even when another howl echoes through the cavernous prison, she remains asleep.

I stride past each sphere as quickly and quietly as I can after checking to make sure I don't see Dash inside any of them. When I notice a male figure with dirty blond hair, I slow down, but as I get closer, I realize the color tangled in with the blond is more turquoise than green. He rolls over as I pass his sphere, confirming for me that he isn't Dash. His eyes meet mine, and he begins laughing. Crazed laughter that should send me scurrying away. But my attention is caught by the markings on his wrists: guardian markings.

"Emerson." My eyes snap back to his, a jolt of adrenalin passing through me at the sound of my own name leaving this stranger's cracked lips. "What a mess we've ... got ourselves into," he slurs. "And the irony. The irony!" he calls out before raspy laughter consumes him once more. "I thought I was ... doing the right thing for ... for once in my life, and look where it got me. Landed me ... right back ... at the mercy of an Unseelie prince."

"How do you—"

"Em?" It's a different voice this time, from the next sphere over. The voice I've been listening for since I descended the stairs.

"Dash!" I hurry to his cell and drop onto my knees. He's lying on his side, his arm stretched out toward me. Bruises mar both cheeks and one side of his neck, and thick stubble covers his jaw. "Are you okay? I'm so, so sorry. You were right about Roarke. He was never going to help me. And then I realized he would never have let you leave, and that you must be imprisoned somewhere, or ... or ..." *Or worse*, I whisper silently to myself. I push my hand through the bars, but I can't reach him. "Are you okay? Are you hurt? I mean, aside from the bruises."

"I'm ... okay." He pulls himself weakly toward the bars,

moving only a few inches before collapsing again. But his hand is close enough now. I can just reach his fingers.

"What did they do to you?"

"I feel … drunk. Sort of."

"What?"

"A potion. A drug. It makes us … weak and disoriented. And my magic. I try to reach for it … and it's almost there … and then it slides from my grasp." His eyelids lower. "Like water … slipping through my fingers."

"Dash. Hey. Wake up." I wrap my fingers around his and shake his hand.

"I'm awake," he mumbles. His eyes open, but he takes a moment to focus on me. "That's the problem. This potion … keeps me drowsy and weak … but it never lets me sleep."

"I'm sorry. That's horrible." He nods but doesn't answer. His eyes close once more. "Dash, what have they done to you? There are bruises all over you. That's … that's not normal for a faerie, right?"

In the next sphere over, the man laughs again. "Not normal," he says. "Definitely not normal. But normal for … for down here."

Dash shifts until he's lying on his back, staring upward. "Sometimes," he says in a weak voice, "they roll the spheres. Or make them swing … back and forth … from a great height." He rolls his head slowly from side to side. "We crash around inside our glass cells. But the glass never breaks. It batters us as our bodies are flung around … but we never die."

"Dash." I squeeze his hand tighter as unshed tears make my throat ache and guilt burns hot in my chest. Isn't this precisely the kind of thing I hoped to avoid when I decided to leave the Griffin rebels' home? "I'm very glad you're not dead. I'm going to get you out of here."

"That would be ... a sweet kind of ... karma indeed," the man next door murmurs. "I save her, and she saves me."

I frown at him before bending closer to Dash's cell. "Who is that man?" I ask in low tones. "How does he know me?"

"We talk ... the two of us ... when no one's around. I must have told him about you." With a great effort, Dash pulls himself up and leans against the glass. "His name is Zed."

"Zed," I repeat. "And how long has Zed been down here? Long enough to begin losing his mind?"

"I can hear you, you know," Zed says, rolling over and blinking until his eyes focus on me. "And no, I'm not the one who's ... lost my mind. That affliction belongs to ... someone else you care about."

I draw even further away from his sphere. Part of me wants to be angry with Dash for telling this stranger about me and my mother, but I can't be. I doubt anyone down here has much control over what they say. And I can't blame Dash for talking to this man when he would otherwise be completely alone. The sphere on his other side, I notice, is empty.

"Dash, we need to plan how we're going to get out of here. I can use my Griffin Ability to open this sphere, but it needs to replenish, and that will only happen tomorrow, late in the morning. And Roarke already knows something isn't right. He came to my room earlier tonight, but I ran before he could see me. He's probably wondering where I am, and if I don't return in the next few hours, he'll send guards out to search for me."

"Everything is ... such an effort," Dash says. "Speaking. Moving. Living."

"Hey," I say, louder than I intended, his words disturbing me than I'd like to admit. "Don't say things like that. That's just the potion talking. You do want to live, which is why you need to help me with our escape plan."

With his eyes closed, he nods. "Roarke doesn't know ... that you know about his prison. He won't look here first. We'll have ... some time."

"Okay. Yes. Hopefully. Then our next problem is that you're drugged and can't use your own magic."

"I can barely even ... move," he reminds me.

"True. So how long does it take for this potion to wear off? Because we're going to have to hide somewhere while that happens. And by the time you're able to move easily and use your magic, Roarke will know you're gone too. We're going to have to find a very good hiding place to wait in while my Griffin Ability recharges and your drugs wear off."

"There's lots of ... waiting ... in this plan," Zed says.

"Well, it isn't your escape plan, so you needn't worry about the details."

"You will ... help him too?" Dash says. "Can't leave him here. He's a guardian. He's ... my companion."

My first instinct is to reject this idea. It will be harder to escape with three of us than with two. But this man has become Dash's friend. I can't leave him behind. But then ... I look around at all the spheres. What about everyone else down here?

No. Stop. You can't go there, I instruct myself severely. I can't save everyone. And many of these people are probably criminals. They must have disobeyed the king in some way in order to have landed up here. If I try to rescue all of them, Dash and I will never get away. "Yes, okay, I'll get Zed out too."

"And what happens," Zed asks, "after all the waiting … and hiding? You know the faerie paths can't … be opened from here … right?"

"Yes, I know that. But my Griffin Ability is more powerful than ordinary magic. I can tell the paths to open a doorway for us, and it should work."

"Don't know … about that," Dash says. "Powerful spells exist … over both royal courts … to prevent access to the paths."

"And you don't think my magic is powerful enough to overcome these spells?"

Dash shrugs. Apparently any more of an answer than that is too much effort in his current state.

"Well, we have to try it," I tell him, "because that's the only escape I can think of. Well, other than stealing a dragon or two and flying out of here, but we're a lot more likely to get caught that way."

Dash nods. "Okay. We'll try … the paths." His eyes slowly close once more. "And what about now?"

"Now …" I wrap my free hand around one of the bars. "I think the best thing for me to do is go back to my room." It's the *last* thing I want to do, but I made my decision when I chose to open the trapdoor instead of the faerie paths. I won't be escaping tonight. "I need to make sure Roarke thinks everything is fine," I continue. "Then I'll sneak away early in the morning before he comes to my room to compel me."

"Don't come until ... mid-morning," Zed says. "You'll miss the guards that way."

I frown at him. "How do you have any idea what time of day or night it is down here?"

"I've been here ... long enough. The guards talk. I listen. They come ... straight after their breakfast."

"Okay. All right." I squeeze Dash's hand, then let go and push myself to my feet. "I'll see you tomorrow." I watch him for another few moments before turning away.

"I'm sorry I ... failed you," he says.

I pause, then slowly swivel around to face him. "What do you mean? This is all *my* fault, remember? I chose to come here. I put myself in this mess, which means I put you in this mess too. *I'm* the one who failed, not you."

"It's been my ... responsibility ... for years. Checking in on you."

"But that assignment—mission—whatever you call it—ended when you brought me to this world. You were done looking out for me." I crouch down and take his hand once more. "Dash, you don't owe me anything. I mean it. I'm the one who owes you. So I'm going to make sure you get out of here alive."

"Does that mean," he asks, "that once this is over ... we can put the cliff thing behind us?"

It takes me a few seconds to remember what he's talking about, and then a smile breaks out across my face. "Consider it far behind us already."

He grips my hand with a little more strength than before. "Looks like you might get to be a hero after all."

I shake my head, but my smile is still in place. "I'm not saving the world, Dash. Only you." I stand and cast a glance at Zed. "Well, and your friend. But that's it. I'm not going anywhere near your hero territory."

I stride quietly past the spheres and back up the stairs, pausing near the top and listening before climbing the final few steps up to the frozen pool. I don't take a straight line back to the palace. Instead, I run a little to the right before turning toward the glowing golden lights in the distance. If anyone stops me now, at least it won't look like I'm coming from the direction of the prison. I start running again, faster and faster, partly because I want to get back inside to the warmth of my bedroom as quickly as I can, and partly because I may need to convince someone I was out here practicing my running, climbing and somersaulting.

But I make it back to the palace without anyone stopping me. I consider letting myself in through one of the ground level doors and walking upstairs, but it's faster to climb. I step back and look up to make sure I'm aiming for the correct balcony, then begin my ascent. It's late—past midnight, I'm sure—so most curtains are closed and no one looks outside as I climb past windows. As I step into my sitting room and silently shut the balcony door behind me, I breathe out a long sigh. I remove Bandit from my pocket and set him down on the table amongst the papers and books that appear to have remained untouched in my absence.

"Emerson."

With a barely concealed gasp, I whip around, slapping my hand against my chest where my heart has already leaped into action.

In the doorway to my bedroom, his arms folded tightly over his chest, is Roarke.

CHAPTER TWENTY-FIVE

"JEEZ, ROARKE, YOU NEARLY GAVE ME A HEART ATTACK." I lower my hand to my side, but my heart continues to race along at a panicky pace.

"Where were you?" His expression holds no hint of a smile, and his tone is deadly serious.

"Oh, just doing a little parkour practice." I shrug out of my coat, leave it lying over the back of a chair, and sit down to pull my shoes off. It's easier to appear relaxed and unconcerned if I keep my hands busy. "You know, the stuff I've been showing Aurora. Running and climbing walls and all that."

"In the middle of the night? In winter?"

"Yes." I look up. "My friend and I used to practice at night all the time. Okay, so we didn't do it in winter. It was too cold. But my days here have become so busy. If I want to keep practiceing, I need to do it at night." I push my shoes aside and cross one leg over the other. "Besides, it gave me a reason to practice that spell that keeps my body warm. I'm getting better at it."

Roarke walks slowly toward me, each step a silent threat. "Do you expect me to believe that? Do you expect me to believe you weren't snooping around, trying to find something *locked* to use your Griffin Ability on?"

I allow all the hurt and horror I felt when reading the witch spell to become evident in my expression. "Are you serious? I thought you trusted me."

"I'm finding it a little difficult right now after you vanished from the room you're supposed to be in every—"

"Oh, *come on*. You keep going on about how you'd never force me into anything, that this is my home now, and that I'm almost a member of your family—and then you tell me that I'm expected to remain in my bedroom every night like a prisoner? That makes no sense. And *you're* the one who decided to compel me to say the word 'open.' I didn't ask for that. And I'm far too afraid of your father to go looking for something that's locked and shouldn't be opened."

"Then what did you use your Griffin Ability on tonight? And don't try to tell me it hasn't happened yet." His gaze moves down to my wrist, where the bracelet is peeking out below the edge of my sleeve. "I can see from the ruby that you've used your power already. It has barely any color in it."

"A flower," I tell him, my voice raised in fake anger. "I used it on a flower, okay? I thought I was being clever, actually, since I was outside and there were no doors to open. I thought I'd just end up wasting the power, directing it nowhere, and then I saw a flower. A closed rosebud. So I looked at it and told it to open, and it did."

Several moments of uncomfortable silence pass as Roarke's eyes bore angrily into mine while I stare defiantly back. "A flower?" he says eventually.

"Yes. A flower." I cross my arms over my chest and direct a frown at the floor between us, hoping Roarke can tell just how much he's hurt his betrothed's feelings by accusing her of lying. "I would happily have told you all about it if you'd just asked instead of accusing me of sneaking around."

After another few moments of staring, he turns away from me without responding. I shouldn't be able to see his expression, but he's facing the mirror above the mantelpiece. In the mirror's reflection, for just a moment, I see his face scrunch up with fierce and terrifying fury. He bares his teeth as his fists clench briefly at his sides. Then he closes his eyes, breathes in deeply, and his anger is replaced by a blank expression.

I would have been utterly confused if I'd witnessed this yesterday. Now, I know better. Roarke's patience is nothing but a ruse, and clearly he's having a hard time reining his anger in right now. How frustrating it must be for him to play the kind yet cautious fiancé when all he wants to do is consume my magic and make it his. How difficult—and yet absolutely necessary—if he's hoping for me to come willingly to him.

"I'm so sorry," he says as he turns back to me, his expression soft now. "I messed up."

Damn right, I want to say. *You're supposed to be wooing me into total compliance, and instead you've upset me and made me doubt that you trust me.*

"I just … I couldn't find you," he continues, "and I was worried that … that maybe you'd taken advantage of me. That maybe you've been lying to me all this time. And I've …" He takes in a deep breath, steeling himself to reveal something. "I've come to care for you more than I thought I would in this short space of time. It hurt to think that you might have betrayed my trust. It hurt a lot more than I expected."

I almost congratulate him on coming up with a great explanation for his anger. If I didn't know the truth, I might almost believe him. "I … I don't really know what to say to that."

"You don't feel the same way?"

It would be easy to say that of course I do, but I can't push this too far or he'll know for sure I'm lying. "I … okay, look. We both know that we're only going through with this union because we'll each get something out of it. Neither of us started out looking for love or anything soppy like that. But … I …" I wish that I could blush on demand. I wish I could look as shy and embarrassed as I'm pretending to be. I glance down, then peek up at him between my lashes. "I do think I actually like you. I expected to hate you, but … but I don't. And the shadow world … I'll admit that it's still a little scary with all the ink-shades, but it's exciting too. I can't wait to see what it will all look like when we've finished building."

Roarke's mouth spreads slowly into a smile. Then, without warning, he closes the distance between us. His hands are gripping my arms, and his lips are pressed to mine, moving hungrily against them. I'm a solid statue, too shocked to move. But I have to give him credit for this. His acting is far better than mine. He seems totally into this kiss, when all I want to do his shove him far away from me. But that isn't the way to play this game. So I try to get into it. I press a little closer to him, place my arms around him, and tell myself to imagine I'm kissing someone else. Someone I might actually enjoy kissing. But it's been a while since I had a crush on anyone, so I can't picture any faces except brief glimpses of hunky celebrities who mean nothing to me. Then Dash's smirking face takes its place at the front of my imagination—which is *super* weird, so I quickly force that thought aside.

"Lady Emerson, are you—Oh, goodness, I'm so sorry."

At the sound of Clarina's voice, I disentangle myself from Roarke. "It's—it's fine," I say with an embarrassed laugh. Fortunately, I'm not the only one feeling awkward in this moment. Clarina's standing in the main doorway to my suite, her gaze pointed firmly away from us and her cheeks turning pink. "We shouldn't—before the union … I mean, it isn't appropriate, is it?" I don't know nearly enough about the customs of this world to know what's appropriate and what isn't, but I'm very much hoping people are more conservative here than in the human world. I might be able to fake a kiss, but I don't think I can fake any more than that.

"Don't worry, my love," Roarke says, taking my hand and running his thumb along my skin. "I don't have any inappropriate intentions."

Right. Except for the intention to steal all my magic. "Okay, well … then I'll see you tomorrow?"

"Yes." He kisses my hand. "I would love it if you'd join me for breakfast in the morning."

"Oh. Um. I was going to have breakfast with Aurora. We have some, uh, girl things to chat about." Hopefully that'll buy me an extra hour or so before anyone comes looking for me.

"Well, I'll see you after breakfast then." He lowers his voice so Clarina can't hear. "We can decide what to build next for our new home."

I watch him brush past Clarina and leave my suite. Without looking at me, she tells me in as few words as possible that she's relieved to see nothing happened to me while I was missing this evening. Then she hurries away before I can ask her how long it took for Roarke to start telling people I was 'missing.'

Finally alone again, I change into pajamas, gather up every spell book I can find in my suite, and climb into bed. I spread the books around me and begin paging through them one at a time. I should be sleeping, but I'm hoping to find some sort of invisibility spell so I can easily hide in the garden tomorrow. I remember Calla concealing us with invisibility when she, Violet and Ryn first rescued me, but she used her Griffin Ability for that, so perhaps invisibility isn't possible with normal magic.

After going through almost all my books and finding nothing, I eventually turn, in desperation, to a book that details some of the less pleasant Unseelie rituals. Among other things, it talks about methods to gain extra power. Certain methods that the Unseelies apparently share with the witches. Finally, I come across a spell that seems useful. It won't make me invisible, but it will help me to be inconspicuous by detecting my surroundings and reflecting them back on me. A form of camouflage, I suppose. I repeat the words over and over in my head until I've memorized them. Then I come to the final instruction, which tells me that I need a 'sacrifice' from my surroundings. This sacrifice will form a bond between me and my environment for as long as I'm holding the spell in my mind.

The word 'sacrifice' makes me feel immediately uncomfortable, as does the word 'living,' which is written in parentheses beside this last instruction. A living sacrifice doesn't sound good at all. I look around, but the only other living thing in my bedroom is Bandit, and there's no way in hell I'm sacrificing him. I wonder if the garden counts as the same environment as my bedroom. How does the spell know if this 'sacrifice' comes from the area I'm in or some other area? Then again, how does my Griffin Ability know exactly who or what I'm referring to when I give an instruction?

Magic makes no sense.

I flop back onto my pillows, about to give up on this camouflage thing. Then I blink at the lights on the ceiling. "Glow-bugs," I whisper. Glow-bugs are living creatures. Perhaps I can use one of them to form this magical bond with my environment. I climb out of bed, stand on the chair in the corner of the room, and unstick a glow-bug from the ceiling. The feeling of its squishy little body between my fingers makes me cringe. I drop it quickly onto the floor and kneel beside it. I can't see a head or legs, only a blob-like body filled with golden light. It's pretty, and I don't want to kill it, but it's essentially just an insect, right? If I was back in the human realm, I'd have no problem swatting a fly or squishing a cockroach. Why is it any different just because this bug has some magic in it?

I remove the heaviest book from the bed. Then I hold my breath and quickly press down on the glow-bug with the book while quietly muttering the spell. When it's done, I stand and look across the room into the mirror inside the open wardrobe door—and suck in a quick breath as I watch my skin and clothing take on the design of the carpet, the edge of the bed, the wall behind me, and a small section of the window.

A small hoot comes from the direction of the bed. Owl-formed Bandit watches me with enormous eyes. "Shh," I tell him. I look at my reflection again and realize the camouflage doesn't cover all of me. Patches of my body still appear normal. I look at the spell book again and re-read the line about the sacrifice. *A sacrifice of adequate size and magical composition.* What exactly does 'adequate' mean? Perhaps a glow-bug isn't big enough. I have no idea what creature I'll use when I'm in the garden tomorrow, but I'll face that hurdle when I get to it.

I release my mental hold on the spell and jump quickly back into bed. I'm torn between elation that I taught myself a new spell and queasiness that I had to kill a creature in the process. *You're going to fit in so well with us,* Aurora said to me only a few days ago. I turn over, ignore the sick feeling in the pit of my stomach, and try to fall asleep.

CHAPTER TWENTY-SIX

SLEEP MANAGES TO EVADE ME FOR MOST OF THE NIGHT, and my eyes are open as the first light of dawn peeks below the curtains drawn across my windows. I get up and witness, for the first time, the way winter melts into the ground and gives way to a fresh and vibrant spring morning.

After admiring the one and only sunrise I ever hope to see from this palace, I cross my room to the wardrobe and dig through it in search of an outfit that might possibly be considered comfortable. Something similar to the pants, shirt and ringmaster coat combo Clarina laid out yesterday, since that proved to be easy enough to run in. I'd prefer to go without the coat—in a few hours it'll be far too warm to wear one, and it might get in the way if I need to run—but I'd be conspicuous without it. According to Clarina, this kind of outfit isn't considered formal enough without the coat. She'd put me in a dress if she knew I planned to be outside any later than mid-morning, but a dress is out of the question. I definitely can't climb in one.

After choosing what I deem to be a suitable combination— black pants, a black shirt with gold ruffles down the front, and a bottle green coat with gold detailing—I dress quickly and slide the stylus I stole weeks ago from Aurora into one of the coat pockets. I've asked for my own stylus each time I've been taught a spell that requires one, but apparently Roarke wanted me to wait until he could gift me a special one. A stylus covered in diamonds and sapphires, or something outrageously unnecessary like that. I know it was only an excuse not to give me one before the union.

I pull on flexible pump-like shoes with no heel, then write a note to Clarina telling her I woke early and decided to return some books to the library before going to Aurora's chambers for breakfast. Hopefully she won't check my story with the guards who patrol the hallway outside my room. I wake Bandit, encourage him to shift into something smaller than a cat—he chooses a tiny hamster-type form with blue hair the same color as mine—and let him climb into one of my pockets. *Not* the same pocket as the stylus; I still don't trust that those things don't have residual magic in them, and I don't want Bandit to accidentally get hurt.

I'm about to walk onto the balcony when I remember the book of witch spells hidden beneath a cushion on one of the chairs. If Roarke finds it, he'll realize Aurora was the one who warned me about his plan. I don't know what he'd do to her if he discovered her betrayal, but I'd rather she didn't have to find out. The fire in the sitting room fireplace has long since gone out, but I stride across the room to it, place the book onto the ash, and add another few pieces of wood. I quietly say the spell to light a fire and step back as a single flame ignites the book's cover. I watch it burning for several moments before turning away.

Outside on the balcony, I look down and around to see if anyone's patrolling nearby. Then I swing my legs over the balustrade and begin to climb down. It's early enough that most of the occupants of the bedrooms I pass on my way down will hopefully still be asleep with their curtains drawn.

I hide in one of the flowerbeds while doing the camouflage spell, using a bird that Bandit catches for me while in one of his cat forms. The bird has a tiny crown of gold ridges atop its head, and its wings are almost transparent with flecks of gold. I feel so sick at having to kill this beautiful creature that I almost can't do it. But I remind myself that Dash will remain a tortured prisoner and probably end up dead if I get caught before I reach the prison.

The spell works. I push my nausea aside as my skin and clothes rapidly takes on the appearance of my surroundings. The dark earth, the green bushes and colorful flowers. The strangest part is looking down at myself as I stand and walk out of the flowerbed—my appearance continually changes so that I roughly blend in with whatever's around me.

Since I have to wait until mid-morning so I don't run into the guards, I take my time walking through the gardens. I look down often to make sure I'm still camouflaged, and I try to ignore the constant low-level anxiety twisting my insides into knots. *Everything will work out fine*, I tell myself repeatedly. When I reach the pool with the fountain—no longer frozen—I hide behind a nearby rosebush with blue flowers. I could probably release my hold on the camouflage spell, but I don't want to risk being seen. Besides, it doesn't feel like it's draining too much of my magic.

The longer I wait, the more anxious I become. The people I care about go around and around my head: Mom and Dash and the Griffin rebels who are probably trying to find their way into this court because Dash never returned home. My imagination shows me the worst things that could happen to everyone, and eventually I have to shut my eyes and tell my mind to go as blank as if someone were leading me through the faerie paths.

Except for the camouflage spell. I can't go blank on that. I open my eyes and look down at the pattern of grass across my hand. I'll focus on that instead.

By the time I hear footsteps, my back has begun to ache and my left leg has gone numb. I shrink further down as I peer between the leaves of the rose bush. A line of about ten guards marches toward the fountain. They come to a halt on the far side where the trapdoor is. The guard at the front leans forward with a stylus in his hand, but once he bends down with it, I can't see what he's doing, and I can't hear if he's saying anything.

I slowly roll my shoulders a few times, check the ruby on my wrist, and remind myself to be patient. I have to wait until the guards are gone and my Griffin Ability has fully restored itself. *Unless ...* I pause with my shoulders pulled back. What if I sneak down now? Right behind the guards? Then I don't have to use my Griffin Ability to open the trapdoor. I won't have to risk accidentally losing all my power in one command and then having to wait until late tonight before freeing Dash and Zed from their spheres.

I bite my lip as I watch the guards descend the stairs one at a time. How close can I risk getting to them? How well does this camouflage spell work? And what if the guard at the end of the line turns back to close the trapdoor?

But ... what if I can't let Dash and Zed out until tonight, and Roarke discovers where I am before then?

I don't give myself another second to think about it. I rise to my feet and tiptoe quietly across the grass. I make it to the pool seconds before the last guard steps down through the trapdoor. With one final glance at my feet to make sure I can't see anything more of them than a faint outline, I step silently through the trapdoor. I pause at the top of the staircase, waiting to see if the guard just ahead of me plans to turn around and close the trapdoor. But he continues descending without a glance behind him.

Holding my breath, I tiptoe down the staircase, shrinking into the shadows on one side when I reach the bottom. I don't dare venture any further into the vast underground chamber while all those guards are still present. They spread out, each heading in a different direction. Here and there, I notice several prison cell spheres slowly descending and disappearing amongst the many other spheres.

In the first row, a guard stops beside the sphere nearest to me. The prisoner inside—the woman who was curled up and sleeping yesterday—scrambles to the other side of her cell. But as the guard flicks his hand, she slides abruptly across the floor and slams against the bars with a groan. The guard crouches down, and I notice he's holding a bottle in one hand. He dips a stylus into the bottle, then reaches through the bars for the woman's arm. He writes a few words across her skin before standing and moving on to the next sphere. Moments later, as the woman slumps against the bars, part of the floor within her sphere shimmers and ripples. A tray of food appears, and after staring at it for a while, she reaches out with a clumsy hand and drags the tray closer.

I wait as the guard performs the same spell on the next prisoner, and then the next. From what I can see down another row of spheres, it looks like the other guards are doing the same thing. By the time the lowered prison orbs rise into the air again and the guards begin marching back toward the stairs, the woman I've been watching has finished eating and her tray has vanished.

I crouch down and keep my head lowered as the guards *clomp, clomp, clomp* their way back up the staircase. Finally, when the trapdoor is closed and I'm certain they're gone, I let go of the camouflage spell I've been hanging onto for hours. I straighten slowly and peer up the stairs once more. Then I tiptoe past the spheres, not wanting to attract the attention of any prisoners in case they start calling out to me and their cries become audible outside the prison.

I run the last few paces toward Dash's cell and crouch down beside his bars. He's lying on his side, his eyes half-closed, one hand wrapped loosely around a bar. "Hey," I whisper to him as I touch his hand. "Ready to get on with this escape thing?"

His gaze shifts to me. He gives me a weak smile. "You made it. No one … saw you?"

"No. I found some sort of camouflage spell in a book last night." I pause, looking hurriedly over my shoulder at the sound of a voice. But it's only a moan from one of the other spheres. "A weird spell that required a sacrifice," I continue, "but I managed to do it."

Dash pushes himself into a sitting position, his eyes widening more than I would have thought possible given his drugged state. "A sacrifice?"

"Just an animal. Not a person, obviously." I push my sleeve back to examine the color of the ruby.

"Em, no," he moans. "You shouldn't have … done that. Especially not here. You don't want to … end up … magically bound … to this court."

"What?" My gaze snaps up. "Is that possible?"

"You're fine," Zed says from the neighboring sphere. I didn't realize he was paying attention to us. "It takes … a lot … to sell one's soul. You're not even … close."

"Still … isn't right," Dash says.

"It was just a bird." Which is what I told myself repeatedly before twisting the poor thing's neck, and it didn't help me feel better at all.

"It isn't *right*, Em," Dash repeats.

"Look, I didn't want to, okay?" I hiss. "It was horrible. But I didn't have many options. I don't have thousands of spells at my fingertips. I'm kinda new to this magic thing, remember? I needed a way to get back to you guys unseen, and that spell was all I could find."

Dash says nothing more. He simply watches me through half-open eyes as he leans against the bars.

I let out a long breath. "I'm sorry. I didn't mean to snap. I just ... feel horrible about the bird thing, so it doesn't help when you keep pointing out that it's wrong."

"Sorry," he whispers. He gestures to my bracelet. "How long?"

"Another hour or two." I squint at the ruby. "An hour and a half, maybe. I can't tell exactly. How long until the magic-impairing drug wears off? I assume that's what the guards were doing?" I add. "When they were writing on prisoners' arms?"

"Yes," Zed answers. "They do it ... twice a day. So it obviously ... doesn't ..."

"Doesn't last a full day," I finish for him. I know they can't help it, but I'm finding it difficult not to get frustrated with their slow, slurred speech. "Okay. That's good."

"Some of the others," Zed says, "are wearing metal ... that blocks magic. A bangle ... a ring ..." He leans back against the curved edge of his sphere. "Seems the Unseelies have ... run out ... of those. This drunken drug thing ... is new."

"It's better," Dash adds. "The metal ... can't easily be removed."

"Okay. So by this evening, you two should be able to move around and use magic?"

Dash nods, then groans and slowly lowers his head to the floor beside the bars. "It gets worse ... now. Straight after ... they write ... on us."

"Spinning," Zed murmurs. As I watch, he slides slowly to the floor of his cell. "Spinning ... spinning ..."

"My magic is ... so close ... yet so far." Dash's hand inches slowly across the floor, as if he's trying to grasp something. "I can't ... touch it ... can never ... touch it."

As disturbing as it is to see him like this, I need to believe that he'll be fine. "Hey, don't worry about it. You'll get your magic back soon. You'll be totally normal by tonight." I scoot closer to his sphere and lean my back against the bars. I pull my knees up, and as Dash and Zed become silent, I prepare myself for yet more waiting. I assure myself once again that everything will be all right in the end. Dash won't remain confused and lethargic forever. We'll both get out of here. We'll return safely to the Griffin rebels. I'll get back to Mom. I'll put this disastrous Unseelie episode behind me and somehow—*somehow*—I'll figure out how to help her.

CHAPTER TWENTY-SEVEN

Some time later, Bandit begins squirming in my pocket. I straighten my legs so he can climb out. In his blue hamster form, he sniffs around on the floor, scurrying further away from me as he explores his strange new surroundings. I have to remind myself—when I start worrying that he might end up lost—that he's successfully followed me across the fae realm numerous times, usually without my knowledge. I don't think I need to be concerned about him.

As I lift my arm to check the ruby, Dash moves and opens his eyes. He holds onto the bars and manages to pull himself up until he's leaning sideways against them. "Hey," I say to him. "I thought maybe you were sleeping." I shift around until I'm also leaning my shoulder against the bars.

He shakes his head. "Can't. I sort of doze, but never sleep."

"Your words sound less slurred now."

"Whispering helps, I think. Takes less effort. My magic is still just out of reach, though."

"Sorry about that. It won't be for much longer, at least."

He nods and closes his eyes for a moment. "I must look terrible, huh?"

"Nah, not too bad." I raise my hand and run my thumb briefly along his stubbled jaw. "You've got that rugged look going on. Some girls dig that. The *smell*, on the other hand ..." I pinch my nose before chuckling. "Well, that's another story."

He grimaces. "Yeah. Lack of showers down here. Not impressed with the ... quality of this ... establishment."

A moment of quiet passes before I ask, "How did you end up in this fine establishment anyway? I was told you were allowed to return home. A guard even saw you saying goodbye to Roarke and climbing into one of the carriages, but that carriage obviously didn't take you home."

"No. Four guards were in the carriage with me. They attacked and stunned me almost immediately. I was completely knocked out until I woke up here. Where are we, exactly?"

"Beneath the gardens. Quite far from the palace. I was running last night. Not trying to get away, just ... I needed to run." I look down at my hands in my lap. "I discovered what Roarke plans to do with me, and I just needed to get out of that palace and figure things out. That's when I found the trapdoor and used my Griffin magic to open it."

Dash narrows his eyes. "What does Roarke plan to do with you?"

"He ..." I bite my lip, then tell him everything about the

witch spell and the words I've been practicing as part of my vows. The words that turned out to have absolutely nothing to do with a union.

"Bastard," Dash breathes when I'm finished.

I look up in surprise. "Bastard? Really? I doubt your mother would approve of that kind of language."

"He wants to *possess your magic*, Em. All of it. I can't even … imagine … how you'll survive that."

I lift one shoulder uncertainly. "Apparently this spell is one of the few ways a person can survive having their magic removed."

"But … your magic is part of … what keeps you alive. What will you be without it? Some kind of … of shell?"

A shiver skitters down my spine. "We don't need to find out, because I'm not going through with the union or the witch spell. So, anyway." I try to brush off my fear. "Did Roarke come to see you? Did he say why he didn't just … kill you? I'm very glad he didn't, obviously," I rush to add. "I'm just wondering why he kept you alive."

Dash's half-open eyes stare past me. "He was here when I woke up. Said he plans to hand me over … to the Guild … and demand compensation for … a guardian getting involved in … Unseelie affairs without authorization. He'll also inform them that … that I know far more than I'm supposed to about … the Griffin rebels. Said he may as well get some entertainment out of … my inconvenient appearance at his court."

"Bastard," I mutter.

Dash hesitates, his green eyes refocusing on me. "Yeah, you're right. My mother wouldn't like that word."

I give him a small smile. "Even if I explain to her that it's appropriately applied in this case?"

"Hmm. She might understand. Just this once." He makes a weak attempt at a laugh, then adds, "You're actually not such a potty mouth anymore. You've improved since arriving in this world."

"You know, I never actually stopped to think about it until you pointed it out." I screw my face up in thought. "I think I remember my mom scolding me years ago when I was little for using bad language, but then I got to Chelsea's, and she didn't seem to care. In fact, she and Georgia used that kind of language all the time, so I ended up speaking that way too." I shrug. "So do most people in my world, I think. It isn't a big deal."

"It isn't a big deal for plenty of people in this world either." His voice is close to a whisper again, which seems to make it easier for him to speak. "My mom's the only reason I don't use bad language."

"The soap spell, yeah. I didn't believe you when you first mentioned it."

"Unfortunately for young fae all around the magic realm, that spell is very real."

I pull my knees up to my chest again and wrap my arms around them. "Your mom must be so worried about you."

He nods. "Probably. But ... she's my mom, and I'm a guardian. So she's always worried about me. And I'm sure she knows that Ryn or one of the others is looking for me. That should give her hope."

"Do you think they really are trying to get into the palace

grounds? Roarke said no one can see the palace unless they're in the company of an Unseelie guard."

"That doesn't mean they'll stop trying to find a way in. And not just for me, but for you too. They would never leave you in the clutches of the Unseelies once they discovered you were here."

I cover my face with my hands, guilt gnawing at me again. "This wasn't supposed to happen, Dash. They were supposed to give up on me and move on to helping someone else. Because, you know, they hardly know me and I've only caused them trouble since I met them. Now they've wasted their time and resources on me. I can't imagine how angry they'll be when you and I finally get back to them."

"Okay, your first mistake," Dash says, "was assuming they'd give up on you."

I lower my hands and look at him. "You mean my first mistake was assuming everyone's as selfish as I am?"

"Em. If you were as selfish as you think you are, you would have left without me."

I look away from his half-drugged gaze and decide not to tell him I almost did leave without him. That most certainly would have given Ryn, Violet and the others a good enough reason to be angry with me. I doubt they would …

Hang on. My thoughts take a detour as something occurs to me. "Hey, Dash," I say to him. "I thought the protective enchantment on the rebels' safe place kept us from thinking or speaking of it to anyone who doesn't already know about it."

"Yes. Something like that."

"But how do they take anyone new there? How did they

take *me* there? How could they think of it when I was with them?"

"The leaders—Ryn and Vi, Chase and Calla, a few of the others—had a different enchanted place on them. They can't speak about the place ... and they can't think exactly of it ... but they can think of ... the area? I don't know the specifics, but they can think of ... the surrounding area ... and once they get there, they can see the actual place. Something like that."

"Sounds complicated."

"Yeah. I guess it needs to be. To keep everyone safe." His gaze moves down. "How long now? For your Griffin Ability, I mean."

"Soon." I push back my sleeve and squint at the ruby. "Half an hour, maybe."

"Okay."

Another few minutes pass with only the occasional sound of a groan or cry reaching us. Then a few repeated thumps, as if someone's banging against the inside of their sphere, and then the muffled sound of crying. As the crying fades once more to silence, Dash asks, "How are you feeling about Chelsea and Georgia?"

Mild nausea lurches in my stomach the way it always does when I think of my aunt and cousin. No one else has asked about them since I told Roarke what happened, but that doesn't mean they haven't been on my mind. "I still don't really know what I should be feeling," I admit. "Whenever I think of them, it's with regret and guilt. Like I should have made more of an effort with them while they were alive.

Maybe I would have discovered they weren't as awful as they always came across. And I should never have let Ada anywhere near their home."

"You didn't exactly have a choice about Ada showing up in Stanmeade. We don't know how she knew you were there."

"Yeah, I know." I nod slowly. "I know it wasn't directly my fault. But still … it all happened because Ada came after me."

Dash hangs onto the bars and pulls himself a little straighter. "Remember I told you about my classmate and mentor who died?"

"Um, yes. I think so."

"Did I tell you it was my fault?"

I hesitate, casting my mind back. "No. I think I'd remember if you mentioned it being your fault."

"It was supposed to be a paired assignment with supervision. Meaning my classmate and I would do it together while a mentor observed. Just in case something went wrong and … we needed help. That's how it works in … the early years of training. Groups, pairs, and a more experienced guardian observing and … getting involved if necessary." He pauses to take in a deep breath. Even whispering, it's clearly still an effort for him to speak. "On the day we were supposed to do this paired assignment, I ended up injured from a training session. My leg hadn't healed yet, so the Guild gave my mentor and classmate a different assignment. Something they thought suitable for one trainee. But it went horribly wrong … and both my classmate and mentor were killed."

"Oh, that's horrible. I'm so sorry." I swallow, then cautiously add, "But surely you can't be telling me you felt like that was your fault? It isn't the same as what happened with Chelsea and Georgia. I basically led Ada to their doorstep. But you couldn't help being injured."

"True. I couldn't. But if we'd all gone on our original assignment together ... maybe they would have lived."

"And maybe they wouldn't have. Maybe your paired assignment would have gone wrong too and they would have died anyway."

"And maybe Chelsea and Georgia ... would have died anyway. A car accident, or ... some other random tragedy."

I look away from him and shake my head. I press my fingers against my temples. "This is a pointless discussion."

"Just like it's pointless blaming yourself for ... something you didn't do. I know, because I had to figure that out for myself. So I could move on." He takes hold of my left hand and gently pulls it away from my face. "You'll figure it out too, Em."

"Maybe," I say quietly, lowering my right hand and wrapping it around my legs. My left hand rests on the floor of the sphere between two bars, still in Dash's grip. I don't pull it away. "But not yet. It doesn't feel right yet to just move on."

"Okay," he says. "That's okay."

"Thank you for telling me about your mentor and your friend. It must be difficult to talk about them."

"It's been a few years since ... since it happened. It's easier now to speak about them."

I lean my head against the bars as I watch him. "I don't think I ever asked you why you chose to be a guardian."

"Hmm. I don't think I ever wanted to be ... anything else.

298

I always liked all the stories my dad told me of the heroic things he did … and the lives he'd saved. I wanted to be just like him. My mother thought … it was a horrible idea. She'd been afraid for years that she might lose him … and now she'd have to be afraid of losing me too. I understood where she was coming from, but … I chose this life anyway. And I've never regretted it. There are lives that might not have been saved if … if I wasn't there to save them."

A few months ago, I would have rolled my eyes at that last comment. But there's no trace of cockiness in Dash's tone. He's simply stating a fact. "And just think," I add with a smile, "of all the pretty young ladies who would have been deprived of swooning over their handsome, heroic rescuer if you hadn't become a guardian."

He manages a quiet laugh. "Exactly. And I wouldn't have met you."

My smile slips away. "Yeah. You wouldn't be locked in a prison right now."

"Ah, well." He looks away as he shrugs. "It's worth it."

Something stirs deep inside me. Something warm and weirdly pleasant. Something I recognize immediately and tell myself it's ridiculous to be feeling right now. "You don't actually mean that, do you?" I say to Dash.

He frowns as he continues staring into the distance. "I wasn't really thinking about what I was saying, but …" He refocuses on me. His hand moves a little over mine, his fingers brushing my skin before becoming still again. "But I think I did mean it. I can't imagine … not knowing you. You've been part of my life for years. A mystery I had no way … of solving, but a mystery I … couldn't stop thinking about. And you looked so beautiful … at the ball. I wish I could have … danced longer with you."

A shiver unrelated to cold or fear races up my arms and neck. I can't help remembering what Aurora said about Dash: *Nobody cares that much. Not unless they're motivated by love.* I argued then that Dash was motivated by his need to be a hero, and I'm still convinced this has nothing to do with love. That drug potion that was written onto his arm earlier probably has a lot to do with what he just said. What it doesn't explain is why *I'm* suddenly feeling like a hundred butterfly wings are fluttering against the inside of my stomach, but that's—

"Hey," Zed groans. He pushes himself up just enough to turn his head and look our way. "Now … is definitely … not the time."

I narrow my eyes at him. "Not the time for—"

"Also … your mother would say … you're too young for a boyfriend, Emerson."

"I—Excuse me?" Fiery flames of embarrassment lick their way up my neck. I pull my hand away from Dash's and wrap it around my legs. "That is *not* what's happening right now. And you have no idea what my mother would say."

"Just trying to … help you avoid distractions," he mumbles. "Don't want this escape attempt going sideways."

I return my gaze to Dash and find him laughing so quietly it's little more than silent shaking. Hopefully he's laughing at himself and the unlikely notion that being locked up in this prison might be 'worth it' because he got to meet me. I clear my throat and look down at the ruby on my wrist. "Oh, hey, it's almost time."

"Good," Zed murmurs. "Guess I'd better … get myself ready." He grips the bars of his cell and pulls himself upright.

"What are you going to say when your power is ready?" Dash asks.

"Um …" I look back at forth between his sphere and Zed's. "Something like, 'Dash's sphere and Zed's sphere, open.' Sounds stupid, but it should work."

Dash nods. "Okay. And what about everyone else?"

With a sigh, I close my eyes. Why did he have to bring that up? I was hoping not to have to think about it again. I don't want to face the moral dilemma I have no answer to. "I don't know if I should do that, Dash. I'm sure some of these people don't deserve to be here, but most of them probably do. How do we distinguish the innocent from the guilty? And I don't know if it's even possible for me to open every sphere. If it requires too much power, I'll end up passing out."

Dash blinks. "Really? Has that happened?"

"Yes. I overexerted myself trying to do too much with one command. I think if I allowed my Griffin Ability to replenish multiple times without using it, I might be capable of doing more, but we don't have time for that now."

"But Em, you … you brought two people back from death. That must have taken … an enormous amount of power. Opening just two spheres shouldn't use … too much. I'm sure you can try to open more."

"And what if I'm freeing criminals?"

"If they're the king's enemies, they're probably on our side."

301

"True," I admit, "but how do I know who should be freed and who shouldn't?"

"We can't save everyone," Zed says. "It isn't possible. They'll—" He cuts himself off, a look of horror slowing spreading across his face. Then he lets out a bitter laugh, staring wistfully into the distance. "Finally, I understand. If only I'd ... understood years ago. I could have ... made them understand too. None of this would have happened." He looks at me. "None of it."

I stare back, completely confused. "Um ..."

"We can't leave innocent people behind," Dash presses, pulling my attention away from Zed.

"Then you can tell your Guild about it when you're safely back home. They'll fix this. That's their job, isn't it? To right these kinds of wrongs."

Zed laughs again. "All those years ago ... they said the same thing. We'll come back for you ... they said. And they never did."

"Hey, I thought you were on my side for this one," I tell him. "We can't save everyone, remember?"

He nods. "We can't save everyone."

"Not everyone," Dash agrees, "but some."

"And then what, Dash? Let's say I let a whole bunch of people free. And then let's say it turns out I actually can't open the faerie paths. Like, I run out of power, or it isn't possible to open them with a Griffin Ability, or something like that. Then what happens to all the people I've freed? They can't use their magic, and the guards are going to come rushing down here to lock them away again. Some of them will fight back, and they

302

might end up dead. Which means *more* people I'm indirectly responsible for killing. I don't want that on my conscience, Dash. Maybe you think I'm a selfish coward for not wanting to free anyone else—and that's probably partly true—but I also don't want people to end up dead because we don't have a proper plan for getting everyone out of here. So I'm only freeing the two of you. We'll escape this court, and you can tell the Guild about everyone down here. *They* can come and investigate."

Dash shakes his head. "It doesn't work ... that way. The Guild can't simply barge in. There's ... a balance. They'd risk starting a war between the courts."

"They don't have to do any barging, okay? They can just ask for details of who's imprisoned and why. Surely they have a right to do that?"

"Maybe, but the Unseelies aren't going to like it."

"Then your precious Guild is just going to have to upset the balance. If loads of people are unjustly imprisoned here, then maybe it's worth starting a war over."

"This ..." Zed says, pointing weakly at me. "This is what we needed ... all those years ago. Someone willing to start ... a war for us. Someone who didn't choose to leave us in prison."

"I'm *agreeing* with you," Dash protests, his breathing even heavier now. "But I'm saying we should ... get everyone out *now*."

"I think he's still confused," I tell Dash. "Too drugged to make sense."

"I am making sense," Zed says, his eyes never leaving mine. "You'll see."

I turn back to Dash. "Please just trust me on this. My Griffin Ability has limits. I need to break open both your spheres, tell the drug potion to leave your systems, and then open the faerie paths. I don't think I can do all that *and* free everyone." I don't add that if any Griffin magic remains after those three commands, I should be able to hold onto it. If I do end up with some leftover power, then we can decide what to do with it.

Finally, Dash relents. "Okay. You know your power better than I do. When I'm back ... at the Guild ... I'll see what I can do about ... freeing these people."

I stand as I sense that shiver of power getting ready to radiate up my spine. I don't know how these spheres would normally open, but I picture the unbreakable glass bars cracking apart and falling away. As my power rushes to the surface, I halt it. It struggles to break free, but I manage to release it slowly as I speak. "These two spheres will open," I say, stepping back and looking first at Dash's round prison cell, and then at Zed's. My voice sounds both far away and right inside my head. "The drug potion will leave your bodies, and you'll have full access to your magic. And faerie paths," I add, turning and speaking to the air itself, "open a doorway."

I swing back around to face the spheres as I hear a crack. Then another crack. Dash's bars snap and tumble to the ground with a several clangs, followed almost immediately by the bars imprisoning Zed. Dash raises his hand, and sparks jump to life immediately, whizzing around his fingers. With a grin, and his eyes alight with life and energy, he climbs quickly from his prison cell and sweeps me into a brief, tight embrace.

A smile stretches my lips as I hug him back, then twist in his grip to look behind me.

The air ripples, distorting my view of the vine-covered wall beyond it. The ripples become waves, undulating repeatedly and violently, as if something is trying to rip through the air itself. My Griffin power begins to drain from my body. I grasp mentally at it, tugging it to a halt as my hands tighten into fists and my body tenses. Success. I can't quantify it, but I sense there's still power simmering beneath the surface of my control.

I relax my limbs and focus on the space in front of me, hopeful that a doorway is about to materialize.

But the seconds tick by, and nothing happens.

CHAPTER
TWENTY-EIGHT

"IT DIDN'T WORK," I SAY, MY SHOULDERS DROOPING AS IF A
weight is slowly crushing them.

"So it isn't possible after all," Dash says quietly.

"I don't understand. I obviously had no way of knowing if
it would work, but I really thought my Griffin Ability would
be powerful enough to access the paths. I mean, it doesn't take
much magic to open a doorway, right?" I turn back to face
Dash.

"It doesn't," he says. "Perhaps it would have worked if the
faerie paths were here to obey your command. But maybe they
don't exist here."

"I thought they existed everywhere."

He shakes his head. "I don't know, Em. Maybe the ancient
enchantments keeping them from being accessed in this part of

the world are so powerful that even your Griffin Ability can't mess with them."

"Emerson," Zed says. I look at him. He moves closer, but stops a few paces away from me. His gaze is intense as he watches me closely. "Thank you."

I wonder if it's disbelief I'm seeing on his face. Perhaps he doubted I would actually free him. "Um … sure. You're welcome."

"So," he says. "Dragons are the only way out, then?"

"You're free," a woman says from somewhere behind us. "How did you get free?"

I look back and see a woman in the sphere beyond the empty one next to Dash's sphere. She watches us with wide eyes, then scrambles to the front of her cell and grips the bars. "Let me out next, girl."

"I … I can't. I'm so sorry. My magic is finished." Which is a lie, of course, but I know we'll need the rest of my Griffin power to escape this palace. "The, uh, the spell I used—the ingredients—I only had enough for two cells."

"Liar!" she hisses. "I heard you. All you did was speak. You didn't apply any additional enchantment. If you could open their cells, you can open mine."

I back away, not wanting to face the guilt of leaving everyone else behind. "I can't. I'm so sorry." I glance around and see other faces watching us. Some visible in the gaps between the Dash and Zed's spheres, other hanging higher up. "Let's go," I mutter to Dash and Zed.

"Wait, please," the woman says, one hand reaching through the bars as her expression changes from suspicion to desperation. "I didn't mean to accuse you of anything. I've just been here for so long. Please help me. Please."

I shake my head. "I can't, but I'll be sending someone back for you."

Her face twists suddenly into a mask of rage. "Let. Me. Out," she hisses through her bared teeth. "LET ME OUT!"

I take another step back as fear weaves its way through my insides. "Why isn't she slow and sluggish like the two of you were?"

"I don't think they drugged her," Dash says.

"They didn't," Zed says. "See the metal band on her wrist? It blocks her magic. She can't access it, but she still has her ordinary strength. She isn't experiencing the fatigue we experienced."

"We need to leave before her screaming alerts the guards," I say, turning my back on the woman. We hurry toward the stairs, but her shrieks only grow louder.

"Don't you DARE walk away! I will KILL YOU, you little WHORE!"

"Whore? Jeez." I throw a glance over my shoulder and see her tugging on the bars of her cell, rocking wildly back and forth.

"I'll kill you, I'll kill you, I'll kill you!" she screeches.

"So how far away are the dragons?" Zed asks as we reach the stairs.

"On the other side of the palace."

"Wonderful," Dash mutters.

"But toward the left. So we don't have to get too close to

the palace itself. Hopefully we can make it there without being seen."

"That's the challenge," Zed says. "Everything in this place is guarded."

"I still have some Griffin power. I've been practicing holding onto it, and I managed to prevent it all from slipping away just now. Maybe I can use it to mimic that camouflage spell. If I have any power left after I've opened the trapdoor."

"If you don't, then we might just have to hide until it's dark," Dash says. "Which we should perhaps do anyway so that no one sees a dragon flying away when it isn't supposed to."

We're about halfway up the steps when I hear a low rumble. I freeze and look up. Bright light shines down from the trapdoor. "Guards," Dash mutters. He spins around, tugging me with him. The three of us hurtle down the stairs so fast I'm amazed we don't trip and tumble over each other all the way to the bottom.

"There she is!" someone yells behind us.

We jump down the last few steps and take off between the rows of spheres. Bright golden light flares on my right, and then on my left. A hurried glance both ways tells me that both Dash and Zed have guardian blades in their hands. The glittery magical kind that appear from nowhere.

"I doubt there's anywhere else to go down here," Zed says as we duck left beneath a low-hanging sphere and race between another two rows. "They'll soon corner us."

"Then we'll fight them off," Dash answers.

"Did you look behind us as we reached the bottom of the

steps?" Zed asks. "There must have been dozens of them rushing through that trapdoor."

"We can handle it," Dash says.

"Have you seen Bandit anywhere?" I ask, suddenly remembering he's no longer in my pocket.

"Little preoccupied here, Em," Dash says, beginning to sound breathless. "But I'm sure he's fine. He's smart. He's probably out of the prison already."

With a wall up ahead, we veer right and turn between another two rows of spheres—and I slam into the back of Dash as he skids to a standstill. At the other end of the row, at least ten guards race toward us. Dash's knives disappear, replaced instantly by a bow. He raises it and—

"Run while we still can!" Zed says, tugging me back between the spheres before I can see where Dash's arrow lands. "Fight when we have no other option."

"I hate running," Dash shouts, but I hear his footsteps pounding the ground just behind us.

"I love running," I mutter.

"Back to the stairs?" Zed calls over his shoulder to Dash. "We'll fight off whatever guards are waiting there for—Aaah!"

Pain crushes my side and the world flips around. My head whacks something solid. I come to an abrupt halt, feeling cold ground along the length of my body. I gasp, my winded lungs desperately seeking air and getting nothing. Scrabbling against the ground, I push myself up and looking wildly around, trying to make sense of things as my lungs cry out for oxygen. I see one of the spheres rolling away from me, knocking into another sphere. All around me, prisoners are screaming.

"Move!" Dash yells. An unseen force shoves me to the side, rolling me over and over into a disoriented heap. I look up in time to see a sphere racing past me at a terrifying speed. It crashes into two more spheres, sending them spinning, which in turn sends more spheres rolling.

"Dammit," I gasp when I can finally get some oxygen. "It's like a giant freaking pool table in here."

Hands grasp beneath my arms and pull me up. I shove backward with my elbow, and my attacker lets out a grunt of pain. "It's just me," groans Zed.

"Crap, sorry."

Dash ducks past a rolling sphere and runs up to me. "You okay?"

"Yeah."

"There are too many to fight," Zed says, twisting around, looking everywhere. Nevertheless, he moves so that his back is against Dash's and raises a glimmering, golden sword in each hand. A crossbow materializes in Dash's grip. I press closer to both of them, my eyes darting around. Everywhere I look, I see men and women in Unseelie uniforms racing toward us between the rolling spheres, weapons raised and magic sparking from their fingers.

"Dammit, dammit," I mutter, wishing I knew how to fight or use combat magic.

"Say something, Em," Dash tells me. "That's the only way we're getting out of here."

"I ... I don't know what to—"

"Anything!"

I allow power to leak into my voice and utter, "The guards

can't see us!" before grabbing onto the last wisps of my magic. Dash holds his crossbow in one hand and wraps the other around my arm. He pulls me swiftly sideways between two spheres that are about to knock into each other. Zed darts after us, and we make it through the gap just before the spheres collide and bounce apart. Guards still surround us on every side, but some of them are slowing down now, and others are looking around in confusion as they run. Not a single one is focused directly on us.

"Are we invisible?" Dash whispers.

"I think to them we are." A brief smile stretches my lips. "It worked."

"Damn, your voice is freaky when you're using your Griffin Ability," Zed says.

"Freaky amazing," Dash says. "Now, if we can just sneak past all the guards, we can make it up the stairs and through the trapdoor."

"Quickly," I whisper. "They're not stupid. They'll block our way out soon."

We slip between spheres and past guards, making our way toward the stairs faster than I would have thought possible. Behind us, the guards shout to one another, quickly coming to the conclusion that none of them can see us.

Then someone yells, "Block the stairway!"

We've already made it to the base of the stairs, though. We race upward without pause. Oddly enough, a squirrel leaps from step to step just ahead of us. "Bandit?" I hiss, and the squirrel freezes. Its tail twitches. Then it jumps up as we run past, landing in my arms in cat form.

Once outside, Dash spins around, sweeps his hand through the air, and the trapdoor swings shut. "Do a locking spell," Zed says immediately.

Dash crouches down, then looks up. "I have no stylus."

"Oh. Here." As if he knows I need my hands, Bandit shifts into a smaller form and scurries up the lapel of my coat. I retrieve Aurora's stylus as quickly as I can. Dash swipes it from my hands and bends down—just as something bumps the trapdoor from below.

"Crap." He smacks both hands down on the trapdoor.

Zed drops to his knees and holds both palms just above the trapdoor. I don't see any magic, but his gritted teeth suggest he's exerting some kind of invisible force on the trapdoor. "Quickly!" he says. Dash writes across the trapdoor, then pulls his hand back. Slowly, Zed does the same. Banging and the sound of shouts reach our ears, but the trapdoor remains shut.

"They'll break through the enchantment quickly," Dash says, rising and stepping backward as he returns the jewel-encrusted stylus to me.

We run through the garden, roughly toward the left side of the palace. We skirt around empty pavilions and leap across streams. Only when we reach a pair of silver trees with elaborate carvings in their wide trunks do we come to a stop to reassess our situation. I take a few moments to catch my breath, leaning against the tree trunk with one hand. When my breathing finally slows and adrenalin is no longer pumping through my system, I'm able to sense it: a glimmer of Griffin magic. I managed to hold onto some of it after telling the guards they couldn't see us.

"Do you think your command applied to every Unseelie guard?" Dash asks. "Or only the guards in the prison?"

"No idea." I look back the way we came, but I don't see anyone hunting through the garden for us. If the guards have managed to open the prison trapdoor, then they're looking for us elsewhere right now. "I don't know exactly what I was thinking when I gave them command, and all I said was 'the guards.' I hope it was all of them, but I think that would have taken more power than I had left."

"We'll find out soon enough," Zed says.

"I'd rather not find out," Dash replies. "Em, do you think we can get to the dragon enclosures now without being seen, or should we wait until dark?"

"Uh … now is probably better. Even if we don't try to escape until dark, there's a thicket of trees just before the dragon pits that hardly anyone ever goes through. It'll be safer to hide there than to hide on this side of the palace."

"Okay. So we move now," Zed says.

We continue our stealthy mission through the gardens, passing nothing more threatening that a few small flying and crawling creatures. "Hey, I never asked what Guild you're from," Dash says to Zed at one point as we pause behind a thick bush to scope out our surroundings again.

Zed rubs his neck as he peers through the bush's leafy branches. "It's a long story, but I'm not affiliated with any particular Guild anymore."

"Oh. But your markings—"

"My markings are still active, yes. But it's a story for another time. Let's get out of here alive first."

I happen to agree with Zed. Especially since I've just discovered our first major obstacle. "Hey, I think we have a problem," I say to them. They're both so intently examining the garden on the other side of the bush that they haven't yet noticed what's happening in the distance behind us.

"What's wrong?" Dash asks, turning to face the same way I'm facing. "Ah. I see it. Where the bunting is hanging between those statues?"

"Yes. A picnic lunch is about to take place there. I just saw the last baskets of food being placed around the blankets, and the first few ladies have just arrived. Oh, and there come more people," I add as a small group of colorfully dressed men and women wander toward the picnic area.

"I assume we were planning to walk right through that spot to get to the dragons?" Dash asks.

"Yep. Unfortunately."

"We could backtrack a bit and go around the other side of the palace," Zed suggests.

"It's a lot longer going that way around," I tell him, "and it takes us past the main entrance where all the carriages drive in and out. We'll have to do almost a full loop of the castle."

"Bad idea," Dash says. "Let's just head further to the left and go around the picnic."

"I've never been to that part of the grounds," I tell him, "so I don't know what we might find there. I have a suspicion there are houses that way for some of the fae who work here, but I'm not sure."

"Well we can't go *through* the palace," Dash says, "so going further left is our best option. Besides, most people should be at work during the day, right? So if there are houses that way, hopefully they'll be empty."

"Fine. But I hope you're ready to fight, because you might have to."

"Have you learned any combat magic since arriving here?" Zed asks me as we sneak out from behind the bush.

"No. Not officially. I tried out some magic on my own, but I doubt I could produce it fast enough to use it in an actual fight." We slip behind our next cover—the first of a row of trees clipped into giant birds—and crouch down. And then … an odd sound reaches my ears from somewhere behind us.

"Oh, fudging heck," Dash says. "The guards are out."

I look around. A wave of uniformed men and women is moving through the garden toward us. They stab their swords into bushes, slash at leaves, and wave their blades beside every tree. "Looks like they're not too concerned about stabbing us or chopping off a limb or two," I say.

"We need to keep moving," Dash says, "or it won't be long before they reach us."

Keeping our heads down, we run alongside the row of topiary birds. The back of my coat drags along the grass behind me. I wish I had time to stop, undo the buttons, and shed the smothering garment. I'm beginning to bake inside it. At the other end, we carefully step out into the open again. We're a good distance away from the picnic, so as long as we make no sudden moves, we shouldn't catch the attention of any—

"There she is!"

The distant shout comes from the direction of the picnic. I freeze and look across the garden. I'm too far away to know for sure, but I think it's one of the guards who's been stationed near my room since the day I got here. He launches forward and runs toward us. Another two guards detach from the gathering and join him.

"Well, that answers our question about the other guards seeing us," Zed says as we start running.

My mind races ahead, trying to visualize a way out of this. If we can beat the guards to the dragon pits, we can jump down into one of them. Hopefully we won't break any ankles or legs, or become a snack for Imperia. Then we can get Phillyp to remove the shield over the enclosure and let us fly away—or threaten his life if he doesn't. Not the best way to go about things, especially since I like Phillyp, but it's our only option now.

Until suddenly, our only option vanishes.

Almost straight ahead of us, from the area of the grounds I've never been to before, dozens upon dozens of guards come racing into view. "Crap," I mutter, skidding to a stop along with Dash and Zed. "Go back the other way. The long way around the palace. At least the prison guards can't see us." We take off in the other direction, but the three guards from the picnic are gaining on us. *Run, run, RUN*, I tell myself, easily keeping up with Dash and Zed. They may be elite warriors, but I feel like I've spent my life training for this moment: fleeing a small army's worth of Unseelie guards.

We hurtle past the front of the palace, providing great entertainment for anyone who happens to be in their suites looking out at the garden. I have no idea what we'll do once we get around to the side where all the carriages drive in and out, and dozens more men and women stand guard along the walls. My mind tumbles through half-formed ideas of what I can use the last remaining part of my Griffin power for.

But I never get a chance to make a decision, because around the corner of the palace comes yet another group of uniformed faeries.

CHAPTER TWENTY-NINE

"DAMMIT!" I CRY OUT. I'M RUNNING SO FAST I ALMOST TRIP over my own feet as I try to stop. Dash grabs onto my arm and tugs me back. "Into the palace," I pant. "We don't have … a choice now. We can hide … somewhere inside."

There are open doors and archways all across the ground floor, and it's far too easy to race into the palace. It's a trap, of course. We're running into an elaborate, lavishly decorated trap. Because once all the doors and windows are sealed off— and I have no doubt the king can do that in a matter of seconds with the aid of magic—we'll have nowhere else to go.

Except …

I stop running halfway across a portrait-lined hallway, and Dash almost collides with me. "What?" he asks. "What's wrong."

"There's a way out."

"Where?" Zed asks.

"It's—wait. Come on." At the sound of running footsteps behind us, we keep moving. I lead the way down another hall, through a small parlor, then take a few turns along increasingly narrow passages, and eventually race past an enormous kitchen. I duck through the first open doorway I see, which turns out to be packed to the ceiling with bags of various kinds of grain.

After peering back out to make sure no one's seen us, Dash quietly shuts the door. He faces me. "Where's this other way out?"

"It's a portal. A gateway into another world." I pause to catch my breath and wipe tiny beads of sweat from my brow. "Not the human world and not this one. The other world Aurora and Roarke took us to. The shadow one."

Deep lines crease Dash's forehead. "That place with barely any color? Where that black shapeless creature chased us?"

"Yes. It isn't a place in this world. It's—"

"Between the worlds," Dash murmurs.

"Yes. Just like you said. There's a portal in Roarke's room that leads straight into that world, and once we're there, we can use the candles to get out."

"Candles?"

"Yes. With—the way the witches—I'll explain later. The point is, we can get out of that world."

"And what about the creatures that rose up from the shadows and wanted to kill us?"

"We can run if we have to. I'm safe, actually." I pull at the chain around my neck and lift the pendant from where it's hiding beneath my shirt. "And you guys know how to fight. So we should be fine. I'd rather take my chances against a bunch of shadows than against an Unseelie army."

"I hope you realize," Zed says, "that whatever the two of you are talking about makes zero sense. A world between worlds? What does that even mean?"

"Now isn't exactly the time to go into detail," I point out, "but it's real. I promise. It came into existence when the veil was torn. And it's the only way I know of to get out of this palace."

Slowly, Zed nods. "Okay. But won't this portal be just as heavily guarded as any other exit?"

"I don't think so. Roarke and his father don't want anyone but their closest guards knowing about the shadow world. And I don't think the king knows about the portal. I'm pretty sure Roarke kept that a secret from him. I know Roarke stationed a few of his men on either side of the portal, but he may not have had a chance to send more guards there yet. If we make it there quickly, and there are only a few guards—"

"We can handle them," Dash says. "Definitely."

"How far to his chambers?" Zed asks.

My enthusiasm wilts a little. It seems impossibly far right now. "Uh … far enough that the chance of being seeing is extremely high."

"The key is to blend in," Dash says. "If we're not running away from anything, we won't catch anyone's attention. We just need to look like your average three nobles wandering around the palace."

"Well, we've already failed then. You guys look awful."

"Thanks," Dash says drily. "But we can't very well shed our clothing. We'll make even more of a spectacle if we wander down the halls without—Oh." His face brightens. "That could work."

"What?"

"Remember where I went when I first got here?"

"Um … no. I wasn't with you when you first got here. You were—Oh, the clothes casters."

"Yes. I had to leave your dress in the chief clothes caster's workroom. And guess where that is?"

I raise an eyebrow. "If the answer isn't 'right next door,' that would be a very sad ending to this story."

Dash smiles. "It's *almost* right next door."

Zed nods. "That's almost as good."

We sneak out of the store room and make it to the clothes caster's workroom without being noticed by anyone. The workroom, by some miracle, is empty, and contains numerous racks of court-appropriate clothing for both men and women. "Perfect," I say. "Too bad we don't have time for you guys to shower. Hopefully the clean clothes will be enough to mask your dirty hair and … you know …"

"The smell?" Zed prompts.

"Yeah."

"No time to shower?" Dash repeats. "Ha. You've heard of magic, right?"

I place my hands on my hips. "Seriously? Faeries have shower spells?"

"Something like that. Not as satisfying as a genuine soak in a hot pool, but it has the same effect."

322

Ten minutes later, after hiding behind a screen and drenching themselves in water and mint-scented soap that somehow never touches the floor and dries almost immediately, Dash and Zed step out as well-groomed members of the Unseelie Court. They just need to take care to keep their wrists covered.

"Right," Zed says. "Let's do this."

It's difficult to walk slowly when all I want to do is flee, but I manage to keep my pace to a casual stroll beside Dash and Zed. Once we've left the storerooms and workrooms behind us and we're strolling the glossy marble hallways once more, Dash moves a little closer and places my arm over his. "Take her other arm," he tells Zed.

"My, what a lucky lady I am," I drawl, sarcasm coating my words. "A man on each arm."

"You're a lot less likely to be noticed as Prince Roarke's future wife," Dash says, "when you have a man on each arm, don't you think?"

"I guess so." I look down and notice magic swirling around his other hand as it hangs loosely at his side. "Getting ready to fight?"

"To stun, actually. It'll be quicker and cleaner."

"Stunning someone means knocking them unconscious with magic, right?"

"Yes. It isn't a quick spell, though. Enough magic needs to be gathered first. It can take—"

"There!" The shout comes from the top of the staircase at the end of the hall. The staircase we need to ascend. Sparks of magic shoot past us as the guards race down the stairs.

We duck down immediately, Zed swearing beneath his breath. "We're gonna have to fight," Dash says.

"Don't waste your stunner magic if you can help it," Zed tells him. "Save it for—" he dodges to avoid more sparks "—for the portal guards."

"Yeah. And Em—"

"I'll be fine." I focus on the railing that runs along the gallery at the top of the stairs. "See you up there." I launch forward with a burst of speed. The guards—just reaching the base of the staircase—might think I'm aiming directly for them. But I duck beneath their sparks and swerve to the side, heading straight for a bureau with a vase of flowers sitting atop it just to the side of the stairs. I leap up, strike the top of the bureau with one foot, and jump again. My fingers grasp the gallery railing. I pull myself up, swing over the railing, roll across the gallery floor, and spring to my feet. A momentary glance back down to the hall shows me Dash and Zed following the same path I took, with guards right behind them and others racing up the stairs.

I spin around and run. Highly polished floors streak by beneath my feet, and I'm grateful my shoes have enough grip to keep me from slipping onto my backside. I risk a look over my shoulder, and Dash yells, "Don't stop!" I sprint toward the final staircase that will take us to royal family's wing of the palace. But of course, it isn't that easy.

Guards are lined up at the top of the stairs, and they're not running down to meet us. I know nothing will make them leave their posts. Magic spins around their fingers as they raise their hands to attack. As colorful sparks fly toward me, I twist one foot, drop down onto my side, and skid clear across the floor beneath their magic. With no time to worry about the pain shrieking at me from my hip and shoulder striking the floor, I scramble through the nearest doorway. Then I'm up and running again along a new hallway, limping only slightly from the pain. "Keep going!" Dash yells, which tells me he and Zed escaped the magical assault.

My thoughts tumble ahead, planning a new path. The only way to the Roarke's suite is up that staircase—unless you count his balcony and windows, which I do. *Go down a level, double back, sneak through someone else's window, and climb up*, my brain instructs. As the pain in my hip begins to dull, I race forward with a fresh burst of speed. I turn a corner and find the winding staircase I was expecting. With every second counting, I don't bother with the actual stairs. I swing myself easily over the railing beside the top step. *Leap, land, shoulder roll, jump up, keep running*, I mentally recite as I execute the maneuver almost perfectly. Despite the life-threatening circumstances, I can't help doing a mental fist pump. Val would be so proud of me.

I run back along halls and passageways until I reach a large parlor that I judge to be roughly beneath the stairway to the royals' wing. From walking through this room before, I know that the various hallways leading off it will take me to the chambers of extended family members and other lords and ladies who live here. A quick look over my shoulder confirms it's still Dash and Zed who are following right behind me. As they reach the parlor, I hurry along another passage, pass two or three doors, then stop. After listening for a moment, I quietly open the door. Dash and Zed reach my side as I peer into the bedroom and confirm that it's empty. We slip quickly inside, and I shut the door behind us.

"Holy freaking crap, Em," Dash says between gasps for air. "You'd make one hell of a guardian if you knew how to fight."

"Yeah. Knowing how to fight might be useful." I swallow and suck in another deep breath. "But I'd rather not be part of any Guild, thanks very much." I cross the bedroom—not quite as lavishly decorated as mine—and look out the window. "Okay, I think we should move over one more room to the right. Once we're directly in line with the snake sculpture out there, we should be below Roarke's balcony."

"We're climbing into his room?" Zed asks.

"Yes. Easier than fighting all those guards, don't you think?"

We move to the next room, which is also empty. Everyone's probably at the picnic. I swing my legs over the windowsill, turn carefully to face the wall, and begin climbing. I edge a little to the left as I ascend, and before long, I'm level with Roarke's balcony. I grab onto the railing and climb over it. On tiptoe, I move toward the open doorway.

"Is this the right one?" Zed whispers from behind me.

"Yes." I recognize the interior of the sitting room.

"Let me go first," Dash says, stepping past me. "We may need to use magic." I notice that sparks of light still dance around his hand. Seems he's managed to hold onto the stunner magic he was gathering earlier.

He creeps inside. I follow him, ready to duck at the first sign of magic. But the room is empty. "The portal is through there," I say in a low voice, pointing to the door leading into Roarke's bedroom. Dash walks ahead of me into the next room, then looks over his shoulder at me in confusion. "The bathroom," I whisper as Zed and I follow him. He nods. I slip past him and stop beside the bathroom door, which is slightly ajar. I look back at Dash. He raises his magic and nods again. I take a deep breath, then kick the door open. He and Zed rush in—and stop.

"There's no one here," Dash says. "But—holy freaking ferret-whistle." His eyes widen, along with Zed's. "That's a portal."

I stride into the bathroom after him. "Yes. That's it. All we need to do is walk through—"

The bathroom door slams shut. Against the wall, standing in exactly the same spot I stood in when I hid here, is Roarke. "Going somewhere?" he sneers.

CHAPTER THIRTY

THE SCUFFLE IS SO QUICK, MY EYES BARELY FOLLOW WHAT happens: Dash flings his magic; Roarke twists away while hurling a crackling mass of power at me; Zed launches himself in front of me, cries out, and drops to the ground. By the time my useless gasp is out of my mouth, the action is over. Dash now holds a protective layer of magic in front of the two of us, and Roarke's raised hand suggests he's doing the same thing. Zed, who took the full force of the magic Roarke tried to attack me with, lies unmoving at our feet.

"Is … is he—"

"Not dead," Dash says, his eyes trained on Roarke. "Stunned."

"Yes," Roarke says. "And the two of you will soon be in the same position."

"I don't think so," Dash answers. "We have the portal right behind us now, and it'll take you far too much time to gather enough magic for another two stunner spells. We'll be gone long before you can carry out your threats."

Roarke lifts one shoulder in an unconcerned shrug. "You're welcome to go through that portal. My guards are waiting on the other side, ready to knock you out the moment you appear. And unlike you and me, they haven't yet used up the stunner magic they've been gathering."

"Well, thanks for telling me exactly what to expect on the other side. Now that I'm prepared, I have no doubt I can stop them all."

Roarke snorts. "Guardians have always been over-confident. I can only hope it gets you killed."

"My over-confidence has served me well so far." With the hand that isn't holding up the shield, Dash pulls me closer to the portal.

"Emerson," Roarke says, directing his hard gaze at me. "Why don't you tell me what all this silliness is about. I thought you and I had an agreement. We both want something, and our union will get us what we want. If you've changed your mind, you'll never get your mother back the way you want her."

"Em, don't listen to him. He's just wasting time so he can—"

"I'll never get what I want from you anyway," I say to Roarke.

"Oh? Is that a lie your guardian friend has told you?"

"I know what you plan to do. I know the meaning of the

words you've been making me memorize, and I know you're planning to take every bit of my magic and make it your own."

Several beats of silence pass as Roarke's cold gaze grows icier. "Interesting," he says, slowly grinding the word out. "However did you discover that?"

I wish I could tell him it was his own sister who shared this information, just so I could see the look on his face. But I won't give Aurora away. Whatever her motives were in going behind her brother's back, she doesn't deserve his wrath. "Everyone's been so insistent that I stuff my head with as much knowledge of this world as I can," I tell him. "Wouldn't want your future wife to be an embarrassment to this court, would you? Well, guess what? In all that reading, I stumbled across the one piece of knowledge I needed more than anything else—the words of a particular witch spell and their meaning."

"A coincidence?" Roarke spits. "You expect me to believe that you stumbled across this spell by *chance*?"

I force a laugh out. "Funny, isn't it? You thought it was silly how much reading I was doing, and yet reading is what ended up saving me."

"Em, we need to—"

"Saving you?" Roarke's quiet laugh chills me. "You think you're going to get away from me? Just like your idiot guardian friend thought he was going to get away from this palace?" He looks at Dash. "You really thought I was going to let you leave in that carriage, didn't you. You *fool*," he hisses. "Did you think you could sneak into my betrothed's bedroom and there'd be no consequences?"

I suck in a breath. "How did you—Wait, you *have* been

330

listening in on me. You disgusting—"

"Of course I've been listening. My father and I make it our business to know exactly what everyone says and does beneath our roof. We have untraceable enchantments almost everywhere." His gaze returns to Dash. "I could hardly allow a filthy guardian to continue sneaking around with my future wife once I knew about it."

"We were *talking*—"

"Em, let's—"

"Ah, but what if talking turned into something else? Something far less appropriate and far more … intimate. I couldn't have someone sullying my bride-to-be."

"We were talking about my family's *funeral*, you sick bastard," I shout, even as my face burns at the thought of what he's implying.

"Yes, and then he was going to sneak around my home and hunt down information he could use against me. Therefore, he needed to be removed from the palace."

"Em!" Dash says, putting more force behind the word this time. At our feet, Zed moans. Clearly there wasn't much magic behind Roarke's stunner spell. "We're leaving now," Dash says. Invisible magic raises the half-conscious Zed into the air, where he flops over Dash's shoulder with a grunt. I look immediately at Roarke to see what he's going to do to stop us.

"I'm not worried, Emerson," he says with a smirk, reading my unspoken thoughts. "My men on the other side of the portal will stop you from getting away."

"They won't," Dash tells him. He takes my hand and pulls me toward the portal. "Get ready to throw some magic as soon as we get through," he whispers to me. "Whatever you can handle. I'll do the rest."

I make my decision then, not giving myself even a second to consider all the things that might go wrong. I tug my arm free, shove Dash and Zed through the portal, and swing back around to face Roarke. He drops his shield of magic, a wicked grin spreading across his face.

But before he can do anything, I open my mouth and speak. I release the final bit of my Griffin Ability, and I say the one thing I've wanted to say since the moment I got here. The words I repeated endlessly the other night: "Tell me every single thing you know about my mother and how to help her!"

Roarke goes rigid. His hands rise to clasp his throat, as if he could possibly stop the words from escaping his lips. Then his mouth twists into an evil smile as a single sentence is ripped magically from him. "I … don't know … anything."

My shock silences me for several moments. "What?" I finally manage to say. How can he lie like that? How is it possible for him to disobey my Griffin Ability? "That isn't true. You *do* know things. You told me things about my mother and her past. You—"

"No." He lowers his hands and rolls his shoulders as he recovers from the magic's effects. "I told you things about the woman who raised you and then lost her mind and ended up in a hospital. I didn't tell you anything about your mother."

I blink.

The full meaning of his words takes its time making its way to my brain, but when it finally gets there, it almost knocks me to my knees. I swallow, shaking my head, refusing to believe him. I've been down this road, and I will *not* travel it again. "She *is* my mother. Everyone thought she was human, but she isn't. We both have magic. We're both faeries, so—"

"Oh, stop," Roarke says in a tone that almost sounds bored. "That's the stupidest logic ever and you know it. Just because you're both faeries she must be your mother? Ha! She could be my mother then, and we both know that isn't true."

"But ... then—"

"No, no, silly girl. It's too late now." Roarke takes a step toward me. "You should have asked the right question while you still had some power in your voice. You should have *thought* about what you were asking. You should have mentally focused on *Daniela Clarke* instead of simply blurting out words without putting any true intention behind them." Another step. "Besides, it wouldn't have helped for me to *tell* you how to heal your mother. I have to do it myself. You might have learned the history of Daniela Clarke, but you would not—" one more step "—have learned how to help her yourself."

Crap. My half-formed plan—to get right up to the portal while Roarke was telling me everything I needed to know so I could rush through it the moment he finished speaking—crumbles to imaginary dust around me. I twist around, throwing my body in the direction of the portal as Roarke lunges for me. He catches my arm, tugging me back and sideways, and we crash to the floor just in front of the portal. With my shoulder screaming out in pain, I scramble away from him. His hand lashes out, twisting in my hair and scratching down the side of my neck before grabbing hold of a clump of my hair and yanking me back toward him. I cry out, reaching up to claw at his arms. I slash my fingernails along his skin, and as he yanks one hand back, I squirm around, pull my legs up to my chest, and kick him as hard as I can. Then I scramble onto my hands and knees and dive through the portal.

* * *

I roll onto the ground in the shadow world to find the dull landscape illuminated by glittering, colorful magic whizzing through the air in all directions. Three guards lie motionless on the ground while Dash and Zed fight two other men. They kick, spin, punch, and dodge amidst clouds of sand, shrieking bats, and flying needles. Through their grunts of pain and cries of anger, I hear Dash yelling, *"What the hell did you do?"*

I know he's shouting at me.

I scramble to my feet and whip around to face the portal. I need magic. Or a weapon. Roarke will arrive at any second. I look down at the rocky ground I'm standing on, searching for a sharp-edged stone—and wondering briefly why Roarke and Aurora transformed part of the grassy world they found into hard earth covered in pebbles and rocks. I spot a suitably sharp stone and bend quickly to retrieve it—

And pain collides suddenly, shockingly with my abdomen. I'm knocked off my feet and hit the ground hard on my left side. I curl in on myself, sucking uselessly at the air and getting nothing. *Breathe*, I tell myself. *BREATHE!* An invisible force tosses me into the air, and as I come to a halt, suspended somewhere above the ground, I see Roarke beside me. With a flick of his hand, I begin moving back toward the portal as he walks alongside me. I'm still gasping for oxygen, wriggling in the air, horrified at how powerless I am against Roarke's magic, when a wordless cry reaches my ears.

A split second later, a blinding flash of white-green light strikes the portal—and the entire thing explodes into yet more light and sparks and spinning glitter. Roarke and I are thrown backward, though his magic seems to cushion my fall. My ears are ringing. My left side still aches. Somehow, though, breathing is becoming almost a possibility. As the flare of light fades away, I push myself up to see what's left of the portal.

It's gone.

Beside me, Roarke curses loudly. I scramble away from him. I don't have time to find a sharp stone, so I aim for the heaviest rock I think I can lift. Without pause, I hoist it up and hurl it at Roarke's head. It strikes exactly where I intended it to. In horror, I watch as he collapses to the ground. Blood begins to ooze from somewhere amidst his hair. "Oh crap oh crap oh crap," I mutter.

And then, after one last thump, everything becomes quiet except for the sound of labored breathing. All the guards are knocked out, and Dash and Zed—covered in scratches and cuts, their clothes partially torn—gather their breath as they stagger toward me. I look back at Roarke, sickened by what I've done. "I didn't kill him ... did I?" I pant.

"No," Zed says. "He'll easily survive that."

"What is wrong with you, Em?" Dash demands. "You were supposed to come with us, not make it easier for Roarke to catch you."

I ignore Dash and keep my eyes fixed on Roarke. "Can we

tie him up? And the guards. I don't want them to get away. Roarke knows things. I … I need to question him still."

"Haven't you done that already? Isn't that why you shoved me through the portal without you?" Dash replies. "So you could stay behind and question him?" Despite his frustrated tone, he crouches down beside Roarke as a glittering rope forms in his hands. Zed does the same with one of the guards.

"I did question him. Seems I asked the wrong question."

Dash looks across at me, pausing with the rope partially wrapped around Roarke's wrists. "You didn't ask about your mother?"

"I did." I focus on the ground at Dash's feet. "I used the words 'my mother.' And that, apparently, was a mistake." My eyes rise to meet his as an unbearable ache forms in my chest. "Turns out she isn't my mother after all."

Dash stares at me with the same kind of expression I probably gave Roarke. "Shoot," he murmurs eventually. "I really thought—after she turned out to be magical—that she must be your real mother."

"Yeah. Me too."

"I'm so sorry, Em."

"This world …" Zed says, looking around. "It's an entirely different realm. This is just … crazy."

"It is," Dash agrees.

"Em." Zed walks closer to me. "Where are the candles you spoke about? We need to get out of here. Once we're somewhere safe, we can talk. I have a lot to—"

"Watch out!" I grab his hand and tug him down as a dark shape swoops over him like an undulating blanket with wispy edges. "Crap, I totally forgot about the ink-shades." I press closer to Dash and Zed as ink-black shapes gather around us. I reach for my necklace—my protection—but my stomach drops when my fingers find no chain against my skin. All that remains are the stinging scratches left behind from Roarke's fingernails scraping down the side of my neck. "Dammit. We need to get to the castle."

"But you're protected, aren't you?" Dash says. "If Zed and I stick close to you, we can—"

"My necklace is gone. Roarke must have broken the chain when he attacked me in the bathroom."

"Terrific," Dash mutters. Then, as the ink-shades swoop closer, he adds, "I think it's time to run again!"

I'm on my feet, racing beside Dash and Zed, hoping Roarke is wearing his amulet. If not, he won't last long, and he'll take all his knowledge of Mom with him. I toss a glance over my shoulder, but all I see are dark figures swooping through the air like misshapen bats. "Aim for the castle's main gate!" I shout as I look ahead once more. "The drawbridge is down."

I shriek in fright as a shadow sweeps right past me. Dash and I veer to the left, while Zed, on the other side of the ink-shade, swerves right. Separating themselves from the ground, a dozen more ink-shades join the one that just startled me. And for some reason, they gravitate toward Dash and me, forcing us further left. "Darn, they're quick," Dash pants. "We can't get around them."

"The tower," I answer between breaths. "The moat doesn't … exist there yet … and the windows are low. We can climb up." With an extra burst of speed, we aim for the tower. "Zed!"

I yell to him, then wish I hadn't when he almost stumbles as he looks around for us.

"Keep going!" Dash yells at him. "Better for him ... to go that way," he adds to me. "He'll make it to the gate."

My feet pound the ground, and my chest begins to burn, but we're going to make it. We're fast, and the castle is less than a hundred yards away now.

And then, in a move that Val most certainly would *not* be proud of, I trip over a clump of grass and land flat on my face. Struggling for air yet again, I manage to turn over. A dark shape swoops down and settles over me, covering me completely. As I scrabble uselessly at the ground, I feel the sensation of cold lips on my neck. All strength drains from my body. My limbs become heavy and cold. My eyelids slide shut as bone-weary tiredness consumes me and a deathly chill pervades my body.

CHAPTER
THIRTY-ONE

THROUGH THE DARKNESS AND SILENCE, A SIZZLING CRACKLE reaches my ears, followed immediately by a piercing shriek. My eyelids spring apart, and I see the dull grey sky far above instead of a cloak-like shape. Adrenalin rushes through me. My exhaustion vanishes. "Come on," Dash says, his hands already around my arms. He pulls me up. "My magic scared it off but didn't kill it. I don't know what spell to use, and—crap, they're already coming back."

We sprint the final distance toward the castle, and though I've always been fond of running, I'm fast approaching the point where I've had enough for one day. I kick off the ground the moment I reach the wall, and my fingers *just* reach the edge of the lowest window. Dash hauls himself up and takes a dive through the window. He jumps to his feet and grabs my wrists, pulling me the final distance. Once I'm through, he reaches up—but there's no window pane for him to pull down. "What the heck? Where's the rest of the window?"

"Not finished," I pant, just as a dark shape separates itself from the wall and rises behind Dash. I tug him forward. "The towers aren't protected yet. Need to get … into a room."

We rush down the stairs, around and around, and almost fall into the sparsely furnished room at the base of the tower. Together we slam the door shut and take a few hasty steps backward. My heel catches on the edge of a rug, and I land on my butt, accidentally pulling Dash down with me. "Are you sure it's safe here?" he asks, his chest rising and falling rapidly.

I nod, only knowing for sure because I've been in this room before. "That thing," I whisper, "was so cold." Dash leans closer and bundles me into his arms, and now that I'm finally still and not running for my life, I realize my whole body is shaking. I wrap my arms tightly around him and don't let go, even when my heart slows and my breathing returns to normal. I finally stop shaking, but still I hold onto his warmth. That creature was *so damn cold*. I don't ever want to be that cold again.

Eventually, just as I'm telling myself I should probably let go of Dash, he asks, "Are you all right?"

I detach myself from him and shift a few inches away. "Yes. I think so. It only got me for a few seconds, right? I felt so cold, so tired, but it was only for a little bit."

Dash nods. "Good. I also meant … about your mother."

Roarke's shocking revelation drops onto my shoulders again. I look away from Dash as I shake my head. I press my hands against my face and rub my eyes. "It feels like I've been on this crazy see-saw of emotion since I discovered magic and the fae world. She wasn't my mother, and then she was my mother, and now she isn't my mother again." I lower my hands. "I suppose I just have to remember all the things I told myself last time. That it doesn't matter how we're related. I still love her the same way. I would still do anything to help her get better. And—Oh! Bandit!" A sudden wriggling against my hip reminds me that I haven't seen him since we escaped the prison. I've hit the ground numerous times, and I haven't heard a squeak from him. What if he's hurt? I gently lift the edge of my pocket and peer inside—and tiny lizard eyes stare back at me. "Bandit," I breathe. "I'm so glad you're okay."

"Wow, he survived a lot," Dash says. "I wonder if he was in your pocket the whole time."

"Yeah, I wonder," I say, my thoughts turning back to Mom again.

"Anyway, we should get back to the oasis. Hey, look at that." He brightens. "I can say the word. *Oasis.*"

The oasis. Surrounded by all these muted tones, I long for the color and warmth of the oasis. Hopefully everyone in charge there will forgive me for whatever trouble I've put them through and allow me to return. "We must be truly alone if we can talk about the oasis. Well, aside from Zed, but I guess he isn't close enough to hear us." I push myself to my feet. "Do you think he made it inside?"

Dash nods as he stands. "Yes. I saw him cross the drawbridge just before we reached the tower."

"If he's found any candles, he's probably gone by now. I

wouldn't hang around if I were him."

"Yeah. I'm sure he's got his own life to get back to. I'll have to see if I can find out anything about him once I'm back at work—if I still have a job, that is. It's strange that he still has his markings if he's not working for the Guild anymore. Usually they deactivate those if a guardian leaves the Guild's service."

"Do you know how he ended up locked in an Unseelie prison?"

"No. He kept saying he'd tell me about it when we were less drugged. And we never really got to the point where that was the case." Dash looks around. "So where are these traveling candles you mentioned?"

"Wait. What about Roarke?" I move to the window and look outside, but we're too far from the spot where the portal was for me to be able to see Roarke. "I need him."

"You *need* him?" I look back and see Dash watching me with raised eyebrows.

"You know what I mean. He can heal my mother. Or—you know—the woman I think of as my mother."

"We're not taking him with us, Em. Even if I wanted to, the protective enchantment around the oasis would forbid it. Once we're near him, we won't remember where we're supposed to go."

"Yes, I know. So the only other thing to do," I continue slowly, knowing that Dash won't like this, "is to bring Mom here."

"You realize that's crazy, right? Your mother is safe right now. If we bring her here, she won't be. And neither will we."

342

"Are you talking about the ink-shades? Because I can command them not to attack any faerie ever again. We only need to wait until tonight for my Griffin Ability to become useful again."

"Not just the—what did you call them? Ink-shades? I mean what about all the people aside from Roarke who know about this world? His sister, his personal guards, his *father*. Em, the Unseelie King himself could show up here at any second."

I lean back against the windowsill and fold my arms over my chest. "The Unseelie King probably thinks we're still hiding in his palace somewhere."

"And when he figures out that we're not? He'll discover that Roarke is missing too, and where is he going to look first?"

"Honestly, I don't think it will be here. He doesn't know Roarke showed me this world. And he won't see the portal because it isn't there anymore. Even if the king does think that I somehow overpowered Roarke with the help of my two prisoner friends, he has no reason to suspect we'd bring him here."

Dash frowns and purses his lips in thought. "I suppose not. So your plan is for us to bring your mother back here, wait until later to command the shadow creatures to leave us alone, then take her to Roarke. I assume you're planning to still have some power in your voice to command him to wake her and heal her?"

"Yes. And we don't necessarily have to wait until we can command the ink-shades. We can look for the underground passages that lead back to the hedges out there near where the portal was. We can get to Roarke that way."

Dash's frown doesn't leave his face. "I'm not sure there's any point in doing that if your Griffin Ability won't be ready to command him."

"Right. That's true." I let my arms fall back to my sides. "Then yes, we'll do as you said: fetch Mom, command the ink-shades, command Roarke. And once he's healed Mom, we'll leave immediately and go straight back to the oasis."

"Where we'll all live happily ever after," Dash finishes.

"Well …" I look away. "Things never work out that simply, so I assume something will go wrong along the way. Someone unexpected will appear out of the blue and try to screw up our plans, and we'll have to fight them off, and *then* we can live happily ever after."

"There's my cynical Em." Dash grins. "I've missed you."

I give him a withering look. "You know I have good reason to be cynical."

"Yes." He moves closer and places his hand on my arm. "But sometimes, Em, things do work out. Hopefully this is your time."

I cover his hand with mine, wishing I could believe him. "Hopefully you're right."

"I am." He rocks forward a little, and for one insane moment I think he means to kiss me. But his hand slides away from my arm and he turns, looking around the room once more. "The candles?" he asks. "Are they around here somewhere?"

"Uh, in the top drawer." I point to the sideboard. It's the only other piece of furniture in this room. Apparently Aurora spent days constructing it while teaching herself the relevant spells. Roarke then added his own personal touch by creating a solid gold snake holding a dagger in its mouth for the top of the sideboard.

Dash crosses the room. "I can't help feeling like this snake is going to come alive and stab me in the hand," he comments.

"Don't worry. I don't think Roarke had time to add delightful enchantments like that to the decorative items in his castle. He was still too busy with the actual architecture."

Dash takes two candles from the top drawer and leaves another few lying on top of the sideboard beside the snake. "In case Zed hasn't found any yet and he comes through here while we're gone." He joins me by the window. "So this is the same way the witch candles work? You light them, think of your destination, and you're taken immediately there?"

"Yes. I think that's how Roarke and Aurora brought us here the first time."

He hesitates. "Perhaps one of us should stay here. Keep watch. Just in case someone unwelcome arrives while we're gone. We don't want any unpleasant surprises when we get back here with your mom."

"Mm. Maybe you're—"

The handle of the door leading to the next room twists. Dash drops the candles. Without thinking, I launch across the room, bring myself to a halt against the sideboard, and yank the dagger free from the snake's mouth. The door swings open.

"Whoa." Zed holds his hands up the moment he sees me brandishing the dagger. "It's just me."

"Sorry." I lower the weapon I would have had no idea what to do with if it hadn't been Zed who walked in. "I assumed you would have found a candle by now and left."

He nods as he heaves a sigh. "I did find some candles. I could have left. I could have vanished and never seen the two of you ever again. But ..." One fist clenches and unclenches as he stares at the ground by my feet. "I owe you, Em."

I focus on that fist for a moment, then again on his face. "You owe me?" My laugh sounds forced. "Because I freed you? I think we're even, Zed. You threw yourself between me and a stunner spell, remember?"

"I wish that made us even. I wish that could come close to making up for the mess of a life you ended up with."

My grip tightens around the dagger's hilt, and from the edge of my vision, I make out something bright and golden blazing in Dash's hands. "Who the hell are you?" I whisper.

"I don't know if this is the best place to talk," Zed says, his gaze shifting back and forth between Dash and me. "Those shadowy creatures are everywhere, and Roarke is still—"

"We're staying exactly where we are," Dash says, his voice low and threatening as he raises a glittering crossbow and points it at Zed.

"How do you know me?" I demand, louder this time.

Zed raises his hands once more. "Almost eighteen years ago," he says slowly, "I was supposed to kill you."

My breathing becomes shallower. My heart pounds harder. But I swallow, steady my voice, and ask, "Why?"

"The people I worked with wanted to hurt your parents."

"Why? Who were my parents? What did they do wrong?"

"It's what they *didn't* do that was the problem. It wasn't their fault, but their inaction led to the pain and suffering of

346

many people—myself included. Years later, those of us who survived couldn't get past it. Some wanted revenge. Some of us …" He shakes his head. "Well, some of us got caught up in finally belonging somewhere and having a purpose again."

I have no words to answer him with. All I can do is stare in horror.

"I was told to kill you," Zed continues, his voice wavering ever so slightly, "but I couldn't do it. I couldn't kill a faerie baby. Especially not a faerie baby who was related to someone who used to be a friend of mine long ago. So I did something else. Something that might be considered even worse."

My heart thunders as I wait for him to continue. "What did you do?" I whisper.

"A changeling spell."

CHAPTER THIRTY-TWO

"HO-LEE SHOVEL," DASH WHISPERS.

My gaze snaps toward him, then back to Zed. "What? What is that? What's a changeling spell?"

"Witch magic," Dash says darkly. "Swapping a faerie baby and a human baby. I thought the witches stopped doing that kind of thing more than a century ago."

"The spell changes the appearance of both the human and the faerie," Zed explains, "so that they look like each other. Over time, that part of the magic fades away, leaving the faerie child looking the way he or she would have without the changeling spell. The faerie's magic remains blocked, though, and he or she will grow up as a human in the non-magic realm, knowing nothing of the world they truly belong to. Usually, the faerie's magic remains blocked for the rest of his or her human-length life. But sometimes, the magic breaks out."

"Which is what happened to me," I murmur. It doesn't seem real. It sounds like the story of someone else's life. The kind of thing I might watch in a movie, sitting side by side with Val and munching on popcorn.

"You forgot to mention," Dash growls, "what happens to the human baby. It doesn't live long. With magic running through its tiny human body, it barely survives a few days."

I'm gripping the dagger so tightly now that my hand begins to hurt. "So you couldn't kill me," I say to Zed, "but you could kill a human baby? You're despicable."

"I know," he says. "But somehow I felt less despicable than if I'd killed you."

This is insanity. This is barely believable. I was born in one world and stolen away to another, and—

"Wait." I point the dagger at him. "If you took a human baby away from its mother and replaced it with me, then why isn't my mother—the woman who raised me, Daniela Clarke—human?"

Zed shuts his eyes and releases a long breath before speaking. "That is where things get a lot more complicated."

"*More* complicated?"

"You'd better start explaining," Dash says, the crossbow still aimed at Zed's chest, "because we're not going anywhere until Em gets every single answer she's looking for."

Zed looks between the two of us. "Can I sit?"

"No," Dash and I say at the same time.

"Okay then." He nods. "I guess I should start with the fact that I'm Griffin Gifted. Don't worry," he adds as I inch back slightly. "I won't be using it on either of you. The effects are just as unpleasant for me as they would be for you."

"Forgive me if I don't take you at your word," Dash says. "This crossbow will be staying right where it is."

"I guess I don't blame you." His eyes move to Dash's empty hand, where magic has begun to gather. Then he focuses on me again. "Almost two decades ago, a group of fae formed based on a common interest: getting revenge on the Guild for leaving us at the mercy of a former Unseelie Prince. You might think I should have felt some loyalty toward the Guild, seeing as I was a guardian for years, but I didn't. I hated them for allowing innocent people to suffer. For their imperfect system that essentially allows them to *choose* who to save." His gaze flicks back to Dash for a moment. "You know I'm right. So we attempted to take down the entire Guild system. But we failed. Then we decided to target specific people instead. That's when I was tasked with killing the child of two guardians. And, as far as the leaders of our group knew, I succeeded. This spurred them on to go after others, but that changeling spell disturbed me more than I wanted to admit. I began to lose faith in our cause. It didn't seem like justice anymore. It just seemed like … murder.

"So I ran, and one of my Griffin Gifted friends—Daniela—ran with me. She'd also lost all interest in getting revenge. She no longer cared whether we killed all the guardians. She didn't care if we made people suffer by murdering their children. She was tired of it all. So in the end, because Dani was the only one I trusted, I confided in her and told her what I'd done. I told her about the changeling spell, and that I hadn't actually killed the faerie child. She was glad. She said I'd done the right thing by not killing an innocent baby."

"You did, though," I remind him. "You killed an innocent *human* baby. Does human life mean less to you than faerie life?"

"It shouldn't," he says, so quietly I can barely hear him. "Years ago, I pledged my life to protect both fae and humans. But by the time I was told to murder a baby, I'd been away from the Guild for so many years that I managed to convince myself that one human life didn't matter."

"That's—"

"I know. All the terrible words you can think of, that's what I am. But just like me, Dani didn't seem to mind too much about that part. So the two of us were on the run. We traveled for a while, and then one day, she asked me to show her the changeling. She said we should check that all was well, and that the human mother hadn't noticed anything strange. We should make sure the child's magic was properly blocked. If it revealed itself, she cautioned, and the Guild ended up getting involved, they might trace it back to us. I didn't believe her, but I took her anyway. The whole changeling concept seemed to fascinate her, and I knew she wouldn't let it go until she'd seen one with her own eyes.

"So we watched them. We watched Macy Clarke and her changeling child Emerson. And they were both completely fine. Dani, though ..." Zed shakes his head. "She wasn't fine. She saw this simple human life, and she wanted it."

"She wanted to be human?" I confirm.

"Yes. Not just human, though. She wanted Macy's life. She

wanted the changeling child, and the lovely little house, and Macy's job, and ... everything."

"But that's ... just ..." I shake my head. "Aside from being totally wrong, that just doesn't make sense. Why would she want to give up her magic, her friends, her own world?"

"If you knew about her past ..." Zed says. "It wasn't good. Her life was horrible. She thought getting revenge on the Guild would make her happy, but it left her feeling even more desolate. She wanted a chance to start over. A new world, a new life. New everything. So she asked me to perform a changeling spell on her. I'd never heard of it being done on an adult, but she was so desperate, so miserable, and she was convinced this would make her happy. I had to figure it out."

"You didn't *have* to help her commit murder and steal someone else's life," Dash interjects. The mass of magic swirling above his raised hand flickers.

"I began working on adjusting the spell," Zed continues, ignoring Dash. "Normally, it binds magic forever but changes the baby's appearance for only a short while—about a year or so—before slowly wearing off. In that time, a baby would grow and change anyway, so the difference isn't too noticeable then. But with an adult ... well, I couldn't have her look like Macy for only a year and then slowly return to her normal appearance, so I had to figure out how to make it last longer. For the rest of her life."

"Which would now be shortened, I assume," Dash says, "without access to her magic."

"Yes. Once I was convinced I'd correctly altered the spell, we went ahead and did it. And as far as we could both tell, it worked. Her name was now supposed to be Macy Clarke, but she didn't like that, so she had it officially changed to Daniela Clarke. I checked in on her every week or so. In that time, we ... well, we started to become more than friends. I fell in love with her. She didn't look the same, but she was still Dani. We had a month or two in which everything was blissful happiness. And then ..."

"Then?" Dash motions with the crossbow for Zed to keep talking.

"The changeling spell that I'd altered so drastically had side effects. It blocked all her ordinary magic like it was supposed to, but somehow it didn't block her Griffin Ability. And her mind ..." He rubs one hand over his face. "It affected her mind. She started forgetting things. Forgetting she'd ever been magical. Seeing things that weren't actually there. Afraid of imaginary things."

"So it's your fault," I whisper. "You're the one who made her crazy."

"I only did what she asked," he wails. "I only wanted to make her happy."

"Your spell drove her mad."

"And I will live with the guilt forever," he whispers. "In the beginning, it wasn't so bad. She didn't get confused too often. Just like her Griffin Ability didn't happen often. But I wanted to help her. Heal her. I tried to convince her that we should find a way to reverse the changeling magic, but she refused. She ended things between us. Told me she was happy with her human life and that she didn't need me to be part of it anymore. But I kept an eye on her. I watched as her Griffin

Ability became ... out of control."

"What was it?" I ask. "What could she—"

"But then it stopped," Zed says, ignoring my question. "Her Griffin Ability disappeared just like the rest of her magic. Soon after that, she snapped completely. I didn't witness it— the day she was hauled off in an ambulance—but I heard about it afterwards. I listened in when the doctors and nurses spoke about her. After that, I consulted healers—a select few that I trusted—but they couldn't do anything. I'd properly blocked her magic when I did that changeling spell, and now her Griffin Ability was gone too. They couldn't sense anything in her, and no one wanted to attempt reversing the changeling spell. No one was brave enough to try to fix the mess I'd made. In fact, they told me it was probably impossible. So, since the healers could do nothing for Dani, I had her moved to a private institution. The best I could find in your world. I was happy to pay for it for the rest of her days. And you—"

"I ended up with an aunt who wasn't really my aunt. Someone who didn't want me. Thanks for that."

"Look, I'll be honest with you, Em," Zed says with an apologetic expression. "I never cared all that much for you. It was Dani I loved. You were more of a nuisance than anything else. You were the child she chose over me. So being able to send you off to your aunt was something of a relief for me. Dani loved you, so I didn't want you to end up a homeless orphan, but I didn't care much beyond that."

I grit my teeth together so tightly my jaw begins to ache. I open my mouth, then snap it shut. I've already told him he's despicable, so there's no point in repeating that.

"I checked in on Dani fairly regularly," Zed continues. "Over the years, the hospital tried to release her a couple of times, but, as you know, it never went well. Occasionally I would try some new form of magic I'd come across, but I was never brave enough to try anything drastic. I didn't want to risk killing her. And with her magic blocked—as far as I could tell—she was as weak as a human.

"We went on like this for years. Then one day, your magic finally broke free of the spell I'd placed on you, and your Griffin Ability revealed itself. Suddenly everyone in power in the fae world wanted to get their hands on you. And I, unfortunately, heard the news too late. The Unseelie King told his son to learn everything he could about you. His search led him straight to Tranquil Hills Psychiatric Hospital—where I was trying to retrieve Dani. She'd always been safe there, but now I needed to get her elsewhere. I didn't act quickly enough, though. Prince Roarke showed up while I was in Dani's room. He captured me and took me back to his home, leaving Dani at the hospital as bait for you, Em. With two potions—truth and compulsion—he forced the story out of me. He discovered that you and Dani were both changelings.

"He brought in a witch then. An old witch well-versed in the magic of her people. Crisanta. He made me explain exactly how I'd performed the changeling spell on Dani, and together the three of us figured out how we could heal her."

"Wait." I hold my dagger-free hand up. "Why would Roarke do that? He doesn't care about my mother. He doesn't need her. He was never planning to fulfill his side of the bargain I struck with him, so why would he go to so much trouble to try and fix her?"

"It was his back-up plan. He thought that if all else failed—if you ended up with the Guild or the Seelies and refused to enter into any agreement with him—he would then steal your mother and heal her. Then he'd contact you, present a fully healed Daniela Clarke to you, and only agree to set her free if you handed yourself over to him."

I find myself slowly shaking my head.

"No?" Zed asks. "You don't think you would have agreed to that? I think you would have."

He's right. I'm not shaking my head because I disagree with him. I'm shaking my head because I still can't quite believe all of this. It's so far removed from anything I've ever imagined for my own life. He can't be talking about *me*. He can't be talking about *my mother*. She wouldn't steal someone else's life, would she? But somehow, deep down in that part of me that recognizes I've been utterly out of my depth since the moment the earth ripped itself open at my feet, I know that Zed's story is the truth. It's my story. It's my mother's story.

"Em?" Dash asks, his crossbow still pointed firmly at Zed. The magic he's been gathering over his palm is almost the size of a bowling ball now. "Everything okay?"

It takes me a few moments to find my voice. "I … yeah. But I have a lot of questions. Starting with my mother's Griffin Ability. What is it? What can she do?"

Zed opens his mouth, then pauses before speaking. "It's … complicated. I doubt you've come across a Griffin Ability like it before."

"I've known about magic for only a few weeks, so there are

many Griffin Abilities I've never come across, Zed. I don't care how complicated this one is. I want to know about it."

"Fine." Zed presses his lips tightly together, then says, "Your mother has ... she *is* ... a split personality."

I shake my head, his words making little sense to me. "What do you mean? Her mental illness is a Griffin Ability? So she was crazy before you messed her up with changeling magic?"

"No, not like that. Not the way you're thinking of it. There aren't just two personalities living inside her. There are two *people*. And those two people—"

"—can separate," a voice says from behind Zed. He spins around to face the door. Someone pushes it open fully, and there stands a woman in an all too familiar silver cloak and black mask.

Ada.

CHAPTER THIRTY-THREE

AND THOSE TWO PEOPLE CAN SEPARATE. DESPITE THE SUDDEN threat of Ada standing in this very room with us, my brain latches onto those words, racing to put together the pieces of this puzzle.

Two people.

They can separate.

Mom and her 'friend' always arguing.

The friend I heard through the walls but never—

"Thank you for sharing that fascinating story, Zed," Ada says in sickly sweet tones.

A knife appears in Zed's hand. Dash steps to the side and aims his crossbow at Ada. "Adaline," Zed grinds out between his teeth. "How nice to see you again after so many years."

Adaline, my brain repeats. Another puzzle piece. I turn it

358

over and around, desperate to make it fit in somewhere. I *know* it fits somewhere.

"I never liked you," Adaline says to Zed as she reaches for the door handle. "I could never understand what Dani saw in you." Glass begins splintering with alarming speed across the door and down to the floor.

My brain abandons the puzzle. My hand raises the dagger. I'm ready to leap over the glass and stab it right into Ada—

But Zed's hand flashes forward. His glittering knife pierces Ada's stomach an instant later. She cries out and doubles over, her hands pressing against her stomach. Her enchanted glass shards stop inches from Zed's feet. He throws his hand up, and a faint ripple in the air hints at the protective shield he's now holding in place.

Ada looks up, her eyes filled with fury. She tugs the knife free, and after it vanishes from her grip, she presses her hands over the wound. "You know you'll have to do a lot more than that to stop me, Zed."

"Yes," he says. "But in order to stop you, I have to slow you down first."

"Hardly," she mutters. "It won't take long for this wound to heal. You don't know what kind of power I possess now."

"I've heard rumors," Zed growls. "Rumors of witch rituals."

"You can hardly judge me, Zed. Not after the witch magic you used." She presses both hands more firmly against her stomach. "Now, I think it's time you finished your story. You were nearing the end, but I'm afraid I interrupted you before you got to the punchline." Her wicked eyes alight on me. "I don't think Em has quite understood yet. And what a delicious punchline it is indeed."

And those two people can separate. My brain fumbles once again with the puzzle pieces it's gathered as Ada raises one blood-soaked hand, pushes her hood back, and removes her mask.

And suddenly I'm looking into the face of my mother.

The dagger slips from my grasp. The air is sucked from my world. My knees begin to weaken. I'm hot and cold and light and heavy and *finally*, all the pieces click into place. "Line," I whisper. That's the only thing I've ever been able to remember Mom shouting through the walls while she argued with the 'friend' I never met. "But it wasn't 'line,'" I say, my voice coming out as a croak. "It was *Adaline*. It was *you*."

Ada nods, her smile slipping away and her gaze turning more venomous. "I couldn't stand the way she used to say my name whenever we separated and ended up arguing. 'Ada*line*,' she used to say. 'Don't be so stupid, Ada*line*. You can't go after the Guild, Ada*line*. Your Griffin Ability is weak and useless. I'm the strong one. What will you do without me? Bury them alive in glass trinkets and ornaments?'" A bitter laugh escapes Ada's lips. "Well, I showed her, didn't I. Once she was too lost in her own mind to control me, I got out. She wasn't strong enough to pull me back inside, and I was finally free once and for all. The witches taught me how to increase my power, and now look where I am. My glass isn't fit merely for tiny trinkets. It's an unstoppable force. And the moment you drop that shield, while the two of you are wasting time with fancy guardian magic you don't think anyone can beat, my glass will get you. It'll crack through you in seconds."

"I doubt it," Dash mutters.

"Ah, and there's that guardian ego we all know and love to use to our advantage," Ada says with a labored laugh. "What will it be today, young guardian? Razor blades, birds, rocks? Glass shards of your own, perhaps? Are you skilled enough to transform your magic at the speed of thought, or are you one of those unimaginative men that likes to throw raw power around?"

"The latter," Dash says. Zed's hand drops to his side, the shield vanishes, Dash throws his arm forward, and all the power he's been gathering since Zed stepped into this room strikes Ada in the chest. A single second passes. Then her eyes slide shut and she crumples to the ground. "Stunner spell," Dash says. "It's amazing how often people forget that one."

"Takes a while to gather the required amount of power," Zed says, kneeling beside Ada and holding her wrists together. "That's probably why."

"Thanks for being so quick with the shield," Dash says.

"Thanks for being so quick with the stunner spell," Zed replies, his hands rapidly looping golden ropes between and around Ada's wrists.

I drop onto my knees as my legs finally give in. "She's … she's my mother. She's *part* of my mother. She's … they're two people. Inside one? That's the Griffin Ability?" I look at Zed for confirmation.

"Yes."

"That's … just … so …"

"Complicated," Zed says. "Super complicated."

"Did you know? Before you did the changeling spell?"

"Yes. Dani told me some months after we met each other. She said that as long as she could remember, she'd been aware of this other presence in her mind. She was seven, I think, when she first split and this other identical person revealed herself. Her parents named her Adaline. Adaline and Daniela. A little bit like twins, but in a weird, magical, share-one-body-most-of-the-time kinda way. Dani was always the stronger one. Adaline couldn't last long on her own. She'd get tired, and the two of them would meld together and become one again. It was strange. I could talk to both of them, and after a while, I could figure out which one was speaking. But if Dani got annoyed with Ada, she could silence her. That was always the way things were."

"Until you messed with their magic and made Dani weak and insane," I say.

"Yeah," Zed murmurs. Finished with the rope, he pushes himself to his feet. "I don't know why it happened that way. Why it affected Dani's mind and not Ada's. Why Ada's magic wasn't blocked but Dani's was. None of it makes sense."

"Sounds like you messed with the changeling spell too much for any of this to make sense," Dash says quietly.

"It changed both their appearances, though," I point out. "They look exactly the same. It's so weird. If I hadn't seen her glass magic, and if I hadn't heard the way she speaks, I would have said without a doubt that this is Mom."

"Yes. They've always looked identical. That's where the similarities end, though. They've never wanted the same things. It was Ada, rather than Dani, who wanted revenge on the Guild. Dani wanted it too in the beginning—Ada obviously couldn't force her—but she grew tired of it a lot faster. Ada wanted to stay. She tried to convince Dani, but Dani wouldn't listen. After we ran, the two of them didn't split as often anymore. It seemed like Ada was sort of ... sulking. Then when Dani asked me to do the changeling spell, Ada was furious. She forced her way out and told Dani how stupid she was being, throwing their magic away for a boring human life. But Dani was still stronger then. She forced Ada back inside. They didn't separate for a long time after the changeling spell, and I began to think that the magic must have blocked Ada. But after Dani began to properly lose her mind, Ada started separating from her again. I saw her a few times, disappearing and only coming back hours later. One day I watched her vanish into the early evening—and I never saw her return."

"So you knew she was out there, then?" I ask. "You knew what she was doing?"

"No. Not for years. I assumed she began a new life in the magic realm, and I was happy to forget about her. I hoped I'd never see her again. But in recent months, I heard rumors about a masked woman who was turning people into glass, and I wondered if it might possibly be Ada. I didn't know for sure until she walked into this room and started speaking. This is ..." He gestures to her. "This is the first time I've seen her since she disappeared."

"So ... when the two of them are together," I say, "their Griffin Ability is that they can split. But when they separate, Ada has her own Griffin Ability: transforming things into glass just by touching them. So does my mother—does Dani—have her own ability when she's on her own?"

"No. Well, not that I know of. The way she explained it to me, her Griffin magic was the ability to split into two different people. The ability to have this other person become part of her while still maintaining a separate consciousness inside her."

"It's so weird," I say again, shaking my head, not moving from my position on the floor. "So super weird. It's like … I don't know. Maybe they were supposed to be twins, and then one of those Griffin discs affected them before they were born, and they ended up in this weird, messed-up, unconventional twin form with one living inside the other."

"Who knows," Zed says with a shrug. "That might actually be what happened."

"And I don't understand why she didn't reveal her face to me before now. She could have pretended to be my mother. I would have been confused, but I'd have gone anywhere with her."

"I don't think so," Dash says. "You're smarter than that. You know now that shapeshifters and illusions are real. You would have suspected some kind of magic. And she didn't actually want *you*; she wanted your mother. So she was probably trying to avoid questions and explanations."

"Then why is she here now?" I murmur, more to myself than anyone else. Dash and Zed don't know any better than I do why Ada might be here. "Anyway." I swallow and clear my throat and prepare to ask Zed my most important question: "Can you heal Daniela Clarke? After spending time trying to figure it out with Roarke and that witch you mentioned, did you discover a way to make her healthy again?"

"We did," he says, and my insides bloom with warmth and happiness. "At least, we think we did. We obviously haven't tried it yet. And there is one catch."

A dark cloud draws across my elation. "What?"

"The changeling spell was applied to both of them. To Dani and Ada. In order to properly remove it, the two of them need to be one again."

I look down at Ada, considering exactly what this means. "She'll never agree to it, obviously, and it sounds like she's strong enough now to resist, but I can command her to do it. To ... reform with Daniela, if that's what you call it." I look back up at Zed. "I assume you know how to wake my mother from whatever spell Ada placed on her? Or I suppose I can just tell Ada to do it. She called it 'irreversible,' but if Roarke was planning to wake Mom, then Ada must have been lying about that part."

"I know how to wake her based on what I overheard from the prince," Zed says. "But perhaps it would be better to command Ada to do it. She's the only one who knows exactly what magic she used."

I glance down at the ruby on my bracelet. "So many things for my Griffin Ability to do." Having recovered from my initial shock—physically, at least, if not emotionally—I climb to my feet. "I'd better go and get Mom so she's here when my ability is ready to be used."

"On your own?" Dash asks, surprise coloring his features.

"Yes. You said one of us should stay here, remember? And that was before Zed ran into the room and then Ada showed up. Now you have to watch both of them, as well as keep a look out for any new dangers. You definitely can't come with me."

"Hey, haven't I proven myself yet?" Zed asks. "I told you the truth. About everything to do with you and Dani and the changeling spell. And I helped stun Ada." He looks at Dash, who is no longer holding a crossbow. His hands are steady at his sides, though, as if he's prepared to grab another weapon at a moment's notice. "You don't have to worry about guarding me," Zed says to him. "I'll watch Ada if you want to go with Em."

"No," Dash and I say at the same time. "I'm not leaving you alone here," Dash adds. "But Em, maybe you should wait. We can go together later after you've used your Griffin Ability to—"

"No. I don't want to wait any longer. I'll be fine, Dash. No one wants to hurt me where I'm going."

"Okay, but your mom is heavy. How will you carry her?"

I walk to the sideboard and pick up one of the candles. "I'm actually not completely useless with ordinary magic, Dash. I can do this—" I snap my fingers and a flame appears atop the candle "—and I can carry my mom."

As bright light flares around me, I squeeze my eyes shut and picture the only other place I can think of that was safe: Dash's parents' home. When I sense grass beneath my feet, I open my eyes and look around. I expect to find the pretty garden—that's what I was picturing—but I'm standing in front of a tall hedge. "Crap," I murmur. I must be outside the property. I look hurriedly around, but there's no one else here. And now that I'm alone, away from Zed and Ada, the protective enchantment over the Griffin rebels' safe place allows me to once again think of and picture the oasis.

I remove Aurora's stylus from inside my coat and replace it with the candle. The candle might work to get me to the oasis, but I'm not sure. At least I know how the faerie paths work now. I bend down and write on the grass while speaking the words I thankfully haven't forgotten. A thrill rushes through me at the sight of a doorway appearing on the ground at my feet; the novelty of performing magic hasn't yet worn off for me. I sit on the edge of the dark hole and let myself slip into it. I might be falling, but I can't tell. Everything is utterly dark and still as I focus firmly on the desert and the dome layer that shields the oasis.

Then abruptly, my feet strike sand and I stumble forward. Hot air smothers me and bright light almost blinds me. I manage to catch myself before tripping onto my knees. After steadying myself, I squint and twist around until I see the faint outline of a dome and hazy shapes within it. When I left, part of me thought I'd never see this oasis again. I knew I might never return from the Unseelie Court. I hoped I would, of course, but I was willing to go through with that union as an absolute last resort if it meant healing Mom.

Now, the thought of that union makes me want to be sick.

I walk as quickly as I can across the hot sand and slip through the dome layer into the fresh, cool oasis air, hoping desperately that no one sees me. I don't have time to answer questions or explain where I'm taking Mom. And I don't have time to apologize—which I definitely want to do properly once this is all over and Mom is safe and healed.

My eyes scan the oasis as I stride quickly—but not too quickly—toward the tree that contains the house I left Mom in. I lower my head and try to remain inconspicuous, but then I remember I'm wearing completely ridiculous clothing, and that of *course* I'll stand out if someone sees me. But it appears to be the middle of the day here, so I guess everyone's busy.

At the base of the giant tree, I pause and look around again. Two kids sit beneath another tree eating something, but neither of them look my way. In the distance, someone leads a large creature—a gargoyle?—out from behind a clump of shrubs. But he or she is too far away to realize I'm not someone who lives here.

My footsteps are silent on the many stairs winding around the tree. When I reach Ryn and Vi's door, I listen outside for several moments, hearing no movement or voices. They're probably far away on some important mission. They might, I realize with a guilty lurch, be searching for Dash and me. I almost continue upward, but my conscience gets the better of me. I duck into their kitchen, then pause for a moment to breathe in the smell of something freshly baked. I look across the counter tops and find a blank scroll and a pencil that keeps changing colors in my hand. Quickly, I scribble a note: *Dash and I are fine. I've taken my mom. Will be back soon. I'm so sorry I left. Em.*

I leave the paper in the center of the kitchen table and place a vase over it just in case a breeze moves through here. Dash would do more than this. He'd go looking for someone he knows here. He'd explain things. He'd make sure that anyone out searching for us is notified immediately of our safety and our whereabouts. But I don't have time for things like that, and I'm already aware that Dash is a better person than I am.

As I head for the door, my stomach grumbles, and I realize suddenly how hungry I am. Hungry and thirsty. Telling myself it isn't stealing—even though it kind of is—I grab the cloth-wrapped loaf of bread from the top of the stove, along with the contents of the fruit bowl, and drop them all into a backpack hanging from one of the chairs. I cast about for something to drink. Do they have bottles in this world? Something I can take with me? For some reason, I doubt plastic exists here. Then I notice an ornate glass shape with something that might be a cork in the top. After removing the stopper, sniffing the contents, tasting it and confirming that it's water—and then taking a second, large gulp—I add it to the backpack.

And that's when I notice three glass vials lined up along the back of the counter. Vials the same size as the one containing the elixir to stimulate my Griffin Ability. Vials, I realize as I bend closer, that have my name written in tiny letters on them. "Perfect," I whisper, silently thanking Ana for making more elixir for me. I remember her saying she would, but I knew I'd be gone by the time she was done with a new batch.

I slide the vials into a pocket inside the backpack and hurry out of the house. I continue further up, just past the simple little tree house that was mine for the brief period I stayed here. Stopping outside the next room, I experience a sudden, irrational fear that I'm going to step inside and find the room empty. I twist the handle and push the door open—and Mom is exactly where I left her. Relief courses through me as I hurry to her side. Looking down at her unconscious form, I'm almost overcome by everything I've learned in the past hour or so. *You don't really know this woman at all*, a tiny voice reminds me. But I can't focus on that thought. For now, I need to get her out of here.

I take a few steps back, recall the early spells I practiced while at the Unseelie Palace, and mutter the words that will lift Mom from her bed. She slides sideways and rolls clumsily into the air. With fierce concentration, I manage to catch her and keep her floating there. Once I'm certain she isn't going to tumble to the floor, I direct her through the air just ahead of me and walk out of the tree house. I manage to successfully make it all the way down the spiral staircase, though it takes me longer than I would have liked.

I realize, as I reach the bottom, that this is probably the last time I'll see this place. I once secretly dreamed of Mom and me living out the remainder of our days in this magical paradise, but that was before I knew she wasn't just one person. That was before I knew that in order to heal her, she'd have to join with Ada, one of the most dangerous faeries I've met in this world. When the Griffin rebels find out who my mother truly is, I doubt they'll let us return.

I walk across the grass, keeping close to Mom as she floats next to me. As I near the dome layer, a shout reaches my ears. I look over my shoulder to see someone in the distance waving and moving quickly toward me. *No time for that*, I remind myself as I step through the protective layer of magic. Heat slams into me as I place Mom on the sand. I kneel beside her, hold tightly onto one of her hands, raise the black traveling candle between us, and light a flame.

CHAPTER THIRTY-FOUR

BLINDING LIGHT BLAZES AROUND US AS I SHUT MY EYES AND picture the room at the base of the tower in the shadow world. After a moment, I sense a hard surface beneath my knees, and the light on the other side of my eyelids begins to dim.

"Em. You did it!"

I open my eyes to see Dash in front of me, a bright splash of color against the muted tones of the shadow world. "No need to sound so surprised." I let go of Mom's hand.

"No, I just mean that I thought someone would stop you. I thought someone—at least one person—would come back with you."

"I didn't see anyone I know," I tell him, leaving out the part about someone running toward me as I left. Zed crosses the room, kneels on the other side of Mom, and takes one of her hands in his. "I guess everyone must be busy at the moment. I did leave a note, though." I can't remember where, now that I'm in the company of someone who isn't supposed to know about the Griffin rebels, but I know I left a note somewhere.

"A note?" Dash says. "That's it?"

"Someone will see it soon, I'm sure. And besides, this will be over soon, right? Then you can return, and I'll find somewhere safe for me and Mom. Hopefully once she's a normal, healthy faerie again, she'll be stronger than Ada, and Ada will never be able to get out again. Mom will be in control, and everything will be fine."

Dash and Zed both look at me with doubtful expressions.

"What?" I demand. "It'll all work out, okay?"

Zed nods, returning his gaze to my mother. "It will. I'm just not sure it'll be as easy as you're hoping."

"Don't worry, I'm used to that," I grumble as I look across the room at Ada. She's lying in the same position I last saw her in, but a semi-opaque spherical shape surrounds her completely. "What's that?"

"I put her in a bubble," Dash says. "A shield. I figured she might wake up quietly without us noticing. She could probably turn her ropes to glass in an instant and shatter them, and if that happens, I want her to remain contained."

"Good thinking." I remove the backpack from my shoulder. "I brought some food. Well, technically I *stole* some food, but hopefully Vi and Ryn won't mind too much. At least we can eat and drink something while we wait for Ada and Mom to wake up."

"Waiting in this world is dangerous," Zed says quietly. "We

should go somewhere else. My home, maybe. No one important knows about it. No one would find us there."

"Great idea," Dash says. "If only we knew we could trust you."

Zed looks up with a frown. "You haven't forgotten that I love her, have you?" he says fiercely. "I'm not going to run away from this. I'm here to fix my mistakes."

"Look, this may be a strange world," I say to them, "but it's the safest place for us to be right now. The Guild doesn't know about it. Most of the Unseelies don't know about it. And the one other place that's properly safe is impossible for us to get to as long as Dash and I are not alone. So let's just be patient until Zed can perform the spell, and then we'll get out of here. Dash, you can return to your Guild job—assuming you still have one—Zed, you can get back to your life feeling a little less guilty than before, and Mom and I ... we'll find somewhere safe to go."

Zed opens his mouth, probably to tell me where he thinks Mom and I should go, but I silence him with a glare. If he's about to suggest we all live together as a happy family after the things he's done to Mom and me, I might have to hurt him.

I move to sit a little further away from Mom, place the backpack in front of me, and open it. "Look what else I found," I say to Dash, holding up one of the three glass vials.

He sits beside me and takes the vial. "Is this ..."

"The stuff that stimulates my Griffin Ability? Yes."

"Awesome." He hands it back. "Now we don't have to wait until tonight."

"Yep. We can get on with things as soon as Ada wakes up."

I remove the bread, fruit and oddly shaped bottle from the backpack. My parched throat is desperate for water, but before I can drink any of it, Dash places both hands around the bottle. He concentrates furiously, and gradually the bottle doubles in size. "That's convenient," I say.

We pass the bottle around, each eagerly drinking from it despite the awkward shape and size. In the silence that accompanies us as we snack on chunks of bread, my mind begins churning over every detail of Zed's story. It's still hard to believe that my mother—Dani—decided to leave her own life behind and take over someone else's. And Zed never mentioned exactly what happened to the original Macy Clarke after the changeling spell. She must have died, but … how long did it take? Did it happen in her own home? Did she know what was happening to her? And what did Zed and Dani do with her body afterwards?

It's so horribly morbid to think of, but I can't help it. Macy didn't do anything wrong. Zed randomly chose her, replaced her baby with an imposter, and then essentially killed her too. And Mom is the one who asked him to do it.

I shrink away from that idea, not wanting to think of my mother as a murderer. She must have had a very good reason for taking over Macy's life. Perhaps it was a reason Zed didn't even know about. Something bigger, something that makes more sense. And she'll probably tell me it was a horrible, awful mistake to have caused an innocent human's death, and I'll tell her not to regret it because it brought the two of us together.

Even though I can barely think the words without feeling sick to my stomach.

"Oh, we shouldn't forget about Roarke," Dash adds, interrupting my thoughts. "And his guards. They're probably awake now, tied up with guardian ropes they hopefully have no way of breaking. I assume they're protected from the shadow beings?"

"Uh, yes." I gladly latch onto this distraction from my disturbing thoughts. "Their amulets will protect them from the ink-shades. They should be fine until we can get back to them."

"Unless someone else finds them first," Dash says. "What about Roarke's sister? She knows about this world. She may have rescued him already."

"Yes, that's possible." I tear the chunk of bread in my hands into two smaller pieces. "Or maybe … there's another woman. I didn't see her, but I overheard her talking to Roarke. She knows about this world too. She might already have found him."

Dash's expression darkens. "If that's the case, then she might still be here. Looking for us."

"See?" Zed murmurs. "Staying here is a bad idea."

"Nothing's going to go wrong," I tell him sternly, wondering if I should get the elixir out of the backpack and put some magical power behind that statement.

Dash nudges my knee with the edge of his shoe. "Glad to see my positive vibes are rubbing off on you."

I roll my eyes. "Don't get your hopes up. That's about as positive as I'll be getting."

Dash gives me a sad face, then pulls the oversized bottle closer to drink more water. I pop a piece of bread into my mouth and chew. Since thoughts of my mother are too confusing to face right now, I let my mind turn back to the start of Zed's story. To the guardian couple he was told to steal a baby from. Fear tangles with a whisper of excitement. Do I want to know who they are? Do I want to know who *I* really am? Do I want to know what my name would have been, whether I have any siblings, where I would have lived?

I clear my throat. "You said you're here to fix your mistakes," I say to Zed. "Do you mean your mistakes regarding my mother and the changeling spell? Or do you mean me as well? Because it wasn't just her life you screwed up. You started with mine."

He looks away from me. "I wish I could say I can fix your life too, but—

"But you only care about Dani."

He sighs. "It's true that she's my first priority. But if I could help you too, Em, I would. I just have no idea where your parents are now, or if they're even alive."

I swallow. "What do you know about them?"

"They were excellent guardians. Two of the best, so I heard, although that wasn't what I experienced when I went to their home to take you. They were unprepared, and it was easy enough to stun them both. I don't know what happened to them after I took you. They were related to an old friend of mine, but I never saw her again either.

"The huge battle on Velazar Island took place not long after that. There were prisoners, guardians, witches, and even Lord Draven himself, with his own army of gargoyles. I still don't know how that was possible; he was supposed to have been killed a decade before that. Some said afterwards it was all a lie, but plenty still believe it was actually him who was burned to death after the veil was ripped. Anyway, my point is that your parents were probably there. They might have been captured by the Guild after the head councilor at the time revealed all the Griffin Gifted. Because they must have had Griffin Abilities themselves," he adds as he gestures toward me. "Your own Griffin magic is proof of that. Or they might have been killed in the fighting. I don't know."

"And you never cared to find out," I murmur.

He shakes his head. "No. You can hate me for it, but I didn't care to find out. I didn't ever want to think of them again."

"What were—"

Crack.

My gaze whips toward the bubble. The rope around Ada's wrists is now glittering glass instead of glittering gold. With another crack, she tugs her arms apart, shattering her bonds into hundreds of shards before climbing upright.

CHAPTER THIRTY-FIVE

ADA'S ANGRY CRIES, ONLY SOMEWHAT MUTED BY THE bubble surrounding her, greet my ears. She pummels the inside of the shield with glass, hail and stones. "And she mocked *us* for wanting to use fancy magic," Dash says to Zed.

"Dash," I say as I fumble with the pocket inside the backpack, "maybe this shield bubble thing wasn't such a good idea. You should have gathered more magic to stun her a second time."

"And then have to wait another few hours for her to wake again?"

"A *small* stunner spell then! But this? She's going to get free." I wrap my fingers around one of the vials and jump upright.

"She won't," Zed says. Both his hands are raised. Hopefully

378

he's reinforcing whatever magic is surrounding Ada.

"Is that Dani?" Ada demands, pausing briefly in her attack of the shield bubble. "You stupid people. You know she can't wake up, don't you? I put her into an eternal sleep!" She continues flinging her magic around, trying to break free.

"Em, are you ready?" Dash asks. "Tell her what you need to tell her."

"Wait. Will my Griffin Ability work through the shield?"

"I don't know! Why wouldn't it?"

"I'm going to kill you!" Ada screeches, reminding me for a moment of the woman in the Unseelie prison. "I'm going to kill you two useless excuses for guardians. I'll hide Dani in a distant hole no one will ever find, and then I'll take what I came for. You!" she spits at me.

"So you've changed your mind about me?" I ask as I pull the stopper from the vial. "Because back in Stanmeade, you made it sound like you didn't have much use for me. But whatever your reasons are for showing up here, Ada*line*, I'll soon discover them all." I tip at least half the vial's contents down my throat.

Ada goes still. She clenches her fists, shuts her eyes, and lets out a blood-chilling scream. Glass explodes from the floor in a ring around her, slices straight through the shield, and embeds itself in the ceiling.

The shield bubble is gone.

She freezes for one second, a triumphant smile on her face and a terrifying gleam in her eyes. Then she raises her hand toward me. That familiar tingling sensation starts at the base of my spine as my Griffin Ability gets ready to rush to the surface.

But it isn't *quite* there yet, and if I can't—

Zed launches across the room and collides with Ada.

"No!" I gasp as the two of them crash to the floor. I expect Zed to turn to glass in an instant. I expect to see all my hopes for Mom shatter to pieces. But the two of them become strangely still as they lie there on the floor. Zed's hand is wrapped around Ada's wrist, but his grip isn't tight, and she isn't fighting him. They're staring at something beyond sight. Twitching, moaning. "No," Ada whimpers, watching something neither Dash nor I can see. "No, please don't. Stop, please."

Frozen in place, without a clue of what to do, I ask, "What's happening?"

"I don't know." Dash inches closer to the two of them.

Then finally, my Griffin magic races to fill my voice with power. Words tumble from my mouth: "Ada, your glass magic has no power in this world." An unexpectedly large amount of magic floods from my body, leaving me a little unsteady. I raise my hands to steady myself. Fortunately, I sense some remaining Griffin magic lingering at the edge of my control. "Ada, you will obey me when I tell you to wake Dani from the enchanted sleep you placed over her," I add quickly. "And Zed, you will answer my questions with the truth, and you'll do everything possible to heal Dani and return her to the way she was before the changeling spell."

My voice has lost its deep resonance for the last few words of my command, but I'm confident I managed to say enough to ensure Zed can't intentionally hurt my mother. Just in case it turns out he's lied about everything so far.

I take a few careful steps closer to Ada and Zed. His hand

slips away from her wrist. Her whimpering ends, and they both lie still, trembling slightly. As Ada blinks and looks around, Dash rushes to her, grabs her hands, and forces them behind her back. Zed pushes himself up, wiping moisture from beneath his eyes. "You swore you'd never do that to me," Ada whispers shakily to Zed.

"I swore I'd never do that to Dani," he answers without looking at her. "I didn't swear anything to you."

"What did you do to her?" I ask, my eyes shifting back and forth between them.

He swallows. "My Griffin Ability. I try never to use it. But … desperate times and all that."

I crouch down in front of them. "What does it do?"

"Nightmares. I can make people relive their worst nightmares." He closes his eyes. "The catch is that I have to feel every ounce of terror they're experiencing. So my Griffin Ability tortures me almost as much as it tortures my victims."

An involuntary shiver crawls across my skin. "That's horrible."

Ada yanks suddenly against the bonds that now hold her hands behind her back. "What did you do to me? What did you say?"

"If you've realized you can't use your Griffin Ability anymore, then you can probably guess what I said."

"You little *cow*," she spits. "How dare you take my own magic from me?"

My gaze hardens. "You've killed people. You were about to kill Zed and Dash. You're the reason my aunt and cousin are dead. Forgive me if I can't muster an ounce of pity for you over the fact that you can't use your horrible glass magic."

Her gaze narrows. "You never loved your aunt and cousin. Your friend always told me that. I did you a favor by getting rid of them."

I stand and take a step back. "What friend? What are you talking about?"

Her glare turns into a taunting smile. "I seem to remember telling you I've always had someone watching you. Someone ready to update me every few months when I stopped by Stanmeade to find out if anything interesting had happened to you yet. I'm not going to tell you *who*, of course. I might need to use that person again."

"You won't," I assure her, "because we're going to make sure you're put back exactly where you're supposed to be."

A frown creases her forehead as she looks between the three of us. Then her gaze settles on my unconscious mother—and I watch as understanding finally dawns in her eyes. "No," she says. "You can't. It isn't possible. Dani has to be awake for—"

"She will be awake. *You* are going to wake her up."

She goes still for a moment, her mouth open, probably ready to refuse. But she can't escape my Griffin Ability. A wordless cry of anger finally breaks free as she begins shuffling across the floor toward my mother. Dash takes hold of her arms and helps her along. He deposits her right beside Mom, where she begins thrashing from side to side. "Dash, her arms," I say, moving closer. "I think she needs to use her hands." He bends as a knife forms instantly in his grip. He cuts the ropes binding her wrists, and she brings her hands around to hover over Mom's motionless body.

382

"Dammit—I don't want—Argh!" She's putting up a good fight against my magical command, but even as her furious cry leaves her mouth, other foreign words begin flying from her tongue. Dash takes a step back and raises a crossbow, pointing it straight at Ada. Zed moves to stand beside him, a short curved blade appearing in each hand. For good measure, I pick up the dagger from the floor and walk to Dash's side.

"We shouldn't need to stop her," Zed says to Dash as the speed of Ada's chanting increases. "I recognize the words. She's saying the right thing."

Dash nods. "Em's voice is hard to resist. But we don't know what she'll try once Dani's awake. Be ready to act."

I tighten my sweaty grip on the dagger's hilt. As Ada chants her spell repeatedly, I sense something different and unnatural pervading the atmosphere. Something that gives me the urge to look over my shoulder to see whether some kind of threatening force is inching closer, about to grab me. I flinch as her chanting reaches a new level of frenzy. She tilts her head back, and an uncomfortable shiver raises the hair at the back of my neck. Dash's hand wraps around mine, and I don't pull away. I want to flee as far as I can from this unnatural magic, but since I can't, it's good to feel the solid, reassuring warmth of someone right beside me.

Suddenly, it's over. Ada lowers her head and stops speaking. Zed drops his knives—which vanish before hitting the floor—and grabs Ada's wrists. She tries to release a few sparks of magic, but he manages to force her arms behind her back without too much difficulty. "Not so dangerous without your glass touch, are you?" he says.

"Why isn't she awake?" I ask, lowering myself onto my knees beside Mom as Zed drags Ada away from her.

"She will be soon," Ada says bitterly.

"How soon?"

She gives me a twisted smile. "You shouldn't be so eager for her to wake up, Em. You know I'm going to tell her what you did once the two of us are joined again. I'm going to make sure she knows all about how you handed her over to me in your weak attempt to save a human town you don't even like. At least I'll get one moment of satisfaction out of this mess: getting to tell Dani that her beloved daughter—the changeling she stole from someone else—betrayed her."

Everything in me longs to lunge at Ada and rip my fingernails down her face, but that would probably give her more satisfaction than it would give me. So I pretend to be perfectly level-headed and sensible, and ask, "Why didn't my Griffin Ability work to wake her?"

Ada shrugs and looks away. "Clearly you're not as powerful as you think you are."

"That has nothing to do with it," Zed says. He looks at me. "People have known about Griffin Abilities for a long time now. Some of the witches figured it out even before Prince Zell began to put the pieces together and started rounding us up for his army. So the witches, who've always been particularly creative with their spells—"

"And particularly evil," Dash adds.

"Creative," Ada repeats with a chuckle. "They certainly are."

"The witches," Zed continues, "came up with a few spells

that are resistant to Griffin Abilities. Not many. Just some basic ones they could be certain would resist any kind of magical influence. Like, for example, putting someone into a permanent sleep."

"Which doesn't seem to be that permanent," I breathe, inching closer to Mom as she begins to stir. I'm so happy that for a moment I forget she'll probably still be confused and scared. I have to remind myself that her mind is still as messed up as the day we rescued her from Tranquil Hills. She may not even recognize me.

"Look at you," Ada murmurs in disgust. "So excited over nothing. You won't win this, you know. You won't stop me."

I grit my teeth and continue staring into Mom's face. "I will."

"You won't. You know why? Because you want your mother. And as long as she's alive, so am I. And as long as *I'm* alive, I'll never give up."

"On what?" I demand, looking up again. "What is your goal anyway? To turn as many people into glass statues as you can and kill them? For no reason other than the fact that you enjoy being in control instead of having Dani control you?"

"You honestly think I don't have a better reason than that? I have a *very* good reason, Em. And seeing as how you've been hunted by the Guild just as I was—just as Zed was—you should understand. Zed understood, once upon a time, and then he got scared off by a *baby*. By *you*."

Dash takes a step toward her, moving his crossbow closer to her head. "All the people you've killed have been related to the Guild in some way. Guardians, former guardians, family of guardians. So is that your goal? You're still trying to get revenge on the Guild, even though the rest of your guardian-hating group disbanded years ago?"

"I'm not just *trying*. I'm succeeding." She directs her glare at him. "What else do I have to live for? It was our life's purpose until Dani decided we should leave magic behind and pretend to be human. Of all the disgusting things she ever made me do against my will, that was the worst. Serves her damn right for going crazy. She deserved it."

"Em?" a quiet, raspy voice says.

Everyone falls silent. My gaze drops immediately to Mom's face. Confusion fills her eyes, but *she recognizes me*! Emotion wells up abruptly, cutting off any words I might have been planning to say. Tears fill my eyes so quickly they spill onto my cheeks before I can stop them. "Mom," I manage to choke out. I blink furiously and clear my throat. "You're awake."

Her eyes slide past me and land on Ada. And that's when everything goes wrong. She shuffles weakly away from me. "What … what's happening? Who are you people?"

"Mom, it's okay." I hold my hands up to show her I mean no harm. "It's just me. It's Em."

"Dani, hey, just calm down," Zed says gently. He takes a step toward her, then stops when she begins scrambling away from him.

She shakes her head. "I don't … I don't know who …"

"Yes you do. You know me. You know Zed. And that's Ada." I point across the room to the exact image on Mom. "You know her too. She's … she's part of you. And we're going to make you one again."

"No, no, no," Mom moans, her terrified eyes fixed on Ada. "She isn't real. I'm seeing things. They keep telling me … that I see things." Her shallow breaths are shaky. "Why are you all … in my room?" She shuffles further back, covers her head with her hands, and presses her back against the far wall.

I bite my lip to keep it from shuddering. I wrap my arms around my middle, attempting to hold myself together, and look at Zed. "Can you just do it please? Start the spell. The reversal—whatever. I don't want to see her like this."

He nods and moves toward Mom without pause, as if the only thing he's been waiting for is my permission. He gently takes her arms and speaks quietly to her, encouraging her to lie down. Dash walks to Ada and pulls her to her feet. "Don't struggle," he tells her. "You'll only make things more difficult."

"I'm happy to make things as difficult for you as possible," she says between gritted teeth as she shoves her elbow into his stomach.

"Stop it," he groans, throwing her into the air.

And there she stays, floating. Wriggling, but unable to get away. With one hand raised, Dash directs her through the air and toward my mother. He lowers her to the ground, where she continues squirming. But his magic must be holding her in place, because she doesn't move anywhere. "I'll break free again," she says. "I swear I will. You can't meld me with *her* and expect me to be the weaker one." She twists her head to the side and glares at Dani. "Look at how weak she is. How pathetic. Useless, insane—"

Zed covers Ada's mouth, cutting off her words with one hand and producing a piece of cloth that's just as golden and sparkling as the rest of the guardian weapons I've seen so far. He places it over Ada's mouth, and despite the fact that she writhes around, the cloth successfully ties itself behind her head within seconds.

"Don't worry," Zed says to her. "Dani may be weak now, but I'll help her to become strong again. And until that happens, I'll personally make sure you don't go anywhere." He turns to Mom. "Dani," he says gently. "Dani, love, I need you to do something." Mom is still crying quietly, but Zed manages to gently pry her hands away from her face. "See this woman? She isn't imaginary. She's real and she's your sister. And all you're going to do is touch her arm, okay? Touch her arm, and don't resist." Mom looks wildly uncertain, but she's spent the past few years doing what doctors and nurses tell her what to do, so perhaps that's why she lets Zed take her arm and extend it toward Ada. "Just relax," Zed says to her. "Relax and don't resist."

Mom's hand touches Ada's arm—and the strangest and most unnatural thing I've ever seen takes place. With a stifled shriek, Ada is sucked into Mom's body. It's over in less than a second. If I'd blinked, I would have missed it.

"Sorry," Zed says, looking up at me. "It's freaky if you're not used to it.

I swallow. "Um … yeah. Definitely freaky." What's even freakier is the way Mom's expression keeps alternating between rage and fear. One moment her lips pull into a snarl, and the next her gaze darts fearfully about the room. As if the two personalities inside her are at war. "Is it … will the spell take long?" I ask Zed.

"Yes, it's a quite complex."

"Are you sure you remember it all?"

"Yes. I made sure to memorize every step while the prince, Crisanta and I were crafting this changeling reversal. I knew he only planned to use it as a last resort. That he'd probably never do it. I hoped I'd be able to get away eventually, find Dani, and perform the spell myself."

"Okay," I whisper. "You can start."

With Mom lying down, Zed places a hand on her arm and closes his eyes. As he begins speaking, I imagine I can see magic seeping from his fingers into her body. Dash moves a little closer and stands beside me. "It's finally happening," he says quietly. "You've wanted this for so long."

I nod, still finding it difficult to speak. "What if … it doesn't work?"

He's quiet for a while before saying, "Then we'll find another way. You're both faeries. You'll both live for many years to come. We've got time to find a solution. Look at the tear in the veil. After it happened, no one had any idea how to fix it. No one knew if it would ever be possible. And now, almost twenty years later, someone found a way to do it."

A hiccup of a sob escapes me, and my next words are stilted as I do my best not to give in to the tears. "I don't want to—wait twenty years. I've waited—so long already."

Carefully, as if he's worried I might shove him away, Dash puts one arm around me. "I know."

We stand like that and watch the spell, and I plead with everything in me for this to work.

After what feels like only a few minutes, Zed stands. "Is that it?" I ask. He made it out to be such a complicated spell that I expected it to take far longer.

"No, that was the first step. I've put her to sleep and initiated the spell. But I need certain ingredients in order to finish it. A few items that are key to the changeling spell, and that Crisanta believed would be necessary in reversing it."

My heart sinks. "You need other ingredients? Why didn't you say anything about that before?"

"Because I knew how that would have sounded. 'Hey, I can heal your mother, but first I need to go home and get some stuff.' You wouldn't have believed me for a second, but I'm telling the truth, Em. I swear I am."

"I know." I let out a resigned sigh. "I commanded you to answer my questions with the truth. And I commanded you to do everything in your power to heal Mom."

He frowns. "You did?"

"Yes. You were lost in a nightmare at the time. You probably didn't hear me."

He sucks in a deep breath. "Okay. That's a little scary."

"Why? Are you planning to hide something from me?"

He answers without pause: "Only things that have nothing to do with you."

I nod. "Seems fair."

He steps closer. "You know I want her to be healed just as badly as you do."

"Yes, I do. But … Zed, what exactly are you hoping to get out of this?" May as well find out what his end goal is. If he's imagining patching things up with his former girlfriend, he'll have to make a new plan.

"I want to finally have peace about all the things I did years ago," he says, not looking away from me. "I hope that Dani will forgive me for driving her mad. I hope you'll forgive me for stealing you from your family. I know I can't expect to get a happily ever after out of this, but hopefully I'll be at peace when I leave the two of you. I'll know that I've done everything I can to fix my mistakes."

I'm glad he doesn't expect to stay with us, to become part of our lives. I suppose Mom could eventually choose that for herself, if she wants, but I hope she doesn't. It's probably selfish on my part, but it messes with the perfect picture I've been working toward all my life.

"Okay," I say to him. "Go and get the things you need. We'll be waiting here."

He nods. "Thank you. And don't touch her. You might disturb the spell."

CHAPTER THIRTY-SIX

"YOU DON'T HAVE TO STAY IF YOU DON'T WANT TO," I SAY to Dash as we sit against the wall beside Mom. "I know you've got your own life to get back to, and you've helped so much already." I almost laugh at my own words. *Helped so much?* Now there's an understatement.

"Are you kidding? I'm not leaving."

I don't want to admit how relieved I am to hear that, so all I say is, "Thank you."

"I'd never pass up the opportunity to defend a damsel in distress," he continues, "and who knows what other dangers might show up before this spell is over?"

I manage to smile, grateful for his attempts to lighten the heavy atmosphere. "Thanks for the reminder that I'm still essentially useless when it comes to normal magic."

"Hey, you know I was just joking, right? You've never been a damsel in distress. Not back in Stanmeade, not in the fae realm, and not here. I have no doubt you'd put up an excellent fight if someone unpleasant showed up."

"Well, I do have a dagger now. I could probably inflict some damage with it."

"Exactly. And also …" He pulls his knees up and rests his arms across them. "I figured you probably wouldn't want to sit here alone waiting for Zed to get back."

"Yeah. Not really. Although I do have Bandit." I watch Bandit, who crept out of my pocket as a lizard about a minute ago, exploring the room in cat form. He sniffs at the candles Dash dropped on the floor earlier, then kneads a section of the rug. When he notices me watching him, he shifts into dragon form—still no bigger than a large dog—and stretches his wings out. He stops, points his face toward the ceiling, and coughs out a tiny flame. "Well done, Bandit!" I open my arms to him, and he shrinks rapidly back into a cat, crosses the rug, and climbs into my lap.

"You guys are so cute," Dash says as he pulls the backpack closer. "Thank goodness I stopped you from selling him."

"Hey." I cover Bandit's ears with my hands. "You know I didn't mean that. I was just being …"

"Contrary?"

"Well, yes." I stroke one hand along Bandit's back.

"Blueberries?" Dash holds a handful out toward me.

"Thanks." I lean my head back against the wall as I chew. Bandit turns around in my lap at least three times before curling up and closing his eyes. I look across at the window. A dark shape floats slowly by, reminding me that I still need to tell the ink-shades never to attack another faerie. Once the changeling reversal spell is done, I'll drink some more elixir and go outside to command them. "You know, I thought I'd have some power left over after commanding Ada and Zed," I say, "but I spent almost all of it telling Ada not to use her glass magic."

"I guess her Griffin Ability is powerful. Makes sense that it would take a lot of your power to stop her power." He looks at me then, his brow creasing. "What did you say to her, exactly? Your glass magic has no power *in this world*?"

"Uh … I think so."

"What about the other worlds? I assume her magic will still work out there."

"Crap. I suppose it will. I'm sorry, I wasn't thinking clearly. But once this spell is complete, she'll be back to her weakened form inside Mom. She won't be able to do much with her magic."

"Yes." Dash nods. "You're right. This is all going to work out fine."

And though I keep cautioning myself not to be too hopeful, I find that I actually believe him. I'm so close to getting Mom back now that there isn't much room left for anything to go wrong.

I allow myself to relax against the wall. It's impossible to know what time of day or night it is by looking outside, but it feels to me like it must be evening by now at the Unseelie Court. I didn't sleep much last night, and I spent half the morning running away from people, so it's not surprising my eyelids feel so heavy.

"You never got to finish asking about your parents," Dash says, rousing me before my head can droop forward. "He said they were a guardian couple, but he didn't mention anything about which Guild they were at."

"No, he didn't," I murmur, blinking and watching Mom again.

"Do you want to know more about them? Once Zed gives us their names, I can look them up. Find out if they're still working at a Guild, or if ... if something else happened to them."

I absent-mindedly run my finger across the soft fur of Bandit's head. "I don't know. Maybe. At the moment, all I can really think about is Mom. But once life gets back to normal—whatever normal ends up being—I think I'll probably be curious. I'll probably want to know more about them."

"Yeah. Well, let me know when you're ready, and I'll see what I can find out. Just imagine," he adds with a grin, "if your parents are alive, how overjoyed they'll be when they find out their daughter is actually ... " He trails off, a frown slowly replacing his smile as he stares at the floor. Then he looks at me, his eyes searching my face for something. "I wonder if ... no. That can't be what she was talking about."

"What? Who?"

"I overheard ... but it was probably something else."

"Overheard what?"

He pulls his head back a little as he examines my face intently. Then he shakes his head. "I can't tell. Your face is too familiar to me now."

"What on earth are you talking about?"

"Nothing. Sorry. Just thinking out loud."

"If you're going to be cryptic and refuse to explain yourself, then perhaps you should keep your thoughts to yourself."

"You're right." He looks away, the shadow of a frown still present on his brow. "I'm sorry."

I nudge his arm with my elbow. "I'm right? Really? That probably isn't something you often say to people," I tease.

He pulls his trademark grin back into place. "I was saving it for you. Since you're so special and all that."

I roll my eyes and shake my head. "Can I please stop being special? It's seriously overrated. I just want to be an average faerie who knows how to use average magic."

"Sorry, Em, but I don't see 'average' anywhere in your future."

"Great," I say with a sigh. "Well if something else exists between 'average' and 'special,' I'd like to aim for that then."

Dash laughs and reaches for the giant water bottle. He hefts it up and offers it to me. I drink a few gulps, then pass it back. "It's probably a weird thing to say, but this—" he gestures vaguely between us with one hand "—feels comfortable. Like, way more comfortable than it would have been a few weeks ago. It's just strange how quickly things can change, I guess."

"Comfortable. Yeah." I nod. "I mean, we're in a world between worlds where shadows rise from the edges of everything while watching my mom, who is actually two people, change back into someone I've never actually met. But … yeah. If this had happened a few weeks ago, we'd definitely be sitting on opposite sides of the room."

396

"Yep. Mortal enemies and all that," he says in a deadly serious tone, before allowing himself a laugh. He drinks from the bottle, then lowers it.

"Sorry. I was really mean to you over the years."

He shrugs. "It's not like I ever gave you a reason to think I was anything other than a jerk."

"True. But at least I know better now."

"Aah, you think I'm better than a jerk?" He presses one hand over his chest. "Emmy, that's so sweet of you. Fills my heart with warmth."

"Shut up."

"Still not a fan of 'Emmy,' huh?"

I look out the window again. "I guess it's not so bad. It's just … it always felt too familiar when you said it to me. Like a nickname that a close friend or family member might give me. But you weren't close to me, and I didn't want you to be."

"Did your mom call you Emmy?"

"Sometimes. Mostly Em, but sometimes Emmy."

He nods slowly, then smiles again. "Well, we can be close friends now, right? Then I can call you Emmy without you wanting to … what did you say before? Hurt me?"

I turn my head to face him, a strange flush heating my skin as part of the conversation we had in the prison comes to mind. He said it was worth it to wind up locked in a prison because he got to meet me. I wonder if he meant that, or if it was simply the drug potion talking. "Is that what you want to be?" I ask quietly. "A close friend?"

"Um …" He shifts and mirrors my position, the side of his head leaning against the wall as he watches me. "Why do I feel like this might be a trick question?"

"I don't know. It isn't." I don't have time for trick questions. Perhaps I would if I were an ordinary girl back in the human world with nothing more to worry about than school and friends and a boy staring at me the way Dash is staring at me now. I could ask trick questions and play hard to get, and then rehash every single second of the exchange with Val late at night, trying to figure out what he meant and what I meant.

But my world isn't like that. It never really was.

"Hmm, let's see," Dash says. "Do I want to be your close friend?"

"Yes or no," I say simply, though part of me is beginning to think it isn't that simple at all.

"How about yes *and* no?"

I narrow my eyes. "Didn't I already tell you how I feel about you being cryptic?"

He nods slowly. "Yeah. You did. Somehow, I'm finding it difficult not to be."

Without warning, a bright green spark skitters across the floor, transforming into green flames that race from one side of the room to the other. I pull my knees up in fright. Bandit lets out a yowl as he winds up half-squished between my legs and chest. "What the hell is that?"

"Uh … I think that was me."

"You *think*?" I jump to my feet as Bandit leaps away from me. The green flames die down and vanish. "What if it wasn't? What if someone else is here?"

Dash remains seated. "It was me. I'm sorry. Just … some

escaping magic. Which is really weird. I thought I'd outgrown that."

After a final look around, I sit again, tiredness already seeping back into my bones. "Outgrown what?"

He examines my face for a while before answering. "I'll explain when you're older."

I muster enough energy to punch his arm half-heartedly. "Idiot."

He laughs. "Fine. You really want to know?"

Bone-weary exhaustion creeps closer. I lean against the wall again. "Mm hmm."

"Well …" He looks down as his hand nudges against mine. After a moment's hesitation in which my heart begins to pump faster and suddenly I don't feel sleepy at all, I let him lace his fingers between mine.

And then, in a blinding flash of light, Zed reappears. I snatch my hand away from Dash's and sit upright. "Did you get everything you need? Did anyone see you? Is everything—"

"Yes, no, and yes, everything is fine. If that's what you were going to ask." I nod as he crouches down beside Mom. He looks around at me. "Can I continue?"

"Of course."

* * *

Part of me wants Dash to finish what he was about to say before Zed returned, but I think I already know, and it isn't something either of us would be comfortable talking about with Zed in the room. Besides, the reversal spell is far more important, so I should be paying attention to that instead.

I watch Zed working on his spell for as long as I can, but after the third time my head droops forward and jerks up again, Dash tells me to stop being silly and just lie down and sleep. "I'll watch Zed," he says. "Make sure nothing goes wrong. I'll wake you when it's over."

"Aren't you tired too?" I mumble. "You didn't sleep at all … in that prison."

"Don't worry about me. I've been a faerie a lot longer than you have. I can survive on barely any sleep."

"That's … not …" I slide down and rest my head on the floor. "I've been a faerie … all my life. Just like you."

"You know what I mean. And here, lie on this." He pushes the backpack toward me, and it feels like the greatest effort in the world to raise my head. "Besides, I'm a guardian," he continues. "I'm used to stressful situations. You're not. Stress and terror are exhausting when they're new to you."

"I'm not … a damsel," I manage to mumble, and I think he replies but I'm already drifting away.

CHAPTER THIRTY-SEVEN

IT FEELS AS THOUGH ONLY MINUTES HAVE PASSED WHEN Dash squeezes my hand and says words my brain is too muddled and sleepy to understand. "Mm?" I manage to peel my eyelids apart and squint up at him. "What?"

"The spell is complete."

"So quick?" I push myself up and rub my eyes.

"It's been about an hour."

"Oh." I blink again and crawl toward Mom.

"Yeah, a regular changeling spell doesn't take as long," Zed says, "but I wanted to make sure I correctly undid every single alteration I made to Dani all those years ago."

I reach Mom's side—and a gasp escapes me when I see her face. "She—she doesn't look normal. What's happened to her face?"

"Her appearance has begun to change," Zed says.

I breathe out slowly. "Right. Of course." In the back of my mind, I knew this would happen. She needed to be returned to her original form, and her original form obviously didn't look anything like Macy Clarke. But it's still hard to imagine looking at a stranger and thinking of her as the mother I've always known.

She isn't the mother you've always known, though, I remind myself. *She was hiding so much from you.*

"Don't worry, you'll get used to her appearance over time," Zed assures me. "She's still the same person inside."

"Well, the same two people inside." Which is still completely freaky to imagine. "How long do you think it will be before she wakes up?"

"I'm not sure. There's a lot of magic working through her system right now. It could be an hour. Maybe more, maybe less."

"Should we leave this world now? In case it isn't safe here much longer. If Roarke is still tied up out there, the king will be searching for him. Eventually, he or some of his guards will show up here."

"I agree we should leave as soon as possible," Zed says, "but I'm not sure we should move Dani until the spell is complete. It *should* be fine, but I'm not certain."

"Okay, then we wait." I look back at Mom, and already her face has changed some more. Even her hair looks lighter than it was a few moments ago. And is that ... pale pink? I lean forward with my hands on my knees and examine the strands of hair lying across her forehead. "Pink?" I ask Zed.

"Pinky peach, she always called it."

I try to imagine how she'll look when the spell is done. "Pinky peach. Sounds like an odd eye color."

"Where you're from, yes," Zed says. "But I always found her eyes quite pretty."

My own eyes are achingly tired. I rub them as I stand and start pacing. Like an impatient child, I keep wanting to ask Zed how long it will be until she wakes up. But I know he doesn't know. I stop moving, fold my arms, and look across the room at Dash. "You must be exhausted by now."

He leans down and lifts the glass bottle, which contains maybe a quarter of the water it contained after Dash's enlargement spell. "I may have placed a small enchantment on this water. An energizing enchantment." He holds the bottle out toward me. "Want to try it?"

"An energizing enchantment? Okay. May as well." I take the bottle in both hands and tilt it over my mouth. The water that runs over my tongue and down my throat tastes a lot like watermelon. I lower the bottle, and it's remarkable how quickly I begin to feel less weary. I drink a little more before carrying the bottle to the sideboard. I check the ruby on my wrist and realize that its color is almost full, which tells me it must be around about midnight back in the Unseelie part of the fae world.

A murmur draws my attention back to Mom. "I think she's waking up," Zed says.

"Crap, crap, crap." I return to Mom's side. "This is so weird. I have no idea how to act around her. I don't know what to say."

"Tell me about it," Zed mutters.

I kneel down and look into the face of a complete stranger. Her cheekbones are higher, and her lips are thinner. Her hair is almost blonde amidst the strands of peach, and a handful of freckles are sprinkled across her nose. This is my mother. This is the person who chose me. The person who chose the simple life we had together while I was growing up.

This is the woman who stole someone else's life, a quieter voice adds. *She stole you.*

I shove the voice away. Mom and I may not have come together in the conventional way, but that doesn't mean it wasn't somehow meant to be. She is my mother and I am her daughter. That's the only thing that's ever felt right in my world.

I reach for her hand and push away the nagging idea that I'm wrong. That maybe *nothing* has ever felt right in my world.

With my help, Mom slowly pushes herself up into a sitting position. She looks down at her hands, her eyebrows drawing tightly together. She pulls her hair over her shoulder and examines the blonde and peach strands tangled together. Her gaze lifts—and eventually falls on me. "Emmy," she whispers, her eyes dancing across my face. She leans forward, pulls me into her arms, and hugs me as tightly as if she's making up for every hug we've missed out on since the day that ambulance took her away. Tears blur my vision as my arms come up to wrap around her. My body begins to shudder as I finally let myself cry properly.

* * *

I don't want to let go of her, but I guess we shouldn't stay on the floor of a half-finished castle in this strange world for much longer. There must be a better place for us to continue our reunion. "I'm so sorry about everything I kept from you," Mom says as we separate. She wipes her thumb across the tears on my cheek and tucks my hair behind my ear. "We have so many things to talk about."

"I know. I have so many things to tell you as well."

"And now we have the rest of our lives."

I nod and smile and try to keep myself from crying more.

We stand, and she looks around the room. "Zed," she says. I watch her face closely as it crumples for a moment, unable to figure out whether she's teetering toward pain or anger. But then her expression smooths into a tentative smile. "You did it. You fixed me."

He blinks away the sheen of moisture in his eyes. "I—I didn't know if you'd want me to."

"I know. For a long time, I didn't. And by the time I regretted my decision and wished I could beg you to change me back, I was already too lost inside my own mind."

"So you ... you remember it all?" I ask.

She nods slowly. "I think so. Most of it." Her eyes fall on Dash. "Do I know you?" she asks. "And where are we?"

"You don't know me," he tells her, "but I'm a friend of Em's. I assisted in your rescue from the psych hospital. And I've been helping out since then." He gives her one of his charming smiles, but I know him well enough by now to notice a brief wariness in his expression before that smile takes over. "It's a long story. I'm sure Em can fill you in at some point." He doesn't mention he's a guardian, which is probably best. If Mom spent a large portion of her life hating the Guild, she probably wouldn't warm up to someone currently employed by them.

"And this is a new world," Zed adds. "A different one. A world that came into existence when the veil was torn. Do you remember that?"

Mom nods as she walks to the window and looks out.

"The ink-shades—those dark beings out there—aren't safe," I tell her. "If we stay here longer, I'll tell them not to hurt us, but I think we should probably leave soon."

She looks over her shoulder at me. "Your Griffin Ability is incredible."

"You know about it?"

"Ada does. Which means I now know about it too."

"Is she … talking to you?" I try not to imagine the weirdness of someone else's voice inside my brain.

Mom's expression becomes thoughtful. "Not really. She's angry with me, I think. Ignoring me. But I'm aware of her memories as if they were mine."

"That's so strange."

"Em?" Dash says. "If you don't need me anymore, I should probably go."

"Right. Yes. Of course."

"Can we … say goodbye?" He motions with his head toward the door. "Out there?"

"Uh, sure." I smile at Mom. "I won't be long." After a hesitant glance at Zed, I follow Dash into the hallway. We walk to the end of it and into a large room furnished with nothing more than curtains. Dash faces me. He starts speaking, and at the same time, I say, "Thank you so much for everything."

We both stop, and he laughs. "You're welcome, Em." He rolls one of the black candles between his palms as his expression turns serious. "Are you sure you can handle things with your mom now? She seems okay, but what if Ada gets out?"

"I think everything will be fine. We've got Zed. He said he'd make sure Ada remained under control until Dani's strong enough on her own. And my Griffin Ability will help. So yeah, don't worry about us. I know you must be anxious to get back to your own life."

"Me, anxious? Never."

I laugh. "Well, anyway, I hope you're not in too much trouble with the Guild when you get back."

He gives me that cocky grin I've become familiar with over the years. "It'll all be fine. The death penalty was brought back especially for Princess Angelica after she tore through the veil, but the next head councilor outlawed it again. The worst I'll get is a lifetime in the Guild's special prison reserved for the worst guardian traitors."

I blink. "You wouldn't seriously land in prison for this, would you?"

"Nah. You know I can charm my way out of anything."

I cross my arms over my chest. "Yeah, I see that worked out really well for you with Roarke."

"Look, if Roarke were a member of the fairer sex, I could totally have talked my way out of that prison."

"Um. I highly doubt that."

He chuckles, rolls the candle some more, and looks everywhere except directly at me. I wonder if he plans to finish what he was saying earlier, or if he thinks now isn't the right time. "Anyway, where will you and your mom go now? I'll need to know where to find you. You know, just in case you want to hang out some time."

"Hang out some time?" I smile. "Yeah, maybe. I'll check my busy schedule and see if I can fit you in somewhere in the next few centuries. And I'm guessing I don't need to tell you where I'll be going, because as long as you're friends with Violet, you can always find me. I mean, once this is gone." My fingers rise to the back of my ear and touch the small circle of metal still stuck to my skin.

"Oh, yeah." Dash's hand rises to the same spot behind his ear. "I need to get mine removed too. Someone at the Guild will be able to do it."

"That's good. I'll have to figure out something else, since visiting the Guild is out of the question for me."

His eyes finally settle on mine. "I have a feeling that if you just *tell* it to remove itself, it will."

"Oh. Yes. Why didn't I think of that?"

"Uh, all of that—" he gestures over his shoulder with his thumb "—might have been distracting you?"

"Yep. I think you're right."

"Well, anyway. I'll see you soon, Em. You should get an amber so we can stay in touch."

I nod. "Okay. Yeah. Hopefully life will be so pleasantly boring from now on that we'll have nothing to talk about."

Except maybe that thing you were about to say before Zed returned to finish the spell.

"One can only hope." He takes a few steps back, putting some distance between us, and raises the candle. He hesitates. "Ah, what the hell." He lowers his hand, walks right up to me, and kisses me. His soft lips move against mine as one hand slides into my hair and the other, still gripping the candle, presses against my back.

I'm so startled that by the time I realize I'm enjoying it, it's over. I blink as he takes a step back. "Um ..."

"There." He grins, then looks down at the ring of green flames that's mysteriously formed around us. The flames vanish an instant later. "Now we'll have something to talk about next time I see you," he says. "And now I can stop torturing myself wondering what it's like to kiss you. Although ..." He rubs the back of his neck. "Now I'm probably going to be tortured wishing I could do it again." He laughs and shakes his head. "Sorry, this is weird. I'm usually way cooler around—"

Without giving myself a moment to think about it, I grab a fistful of his shirt, tug him closer, and kiss him again. His lips are parted this time, and his mouth tastes faintly of watermelon. As he tugs me closer, pressing his fingers into my back, shivers of hot and cold race across my skin, and bright light pops beyond my closed eyelids. I'm probably imagining it, but I think something almost ... *electric* zaps across my tongue and lips. I pull away from him, look into his bright eyes, and give myself a moment to catch my breath. "You're cooler when you stop trying to be cool."

He swallows, looking completely ruffled, and I like it way

409

more than the cocky, self-assured Dash. "Right." He clears his throat. "Okay. We definitely have something to talk about next time I see you."

I shrug, feigning indifference. "Maybe. I guess we'll see."

His confident smile returns. He lifts my hand and kisses it, keeping his eyes on mine. "Bye, Emmy. Don't miss me too much."

I shove him playfully away. "Dumbass."

"Save me a kiss." He winks as he steps further back and raises the candle.

I shut my eyes against the bright white light. When it fades, I open my eyes to an empty room. I wonder if I should regret acting without thinking, but I don't. A bubble of laughter escapes me. Maybe that kiss meant something big and maybe it didn't, but so what? Ada's glass magic is basically gone. Mom is healthy. No one's trying to lock us up or hurt us or use us, and soon we'll be hidden far from anyone who might want to do those things. *And* I got to kiss a hot guy. Twice.

All of a sudden, life is good.

Well, except for the part where Roarke wants to tear the veil further open instead of allowing the Guild to close the gap. But I can command him not to before Mom and I leave this world. And if somehow he's already gone, then the Guild can stop him. Mom and I don't have to get involved.

With my joy somewhat dampened, I head back for the room at the base of the tower. "And you're sure she's not struggling to get out right now?" Zed asks Mom as I walk in.

"Yes, I'm sure. I could always tell, remember? I'd get kind of twitchy if I was trying to hold her back and she was trying to get out. Like that night at the Punk and Mouse Face concert, remember? But I'm totally fine now." She holds both hands out and looks at them. "See, no shaking."

A slow smile takes the place of Zed's anxious expression. "I can't explain how strange it is to see you like this again. If I try hard enough, I can almost imagine the past seventeen or so years never happened."

Mom's smile is sad. "But they did. And we've both changed."

"I'm so sorry for everything you went through, Dani."

Looking a little confused, she asks, "Were you expecting me to be angry with you?"

"Yes, of course." Zed's brow furrows. "You ended up going crazy because of a spell I cast over you. You *should* be angry with me."

She shakes her head. "I thought *you* would be angry with *me*. I was the one who insisted you do the changeling spell. You never wanted to do it. I thought you'd be shouting 'I told you so!' right now."

"I would never say that to you, Dani."

I edge a little further into the room. It feels rude to interrupt them, but, selfishly, I want my own time with Mom now. Noticing me near the doorway, Mom waves me over. "Anyway, Zed," she says as I reach her side, "I think you and I should probably part ways now."

"Oh. I thought—maybe—"

"Look, our relationship wasn't healthy. I think you know that. So it probably isn't wise if you're around while I'm trying to figure my new life out. Figure *our* new life out," she corrects, smiling at me. "It would just confuse things," she continues, looking at Zed once more. "Don't you agree?"

"I do," he says carefully, his eyes swinging back and forth between Mom and me, "and I'm not asking for the kind of relationship we had before. I'm just worried about you, and I want to help you get back on your feet. There are so many things you don't know anymore. Our world has changed."

"It can't have changed that much. I'll figure things out. And if I really am lost, I'll come find you. Or perhaps catch up with some old friends."

He frowns. "You don't mean …" He pulls his head back slightly. "That group doesn't exist anymore, Dani."

"Not *them*. I had other friends before I took up with those guardian haters. I had other friends before you, Zed. Things will work out." She puts an arm around my shoulders. "Em and I will make our way in the world together."

I smile at her. I thought she'd wake up from the changeling reversal spell a little confused. Or at least in need of some direction. But she appears fairly certain of her thoughts and feelings. It lifts a weight of responsibility off my shoulders. For so much of my life, I've been trying to figure out how I'd take care of Mom one day. I didn't believe until recently that she'd ever be normal again. And now that she is, it's incredibly freeing to realize she's able to take care of herself. And not just herself, but me too, perhaps. She doesn't *look* anything like the person I remember, but Zed was right. She's the same inside. I recognize the way she speaks, and this is the quiet confidence I remember my mother possessing before she began to lose her mind.

412

Zed, however, doesn't seem convinced. "But what if … what if Ada gets out?"

"Zed, you've restored things to the way they were before. She's the weaker one now. Yes, she might get out on occasion, but it won't be for long. You remember how things were. She couldn't remain separate from me if I didn't want her to."

"Yes, I remember. I'm still worried, though. I'm not saying I want what you and I had before. I'm not asking you for anything. Why don't you just stay with me for a few weeks until we can be certain you're in control? You'll be safe at my place."

Instead of arguing, Mom turns her gaze to me. "Em, what do you think?"

Surprised to be asked my opinion, I take a few moments to formulate my response. I know Zed isn't lying. I know he's only suggesting we stay with him because he's worried about Mom. But I don't think he has anything to be concerned about. More importantly, he doesn't belong in the picture that I—and Mom, it would seem—have of the future. "I appreciate your concern, Zed, but I think Mom and I are fine without you. You've righted some of your wrongs, and I think that's enough."

With a weary sigh, he nods. "Okay. I suppose you've got your Griffin Ability. If Ada gets out, you can tell her not to hurt you or your mother or anyone else. But you know where to find me if you need help, Dani," he says to Mom. "Orangebrush Grove. In case you've forgotten." He crosses to the sideboard and picks up a candle. He looks at me. "Orangebrush Grove. Tell the faerie paths, and they'll take you there. If you ever need help."

"Thanks." I hope I'll never need his help again, though. Mom and I wouldn't have needed it in the first place if he hadn't messed with our lives to begin with. "Oh," I say, raising my hand to stop him, remembering suddenly that I never asked him the names of my birth parents. But the candle is already lit, and he's gone in a flash of light.

"Did you need something?" Mom asks me.

I turn to face her and realize that everything I need is right here in front of me. "No. It wasn't important. We'll probably see him again some time, so I'll ask him then."

"Maybe," Mom answers. She tilts her head back, lets her eyes slide shut, and breathes in deeply. Then she laughs and focuses on me again. "I can't wait to spend hours and hours just talking, catching up on everything from the past few years."

A wide smile stretches across my face as I watch her. "Where shall we go? We can go *anywhere*, Mom. Anywhere in any world. Or ... do you have a home somewhere? From before?"

"I did, but ..." She turns slowly on the spot, looking around. "Why don't we stay here? Make this our home."

"What? But ... this is hardly a home. It's a half-formed world. A *tiny* half-formed world. And it isn't safe."

"We can make it safe." Her hands clasp my upper arms as she gazes proudly at me. "*You* can make it safe."

"I suppose I can."

"And we can fill it with life. Your power can create almost anything, and my magic can help. In small amounts," she adds with a laugh. "It doesn't matter that it's a small world. It only needs to be big enough for the two of us—and maybe a few other people over time. And you can *tell* it to belong to us, so no one can ever try to take it away." Her hands slide down to grip mine. She swings our arms back and forth between us the way an excited child would. "This will be our home, Em. Our fresh start. What do you think?"

I don't know if it's reckless or stupid, but suddenly I don't care. Mom's enthusiasm is contagious, and the way she says it, it sounds like a perfect idea. "Yes. Okay. Let's do that."

And so, about fifteen minutes later when the color has filled my ruby completely, Mom and I stand at the window together, looking out at our wispy grey surroundings as power fills my voice. "The shadow world is ours. Yours and mine. The Unseelies will never enter this world. The Guild and its members will never enter this world. Only those we give permission to can enter this world. The ink-shade creatures will never attack anyone here. We will be safe."

In the distance, a ripple of magic races along the horizon as my Griffin power rushes out of me, leaving me weak but happy, knowing the shadow world is about to become our home.

PART IV

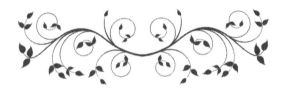

dash

CHAPTER THIRTY-EIGHT

THE ONLY PLACE DASH WANTED TO GO WAS HOME. FIRST, to reassure his mother he hadn't met a horrible end at the hands of the Unseelies, then to send a message to Ryn, and lastly, to enjoy a proper shower and a good sleep. But he knew that after almost a week of unexplained absence, he needed to report to the Guild first. So, with the traveling candle blazing in his hand, he pictured the inside of the Creepy Hollow Guild's entrance room—and that's exactly where he appeared moments later.

The light faded to reveal two guardians with weapons pointed directly at him, probably due to his unorthodox arrival. "Dash?" one of them said, lowering her sword. "You're not dead."

Dash raised both eyebrows. "Nope."

"Is that a candle?" the guy next to her asked, his knives vanishing as he let go of them.

"Yep. No stylus. I had to improvise." Dash headed through the archway—which would scan his wrist markings to determine he wasn't an imposter, and would detect any other dangerous enchantments that might have been placed on him—and into the main foyer. He hastily made his way upstairs. The sooner he explained himself to a Council member, the sooner he could get home. But he expected his report meeting would take a while, so if he could send a message to his mother first, that would be great.

Reaching the open-plan office area he shared with several other junior guardian teams, he rifled through his desk drawers, searching for an old amber. Or perhaps he had a mirror here somewhere. He could make a quick call while on his way to the Councilors' level.

"Dash!" He looked up and saw Jewel across the room. He expected her to run over and hug him, but her delighted expression soon turned to wary confusion. Guilt stirred uncomfortably in his chest. He'd abandoned his team—including one of his best friends—to go on this unofficial mission. Hopefully they'd understand why he did it, once he explained himself, but he still felt bad about whatever worry he'd caused them.

"Dash?" A different voice uttered his name this time, and he turned to the side to see Councilor Delmore walking through the door, accompanied by several senior guardians. "I'm glad to see you've returned safely," she said, though her eyes lacked their usual warmth. "We need to talk."

"Great timing," he said. "I was just about to come looking for a Council member. I have a lot to report."

"Good," she says. "We have a lot to ask you."

"I'm just calling my parents first," Dash added, his fingers finally locating the edge of a mirror in one of his drawers. "They don't know I've returned."

"We'll get a message to your father," Councilor Delmore said. "He's on duty nearby in the forest. Your debriefing is more important."

Dash hesitated for a moment, then moved to walk beside her. He wondered at the presence of the additional guardians who accompanied her, but he told himself there was no reason to be concerned. He assumed they already knew he'd been with the Unseelies—he'd told his mother not to lie about that part seconds before he climbed into the Unseelie carriage—so they were probably here to ensure there wasn't some form of dangerous magic lingering about him.

But a minute later, as he and Councilor Delmore sat across a table from each other in one of the oval conference rooms and six guardians lined up along the wall, his apprehension returned in full force. There was definitely something different about this debriefing.

"I'll get right to the point, Dash. We received correspondence from the Unseelies this morning regarding your unauthorized presence in their court."

"Okay," Dash said with some uncertainty. "But you were already aware of that, weren't you? Didn't my mother inform you straight after I left her studio for the Unseelie Palace?"

"She did."

"I know it wasn't an authorized mission," Dash hurried to explain, "but I couldn't pass up the opportunity. I'd heard the rumors about a new young lady at the palace and the royal family's interest in her. I strongly suspected it was the Griffin Gifted girl, Emerson. I discovered at the last minute that my mother was handing over a dress to one of the Unseelies, so I had to act immediately. There was no time to alert the Guild or make an alternate plan. I'd hoped to correspond with you from there, but the prince took my amber when he discovered I was a guardian. Oh, and this?" Dash tapped the piece of metal behind his ear. "The prince added this special little touch to make sure you couldn't summon me if I was tagged. And then I was thrown into their prison. Which, I might add, we knew nothing about. I think there are plenty of people imprisoned there who shouldn't be. The Guild needs to get involved."

"Well, we'll be sure to look into that," Councilor Delmore said. "But for now, I'm far more concerned about the part of the letter than implied you have inappropriate connections to the Griffin rebels."

Dash's stomach lurched. After a beat of silence, he said, "What? That's insane."

"The Council has reviewed the letter, and we believe we have sufficient cause to question you under the influence of a truth potion."

Crap, crap, crap. Dash tried to keep the alarm from showing on his face. "Woah, seriously?" He laughed her words off in his usual manner. "You're going to believe the Unseelies over me?"

She sighed, leaning back a little and regarding him with an

almost apologetic expression. "Dash, I've known you since you began your training here. I don't believe you'd work against us like this. Not for a second. But it would be remiss of us not to be absolutely certain. And the fact that you've been missing for days …" She lifted her hands from her lap and placed them on the table, revealing a tiny bottle in her grip. "We just need to know what's going on. I don't want any unpleasant surprises further down the road."

Dash swallowed, his eyes on the bottle of truth potion. He couldn't refuse. He could only hope that the protective enchantment would keep him from revealing anything too important, and that any other questions would be vague enough for him to avoid giving away too much information. "Well, let's get this over with then," he said, holding his hand out for the bottle. "We've all got work to get back to." He opened the bottle, allowed a few drops to fall onto his tongue, then passed the bottle back. Behind him, he heard the door open and a few more people walked in.

"Councilors," Councilor Delmore said with a nod, and Dash decided not to look over his shoulder to see who, exactly, had joined them. He needed to appear unconcerned. So he leaned back and loosely folded his arms, giving Councilor Delmore an expectant smile. He would feign innocence as long as he possibly could. Across the table, she laced her fingers together and asked her first question: "Are you keeping information from us about the Griffin rebels?"

Damn. There was no avoiding that one. Dash tried to clamp his mouth shut, but he couldn't. He *couldn't*. His answer left his mouth almost as a grunt. "Yes."

Councilor Delmore blinked. In her eyes, Dash saw not only disappointment, but sadness as well. She shook her head and looked away. "Do you know, I didn't actually believe it until this moment."

He wanted to cry out that he wasn't the traitor she thought he was. The Griffin rebels were *good people*. He was doing the right thing by helping them. But he'd only dig himself into a deeper hole, so he bit his lip and remained silent, waiting for the next question.

"What do you know about the Griffin rebels?"

"I ... mmm." He pressed his lips tightly together, breathing out sharply as he struggled against the barrage of information that longed to pour free from his mouth. There was certain information he'd never be able to give away, but there were *so many other things*. It was too much. Far too much for one answer. He wouldn't even know where to start, and that—he realized with relief—was what helped him to fight off the potion's influence.

But Councilor Delmore was smarter than that. "Sorry. That was far too broad." She paused, then asked, "Where are the Griffin rebels based?"

"I don't know."

"Are they planning a move against the Guild?"

"No."

"Are they planning to interfere in the veil restoration ceremony?"

Interfere. Focus on interfere, he instructed himself. They weren't planning to interfere. They were only going to watch. He'd suggested it, and he knew they agreed it was a good idea.

They would be back-up. Just in case something went—No! Nothing would go wrong. They wouldn't have to interfere. "Nnnnno," he managed to force out.

Councilor Delmore's eyes narrowed. "You didn't sound like you entirely meant that, Dash."

"They don't plan to interfere," he said, the words tumbling quickly from his lips.

She nodded slowly. "I see." Then she asked, with far more emphasis on each word, "Do they plan to be there?"

Dash squeezed his eyes shut, gripped the chair's arms fiercely, and tried with all his might to force the answer down. But it slipped from his mouth anyway. "Yes."

Footsteps sounded behind him as someone moved around the table. Head Councilor Ashlow, with her stiff posture and her unreadable expression. She nodded as she stopped beside Councilor Delmore. "Good. Now we know who it is. This confirms what the Seers have Seen and filled in the specifics that weren't clear to them." She looked across the table. "Thank you for being so helpful, Dash. We'll question you further at another time."

As glittering handcuffs snapped around his wrists and rough hands tugged him to his feet, Dash shut his eyes and let the horrendous guilt at having betrayed his friends sink into him.

CHAPTER THIRTY-NINE

BANDIT PRANCES FROM ROCK TO ROCK ACROSS THE POOL of water I created earlier, leaping from the last rock into the air and landing in my arms as a cat. Mom laughs at him. "He is very sweet. Where did you say you found him?"

"The forest outside Chevalier House. And it would probably be more accurate to say he found me. He's been following me ever since."

"Lovely," Mom says. She leans back in one of the two beach chairs I spoke into existence earlier and looks out at what we've achieved in our first day together: a river that leads away from the rock pool, clouds that change shape, drift across the sky, and never actually disappear, and a new section of the castle. Plus what isn't currently visible: the two wardrobes of normal, court-inappropriate clothing back inside the castle.

My command to the shadow world late last night sapped me entirely of my Griffin power, but I took one of the elixir vials from the backpack and walked to where the portal used to be, planning to command Roarke not to interfere with the veil. I was then going to light a candle and tell it to take him and his guards back to the Unseelie Palace. But I couldn't find him or his men. Perhaps Aurora or some of the Unseelie guards showed up and took them away while we were hiding inside the castle. Or perhaps it had something to do with the command I gave this world about Unseelies not being able to enter. Either way, Mom and I now seem to be the only ones in this world.

So I returned to the castle, where Mom had chosen two bedrooms near each other that were mostly furnished, and prepared one of the beds for me to climb into. I almost cried when I saw it. I decided to blame my emotional state on exhaustion, but I knew the real reason: my mother was finally here to take care of me.

I slept for so long that my Griffin Ability was almost replenished by the time I woke up. After using it for the big things—the river, the clouds, the castle, and telling the dim light in the sky to mimic the day and night of the Unseelie Court—Mom taught me a few things with ordinary magic. Like changing the patterns on our bedspreads, using an organizational spell for all the food we found in the pantry, and getting a cleaning spell going in the kitchen to take care of the dirty dishes left behind by Roarke's guards. And all the while we chatted endlessly. I decided not to go for any of my big-deal questions yet—like 'How could you allow a human to die so you could take over her life?'—choosing to stick to less serious topics until Mom and I get to know each other a little better.

Now we're sitting by our little rock pool drinking something Mom concocted as the light around us gradually grows dimmer. I'd love to watch a real sunset, but I'll have to make do with the enchanted lighting. Perhaps I can add color to it when my Griffin Ability next refuels itself. Or I could use the elixir, but I'd rather save that for emergencies.

As I sit in my comfy chair with Mom right beside me, Bandit on my lap, and a strange yet tasty drink in my hand, my thoughts turn toward Dash. He may have been joking when he said he'd wind up tortured wishing he could kiss me again, but I'm starting to feel a little tortured myself. It's not as though I've never kissed anyone else, but none of the boys in Stanmeade can quite match up to a guy with magic racing through his veins. I've replayed that kiss over and over in my mind, and each time I remember something else that seems sort of … magical. And not in the corny, figurative sense. I mean *actual magic*. The flashing lights I noticed through my closed eyes, the sensation of sparks on my tongue, the hot-cold shiver that didn't quite feel like a normal shiver. Not to mention the flames that briefly encircled us.

Interesting. Very interesting. Like Dash said, we'll definitely have something to talk about the next time we see each other. I probably shouldn't get too attached to the idea of him, though. He might have already moved on to whatever new guardian girls have arrived at the Guild in his absence. It may feel to me like we've created some kind of bond while surviving life and death together, but he's probably experienced the same thing with plenty of other guardian females. Life and death situations are an everyday occurrence for them, right?

"Everything okay?" Mom asks, and I realize she's watching me.

"Yes. Better than okay. Why?"

"You just had this frown on your face, that's all."

"Oh." I make sure I'm smiling instead. "Sorry, I didn't even realize."

"Do you have more questions?" She shakes her head. "I mean, of course you have questions. But is there something in particular you were wondering about right now?"

"Um …" I suppose I could ask her about the magical side-effects of kissing, but I don't feel entirely comfortable about that. Right now, it still feels like something private that I want to keep between Dash and me. So I decide to ask a different question instead. "You said you have Ada's memories of the years since the two of you separated, right?"

"Yes."

"Can I ask you some things?"

"Of course, honey." She turns a little in her chair to face me. "I've been waiting for you to ask more about my Griffin Ability and Ada. I thought you'd be more curious."

"I am curious, I just didn't know if it was something you'd want to talk about."

"Em, I'm happy to talk about anything with you." Her smile crinkles the skin around her strange peach-colored eyes. "No more secrets, okay? I want everything out in the open."

"Okay. So … how did Ada know about this world? I

thought it was just a few of the Unseelies and their guards who knew about it."

Mom pauses for a few moments, perhaps digging through Ada's memories to find the answer. "It seems she discovered it by accident, actually. She wanted to, uh ... Ugh, this is horrible. She wanted to kill the guardians stationed by the veil tear. But they saw her coming and chased her with magic. She escaped into the faerie paths, but the guardians were so close behind her, she was worried they might actually be able to follow her through. So she stayed inside the paths. Which, in case you don't know, is a difficult thing to do," Mom adds. "And while she was hiding there, she began to notice light in the distance. She thought that was odd, since the faerie paths are supposed to be completely dark, so she followed the light, and she discovered this world. There was a wall and a door, and once she went through it, she found a half-formed castle, and soldiers or guards in the distance. She didn't stay long, but I can tell from her memories that she's been here a few times since, just to see what's going on."

Suspicion has been growing inside me while Mom's been talking. "That's very weird," I say when she's done. "That's almost exactly how Roarke and Aurora discovered this world."

"Oh." Mom tilts her head to the side. "That is strange. I wonder how many other people have also accidentally stumbled into this world, probably not even realizing what it is. It's a good thing you told this world it belongs to us. Now we don't have to worry about random strangers wandering through our home."

"Yeah ..." I say, though there's definitely an edge of doubt to my voice. "Wait, but how did Ada know I was here yester-day? She arrived and basically said she came for me."

"She …" Mom screws her eyes shut, then breathes out sharply as she opens them. "She's keeping certain things from me."

"Is that possible?"

"Yes. If she chooses to deliberately not think of certain things, or cover them up by firmly thinking of other things, then it's difficult for me to access her memories."

"Is she … gaining control?"

"No, no. She's just hiding a few things from me."

"Oh. Okay." Nevertheless, my eyes scan Mom's body for signs of twitching. That's what she said to Zed, right? That she used to twitch when she was struggling to maintain control?

"I'm fine, Em, I swear," Mom says, noticing me watching her closely. "And I'll figure out what Ada's hiding. She won't be able to keep things from me for long."

"Okay." I sip my exotic drink and find my mind turning back to the changeling spell. I want to understand why Mom decided it was okay to steal someone's life. She must have known Macy Clarke wouldn't survive the spell. So it was more than stealing, actually. It was *murder*.

I shove away the image of my mother as a murderer. I know that isn't who she is. She was just confused and lost at the time. And maybe she didn't know what would happen. Surely it isn't possible for every faerie to know every spell that exists, so maybe Mom had never heard of a changeling spell. And maybe Zed left out the part about Macy ending up dead. That seems far more likely to me than Mom agreeing to murder.

Movement catches my eye. I look to the side and see Mom holding her glass toward me. I raise mine and clink it against hers, smiling as I force all my doubts to the back of my mind.

* * *

By the end of the second day, when Dash hasn't returned yet, I suddenly remember that I told this world no member of the Guild would ever come here. So before I climb into bed, I drink a tiny bit of the Griffin Ability elixir and listen to my oddly distorted voice saying, "Dash Blackhallow is allowed to enter this world."

Then, since there seems to be a little bit of my Griffin power left over, I look down at my feet and tell them they're wearing unicorn slippers. Fluffy white fabric wraps itself around my feet while filling with some kind of padding. Silver wings pop out the sides, a head bulges over my toes, a mane of fuzzy rainbow hair appears, and a gold horn materializes on top of each unicorn head. Peering down in delight at my latest creation, I clap my hands together and laugh. Then I imagine what Val would say if she saw me wearing *unicorn slippers*, of all things, and I laugh harder.

I hurry down the passage to Mom's room and offer to make a pair of unicorn slippers for her too with the last remaining shred of my power. Once her slippers are done, I climb onto her bed. We stretch out our legs so we can wiggle our feet back and forth in front of us as Mom shares stories from her past. I remember Zed mentioning that her life was horrible, but if that was true, she doesn't speak about it. She tells me only the fun things about her childhood. Faerie school, and getting her first stylus, and the rules she loved to break. I'm happy to sit here and fall asleep to the sound of her voice.

My eyes are half-closed when Mom quietly says, "I wasn't sure if I should bring this up, but I meant it when I said I don't want there to be any secrets between us."

I blink, open my eyes fully, and push myself up a little straighter. "Okay. What is it?"

She looks down at her lap. "I know what happened outside Chelsea's home. When Ada came for you. I know you gave me up."

My stomach plummets instantly, weighted down by guilt. "Mom, I'm so sorry. It wasn't like that—"

"I know, honey."

"She was going to kill my new friends. She was going to wipe out the whole of Stanmeade. And the last thing I wanted to do was tell her where you were." I reach for her hand. "I swear, Mom, if my heart could literally have broken, it would have. But I couldn't—"

"I know, Em, I know." She strokes my hair as if I were a small child. "You couldn't let all those people die. You had to choose them over me."

"It wasn't that I was *choosing* them—"

"Sweetie, I know. I understand." She kisses my forehead. "I forgive you."

It should be a relief to hear those words, but I feel even worse. She shouldn't *have* to forgive me. I should never have done something to her that would require forgiveness.

We say goodnight, and with a heavy heart, I return to my

bedroom. I pull Bandit closer and snuggle him against my chest, trying to tell myself not to be silly. Mom forgave me, so I should be able to forgive myself too, right? It was an impossible situation. I *had* to choose to save a whole town of people over saving just one, right? Even if that one person was my own mother ...

I sit up and walk to the mirror over the dresser. I haven't tried the spell to call anyone, but I know the words. I touch the mirror, thinking of Dash, then immediately withdraw my hand. I doubt he'd want to hear about my troubles. He's probably busy saving someone else's life right now. A damsel in distress. He wouldn't appreciate the interruption.

The only other person I want to talk to is Val, and that's impossible right now. My best friend would have a heart attack if her mirror started talking to her, and I don't know if the spell would even work on an ordinary mirror in the human world. Or if it would work in the shadow world, for that matter. But that doesn't stop me from longing to tell her every single thing that's happened since that horrible night at the party.

I return to bed without attempting to call her. One day I'll go back to Stanmeade and explain my disappearance as best I can, but now isn't the time. I need to focus on the new life Mom and I are building and shove the past far behind us.

CHAPTER
FORTY

BY THE END OF DAY THREE, OUR WORLD IS EVEN FULLER. I closed up the side of the castle, added some rose bushes and other flowers alongside the river, and spoke a golf cart into being. Mom thought the golf cart was a bit strange, especially in a world of magic, but I thought it would be fun to drive around our land. She reminded me that we have nowhere to plug it in, and I reminded her that we can make it move with magic. Then I used the last bit of my morning's Griffin power to tell two ink-shades to take on the form of dragons as large as Imperia—just to see if they could.

And they did. I bounced up and down with sheer excitement before climbing onto one of them. After I got past the odd sensation of sitting on a cloud of icy air, I flew around and around our little world, only landing when Mom told me to come down and learn how to transform some pillowcases into curtains for our bedrooms.

I wish I could show Dash everything we've done, but he hasn't returned. Totally understandable, I keep reminding myself. He probably has a ton of work to catch up on after being AWOL for days. Still … I kinda miss him.

* * *

I walk into the castle's enormous kitchen to help Mom with dinner. "Can I chop these veggies?" I ask, pointing to the pile on the counter beside the stove.

"Yes. Thanks, sweetie. You remember the chopping spell?"

"I think so." I move a few potatoes, carrots, and something that looks like purple celery to another counter, marveling at the simple fact that I can stand in a kitchen with my own mother while we prepare a meal together. I push the veggies aside to make space for my chopping board—and that's when I notice two perfect glass roses in a vase on the windowsill.

My blood chills instantly. "Mom," I say carefully. "What's this?"

"Hmm? Oh, I wanted to add some flowers to the kitchen, but I didn't feel like walking out to the rose bushes by the river. Don't you think the glass ones are pretty?"

Swallowing, I turn slowly to face her. "Did Ada make them? Did you … give her some control so she could do these?"

"What?" Mom's eyes widen. "No, don't be silly. I made those."

"But she's the one with the ability to—"

436

"Em, honey, she doesn't have a monopoly on glass magic. She can do far more with it than any ordinary faerie, but the rest of us can still make use of simple spells involving glass. And you know I like glass trinkets as much as she does."

"Yes, but ... okay." These roses look far from simple to me, but I suppose that's because I'm still new to most magic. "Sorry, I guess my first response is to freak out when I see something I don't expect that's made of glass."

"Understandable," Mom says with a laugh as she turns back to the stove.

"I guess we'll need to go shopping for more food soon," I say. "I thought we could create a veggie garden here, but then I remembered we don't actually have a sun in this world, so that wouldn't work. Oh, and while we're on the topic of no sun, that isn't exactly healthy, is it? We should probably go back into one of the other two worlds at some point just to get some sun."

"Good idea. And you're right about the fresh food too. It won't last much longer."

"Yeah." I'm starting to think that living in this world isn't a viable long-term option, but I decide not to voice that opinion just yet. Mom seemed really keen on the idea, so I'm happy to stay here for now. Maybe until everyone out in the magic realm forgets about me and I don't have to worry about looking over my shoulder wherever I go.

I get the chopping spell started, then wander into the pantry to check out the state of our supplies. "When do you think we should go?" I call to Mom. "To get more food, I mean. And should we go to the human world or the faerie world? Oh, and what about money?" I walk back into the kitchen. "Crap. That could be a problem."

Mom sets up a spoon to stir the pot by itself before facing me. "Em, I was thinking I should go without you. I know you want to see the fae world, but I don't think that's wise at the moment. It isn't safe out there. People are still looking for you."

"I know, but it won't be for long. And we can go to an area I've never been to before, so there's no risk of anyone recognizing me."

"Em." She gives me an indulgent smile. "You know that isn't a good idea. At least not yet. The Guild has other ways of finding people. Rather wait a bit longer until they've begun to worry about other things."

"Um, okay."

"Hey, come here." I cross the kitchen and she puts her arm around my shoulders. "You know I love you, right? You're the most important thing in the world to me. In any world."

"Of course. I love you too. More than anything and anyone." It's still a little weird to say that to someone who doesn't look like my mother anymore, but I still mean the words.

"Good." She rubs her hand up and down my arm. "Then you know I only want to keep you safe."

"Yes, of course. But … you know I've been looking out for myself for a long time, right? I think I'd probably be fine out there now that I've got a better grasp on my magic."

"I'm sure you could, hon, and I know you can take care of yourself. But I've missed out on so many years of taking care of you. Why don't you let me do it for a little while? Let me make up for all the years I didn't—"

"Mom, you don't have to make up for anything. Seriously."

"Em, please. Just let me do this."

After a moment, I give in with a smile. "Sure. Of course." It seems silly to me, but if this will help her feel like my mom again, then cool. I can handle that for a while.

The silence is awkward for a few minutes as we continue preparing dinner, but soon we begin talking about other things. I don't mention the money problem again, but that doesn't mean I don't think about it. What will we do when we need to buy food? I don't particularly want to create money from nothing with my Griffin Ability. It wouldn't be *stealing*, but somehow the idea doesn't feel right either.

The dining room is empty except for the long table Roarke built in here, but Mom and I dragged a few chairs in yesterday from other rooms. I'll get around to furnishing it properly at some point. For now, Mom and I sit next to each other in mismatching chairs, and Bandit sits on the other end of the table in monkey form with a collection of fruit in front of him.

"Your Griffin Ability is already so impressive," Mom says when we're halfway through dinner, "but I wonder what more it could achieve. I think if you had more power—if your base magic levels were higher—you could probably do even greater things."

"Maybe." I finish another mouthful of food, then add, "I thought if I could save up my Griffin Ability's power instead of using it, then once it's replenished a second time, I'll hopefully have twice as much power."

"But that would take so long," Mom says. "It would be a lot faster to draw magic directly from another source."

"Okay. Like what?"

"You know, the way the witches draw power from other beings." She pauses to sip her faerie wine. "I can see exactly how to do it from Ada's memories. I'm sure that would power-up your Griffin Ability much faster."

I laugh at Mom's crazy suggestion. "We can't do that."

"Of course we can." She returns her glass to the table. "We'll find some people who don't matter. Some humans."

I slowly lower my fork, realizing that she might not be joking. "*All* people matter, Mom. Including humans."

"Not the bad ones. There are humans who've done terrible things. We'll look for those ones. Raid a police station or something."

I stare at her for several moments. She continues eating as if nothing is wrong. As if she hasn't just suggested something horrendous. "You're not serious, are you?"

Confusion colors her expression. "Of course I am."

"We can't do that, Mom. Seriously. It's not happening."

It's her turn to lower her cutlery. "I don't understand what the problem is, Em."

"The problem is that we can't *kill* people just to get power."

"Em, we're talking about people who are going to die anyway. You know, people who've been sentenced to death. Their energy may as well be of some use to us before they die."

"I … I can't …"

"I'm sorry, Em, I didn't realize you'd have such a problem with this." She places her hand over mine, and her thumb rubs back and forth across my skin. "We can wait a bit longer until you're okay with it."

I pull my hand away. "I'll never be okay with it."

Her expression slowly becomes stern. "I don't remember you talking back to me like this before."

"Probably because you never suggested we go out and kill people together."

"Em, I'm your mother. You need to trust that I know better than you about certain things."

"I don't think you do, actually."

"Emerson!" Mom smacks her hand down on the table.

Bandit shifts rapidly into a dragon and snarls at her, letting loose a small stream of flames.

"Down!" Mom shouts, sweeping her arm through the air. A flash of sparks swipes him across the face and knocks him backwards. He tumbles off the table, shrinks into a cat as he hits the floor, and whimpers.

"Bandit!" I jump up and rush to end of the table, dropping onto my knees beside him.

"Em, I'm so sorry," Mom says. Her chair scrapes the floor as she rises. "I'm still getting used to having magic again. I don't know my own strength. I didn't mean to hurt him."

Bandit crawls into my hands as a mouse, where he repeatedly licks his front paws and rubs them over his ears. "I think he's okay," I say quietly. I stand and place him inside my hoodie's front pocket. Then I look at Mom.

"I really am sorry, Em. Please come back to the table and finish dinner."

"Yeah," I say quietly, still trying to make sense of the highly unpleasant turn our discussion has taken. "Okay."

I sit and pick up my fork, and Mom says, "I'm sorry I lost my temper. I'm just trying to do what's best for you, and I don't know why you're fighting me on this."

"Because you're talking about mur—"

"We've had horrible lives, both of us. You lived with that awful human sister of Macy Clarke's. And I suffered with the changeling spell tormenting my mind for years. And then I almost ended up unconscious for the rest of my life because—" She cuts herself off, closing her eyes briefly and biting back the words I imagine she wants to say: Because *I* gave up her location to her dangerous other half.

Sickening guilt twists inside me once again as I press my lips together and stare at my remaining dinner. My hand clenches around my fork.

"My point is, Em, that this is our chance to make everything so much better. So you need to stop questioning me. I'm your mother, and I know what's best for both of us. So we're going to increase your power, okay? I'll give you some time to get used to the idea and to understand that it's a totally normal part of our way of life, but then we're doing it. No more arguments, okay?"

I force myself to look up at her and nod. I even manage a small smile and a resigned sigh. But inside, I can't stop shaking.

CHAPTER FORTY-ONE

I MANAGE TO PRETEND EVERYTHING IS FINE UNTIL WE'VE finished eating dinner. After cleaning up, I give Mom what I hope is a cheerful smile and tell her I'm going to relax in the pool in my bathroom for a while, now that I've learned a few spells for changing the scent and color of bubbles. But the moment I'm up the first flight of stairs, I run. My feet don't stop pounding the floor until I reach my room. My hands shake as I pull a jacket on over my hoodie and snatch a candle and stylus from the drawer beside my bed. I double-check to make sure Bandit is still in my pocket.

Then I freeze, completely lost for a moment as to where to go or what to do.

Mom wants me to *kill* people? What the freaking hell?

The picture I have in my head of the perfect life the two of us are supposed to have now has suddenly become as brittle as the glass ornaments Mom and Ada love so much. It's balancing on the edge of knife tip. About to fall. About to shatter.

No. Everything will be fine. This is merely … a hiccup. A misunderstanding. Ada's influence, most likely.

With a snap of my fingers, the candle is alight. I close my eyes and concentrate fiercely on the one place I know we can still be happy: the home I grew up in. Number twenty-nine Phipton Way. Bright light flashes beyond my eyelids. As it slowly fades away, peace begins to soothe the shivering fear in my heart. Soon, I'll be home. Soon, everything will be okay.

When I feel solid ground beneath my feet, I open my eyes. I'm standing outside number twenty-nine in dim light that reminds me all too much of the shadow world. The wet road and the smell of damp earth tells me it recently rained. Pushing the remaining piece of the candle into the front pocket of my jeans, I take a step closer to the wooden fence. It's tangled with bushes, just as it was before. More overgrown now than I remember, but that's okay. My heart thumps uncomfortably against my ribcage as I walk toward the pedestrian gate. The crunch of my shoes against the damp road seems overly loud in this quiet neighborhood.

Bandit twitches, climbs out of my pocket, and scurries up my arm to my shoulder. I reach the gate and find its hinges rusted with age. The number twenty-nine painted onto a block of wood and nailed to the gate is so faded I can barely read it, and the wood itself is split in various places. *Not right*, my mind whispers to me. *It isn't supposed to look like this.*

I swallow the painful lump in my throat before stepping

forward and pulling the gate open. It screeches on its rusty hinges. Once inside, I look around as my heart continues to sink lower and lower. "This is all wrong, Bandit," I murmur. The setting sun should cast warm light across the garden instead of being hidden behind grey clouds. The grass should be cut short, not growing wildly out of control. The rose bushes should be neatly pruned, not choked to death by weeds. This nightmare of a garden is nothing like the perfect home from my memories.

But then, with slow and horrible clarity, I begin to realize that it never was.

I push my hands through my hair as the rosy memories begin to crack and darkness appears in the gaps. I remember now that it wasn't always sunny, and Mom wasn't always happy. I'd find her outside at night, brandishing a broomstick or garden shears, shouting at no one. She wouldn't come inside, so then I'd start crying. Eventually she would drop her weapon, tug me inside, and lock every door. We'd huddle together, and sometimes she'd cry too, and she'd swear to protect me from the bad guys. The first few times, I was terrified along with her, but I soon grew to realize there was no one there. The things that frightened her existed only in her mind.

I drop my hands to my sides. As if in a daze, I walk back to the gate. I turn and face the house once more, realizing finally that it was never the safe place I thought it was. And it was never *ours*. This was Macy Clarke's home. This was the home Dani stole. This was the *life* Dani stole. This is where the real Macy Clarke and the real Emerson never got the chance to live their lives. The only thing I see when I look at it now is loss and misery.

And I don't ever want to see it again.

My feet turn me around and carry me out through the gate and into the road. I keep walking, though I have no idea where I'm going. I think I want to cry—I feel like I *need* to cry—but I'm too empty even for that. I walk to the end of the road. Then I place my butt down on the hard wet curb and rest my head in my hands.

I must have been in a dream the past few days. A silly happily-ever-after kind of dream that could never exist in real life. How could I have let myself get caught up in it? I should have known better than to believe it. I drag my hands down the sides of my face and try to picture my future now, but where there used to be a solid goal to work toward, there now exists a void where my life should have been. The life Zed took from me when he stole me from my real parents and my real home.

Zed.

I look up as the tiniest glimmer of hope lights the darkness in my heart. Zed stole my life, which makes him the one person who might be able to give it back to me. He doesn't think he can do anything else to fix the mess he made, but he hasn't told me the one thing that could make a difference: who my real family is.

* * *

446

I have no coherent plan. I don't know what I'll do with the information Zed gives me. I don't know what I'll say to Dani when I get back to the shadow world. I can only think of one step at a time. And the current step is this: find Zed and ask him who my real parents are.

I stand and return Bandit to the shelter of my pocket. My sleeve slides back a little, so I check the ruby. I estimate it's about an hour or two away from being fully colored in. I probably should have brought some elixir with me, just in case I need to get out of a sticky situation before returning to the shadow world, but I wasn't exactly thinking clearly when I left the castle.

I pull Aurora's stylus out and remind myself what Zed told us just before he left. Orangebrush Grove, I think. That was all. No street name, no number. *Well, here goes.* I open a faerie paths doorway on the sidewalk. I don't know what to think of, so I try to think of nothing as I slide into the darkness while repeatedly whispering, "Orangebrush Grove, Orangebrush Grove." It almost becomes a tongue twister, but I don't stop saying the words until the darkness begins to melt away around me.

I find myself on a piece of land containing a few scattered houses amidst tall trees, with rolling hills and horse paddocks in the distance and a setting sun bathing the scene in rose-gold warmth. If I'd had the time to formulate some kind of expectation before getting here, this would not have been it.

I approach the nearest house, looking around as I go and seeing no one else. I avoid the front door; I'm not going to knock when I don't know if this is the right house. Instead, I edge around the side and peer in through a half-open window. An unmade bed stands on one side of the room, and clothes are strewn across the floor, but none of it tells me whether this house belongs to Zed or not. I move to the next window, but the living room furniture doesn't give away much either, aside from the fact that it's worn and outdated. I'm about to move on to the next house when I see it: formal Unseelie clothing draped over the back of an armchair. The clothing Zed was wearing when we escaped from the Unseelie Palace.

Yes! I mentally congratulate myself for finding the right house. Then I head back around to the front door and knock. After waiting a few moments, I knock again. When it becomes clear that Zed isn't home, I walk around to the half-open window, hoist myself up, and swing my body inside. Trespassing isn't cool, I guess, but I'm not waiting outside the front door. Not when I have no idea who else lives around here. And why did Zed leave his window open anyway? I thought magical homes had better security than this. Although, now that I think about it, I have no idea if I'm in the magic or non-magic world.

I walk through the bedroom and into the living area. Still wary of the types of neighbors Zed might have, I choose a chair that can't be seen from the window and sit down.

And I wait.

And I try not to think about my mother, because dammit, I don't know what I'm supposed to think anymore. I spent so many years wanting her back the way she used to be, only to discover that that person never actually existed. It was all a facade. She was a faerie pretending to be human. She was two people pretending to be one. And, worst of all, she was pretending to be my mother.

Crap. This *not thinking about her* thing isn't working out well. I lean forward in the chair and dig my fingers into my hair. "Dammit, dammit, dammit," I mutter. Why did someone have to invent a changeling spell in the first place? What a seriously messed-up idea.

Bump.

My head jolts up. I freeze. I'm sure it's only Zed, though. But I wait a few seconds, and no other sound reaches my ears. No door opening, no footsteps. *Holy crap*, I whisper silently to myself. What if someone else is here? What if Dani was right about the Guild having other ways of tracking me down, and now that I've left the shadow world, they've sent someone after me?

I rise silently from the chair, tiptoe across the room, slip behind a curtain, and flatten myself against the wall. My blood rockets through my veins, and my hand moves to the candle in my pocket. How quickly would I be able to light it if someone came into the room? And could I get away before setting the curtain on fire?

Then I hear the sound of a key in a lock. A door opens and closes. Footsteps cross the wooden floor. Surely this must be Zed? But the person or thing that caused the bump must still be in the house somewhere. Or perhaps it was nothing more than a bird or a squirrel or some other animal on the roof. Or maybe it was one of those noises that old houses make sometimes.

I risk moving my head a few inches to the side so I can peek

the curtain. When I see Zed shrugging out of a
, tossing it on top of the Unseelie clothes, I almost
ı relief.

ɔon't. Move."

I freeze.

So does Zed.

"Raise your hands," a woman's voice says from the direction
of the bedroom.

Again, I don't move an inch. Zed, however, does as he's
told. "Who's there?" he asks, twisting his head to the side as he
tries to see over his shoulder.

"You're an exceptionally difficult person to find, Zed," the
woman says, stopping in the bedroom doorway with a shadow
across her upper body and light illuminating a knife in one
hand and a throwing star in the other. "I didn't think I'd have
this much trouble locating you." She moves fully into the light
of the living room, and finally I see who she is.

"Calla," Zed says, turning to face her.

What the actual heck? I demand silently. Even if I wanted to
reveal myself right now, I don't think I could. My body is too
shocked to move.

"Don't be too hard on yourself," Zed adds. "I've been
hidden recently. Magically hidden. Against my will."

"Yes. At the Unseelie Palace."

"You know about that?"

She narrows her golden eyes at him. "Why are you surprised? You know I can find out pretty much any information I
want. All it takes is the right illusion."

He nods as he slowly lowers his hands. "True. I guess I'm

not surprised that you know exactly where I've been recently. But I am surprised it took you this long to come looking for me. I thought you'd catch up to me years ago. Or, at least, I thought someone from your family would."

Calla crosses the room in about two seconds. Her knife flashes through the air and comes to rest firmly against Zed's neck. "Someone from my family almost did. Someone from my family wanted to rip you to shreds for what you did. I'd be lying if I said I didn't want to do the same thing."

Zed makes no move to get away or fight back. "Then why haven't you?"

Calla steps back. She spins the knife in her hand before pointing it again at Zed. "What did you do to Victoria?"

"I suspect you already know, or you wouldn't have come looking for me after all this time."

"Tell me what you did!" she shouts.

His exhale of breath is slow. He swallows. "A changeling spell."

I watch as her breathing becomes shallow and she slowly lowers her hands to her sides.

"I took the baby and replaced her with a human one," Zed continues. "Victoria grew up in the human world."

"So it's true," Calla whispers, turning slightly away from Zed. Almost in slow motion, she drops onto her knees. Her weapons clatter to the floor beside her as she stares unseeingly past Zed.

"I'm so sorry," he says, showing emotion for the first time since she appeared. "I'm so, so sorry for what I did. But I can show you—"

.king." Calla takes another shuddering breath,
,asp this time. She runs her hands through her hair,
ns forward and presses her palms flat against the floor.
i't believe it. When I saw the birthmark, I knew. But I
ited to be sure. I had to be sure. She didn't die. All this
.me ... all this time, and she was actually alive."

As she repeats the same thing over and over, I push the curtain aside and step forward. I'm fairly certain—unless Zed is some kind of serial changeling creator—that the baby they're talking about is me. But they still haven't said enough for me to understand who I am and how Calla knew me back then. "Please explain," I say.

Zed whips around to face me. Calla's response is slower. She freezes, her palms still flat on the floor, before slowly raising her head. She stares at me between the golden strands of her hair, her eyes wide and red, her cheeks tear-stained. Then she stands and rushes toward me. Her arms are wrapped around me before I can move away, and she hugs me tightly, crying into my hair. "You're alive, you're alive, you're alive."

"Um ..." I don't know what else to say.

"We saw your note, and Vi tried to find you, but she kept seeing a shadowy place she couldn't get to, and we still haven't heard from Dash, and ... holy flip, you're ALIVE."

"I ... I am. Yes."

"And *you*!" she hisses, lurching away from me suddenly and advancing on Zed. "How could you DO THAT? How could you KILL A HUMAN CHILD?" Her words are punctuated with sparks of magic that fly from her fingers and tongue, striking Zed.

"Hey, I did what I had to in order to stay alive. I didn't—"

"You didn't *what?*" she spits as magic skitters across the floor all around her. "Have a choice? So you decided to go ahead and ruin two families?"

"I made the best of a bad—"

"You COWARD!"

I don't know who moves first, but suddenly they're fighting. Bare fists and blinding sparks, flying furniture and grunts of anger, dodging and ducking and punching. Calla spins around and lands a kick directly in the center of Zed's abdomen. He crashes to the ground. She grabs a chair, swings it toward him as he tries to get up, and whacks him solidly across the head.

He slumps to the floor and doesn't move.

"I've been wanting to do that for years," she breathes as she lowers the chair. Then she twists around and pulls me into another hug. It only lasts a few seconds, though, before she pulls away from me, wipes at a few stray tears on her cheeks, and smiles. "I'm sorry. You must have so many questions."

"Only one, really," I say in a shaky voice. "Who the hell am I?"

Her smile stretches even wider. "You are Victoria Larkenwood. Violet and Ryn's daughter."

CHAPTER FORTY-TWO

VICTORIA LARKENWOOD. VIOLET AND RYN'S DAUGHTER.

I have to repeat the words several times in my head before they can begin making even the tiniest bit of sense. Calla is saying something, and I'm staring dumbly at her, and still the words are trying to sink their way into my brain.

Victoria Larkenwood. Violet and Ryn's daughter.

I have parents. I have a brother. I have an aunt who's once again hugging me tightly. And the weirdest part is that I've met them all already. I've talked with them, shared meals with them, tried to figure out my past with them, and not once did I ever imagine I might belong to them. I'm probably supposed to be happy. Overjoyed. But I'm too stunned to feel much of anything.

Except … sick?

I pull away from Calla and press one hand against my stomach. "Em?" she says. "What's wrong?"

"I feel ... squeezed? I think?" I double over as nausea overwhelms me. Dizziness spins my brain around. I throw my arm out to steady myself against something.

"Em, what is it?" Calla catches hold of my hand. "Oh ... shoot."

"Dizzy ..." I manage to mumble.

"I think someone's using a summoning spell on you."

"Everything is ... pressing in on me."

"Resist," she instructs. "It's a difficult spell to get right. You can resist it. Just be strong. Root your mind and body firmly here. *Resist*, Em!" Her hand tightens around mine.

Then everything goes dark and I'm squished, squeezed, and tossed around through nothingness. The force pressing in on my body is almost unbearable. Just when I think I'm about to explode, the pressure releases. Everything finally stops moving and the nausea begins to ease—but Calla's grip on my hand is gone. She isn't here.

And where is 'here'?

I'm kneeling on the ground, my hands pressed into grey grass. Tendrils of inky blackness rise between my fingers, giving me my answer: I'm back in the shadow world. I pat my front pocket—but Bandit isn't there. "No!" I whisper. If that summoning spell did something to him, I'm going to have to hurt the person who cast it. I push myself to my feet and turn around—and find myself faced with dozens upon dozens of men and women in Unseelie uniforms.

My heart jolts. I take a step back.

Unseelies. In my shadow world. How did they get here?

"Em, I see you decided to take a little trip." My eyes dart to the side at the sound of Dani's voice. "Let's make sure you can't do that again." My hip is tugged forward as the candle flies from my pocket. I steady myself. Then, looking up, I see Dani raise her hand toward me—

Flames fly across the ground, racing to form a blazing circle around me. I shy away from it, but I have nowhere to go. Then a glistening ripple rushes through the air, forming a layer just inside the fire circle. The indistinct ripple spreads upward, enclosing me completely in a hemisphere. She's imprisoning me in magic.

But on the other side of the magic layer and the waist-high flames, Dani looks confused. She narrows her eyes at me. "When did you learn a shield spell?"

I blink at her as something suddenly becomes painfully obvious. "When did Ada become the one in control?"

She cocks her head. "Really, Em? Are you that stupid? I've been in control since the moment I woke up from Zed's reversal spell."

"But … it was my mother—it was Dani who—"

"What, you think I can't act? You think I can't pretend to be exactly like her after sharing my body with her for most of my life?" She stands a few feet away with her hands on her hips and light flickering across her face. In her jeans and shirt, it's difficult to imagine her as the deadly glass faerie in the sliver cloak and black mask. But it's her, no matter what she looks like now. "You're an idiot, Em. An idiot for believing Dani would ever be strong enough to take control of our body after

456

we merged again. She's so weak, I can't even hear her. She may as well be dead. And since I'm the one in control now, she'll never be able to use her Griffin Ability again. She'll never be able to force us to split."

"If you're so brilliant at acting like her," I say bitterly, "then perhaps you shouldn't have suggested that our mother-daughter bonding include *killing people*."

Ada rolls her eyes. "If you knew Dani as well as I do, you'd know that she'd be just as likely to suggest using an insignificant human to gain power. But you don't, Em. You've never known what she's really like."

"But *you* should have known *me*," I tell her. "I grew up in that world. Did you really think I'd be happy killing one of its inhabitants? *You're* the idiot, Ada."

She shrugs. "Yeah. I'm the idiot with an Unseelie army on my side."

I look out at them again, fear tightening my stomach. "It shouldn't be possible," I murmur, trying to fathom how they can be here. "I said they would never enter this world."

"Yes, but you also made the mistake of saying this world belonged to me as much as it does to you. So I gave the Unseelies permission to enter. As easy as that." She twists her hand in the air, and a small sandstorm attacks the shield layer. I duck down, but the shield remains intact. "Impressive," Ada says. "You clearly forgot to mention you learned how to cast a shield."

I say nothing as I straighten. I have no idea where the shield layer came from, but I'm not complaining about it as long as it separates me from Ada and the soldiers behind her—and the

457

heat of the flames. "You should hate the Unseelies, shouldn't you? Zed said you guys were tortured by a former Unseelie Prince. So why would you bring them here?"

"Come on, Em. I can't hold an entire family responsible for one prince who decided to go rogue and build an army to take power for himself. That would be unfair of me. The people I *do* hate, however, are guardians. There are plenty I still need to get rid of, and that kind of thing is easier when you have friends to help you. Ah, and there he is," she adds, looking past me. "One of my newest friends."

"Guardians are gathering at Velazar II," a voice says from behind me. A voice I've come to hate. "They'll be starting the ceremony soon. Ah, you retrieved Emerson. Well done." Roarke strides past the fire circle and stops beside Ada. And with him is—

"Clarina?" I say.

Still in her handmaid's uniform, Clarina folds her arms across her chest and stares directly at me. "I think I'm enjoying this shocked expression I keep seeing on people's faces. Aurora, these men and women behind us, and now you. It almost makes all the years of waiting worth it." Her voice is devoid of its usual respect. I realize abruptly that this is the woman I overheard in Roarke's bedroom.

"Wow," I say, shifting my attention to Roarke. "I didn't take you for someone who'd fall in love with a lady's maid."

Roarke snorts. "Clarina isn't a lady's maid. She's a spy. *My* spy."

"And I am, in fact, of noble birth," Clarina adds.

"Ah, well that makes sense then. A prince of the Unseelies

would never shack up with the hired help." I look at her, thinking of all the times she's seen Roarke and me together. Not once did she seem upset, even when she caught us kissing. "You're a good actress. I'll give you that, at least."

"I'm a *very* good actress," she corrects. "And now the pretense is finally paying off."

"Why? What was the point?" I look at Roarke. "Who were you spying on?"

He smiles. "Everyone."

"Where's Aurora?" I ask, suddenly realizing I haven't seen her since the night she warned me about Roarke's plans. "Is she also—"

"It's none of your business, actually," Roarke continues, "and we have more important things to do now than tell stories. I would take you with us, Emerson—I suspect your Griffin Ability might actually be powerful enough to tear the veil open further—but I can't risk losing you to the Guild. I might never get you back, and you'll be worth more to me in the future than you would be today."

"And why bother with Em when you have me?" Ada adds. "I've gathered far more power than she'll probably ever have."

"That's true. For now, at least." Roarke breathes in deeply. "Okay, get rid of that shield of hers," he says to Ada, "then hand her over to Clarina. She knows where to lock her up."

"With pleasure," Ada answers, raising both hands. Behind her, several soldiers do the same. I duck down again as hundreds of stones bombard the shield. Within seconds, the rippling shield magic vanishes with a flash. Heat sears the air around me. I carefully raise my head enough to peer over the top of the flames, already planning my escape route.

"Where the hell is she?" Roarke yells, his eyes sliding past me.

What? I look down, but as far as I can tell, I'm still visible.

"Dammit, where did she go?" he shouts, walking right up to the circle. Is this world protecting me, perhaps? Because I told it I'd be safe here? I don't know, but I'm not wasting this opportunity. Turning away from Roarke, I bend my knees, then kick off the ground with as much force as I can muster. My knees come up to my chest as I sail across the fire circle, clearing the ring of dancing flames. I hit the ground with both feet and straighten immediately. Then, with no candle to get me out of here, I take off in the direction of the wall that conceals the veil tear.

"Find her!" Roarke shouts. "And the rest of you, follow me to Velazar."

Crap. That's the same way I'm going. A glance over my shoulder tells me the soldiers aren't marching slowly; they're running. And Roarke and Ada are rising into the air on the back of my ink-shade dragons!

Anger flashes through my chest. *Those are mine!* I want to shout at them. But I need to get to Velazar before they do, so I force my legs to move as fast as I know they can. Roarke may have forgotten what time of night it is, but I haven't. My Griffin Ability is almost ready to be used, and if Roarke thinks my magic is powerful enough to open the veil further, then it must be powerful enough to close it. All I need to do is hide somewhere and say the right words as soon as I'm able to, and I could save countless lives on both sides of the veil.

An unexpected thrill races through me, along with the terrifying thought that I might be edging near hero territory. If I had enough breath left in my lungs, I'd probably laugh at myself. Does it count as being a hero if you hide while you're saving the world? I don't think so. I think it just counts as doing the right thing.

With ink-shades streaming past me on both sides, I push myself faster than I've ever run before. I slow a little as I reach the wall and veer to the side so I'm running along it. When I reach the door, I tug it open, run through, and slam it shut. Then I face the great big gap in the sky, my lungs burning as I gasp for air. As I stop near the edge of the opening, I see figures in black, some lined up, others walking around. While it's almost midnight in the shadow world—at least, the enchanted version of midnight—it looks like late afternoon over Velazar II Island.

Hoping that I'm still somehow invisible to everyone else, I step quickly onto the monument, swing myself around the trident, and jump to the ground behind it. I crouch down, listening carefully through my heavy breaths. When I don't hear any shouts or hurried footsteps coming my way, I relax a tiny bit.

"Don't scream," a voice says right beside me.

I can't help my involuntary gasp as Calla appears out of thin air right beside me. "What—where did you—"

"I've been with you since you were summoned," she whispers. "I masked myself with invisibility."

"So—the shield was yours? And now, when they couldn't see me ..."

"Yes, that was me. Sorry I didn't conceal you sooner. I needed to find out what was going on, so I shielded you instead, hoping they'd tell you something useful. And they did." She leans a little to the side and looks past the monument. "I need to warn the others."

"Others?"

"Yeah, they're here somewhere, watching. Keeping an eye on things."

"Violet and Ryn are here?"

Calla looks at me. She places her hand on my shoulder and squeezes it. "Yes. And we're all going to get out of this alive. You'll get your family reunion, okay? I'll make sure of it."

"Before we begin," a voice shouts out, "there is an important matter we need to take care of." I lean far enough to the side to catch a glimpse of the person standing in front of the monument addressing everyone. I recognize her as the woman who came to Chevalier House to take me away after I revealed my Griffin Ability to everyone there. Head Councilor Ashlow. She nods toward someone I can't see—

And then the strangest thing floats into view just in front of her: a chair with a man securely tied to it. And though he's facing away from us, I can see enough of the side of his face to recognize him.

Dash.

CHAPTER FORTY-THREE

"GRIFFIN GIFTED REBELS," COUNCILOR ASHLOW SHOUTS IN a magically magnified voice, "we know you're hiding here watching us. We know that Dash Blackhallow has been working with you. And if you don't hand yourselves over to us now, we will kill him."

I clap one hand over my mouth. Calla's grip on my shoulder tightens.

"You have two minutes," Councilor Ashlow adds. "Then we will carry out the execution."

"How can they do that?" I demand in a low voice. "Surely that's against the law, even for people who *make* the laws."

"They're desperate," Calla says darkly. "They're so afraid of us that it seems they'll do anything these days to apprehend us." She pulls her head back behind the monument, adding,

"Chase needs to be here." She retrieves her amber and stylus, scribbles a few words, then returns both to her pocket. "Okay, I need to help the others. And you need to get away from here. Do you have a stylus?"

"I—yes, I do, actually."

"Open a doorway and get yourself back to safety."

"But I can help—"

"No. I refuse to lose you again, do you understand me? If Ryn and Vi were hiding here with us instead of somewhere else on the island, they'd say the same thing."

"But my Griffin Ability can—"

"No, Em. I mean it. We can stop Roarke and his soldiers without you. His army isn't that big. It's nowhere near the size of the entire Unseelie army. And you are too important to us."

I know there's no time to argue, so I don't. I nod, even though I have no intention of leaving this place. If Roarke tears the veil further open and this island is consumed, the majority of the family I have left will die. There's no way I'm letting that happen when I know I can stop it with only a few words.

"Okay." She gives me a brief hug. "See you when it's over." Then she vanishes. I don't hear her footsteps, but, looking closely at the rocky ground surrounding the monument, I see small pebbles moving here and there as she walks away.

Since I'm not leaving the island, I should probably find a better place to hide than right behind the monument the Unseelies will be targeting the moment they get here—which, now that I think about it, should have happened already. Where are they? Those soldiers were moving almost as fast as I was, and the ink-shades can be quick when they want to be.

I look around. The closest form of cover is a collection of rocks a short distance away. The only problem? I'll almost certainly be spotted as I run toward it.

"Is no one interested in saving the life of this young man?" Councilor Ashlow shouts. She waits another few seconds. "No? Well then. I guess we'll get started with both the execution spell and the veil restoration spell."

Several guardians form a tight ring around Dash while another few climb onto the cylindrical base of the monument. I can no longer see what's happening to Dash, but I tell myself not to panic. Calla won't let anything happen to him. Neither will any of the other Griffin rebels. They must have a plan.

I throw my hands out as the ground suddenly shudders beneath me. I push myself a little further away from the monument and look up. The gap in the veil is difficult to see from this angle, since it's almost directly above me, but I think the edges are beginning to move.

A loud cry makes me look around the side of the monument again. *Not Dash, not Dash*, I plead. But it's Councilor Ashlow, flat on the ground with blood seeping from her shoulder. Guardians rush to her side, while others raise their weapons toward the slowly diminishing gap. And then, with a cacophony of whoops and roars that chills my blood, the Unseelies leap through the tear into this world, brandishing their weapons.

Chaos follows, and in the midst of it, I jump up and run to the rocks, hoping like hell that no one notices me. I drop down behind the rocks and press my back against them. I look up and around, but I don't see any ink-shade dragons. They must have remained in the shadow world. My gaze drops then to the ruby, but its color isn't quite full yet. So I press my hands against my ears, trying to drown out the clash and clang of blades, the roar of wind, the shouts of men and women. *Come on, come on, come on,* I silently urge, as if that might possibly help my Griffin Ability replenish faster.

"Stop her!" Someone's voice rises above the noise. "STOP HER!"

I risk a glance around the side of the rock and see a woman—Ada—racing for the monument with glass slivers streaming from her fingertips. And Ryn, sprinting just behind her, expertly dodging the glass. *No!* I want to scream. *Don't touch her!* He lunges for her, brings her crashing to the ground, and she kicks him in the face and scrambles away—which I'm almost thankful for because it means she hasn't turned him to glass. Ada throws herself forward, grabs hold of the edge of the monument, and the entire thing becomes gleaming, faceted glass. She pulls herself up and gives the monument a good kick accompanied by a flash of magic. A crack zigzags all the way through the monument. Then she dances away from it, glass shards raining down from her fingers and rushing to form a glass wall. I suck in a gasp as Ryn rolls out of the way just in time. He leaps to his feet just as the monument shatters into thousands of glass pieces on the other side of Ada's wall.

I look up. My stomach turns. The gash in the sky is now growing larger instead of smaller. I see the field on the other side, and it seems to roll toward us as both worlds are consumed by the shadow world. I grasp my wrist and look down, but the darn ruby is still missing a fraction of color.

"Dammit!" I moan, tears of frustration welling in my eyes. "Just *hurry up*!"

With my hands tugging uselessly at my hair, and almost everyone else on the island still fighting each other, I watch the hole in the sky widening and moving closer. It reaches Ada's glass wall—and it stops. "What the ..." I mumble breathlessly. I don't understand why. The monument had ancient power or something, but Ada's glass wall has ... what? The power of all the people whose energy she's consumed recently?

My momentary relief vanishes when I realize the human world is still being consumed. Our world is fine, but the other one still seems to be slowly rolling toward us. The field is gone now, and then the road, taking two people with it. Then another field, and a tractor with a man on it, and the side of a building—

I can't look. I pull my head back behind the rock, hating myself for being such a failure. I have *so much power*, yet I can't do a damn thing right now. I grit my teeth and clench my fists and try not to count every second that passes. Time goes on. And on. And on.

Then finally—*finally*—that familiar tingle radiates throughout my body. My eyes close for a moment, forcing tears down my cheeks as I relax for the final few seconds it takes for my power to reach my voice. Then I twist around to look at the veil. I don't shout anything out. I don't move any further away from the rock. I simply focus fully on that rapidly increasing gash in the sky and say, "Stop growing bigger. Start closing instead. Close completely so that the veil is fully restored."

I slump sideways against the rock as my power rushes out of

me to do my bidding. All of it in one go. Dizziness wraps around me, but it lasts only a few seconds. The fighting pauses. The island becomes almost quiet. We watch as the edges of the tear move rapidly toward each other. They meet, light flashes in a jagged line, and then it's over, leaving no sign that there was ever any imperfection in the sky.

It's done.

I did it.

I experience a single moment of satisfaction before noise assaults my ears once more. I look further past the rock and realize that despite having succeeded at something so huge, my world is about to shatter anyway. Because everyone is fighting with renewed fervor instead of retreating, and near the edge of the island, Ada's got a circle of glass enclosing Dash. And beside him, standing back to back with glittering weapons raised, are Violet and Ryn.

No no no no no. I press my hands against my cheeks, searching the battle for the other people I know. Where are Calla and Chase? Or any of the other rebels I met? There must be more of them here. But there are so many people, so many weapons, so much magic flying around. How the hell does anyone know what's going on? And why doesn't anyone seem to care that the veil is now *closed*, dammit!

Then I notice the other movement inside Ada's glass circle, and my anxiety ratchets up a notch. *What the heck is that?* They look like the people I've seen Ada transform into glass statues, except they're moving. She must have *animated* her statues instead of shattering them. And I see at least seven—eight— inside the glass circle with Violet, Ryn and Dash. Dash is free of his bonds, so at least he can fight, but the glass statues seem, oddly enough, just as quick as if they were made of flesh. They dodge the glittering weapons and block the magic hurled at them.

Ada pumps her fist in the air, as if she's cheering them on. As if this is a game. Then, because it probably is a game to her, she waves her fingers through the air in a graceful motion. As I watch, the jagged glass circle begins splintering inwards, growing rapidly smaller.

Crapping hell. I'm not hiding any longer. I launch up from behind the rock and bolt past the fighting toward the edge of the island. The glass circle reaches the first statue and crunches it to pieces. The other statues edge closer to the center, where Ryn, Vi and Dash slice through the air with their weapons and spin and throw their magic. They manage to shatter one of the statues, and then another. They could probably knock each one down almost instantly in hand-to-hand combat, but I can tell none of them wants to risk touching Ada's glass.

The circle grows smaller, and Ada's grin grows more twisted, even as she watches another one of her own statues taken down by the encroaching edge of her circle. "Stop!" I scream as I get closer to them. "Ada, stop!" She cocks her head to the side, then turns enough to look at me. Her magic, however, doesn't change. "Ada, please," I gasp, slowing down and hoping to appeal to whatever part of Dani is left inside their body. The only part that might still care about me. "Stop, please!" I shout again. "They're my parents!"

I come to a halt a few paces away from Ada, my chest heaving as I catch my breath, my words still ringing in my ears.

In the center of the circle, Violet and Ryn stop fighting. Their eyes lock onto me, and on their faces I see ... blank shock.

A solid glass arm swings toward them. Dash jumps forward, brings his sword down, and slices clear through the statue's arm. At the same time, Ada charges at me. Her magic lashes out, slapping me across the face and knocking me sideways. My knees and palms scream out at me as I land hard on the ground. Hands grip my shoulders and shove me over onto my back. The next thing I know, Ada's leaning over me, both hands around my neck. "Are you kidding me? You tell me that those guardians are your parents, and you expect me to *stop* attacking them? How stupid are you?" She squeezes harder. "Those are the two people who left us to suffer at Prince Marzell's hands. Now I *definitely* want to make them suf— Argh!"

Her hands disappear from around my neck. She twists to the side, and as I cough and gasp for air, I see a glowing arrow protruding from her shoulder. "Damn guardians," Ada hisses, looking behind her. I push myself up and follow her gaze. At the center of the glass circle I see Violet—my mother—with a fierce expression on her face, and her bow and another arrow pointed straight at Ada.

Ada rolls instantly away from me, and I duck down too, just in case Vi lets that arrow go. I'm about to scramble back toward the circle when something grabs onto my ankle and drags me back. "Where do you think you're off to?" Ada asks. The arrow is gone from her shoulder, which means she must have somehow ripped it free herself. "I'm not done with you. And don't—" she adds, grabbing my jaw and forcing me to face her "—worry about your parents. My glass guardians are making sure to inflict as much pain as they can."

I swat her hand away, then swing my arm around and punch her face as hard as I can—which probably hurt me as much as it hurt her, but was worth it to see the look on her face.

"Oh, you little—"

"Get the hell off me!" I yell at her, kicking with both my feet. She slides a little further away from me toward the edge of the island, and by the time she sits up again, I've got the smallest glimmer of magic zapping back and forth between my hands.

She laughs at me, which I suppose is warranted. "What are you going to do with that, Em? Tickle me? Because that's about the only thing such a pathetic amount of magic can achieve."

I imagine digging down deep to wherever my core of magic is, and pulling it free. More and more and more. It doesn't seem to make much difference, but *any* difference is better than none.

"You know what, Em?" Ada says, unconcerned by whatever power I'm gathering between my palms. "I don't particularly care if you survive this battle or not. The prince asked me to retrieve you, so I did. But he isn't watching right now, so I can easily say it was someone else who did it when I bring your dead body back to him in multiple pieces."

"You're sick."

"Nope, just looking out for myself. Something I'm sure you can identify with."

"Not like this." Behind her in the sky, I notice strange ovoid shapes moving toward us. Shapes that look like they have people inside them. *Crap.* Who do we have to fight off now?

"He wants us both to use our powers for him, did you know that?" Ada says. "And while that might be a great idea for him, I don't see that working out so well for me. I wouldn't want to have to compete to be the favorite weapon, you know? So." She stands up and shoots a stream of glass at me. I scoot to the side, and it narrowly misses me. "While I like this kind of game, I think we should probably bring it to a—"

I hurl everything I've got at her. It's pathetic, probably not even enough to stun her, but it knocks her down, spins her over twice—and rolls her clear off the edge of the island.

"Holy crap," I gasp. "Crap, crap, crap." I push myself up and rush to the edge. Far below, I can just make out the white bubbles from the splash where she must have landed. Is she dead? Or is this another thing a faerie can easily survive? And why the hell do I care when *she just tried to kill me*?

I turn and race back toward the only people who matter now: Vi, Ryn and Dash, who are—where? I skid to a halt. A pile of shattered glass sits in the middle of the enclosing circle. Hell, if they're part of that pile of glass, I might have to—

"Em!" Violet shouts my name from the other side of the circle, where she and Ryn are fighting off another three glass statues. I take off toward them—

And I'm knocked to the side by a bright bolt of magic.

Moments later, darkness clears from the edges of my vision. I find myself face-down on the ground, horrendous pain

472

burning my side. I manage to roll over and sit up. My hand comes away from my side covered in blood, but I try not to panic. *Faeries can heal easily*, I remind myself. *This is totally fine.*

"Emerson!" someone screams.

I look around. The ovoid shapes I saw in the air have landed on the island. They remind me a little of the prison cell spheres, although the glass isn't as dark, and there are no bars anywhere. On one side, I notice a gold emblem I might possibly have seen on uniforms at the Guild.

"Em!" someone shouts again. Amidst the chaos of Unseelies and guardians running everywhere, I finally see them: Violet and Ryn, their hands and feet bound, being tossed into one of these ovoids. Dash, similarly restrained, is already inside.

"No," I mumble, managing to get to my feet. I stagger a few paces toward them. "No. Let them go." I raise my voice. "Let them go!"

The side of the ovoid closes up, and it rises a few feet above the ground. "No, stop. Stop!" I shout, pressing one hand against my wound and moving more quickly toward the vehicle. It skims above the ground, gaining speed, and then it's off the island, gliding away from me, and the last I see of my parents is their faces pressed against the glass as they shout words I can't hear.

I drop onto my knees. I strike the ground with one fist and let out a furious cry. "Come back!" I yell. Anger, desperation and a heartbroken sob mingle together, making my voice crack as I scream even louder: "COME BACK!"

Hands grab hold of me, and that voice I hate so much speaks into my ear. "Time to return to our shadow world, my dear. Wouldn't want the guardians getting their grubby hands on you."

"NO!" I thrash against Roarke. Then my head jolts forward abruptly. Sickening pain radiates through my skull, and—

Darkness.

CHAPTER FORTY-FOUR

I WAKE IN A ROOM COVERED ENTIRELY IN PADDING. THE floor, the walls, even the ceiling. It's probably Roarke's idea of a sick joke, given the type of institution my mother—nope, not my mother. *Dani*—spent the past five years in. Either that or he honestly thinks I'm so depressed about the current state of my life that I'm planning to hurt myself by ramming into walls.

He wouldn't be entirely wrong there.

Not about the wall-ramming part. That would be excessive. But the depressed part isn't far off. The same thoughts have been tormenting me since the moment I woke up. The same images. Vi and Ryn's shock when I shouted, 'They're my parents!' Their bodies pressed against the glass as that oval-shaped vehicle carried them away. Their silent shouts.

I saved the veil, but I couldn't save my own family. That's how messed up my magic is. I have a super powerful Griffin Ability, but when I can't use it, I'm essentially useless. I keep thinking of all the ways things might have ended differently for us if I knew what to do with my own magic. I could have attacked Ada from a distance. I could have helped to fight the glass statues. I could have protected someone with a shield while they fought someone else. I might, at this very moment, have been sitting with my family in the oasis, finally reunited after almost eighteen years.

I also can't help thinking about how things would have turned out if I *hadn't* been there. I wouldn't have distracted Violet and Ryn. They might have fought their way past the glass statues sooner. They wouldn't have been so worried about what was happening to me that they let themselves get caught by the Guild. They'd probably be back at the oasis by now, and hopefully Dash would be with them.

Although, if I hadn't been at Velazar today, what would have happened to the widening gap in the veil?

And of course, there's the continual guilt regarding my mother. Dani. The person who became so weak she's now locked inside the body she has to share. She isn't the innocent person I always believed her to be, but I don't think she's anything like Ada either. If I'd had the chance, I could have commanded them each to have their own bodies. She and I could have had a second chance to get to know each other. Instead I pushed her over the edge of an island floating high up in the sky.

I might possibly have killed her.

And then there's Dash. Dash who only ever wanted to help me. Who ended up in trouble because he braved the Unseelie Court to come and get me out. Who is now a guild prisoner just like my parents. I want to see him almost as badly as I want to see Violet and Ryn.

And Bandit! Where is my Bandit?

I tilt my head back against the padded wall, screw my eyes shut, and let my tears fall. What an absolute mess I've made.

A bang on my cell door interrupts my crying. I wipe my hands quickly across my cheeks and stand. The padded door swings open and Roarke walks in. My hatred of him rears its ugly head instantly. I almost lunge at him, but then I notice the slight shimmer in the air that tells me he's placed a shield between us.

"I trust your wound has healed?" he asks.

I nod. Barely a hint of a scar marked my skin by the time I woke up earlier. Now, two or three hours later, even the faint scar is gone. I sniff and ask, "Where am I?"

"The shadow world, of course. I told you about these underground passages, didn't I? Though I probably chose not to mention the prison cells."

"I wonder why," I say, my voice weighted with sarcasm. "So, what are you doing here in my lovely cell? Got any more marriage proposals for me?"

"No. That plan always hinged on your complete willingness. It would never work now. I'll marry Clarina, which was always my ultimate intention. We needn't wait any longer, now that we've relocated to this world."

"You've relocated? Officially? But this world belongs to me, not you. I claimed it."

Roarke looks almost amused. "You're in a prison cell, and I'm in control. The necessary rituals still need to be performed, but for all intents and purposes, this world is already mine."

I cross my arms. "Your father must be thrilled about that."

"Not particularly. But I'm not here to talk about my family. I'm here to talk about yours."

"Where's Aurora? She said she didn't want to choose sides, but I assume she'll have to now."

Roarke's composure flickers for a second. "More specifically," he continues, ignoring my interruption, "I'm here to talk about what an enormous disappointment it must have been for you to discover what kind of person your mother really is. You—"

"*Is?* So she's still alive?"

Roarke's narrowed eyes tell me he doesn't appreciate being interrupted again. "We'll find out soon enough, I suppose. But either way, you must feel so lost now, when your life's purpose has always been to return your mother to exactly the way you remember her." He takes a few steps closer to the magic layer that divides us. "You need a new purpose, Emerson. And I would love to give you one."

"You can take your new purpose and shove it up your—"

"Let me remind you," he says, speaking over me, "that you have nothing else left."

"I have a family. I have real parents who—"

"Who are probably being executed by the Guild as we speak."

"Liar!" I walk right up to the shield layer and ball my hands into fists as I stare defiantly back at him. "The death penalty doesn't exist anymore."

"True, but the Guild has been known to make exceptions. And, given how they feel about these Griffin Gifted rebels who've evaded them for years, I'm almost certain this will be one of those exceptions." He folds his hands neatly together. "The Guild will kill them. Then they'll find the rest of your Griffin rebel friends and lock them up. You will have no one and nothing. All you will know is the inside of this cell. And when you are finally broken, Emerson, then we can start again. We can build you a new life with a new purpose. One that involves serving me."

"Yeah, and pigs might fly."

He smiles. "Well, there's always compulsion potion if you insist on being difficult. I'll make sure your first compulsion command includes telling pigs to fly." And with that, he walks out of the room.

I return to the wall, slide down against it, and pound the padded floor with my fists a few times. But my anger dissipates quickly, my misery returning to take its place.

"Don't scream."

"Holy CRAP!" I gasp, my heart thundering instantly in my chest. I look across the room at Calla leaning against the wall. "What are you … are you real?" I wouldn't put it past Roarke to play magical mind games with me.

"Of course I'm real," she says in a low voice. "I followed you and Roarke back here from Velazar Island. I've been waiting outside your cell for hours. I came in just now when he opened the door."

I push myself hurriedly to my feet. With my emotions so close to the surface, I can't help the words that tumble from my mouth: "The Guild took them. They took Ryn and Vi, and I never—I didn't get to speak to them—or … or even touch them. I tried so hard to get Ada away from them, and then they were gone. And Dash said the Guild has a special prison for the worst traitors, but Roarke said sometimes they just execute people instead. And they have Dash, and they know he's been helping the Griffin rebels, and what if the Guild executes all three of—"

"Stop," Calla tells me firmly. She crosses the room and places her hands on my shoulders. "Stop. Breathe. Calm down. We're going to get out of here. Then we're going to get Ryn, Vi and Dash back. And then we're going to kick this prince's Unseelie ass. Okay?"

I breathe out a long and shaky breath. "Okay. That sounds good."

"Oh, and I thought this might help you feel a little better." She unzips her jacket, and nestled against her stomach is a black rabbit.

"Bandit!" He jumps into my arms, and I almost start crying as I hug him close and rub my cheek against his soft hair.

"He leaped away from you after Ada summoned you earlier, but I caught him and concealed him. He was with me the whole time at Velazar."

"Thank you for keeping him safe."

"Of course," she says with a nod. "Now, help me decide on the best illusion to get us out of here."

LOOK OUT FOR THE
NEXT BOOK IN THE
CREEPY HOLLOW SERIES!

ACKNOWLEDGEMENTS

Wow. That turned into a long one! My unending thanks go to:

God, for creating stories in the first place, and for helping me imagine yet another one.

Heather and Krista, for your helpful feedback and editing notes.

Early readers who take the time to let me know about the typos I've missed.

Creepy Hollow fans, for continuing Emerson's journey with me.

And of course, to Kyle, for understanding that I will *always* take longer than I say I will when I disappear into my fantasy worlds!

© Gavin van Haght

Rachel Morgan spent a good deal of her childhood living
in a fantasy land of her own making, crafting endless stories of
make-believe and occasionally writing some of them down.
After completing a degree in genetics and discovering
she still wasn't grown-up enough for a 'real' job, she decided
to return to those story worlds still spinning around her
imagination. These days she spends much of her time
immersed in fantasy land once more, writing fiction
for young adults and those young at heart.

Rachel lives in Cape Town with her husband and
three miniature dachshunds. She is the author of the
bestselling Creepy Hollow series and the sweet
contemporary romance Trouble series.

www.rachel-morgan.com

Made in the USA
San Bernardino, CA
04 March 2018